KEYSTATE

A Novel By

Damon Rodehorst

Copyright ©2012 by Damon Rodehorst

All Rights reserved.

Published in the United States of America.

ESBN 978-1-300-80310-2

Second Edition. XI MMMXIII

For the unwitting.

Prologue

Alexandar stuck to the shadows as he made his way toward the river. It was clear and a sliver of a moon hung low over the southern sky. There was no wind and very little noise save for the far off hum of traffic and throb of adjacent factories. The path to the river took him past the tank farm that rose high above the plant. He stopped at the base of a ladder welded to the side of a large steel tank.

A former special forces soldier, Alexandar was massive, strong and agile. Even so, the body slung over his shoulder would make reaching the top of the towering tank an almost impossible task. Several agonizing minutes later, he perched on the top rung of the ladder to catch his breath before pulling himself onto the domed top of the tank.

The unconscious man grunted and moaned softly as Alexandar jostled him across his broad shoulder before starting the hazardous trip across the tops of several adjoining tanks. After reaching the far side, he slid the body onto the steel decking of a mezzanine before stepping to look over the edge. He estimated the drop to be about fifteen meters. Enough to kill someone if they fell on their head. But only if they fell on their head. He had to go higher.

A makeshift ladder fastened to a tank at the far end of the mezzanine led up to the next level. Alexandar stepped over the prostrate body and, as he walked toward the ladder, rolled his neck and swung his arms to loosen muscles made tight by exertion. Alexandar stopped at the base of the tank and, hands on hips, leaned back to stretch his lower back and look up the ladder and past the top of the highest tank to the stars beyond. It struck him that it looked like the night sky in Afghanistan.

It was his last pain free thought.

Chapter One

Doug Reardon stood looking up. The tank farm at Keystate Oil was a maze of storage tanks, pipes and walkways. New equipment had always been installed where it was most convenient and the old removed only if it was in the way or could be sold. After forty-plus years, the oil and chemical laden storage facility was a labyrinth. Doug hadn't taken the time to count, but there had to be more than seventy-five tanks of various sizes. Smaller tanks were stacked on top of larger to a height of about sixty feet. Doug was looking for the best path to the top. His gaze, following a path of ladders, catwalks and mezzanines, stopped at the rusted, red tank piqued his curiosity whenever he walked past. It was obviously no longer functional; the explosion that blew a gaping hole had been mortal.

He started climbing after determining the easiest route. It took a few minutes to reach the top of the first level. He had to walk across the tops of six tanks to a mezzanine That held the uppermost tanks. Doug couldn't help but feel a little unnerved. The tanks were crowned and exposure to the sun had made them chalky and slick. Worse, there were rusty patches every so often. He considered the possibility that he might break through and be pickled in methanol or ethylene glycol.

He pushed that out of his mind and crossed the tanks. As he walked the length of the mezzanine, Doug passed the rusted hulk of the destroyed tank. The gash that ran up most of one side and cut into the top revealed that it was really two tanks - one inside the other. The inner tank had taken the brunt of the explosion. It was a mangled mess of distorted metal and jagged edges. The outer shell looked like it had been deliberately cut and peeled open. Doug was no closer to understanding what had happened to it.

Reaching a makeshift ladder of welded rebar, Doug climbed to the top of the highest tank. Fortunately, someone had installed safety railings so Doug was able to get a literal and figurative grip. As he caught his breath and settled his nerves, Doug looked around. He was glad he made the climb.

Keystate Oil was located on Neville Island just below where the Allegheny and Monongahela rivers converge to form the Ohio. There was a slight breeze coming from the west and the air, which at ground level stung from the acrid smell of chemicals and industrial grime, was fresher and smelled of the river. From this height, Doug could see straight into downtown Pittsburgh. His line of sight passed over Heinz Field - the replacement for the much more famous and revered Three Rivers Stadium. Adjacent was PNC Park, the equally new home of the Pirates.

It was an early evening in mid June and the setting sunlight bounced off the PPG Place towers. Now a general commercial property, PPG Place once headquartered the glass and chemical company of the same name. It looked like a fortress complete with crenelated roofline and towers. As befitting one of the world's largest glass companies, the entire building was clad in mirrored glass. It glowed orange-red in the fading sun. Farther east, One Mellon Place, the city's second tallest building gleamed. Just north stood the U.S. Steel building.

The tallest building in Pittsburgh, it was literally a rusting behemoth. The surrounding sidewalk was stained the color of dried blood from rain washing down the sides of the building. No flaw, the building was designed to rust as if to proclaim to passersby that this was Pittsburgh – a town built on sacrifice, sweat and blood and damn proud of it.

Of course, that was decades ago. These days, the mills were closed. Their former locations, once gritty, toxic sites, had been replaced with retail shops and commercial businesses. Pittsburgh was now a high tech hub and center of advanced engineering and finance. There were still plenty of blue collar jobs around. Doug was reminded of that as he looked down and across the parking lot to the smoker's shack. There, three or four plant workers were having a cigarette. One he recognized as Stoli, the chief blender.

His name wasn't really Stoli. It was Jack Stalich but, because he was second generation Russian and liked vodka, everyone called him Stoli. Like most everyone else in this football rabid town, he was a Steelers fan. Also, like most factory workers, he had an array of Steelers baseball caps. He was, however, one of the few that had a bright yellow one with a Harley Davidson patch on the back. It was the bright yellow cap that Doug recognized. That and the fact that Stoli had a sizable pot gut, long graying hair and a scraggly, salt and pepper beard.

Stoli was one of the key men in the plant because he knew how to blend up the different oil and chemical products and was intimate with all the piping and valves that controlled the flows of the various liquids. The two men talked a lot during the time Doug had been at Keystate. Doug knew that, despite his disheveled appearance, Stoli was whip smart and a hard worker. As Doug looked down, Stoli looked up and, across the distance, they gave each other a nod. Then Stoli gave an amused shake of his head.

Looking back up, Doug scanned the roof that covered the more than three hundred thousand square feet of factory and warehouse. He saw the couple of areas where he knew the rain was coming in. Ostensibly, that was the reason he climbed up; he told himself he wanted to survey possible maintenance needs. He knew the real reason was that, like any newly installed regent, he wanted to look over the entirety of his new realm. Earlier that day, Doug Reardon had become president of Keystate Oil Company.

Keystate Oil was a private company. The owners, Ken Dawson and Jim Harding, were the two smartest business people Doug knew. He first met them when they all served on the board of directors at the Oakdale Country Club. Doug got his seat on the board because he was the club's best golfer, was an expert on the game and generally liked by the membership. Ken and Jim were on the board because, though lousy golfers and not particularly social, they provided a lot of money to fund the club's many capital projects. Located just southeast of Cleveland, Oakdale was one of northeast Ohio's oldest, most venerated clubs. The "venerated" part ensured a waiting list of potential members. The "old" part ensured a longer list of maintenance projects.

Doug got along well enough with the two millionaires but he wasn't close to being in the same financial league. He was more familiar with Jim who, for a time, had part ownership in a plastics company where Doug worked as the sales manager. The two spent time together on customer visits and one long weekend at a trade show in Las Vegas. Eventually, Jim sold his interest in the company but not before installing Doug as the chief operating officer. Jim also arranged an invitation for Doug to join Oakdale. Things were great for a few years after that. Doug was very good at his job and his personal and social life clicked. Then the shit hit the fan.

Doug grew a bit too big for his britches and got into an argument with the remaining owner. There was a point during the argument when Doug said he'd happily agree with his boss' position but then they'd both be wrong. He half meant it as a joke. His boss didn't take it that way and fully meant it when he fired Doug. Shortly after, Doug's wife, Julie, showing an equal lack of humor, moved out.

Doug and Julie had been married for nearly ten years before the split. They met while working on their MBA's at Case Western Reserve University. Both had full time jobs and the accelerated program was grueling. When they weren't working for a paycheck or towards their degrees, Doug and Julie slept. At some point, they started sleeping together and eventually fell in love. Six months after getting their diplomas they got married. For a while, shared interests like local families, friends, social circles, favorite restaurants and haunts kept alive the illusion of shared goals and dreams. After a couple of years, however, fundamental differences started to outstrip the shared interests.

Doug had never aspired to any particular calling. He was best described as an adroit problem solver. Given enough time and thought, there weren't many things he couldn't figure out or perform competently. He was very good at everything to which he put his attention and hand. Unfortunately, once he got a handle on a task or concept, he got bored. Something new came along to grab his attention. As a result, Doug knew a lot about a lot but excelled at nothing.

Julie was ambitious, focused and goal oriented. She liked the money that came her way because of what she accomplished at work. She had no trouble recognizing the connection between her efforts, the company's profits and her continued employment and prosperity. She didn't care much for those that couldn't - or wouldn't - make that connection. Nor did she care much what others thought of her - especially if they disagreed with what she knew to be correct.

Julie couldn't understand Doug's cavalier attitude about money or his inability to stay focused on a job long enough to make it a career. Doug perceived her as increasingly critical and unappreciative of him, his efforts and his abilities. In order to divert her more acerbic criticisms, he'd lied to her on a couple of occasions about the significance of his work and the amount of money he would make. When, inevitably, the truth came out, her trust was broken. The periods of anger and silence became more protracted.

Because they were a working couple with active travel schedules, it was easy to find excuses to be apart. When they were together, they seldom had sex and eventually stopped altogether. The death knell came when Doug got canned from the plastics company. Julie moved out and Doug, not really caring about the marriage at that point, didn't put up any objections. About the only consolation he had was that she didn't leave him for somebody else. That rejection would have buried him.

Doug wasted two months moping about his losses and another four months looking for a job. He was about ready to completely chuck the business world, go south and find a job as a country club pro when Jim Harding approached him about Keystate Oil.

Jim and Ken bought the company about the same time Doug's marriage was breaking apart. They purchased the company out of bankruptcy and it took about six months to realize they lacked the expertise or time to turn the business around. When the discovered Doug was available, they asked if he'd look into it for them.

It took a few weeks for Doug had sorted out what was needed to set the company straight. The business was fundamentally sound. The building, equipment and employees were intact. The suppliers and customers, albeit put off by the bankruptcy, were willing to talk. Most important, the location on Neville Island made it possible to purchase barge loads of chemicals and lubricants. This bulk purchasing provided low raw material costs and allowed the company to compete on price. The missing ingredient was the leadership

Ken and Jim and they offered him the job as president. The following day, they drove to the plant, installed Doug as the president, committed to ongoing financial support as long as the business showed progress then got in Ken's Land Rover and drove back to Cleveland. They were in and out in two hours.

Doug called another meeting after shift change to bring the second shift operators up to speed. An hour later, he was on top of the tank farm. Doug took another look around to enjoy both the view and the fact that, at age forty-five, he was president of a twenty-five million dollar company. It wasn't General Electric or Ford but it was something and he felt the right to be a little proud. After a couple minutes more, he headed down. Stoli was waiting for him when he stepped back on the ground.

"Is there a reason you took the long way up?" Stoli asked. "There's a ladder next to the building that goes to the mezzanine. You shouldn't walk across the tanks the way you did."

"Now you tell me," Doug replied. "Why didn't you say so before?"

"You didn't ask. Besides, you made it up and down in one piece. Did you enjoy the view?"

"Yeah, I did. Enjoy your smoke?"

"Not really. But I needed to get out of that sweatshop you're running. Are you ever going to install air conditioning?"

Doug had to laugh. He and Stoli often bantered like this. It was bound to get worst now that he was in charge. In addition to being the lead blender, Stoli was the union steward. Doug had worked with several unions in the past and had never had any real problems. Doug had seen no evidence of union activism in the three months he'd been at Keystate. There had only been a couple of minor grievances and some huff about cross-classification seniority for overtime. Certainly nothing to get excited about.

"Well, I'll tell you what," Doug answered. "If we start making money, I'll think about keeping your ass cool. If we don't start making money, both our sweaty asses will be looking for jobs!"

"Not likely. If this shithole can make money, you and your bosses will just buy fancier cars and better booze," Stoli retorted.

"Probably. If we do, I'll give you a ride sometime. I might even buy you a bottle of Grey Goose so you can see what good vodka tastes like."

Doug thought he'd change the direction of the conversation and, pointing up the ladder he'd just come down asked, "When's the last time you went up there? It looks like we could use some serious painting and maintenance. And what's the story on that blown up tank?"

Stoli's face lost expression for a second and then looked profoundly sad.

"I never go up there."

He turned on his heel and walked away without another word leaving Doug stunned. It was a strange end to an interesting day.

Chapter Two

At the same time, and three hundred miles away, Carmen Risotti sipped his Glen Fiddich. From his apartment on the Upper East Side, he looked down on the Queensborough Bridge and across the East River. Through the trusses and cables of the bridge superstructure, he could just make out the red sign of the Silvercup Studio. He bought the apartment specifically for this view. The first time he saw it, he felt immeasurably proud. Carmen had grown up in Queens and spent much of his youth plotting to leave, cross the river and live in Manhattan. Doing so by his early thirties marked the greatest accomplishment of his life. It represented years of struggle and hard work.

He was twelve when he started earning money for college. He literally saved every penny. He was smart. Smart enough to excel in academics and smart enough to know that his parents would never be able to send him to any of the Ivy League schools he ached to attend. He was awarded an academic scholarship at Columbia which, along with his savings and part time jobs paid for a business degree.

The fact that he was Italian, from a working class family and worked his way through school earned him the distain of many of his peers. That added fuel to his burning desire to succeed. He often thought of them when he looked out his window and into the neighborhood of his youth. He wondered how many of those bastards had a similar view. He hoped none of them.

Carmen was the most prodigious loan officer at Empire State Bank and a rising star. His high six figure salary and incentive pay allowed him a lavish lifestyle even by Manhattan standards. He was aggressive, tireless and smart. Over a decade, his portfolio of clients grew remarkably fast. Unfortunately, his success fueled both his appetite for more deals and a sense of invulnerability. He started taking risks that became more and more tenuous.

His first foray into riskier ventures was summarily shot down by the bank's loan committee. He'd been approached at a party by an erstwhile theatrical producer looking for financing. This was decidedly outside the pale for a bank focused on brick and mortar clientele so Carmen had to decline. However, the conversation introduced Carmen to the New York theater crowd; a crowd into which he enthusiastically dove.

He was soon a regular on the bohemian party circuit. He dated starlets with various degrees of fame and got his photograph on the society pages a few times. This raised eyebrows with his superiors but, since his productivity didn't suffer, they let it slide.

Eventually, Carmen developed an infatuation with the one girl he would marry. He even followed her to Los Angeles when she landed a supporting role in a feature film. They did the transcontinental relationship for the several months it took to shoot the film. After that movie wrapped filming, she tried unsuccessfully to get other roles. When nothing panned out, she returned to New York disillusioned and depressed. Perhaps it was that state that prompted her to marry Carmen. In addition to the financial security he provided, Carmen made possible a bicoastal lifestyle that kept her dream of Hollywood stardom alive. While she was busy trying to get movie roles, Carmen, always on the prowl for new business opportunities, met several people on the commercial side of the camera.

One of them was a young woman that specialized in special effects and computer imaging named Marcie Wright. Marcie had developed several techniques that revolutionized computer generated imagery and – she claimed – would eventually obsolete human actors. While Carmen couldn't quite see that happening, he did see the huge potential of the technology. More, this would be a business aligned with the bank's client profile. Carmen presented it as such and the loan committee approved the deal. Out of gratitude for his help – and for lack of a better name – Marcie named the start-up company CARMA.

It wasn't a big deal in the scheme of things but it did offer Carmen and his new wife the opportunity to stay involved with a life they'd very much come to enjoy. They became a regular part of the party crowd on both coasts. Not only was Carmen having a great time but, because the Los Angeles social set were also industry movers and shakers, he made several new business contacts. He used these contacts to orchestrate several new loans all of which involved the technical side of filmmaking. As such, they were businesses his bank would support. He opened up a new market for the bank and his star continued to rise.

CARMA experienced significant growth and needed a cash infusion. Empire did not want to extend more credit but did offer investment banking services. Since Carmen already had the relationship, he would lead the effort. He organized a prospectus meeting at the Beverly Hills Hotel and sent invitations to several public and private investor groups..

The meeting was well attended and Carmen did a masterful job presenting the history and potential of CARMA. Marcie came across as an earnest if somewhat whacky entrepreneur and creator. A month later, ten million shares of CARMA stock were offered for sale at fifteen cents apiece. At the end of the day, they'd sold almost three million shares at an average price of just over thirteen cents a share. CARMA raised almost four hundred thousand dollars.

One investor, a lawyer named Michael Cole, bought one million shares at prices between twelve and thirteen cents a share. The total investment of one hundred and twenty-six thousand dollars made him the single largest investor. As such, he became a person Carmen very much wanted to meet.

They met for lunch at Wolfgang Puck's Spago restaurant in Beverly Hills. The eatery had been open for a few years and was deservedly one of the best restaurants in the country. Carmen had become a well liked regular though his blue blazer, khaki pants and deck shoes clashed with the attire of the usual clientele stepping out of their Ferraris, Jaguars or Mercedes perfectly coiffed and in designer clothes.

Michael pulled up to the valet in a silver Mercedes CL600. It was a rental. Michael lived in Philadelphia and was in Los Angeles on one of his frequent business trips. He was wearing Armani. He was also fifteen minutes late. He hadn't really wanted to meet with Carmen but agreed to have lunch that particular day because he had an afternoon appointment one street over on Rodeo Drive to pick up a new suit. The two made an incongruous pair and it was almost more than Michael could bear to sit across the table from the disheveled Carmen.

Carmen relished Michael's obvious discomfort and palpable condescension. He was there to gather information and it wasn't the first time he'd used his appearance to disarm someone in order to get a read. In Michael's case, Carmen's antennae went up immediately. Michael's ambiguous answers to Carmen's benign questions about CARMA and computer imaging in general indicated he didn't know much about the industry into which he'd invested. In fact, it didn't seem that he knew much about business in general.

About the only thing Carmen learned was that Michael was an attorney that was investing in several small, start-up companies. Not yet forty years old, Michael had all the trappings of a wealthy man. Carmen's research hadn't revealed the source of his money. Michael wasn't a trial lawyer and was too young to have made any real money as a corporate attorney. There was no record of any business that Michael started, owned or sold. Whatever the source of Michael's money, Carmen concluded that it was not legitimate. That begged the question of what was Michael doing and whether he posed a risk to CARMA and, more important, to Carmen?

Three months later, Carmen's suspicions were confirmed. As the administrator of the CARMA investment, Carmen saw a trade cross his desk whereby Michael netted a thirty thousand dollar profit by selling four hundred thousand shares to an investment company in the Cayman Islands. Michael netted a profit of thirty thousand dollars. Two weeks later, a different investor, also located in the Caymans, bought another two hundred thousand shares; Michael profited fifteen thousand dollars. Carmen really knew something was up when, a week later, Michael bought back five hundred thousand shares only to sell them the following week to the initial Cayman group. The possibility of stock manipulation was so strong that

Carmen immediately started calling his cronies to get the lowdown on the Cayman-based investment groups. What Carmen discovered really set him back on his heels. It turned out that both of the Cayman companies had fairly deep ownership trails. Each was a subsidiary of independent parent companies. Those parent companies, however, were both owned by a company called Lindsey, Ltd. Also incorporated in Grand Cayman, Lindsay was owned by a company incorporated in the United States named Belausa. The sole owner of Belausa was man named Yuri Pandropov.

Carmen was stunned. There could only be one person in North America with that name and Carmen knew him well.

Chapter Three

Yuri Pandropov served in Afghanistan during the
Soviet Union's sorry occupation of that dismal
country. His assignment to the war had been a
bitter blow. His father was a diplomat and Yuri had
been trained and expected to serve as the military
attaché to a Soviet embassy in Europe or America.
He was fluent, or at lease conversant in English,
French, German and Spanish. He didn't know a
single word of Pashto, Dari or any of the other
forty-plus languages in Afghanistan.

His translator turned out to be an enterprising
young man and the nephew of one of the more
powerful warlords in the Kandahar province. Like
most powerful men, this warlord was more
interested in maintaining power than ideology. He
left the theology to the mullahs and focused his
attention on making money. In that part of the
world, money comes from poppies.

The sap from spent flowers is converted to a paste
and, eventually, heroin. The warlord's wealth and
power stemmed from the sale of the paste. The
buyer of the paste was a Soviet army major who
used military planes to carry it out of the country.
That officer was killed when his helicopter blew up
mid-air; an errant shot of a Stinger missile by one of
the warlord's mujahedeen. While unfortunate for
the officer - and the mujahedeen who was
summarily shot by the warlord – it was very
fortunate for Yuri. The nephew translator made
discreet introductions and Yuri quickly found
himself in the very lucrative, albeit dangerous, drug
trade.

Yuri left Afghanistan at the beginning of the Soviet withdrawal in late 1988. By then, he had secured his relationship with the warlord and expanded his heroin trade to include refining and packaging sites in East Germany and distribution outlets in Brussels, Paris and Vienna. Yuri retired from the military as one of the very few millionaire colonels in the Soviet army. Three years later, the Soviet Union collapsed.

While looking for a method to expand his distribution into North America, Yuri came up with the idea of secreting heroin inside crates of farm equipment. Belarus tractors were being marketed in America with minimal success. In addition to taking an equity stake in the newly privatized Minsk Farm Products Company, Yuri offered to set up and fund a distribution center in the United States. This idea had a second – and to Yuri, more important – benefit. It was a way to launder his drug earnings and make money conducting a legitimate business. In addition to acquiring wealth, Yuri had acquired a family and, for his children's sake at least, he craved the semblance of legitimacy.

In the fall of 1998, while Yuri was in Vienna looking for legitimate financing for the distribution venture, he first met Carmen Risotti. Carmen didn't know much about farm machinery but he had heard of Belarus tractors. Besides, Yuri oozed wealth. This was well after the disintegration of the Soviet Union and Carmen had rightly assumed that Yuri was one of the new capitalists that had risen to the top.

Carmen also assumed that Yuri was dealing in something other than farm equipment. Carmen's nose for money told him that Yuri's wealth was much greater than he let on. Carmen suspected that Yuri, with his former connections to the military might also be dealing in military equipment and weapons. Carmen would have been surprised to learn how close to the truth he was. Except Yuri's wealth didn't come from distributing tractors and military hardware. He'd done it distributing tractors and heroin.

The two men couldn't have been more different in appearance and manner. Yuri had the ramrod posture and disciplined demeanor of a career military man. He was just shy of six feet two inches with grey flecks in his hair and bushy eyebrows. Under his heavy brow were two black, penetrating eyes that looked out over a nose that was just beginning to show the bulbous signs of age and the Russian penchant for vodka. He rarely smiled and when he did his teeth showed the effects of chain smoking. Perhaps because of the smoking, he was trim with only the slightest sign of a paunch at age fifty-four. When he walked into a room, it was done with a purposeful stride and confident air. He was an impressive man.

Carmen, on the other hand, was not. Just over five feet seven inches, he carried two hundred and ten pounds on his fifty year old frame. He had a full head of hair but, unlike Yuri's, which was immaculately coiffed, Carmen's was on the long side and always looked like he'd just come in out of the wind. His hair was dark brown except for the temples which were white. So, too, were his eyebrows which - like Yuri's – exploded from his forehead. Carmen had an almost cherubic face with an upturned nose and pouty mouth. He smiled a lot to show off his perfect white teeth. In addition to the bushy eyebrows, the two men shared two other characteristics. Like Yuri, Carmen had jet black eyes. In both men, the eyes were impossible to read except when angry or exploitive.

The other feature they shared was not physical or even visible. They were both morally bankrupt.

Inevitably, they hit it off at their first meeting.

Later that year, Yuri travelled to the United States to develop plans to distribute his legal and illegal products. While there, Yuri met with Carmen in New York City and they came to an agreement whereby Empire State Bank made available a six million dollar line of credit. The bank also offered an attractive mortgage for the property Yuri bought in Erie, Pennsylvania to house the business.

The city offered a seaport via the St. Lawrence Seaway to bring containerized product directly from the North Sea. While not the vast agricultural lands of the Prairie States, there was an ample market selling to farmers in New York, Pennsylvania and Ohio. The location was even better for his illicit trade. Heroin shipments coming into Erie had direct routes via the interstate highways east to New York, Boston and Philadelphia and west to Cleveland, Detroit and Chicago.

At the outset, and as he set up his heroin distribution, Yuri had trouble with established drug networks. Because of his access to large quantities of quality product he had no problem competing on supply and price. However, in an illegal trade, there is no illegal competition. Threats, extortion, kidnapping, battery and murder are all allowable tools of the trade. Yuri took this in stride. Having turned the horrors of Afghanistan to his advantage, Yuri was more than prepared to handle the tribal conditions of the urban drug trade. He noted that the only real differences were clothing, facial hair and weapons. Afghanis carry mostly AK47 assault rifles while the Americans preferred handguns.

He negotiated when he could and strong-armed when that failed. He was well prepared for either outcome. What had become known as the Russian Mafia was largely peopled by former Soviet military. Most of these people had families. Some of these families extended to Russian émigrés in Erie and Buffalo. Yuri tapped into this resource and recruited several local toughs to establish and protect his burgeoning interests. Key positions he filled with his own extended family and trusted subordinates from his days in the military.

Once fully entrenched as a major heroin supplier for both Europe and the United States, Yuri became a very wealthy man. Had he been legitimate, he would have easily ranked as one of wealthiest people in the eastern United States. As it was, he was measured only by his reported net worth from importing Russian built farm equipment. This irked him for three reasons. First, he craved the recognition that only the fabulously wealthy get. He knew this impulse was irrational but he wanted it anyway. Secondly, because his vast wealth was ill-gotten, he couldn't exploit it the way he wanted. The Pandropov family lived in a beautiful, lakefront house just west of Erie. They also had houses in New York, London and Vienna – the last two titled under the names of shelter companies. When the family travelled, it was by commercial airline, albeit first class. When the kids – two boys and a girl – were growing up, they took a couple nice vacations a year to the Caribbean or Europe. Yuri wanted to live the extravagant lifestyle his fortune would permit. He wanted exotic cars, private jets, helicopters, a luxury yacht and palatial estates around the world. However, there was no way to do that on the reported income of a tractor distributor. The IRS would have been on him in a heartbeat. The only way to live up to his wealth was to somehow convert it to legitimate income and assets.

The final reason was not completely self serving. Yuri wanted legitimacy as an inheritance for his two youngest children. It was already too late for his wife and eldest son. Josef, was twenty-eight and already part of the illegal business. He lived in Manhattan and ran the east coast distribution. Yuri's wife, Elena, also knew of the drug business and had from the outset. That knowledge was killing her. She was to the point that she feared only two things: losing all the material luxuries that the trade provided and spending too much time thinking about it. Her cure for the former was spending an inordinate amount; for the latter – booze. Elena was a drunk.

Yuri kept the younger two kids out of the trade. Samuel was twenty-seven and on his way to becoming an oncologist. He was doing his residency at the Cleveland Clinic. Lindsey, the youngest at twenty-four, was Yuri's pet child and the only person that could soften his otherwise impenetrable eyes. Pretty, smart and outgoing, she had been spoiled and, at this point, was adrift. She recently graduated from Allegheny College and was filling her time doing clerical work at the tractor business.

For these reasons, Yuri wanted to ease out of the drug trade and into something more legitimate. He had dabbled in the stock market and a couple of minor forays into venture capital. He hadn't been very successful with either effort but it had focused his thinking about ways to game the legitimate world of business. He came to think of it as his 'legitimization strategy.'

Michael Cole was an integral part of that plan. Yuri had retained him on that first trip to the United States to set up the corporate structure for his tractor distributorships. Over time, Michael proved that he possessed two traits that Yuri valued: secrecy and greed. The first was a job requirement. The second was the means by which Yuri maintained control. Later, when Yuri wanted to accelerate his legitimization, he approached Michael with an exclusive offer. With Yuri as his only client, Michael got rich by keeping his mouth shut while he devised and executed strategies to convert Yuri's ill-gotten gains into legitimate business and investments. Thus far, however, progress had been frustratingly slow. They'd been able to clean only a few million dollars. Yuri needed specialized help if he was to accomplish his goal before he died of old age. He was about to rediscover someone with those unique skills.

Chapter Four

By the time Carmen walked the block and a half from his apartment on East 61st St. to Campo di Bocce, the rain had turned to snow. It was ten past seven and, as intended, Carmen was late. He was greeted royally as he entered the eatery. Campo di Bocce had been his regular haunt since he'd move to Manhattan ten years earlier. He was more than a regular; he was a *preferred* customer. One attained that status only by first crossing three bars. First, you had to be first or second generation Italian. Second, you had to live in one of the boroughs. Third, you had to throw an acceptable game of bocce. Campo di Bocce had the oldest – and only indoor – bocce court in Manhattan.

There was only one other way to approach preferred status and that was to be a national - and bonafide - celebrity. This class was made up almost entirely of famous actors and musicians. Politicians and flashes-in-the-pan never made the cut unless the first three criteria were met. The fact that Carmen occasionally brought members of the Hollywood and Broadway set to Campo di Bocce, put him in a supernumerary category. He covered all four bases. More than a preferred customer, he was royalty. Before he'd been escorted to his table, the sommelier was topping off a glass of his favorite Chianti and the waiter was headed to the table with plates of piping hot calamari and anti-pasta.

Michael was already seated, facing the wall with his back to the entrance. He was not happy to be there. He had to postpone a trip to the West Coast for this meeting with Carmen. When Michael balked at the invitation, Carmen expressed his concern about the appearance of Michael's recent trades and suggested that a friendly dinner would be much more pleasant than a meeting with the Securities and Exchange Commission. Michael grudgingly agreed to meet..

"Sorry to keep you waiting," Carmen said as he slid into his seat. Turning to the wait staff, he thanked them for his wine and appetizer. Lifting his glass, he extended it to Michael in the form of an informal toast. Michael lifted his half consumed Manhattan and touched glasses in a wary response.

"I hope I didn't keep you waiting long. It was a little slippery walking here tonight and I was on the phone. Sometimes, I can get so distracted when I do that. I've been known to stop in the middle of an intersection when I'm on the damn thing! Did you have any trouble finding this place?"

"No," Michael responded. "The cabbie knew exactly where it was. I had a bit of trouble getting in the door, though."

Carmen had to suppress a smile.

"Why? They didn't make you wait outside, did they?"

"As a matter of fact, yes. Some bullshit that they didn't know me. I thought this was a restaurant. You didn't say anything about this being a private club!"

"It's not, technically. They just have strict, albeit unwritten, rules about who they let in. I'm sorry, I should have told you to use my name."

"I did."

"And...?"

"Once they tied me to you, they almost dragged me in the door, gave me this drink and sat me down."

As usual, the restaurant was busy. Carmen was the last person to be seated in the filled room. It was his customary seat with his back to the wall. The walls of the restaurant were covered with photographs of the clientele. Most were celebrities but there were a fair number of nondescript faces belonging to the regulars. Directly over Carmen's head were several photos featuring him and sundry famous people.

The point was not lost on Michael.

"I see you eat here a lot," He said pointing to the wall behind Carmen.

"I don't always eat," Carmen responded. "Sometime I just meet people for a drink and a talk. It's a great place for that. Nothing that's said in here ever gets out of here."

It was true. Campo di Bocce had become known as neutral turf for private commercial or financial discussion. Many deals that would eventually become public were first hashed out over anti pasta and a drink. The same was true for the deals that would never see public light. Tonight's dinner conversation was to be one of those.

"Did you get a chance to look over the menu?"

"Yeah, but I didn't see any kreplach listed."

Carmen allowed himself a chuckle.

"No. But there's a deli the next block over, I could send someone for lox and bagels or corned beef, if you like."

"Thanks, but no. I'll just have the lasagna. That's almost the Italian equivalent of kreplach, isn't it?"

Carmen's look at the attending waiter summoned him from the shadows to the table.

"Yes, Mr. Risotti?" His English was heavily accented.

"Pepe, please bring me the bottle of Chianti from this glass. It's very good." Looking at Michael, he asked, "Would you like a glass of wine to go with your appetizer? It's almost considered a crime if you don't."

Michael agreed and the waiter slid away.

They sat in silence for a few moments while Michael looked around the room. Finally he looked Carmen in the eye and said "My congratulations on an excellent job of staging."

"What do you mean?"

"I mean you brought me onto your turf. That means you think you hold the high ground while I'm at a negotiating disadvantage. Here you're treated like a god." Pointing to the pictures, he continued. "Hell, you're surrounded by icons to yourself. Me? I have to wait out in the cold and rain until your mignons allow me to approach. Don't get me wrong, I appreciate the effort and execution. I'll probably enjoy the meal. But don't mistake me for a piker."

Carmen was able to hold his expression although he was taken aback by how easily Michael had neutralized his home field advantage. Hoping to regain it, he responded.

"I won't insult you by denying what you said is true. I'm sure you'd do the same. In fact, you did the last time we met in Los Angeles. However, there's nothing wrong with discussing business in comfortable surroundings. I am very comfortable here – as you can see. Relax. You might find you like it, too."

Carmen paused while Pepe brought the wine and poured. When he withdrew, Carmen continued. "I won't make the mistake of underestimating your negotiating skills. However, I do question your wisdom in how you transacted shares of CARMA. That was heavy handed and amateurish. I know it and you know it. Otherwise you would never have taken this meeting."

Michael glanced away, conceding the point.

"That's true," He said. "You got my attention when you brought up the SEC. Although I'm not saying I did anything illegal or wrong with those CARMA transactions, I'm not interested in having regulators looking over my shoulder. Is there any chance that could happen?"

Carmen felt the ground rising under his feet. He took the opportunity to plant a little seed of concern.

"It's possible," He said and covered the seed with a follow on. "But not likely. I discovered what you were doing because it's my business. I regularly keep track of my clients' transactions. Especially in the early going. That's usually when something funny is likely to happen."

Carmen put down his knife and fork to pick up his wine. Swirling the glass, he let a few seconds pass before he continued. "I won't judge whether you did anything illegal but you sure did something wrong."

The brief glint in Michael's eyes let Carmen know that the flush reddening his face was anger and not embarrassment. Michael was mad at himself because of his clumsy financial maneuvering. He was angry that Carmen detected it so easily but he also knew in a flash that Carmen wasn't going to report it. That instant let Michael know that Carmen wanted something from him. What did he want in return for his silence?

"I'll bite," He said. "What did I do wrong?"

"Well, for starters, you made too many transactions in too short a time. Second, there were too few entities making deals and, third, the sizes of the transactions were too large. Any one of those will get people curious. All three of them concurrently are bound to start an investigation."

Planted, covered and watered. Now Carmen just had to wait for the seed to sprout. It didn't take long.

Michael went for his Manhattan; a sip of wine was insufficient to cover Carmen's comment. This time when he looked at Carmen his eyes held fear.

"You just said it was unlikely anyone would look into it," He had to ask. "Are you going to report it?"

"No." Carmen gave him a moment's reprieve and then hit him again. "But that's no guarantee the SEC won't stumble across it. If they do, I may be able to take care of it."

Michael took a sip of wine. He realized that Carmen had significantly upped the ante. The price was now his continued silence and promise to run interference should the Feds come knocking. It was time to find out what Carmen was after.

"Why would you do that... assuming there is anything wrong with what I've done?" He asked.

"Because I want you to introduce me to your boss."

Carmen's statement had been delivered in an off-handed manner but there was no mistaking the predatory look on his face.

Michael's mind froze for an instant of abject fear. He had been prepared to parry with Carmen about *his* clumsy trades and *his* possible exposure to SEC scrutiny. He had considered the possibility that an SEC probe might discover the full extent of his dealings with CARMA. However, he felt confident in his obfuscation of any connection between CARMA and the real investor. He hadn't considered that Carmen might actually discover the existence of the third party. Keeping that secret was more than just a matter of client privilege. It was a matter of life and death.

He then took another sip of wine before responding.

"What do you mean?" He got out as nonchalant as he could manage. "We were talking about my investment in CARMA. I don't have any client relationships where that is concerned."

"I happen to know you do. And, although someone seems to have gone to a lot of trouble to create shelter companies, they are all controlled by Yuri Pandropov."

Michael dropped his fork. This time, there was no disguising his naked fear. If Carmen knew that Yuri Pandropov was behind the deal, Michael was in mortal danger. Yuri Pandropov had made it clear that his role in CARMA, or any other, deal must never come to light. He paid Michael a lot of money to do just that. Michael knew that the price of failure would be inversely commensurate. Carmen may have him by the balls but Yuri Pandropov had him by the throat. He was terrified what would happen when Yuri learned he'd been exposed.

Michael was brought back into the moment by Pepe's return to clear the table. Carmen was done with his appetizer but most of Michael's remained. Pepe was a little taken aback. "Mr. Risotti, is your guest all right?" He asked. Michael's face was drained of color.

"I think so, Pepe," Carmen answered. "Say, would you please bring us both a cup of coffee and the dessert menu. I think we'll skip the entrée tonight. Maybe Mr. Cole just needs something sweet to digest. I think you can take his plate."

Then, noticing his wine was gone, he added: "Bring me a glass of port, will you?"

Turning to Michael. "Anything for you?"

Michael just shook his head. Then, with Pepe out of earshot, Michael looked at Carmen.

"Why do you want to meet Mr. Pandropov?"

"Didn't I tell you?" Carmen started innocently, "Yuri and I are old friends. I was the banker that helped him finance Belausa. His friendship, although it means a lot to me, could mean a lot more. I always felt that there was another side to Yuri that I never got to know. I think you can help me do that."

There it was. The final demand – for now. In exchange for his complicity in hiding the CARMA transactions from both the SEC and Yuri, Carmen wanted Michael to open the door to the illicit side of Yuri's business. But why? It would be dangerous for both of them.

"If you and Yuri are old friends, why don't you just call him? I'm sure he'd find time to meet with you."

"That's true," Carmen replied. "But he wouldn't want to talk with me on a subject I'd like to discuss. He doesn't think of me in those terms."

"What is it you'd like to discuss?"

"Laundry."

"What?!"

"Laundry. You know, cleaning items that are too dirty to use. I have given this a lot of thought and have come up with a fool-proof method. It works and its subtle. Yuri would find it very effective. I just need someone to carry the message to him. That someone is you."

"But why would you take that risk? You look like you're doing alright as you are. Do you really need more money?"

Carmen looked into Michael's eyes. They were no longer angry or afraid. Now they were just questioning.

"You answered your own questions. I take the risk because I want more money and, no, there is no such thing as too much."

On this, they could agree. They spent the next hour over coffees, tiramisu and several brandies as Carmen laid out in detail how his scheme would work.

Chapter Five

Carmen sat at his desk the following Monday. He was going over some mundane correspondence when his computer chimed an incoming email from the CEO. Carmen had been invited to a special meeting of the board at ten o'clock that morning. Looking at his watch, he saw that he had half an hour to try to figure out why the meeting was called and why he was to attend. It was the first time he been invited. He had a passing thought that the topic might be some modifications to the annual bonus program. The payout percentages had been announced earlier in December but there always were some minor adjustments. He hoped he might be up for an additional bump.

At three minutes before the hour, he walked off the elevator on the fiftieth floor and down the plush, carpeted hallway to the boardroom adjacent to the CEO's office. At precisely ten o'clock Carmen walked into the room. He was always exactly on time when summoned by the CEO and he got satisfaction by watching those that came in late. This time, he was the last to arrive. He could see that it was just the executive committee and, ominously, the VP of human resources. The CEO asked him to take a seat.

"Carmen," He began. "This isn't going to be easy or pretty so I'll get right to the point. You're being terminated for behavior unbecoming an officer of the bank."

Carmen felt that he'd been hit in the head by a sledge hammer. It was almost as if he'd been knocked unconscious. Worst, he had to fight the urge to cry. Struggling mightily, he regained some measure of composure.

"Why?" Was all he could get out.

"As you know," The CEO responded mechanically. "This board has always been concerned with your style of doing business and some of the proposals you've brought us. As you also know, your record of success was sufficient to convince us to tolerate your methods."

The positive comments helped Carmen regain some composure.

"If that's true," He replied. "What has changed that puts me here... now? I haven't brought you any new projects for a month. Is that it? Are you concerned that I haven't been performing? If so, give me a break, it's the holidays. Nobody wants to work any deals this time of year."

"No, Carmen." This time it was his direct boss, the COO. "It's what you've done, not what you haven't done. You've always been a high level performer. Unfortunately, you've gone over the line of what is acceptable in performing your job. We can't ignore it. It's bad for you and it's bad for the bank."

Carmen felt like puking. He could see where this was going but had to ask, "What is it that I've done that you think is so wrong?"

This time, the legal counsel answered, "It was more than wrong. It was illegal. You used your contacts to make illegal inquiry into transactions pertaining to CARMA. Only those here present, and the contact you used are aware of this. We do not intend to report it. The bank does not need the adverse publicity. You will be allowed to resign. I suggest you indicate in your letter of resignation that you are leaving to pursue interests outside banking. There will be no severance agreement because we require nothing more from you. We don't wish a non-compete agreement from you because I doubt you will find a similar position anywhere in the industry."

Carmen looked around the table taking in the face of each man. There were five: the president and chairman, the CEO, the COO, corporate legal counsel, and the VP of human resources. They all wore the same practiced expression of dispassionate aloofness. Carmen knew there was no recourse past this meeting. He stood to go; none of the others stirred. Carmen walked to the door and pausing, turned around.

"Tell me, who is going to fire all of you? You accuse me, try me and judge me unworthy to work in this bank or in this industry. But since you will not report my alleged crime to the authorities, you become accomplices in anything I might have done. I have done nothing that has accrued to my personal wealth. Can you say the same? You get rid of me because my presence might embarrass the bank which could have a negative effect on share value. What would that do to your compensation?"

He paused for a breath before continuing.

"I really should thank you. A minute ago, I was working for you. Now I can start working for myself. We should get together a year from now to compare notes on how we've done without each other. I'm sure I'll be much better off. One thing for sure, none of us will be guiltless. If I've done anything illegal, so have you by your silence. I can live with that. Can you?"

With that, Carmen walked out of the room, the building, corporate banking and legitimate business.

For the next four months, he had to deal with the mess of his broken marriage and cleaning up what resources were left to him.

His tenuous marriage came to a crashing end. He had never really loved his wife for anything more than her looks and libido just as she loved only the lavish lifestyle. She moved out the day Carmen got fired and filed for divorce within a week. It took somewhat longer for her to clean him out.

She wasn't totally heartless in that she let him keep the apartment although she took the lavish furnishings. Once decorated in a manner both contemporary and chic, it was now desolate and bare. A well-worn Barcelona chair was one of the few remaining pieces of furniture in the sparsely decorated living room. There was a matching foot stool, a glass top coffee table, a flat screen Sony, a floor lamp and a nearly dead plant. Two of the three bedrooms were completely empty and the master contained only a king-sized bed, a nightstand and a dressing table that doubled as a desk. The walk-in closet was empty save for six navy blazers, a couple of heavy coats, several pairs of khaki pants and sundry shirts. There was a built in dresser that held underwear and socks.

Carmen had called Michael several times during this period to arrange a meeting with Pandropov. The first few times, Michael said he hadn't found the right opportunity to approach Yuri. Eventually, Carmen got the feeling he was being brushed off. Apparently, Michael figured that if the SEC hadn't sniffed around the CARMA deal yet, he was free and clear.

It took Carmen only a couple of minutes to disabuse him of that notion. He reminded Michael that the SEC had seven years to act before the statute of limitations expired. There was plenty of time. Besides, Carmen reminded, Michael had much more to fear from Yuri than he did from the SEC. Michael promised to make the call.

In early May, Michael called to tell Carmen that he'd just left Yuri's house. Michael told Carmen he was surprised when Yuri met him in the driveway wearing muddy work clothes and boots. Yuri explained that he was having a boathouse built near the beach. They had walked to the work site while Yuri described how the completed project would appear. Michael had a hard time visualizing the finished building. He just saw muddy guys with lumber and tools. As they headed back to the house, Yuri explained that his kids talked him into buying a small boat. That, of course, required a boathouse.

None of this registered with Michael. He wasn't married and had no desire to have kids. Besides, he was preoccupied trying to find the right moment to bring up the topic of Carmen Risotti. On the way to the house, they started talking business. They were in the garage and Yuri was kicking off his muddy boots when the subject of Yuri's investment in CARMA came up. As nonchalantly as possible, Michael mentioned his two meetings with Carmen

Risotti. Yuri's reaction was anything but nonchalant.

"What has Carmen Risotti to do with CARMA?" Yuri asked.

"He was head of investment banking at Empire Bank."

"Hmm. I knew Carmen when he was in the commercial loan department. I didn't know he'd changed jobs. Why did he want to meet you?"

"I – by that, I mean you - am the single largest investor in CARMA. We met the first time in Los Angeles. It was nothing but a casual lunch between an investment banker and a large shareholder."

"And you met a second time in New York? Why?"

"To caution me." Michael started to feel the earth shift under his feet.

"About what?"

"About what he thought were a series of peculiar trades early on." Another seismic bump.

"CARMA trades?

"Yes."

"What did he say?

"He said that, although the trades were legitimate, they were of a nature that could get SEC scrutiny."

Michael felt a full blown earthquake now. All he could do was hold on to see what might fall on him. By this time, they had made their way to Yuri's study at the back of the house. Yuri walked over to a window and stood looking toward the lake and the crew framing the boathouse. His hands clasped behind his back, he said nothing for a few seconds. Michael could see Yuri's knuckles turning white as he clenched his fist and crushed the filter of the cigarette. Michael's stomach felt as if the clenched hand gripped his guts. Turning back, his black eyes riveted on Michael's pale blue, Yuri walked to within a few inches of Michael's face.

"Did they?"

"Did they, what?" Michael flummoxed.

"Did they get SEC scrutiny?"

"No. If they did, Carmen said he could take care of it."

"He did?" Yuri's impressive eyebrows shot up in surprise. "Did he say how he would do that?" To himself, he asked, '*Why would he do that?*' The answer came to him immediately and caused a fleeting smile.

Michel answered the spoken question. "No, he didn't say."

Yuri crossed back to the window. This time he asked over his shoulder. "Did Carmen tell you he knows me?"

"Yes"

"And you didn't think this was something I should know?

By this time, Michael wished a real earthquake would open a hole in the floor and swallow him.

"Carmen is no longer with Empire Bank. He got fired around Christmas. I haven't heard from him since." He lied "And I changed the way I was doing trades; much smaller and less frequent transactions. I thought it unnecessary to bother you."

"Did you?" Replied Yuri. "Perhaps your new manner of making transactions is why I am making almost no progress in generating clean cash. It was generous of Carmen to warn you about what you were doing. Did he say anything else to you?

"He said he always enjoyed doing business with you and would like to do so again."

That was the message that Carmen wanted Michael to deliver. Though scared shitless and the danger still real, Michael had delivered it the only way he could. He prayed Yuri would receive it favorably.

If he did, Yuri didn't let on. He had one more question and it was particularly dangerous.

"He got fired right after your last meeting. Do you know why?"

"No." This was true. Carmen wisely hadn't told Michael why he got canned. If Yuri discovered that Carmen was fired because of his association with Michael, there would be little likelihood of them working together. In fact, there could be a real possibility that Michael and Carmen might just disappear.

"Michael," Yuri said. "I will not say this to you a second time. I am very disappointed that you did not tell me of this sooner. I suppose since you're a lawyer, you've been trained to respond only to direct questions. Just like the military. I also respect a man that can keep his mouth shut. In our line of work, it's a most important ability. Frankly, it's why I chose you to lead my legitimization activities. However, in the future, you will tell me everything that pertains to my business. I will determine whether it is important.

Michael felt the ground start to stabilize under his feet. Although it had been dicey for a minute, he felt that he was safe. A second later, he wasn't so sure.

"I am disappointed that we have made so little progress in processing my cash," Yuri continued. "I think your plan to manipulate equities is good and you possess the skills to set up shell companies to make the transactions. Maybe we need someone that knows more how equity markets work. Maybe Carmen is a man that can help get this done. Is there anything else he said that I would want to hear? This time, don't make me ask so many questions."

Yuri sat at his desk and lit a fresh cigarette as Michael related the rough outlines of Carmen's plan. He listened intently, nodding his head on occasion. Michael didn't know if the nods indicated understanding or agreement. It took ten minutes for Michael to lay out the scheme. Yuri didn't interrupt and, after Michael finished, sat silently staring into space. After a couple of minutes Yuri leaned forward to put out his butt in the already overcrowded ashtray.

"Yes, I think Carmen Risotti could be very useful," He said as he picked up a half empty pack and shook out another cigarette.

Michael finally breathed full sigh of relief. "Would you like me to call him and set up a meeting?" He asked.

"No, no." Yuri stood as he lit up. "I want to think on this some more. When I'm ready, I'll contact him."

Then, putting his hand on Michael's shoulder, he said: "Remember, I don't like the way you did this. But I'm glad you did."

****** ****** ****** ******

Carmen Risotti sipped his Glen Fiddich. From his apartment on the Upper East Side, he looked down on the Queensborough Bridge and across the East River. The phone rang. It was Yuri Pandropov.

"Hello, Carmen," He said with his heavy accent. "I understand that you are looking for a new direction in life. Perhaps we should talk. I will be in New York next Tuesday. Are you free?"

"Yuri, you know that I'm never free. I am, however, affordable. Where do you want to meet?"

They made plans and said their goodbyes. The conversation lasted less than two minutes but it was the best two minutes Carmen had had in six months. Draining his scotch, he raised his empty glass to the view from the window.

"Fuck you, Queens," He growled. "Not this time and not ever!"

He poured his third and final drink of the night and trundled off to bed.

Chapter Six

Doug Reardon stood looking up. Above, one of the maintenance guys sparked an acetylene torch to life while two others stood by with fire extinguishers. A mobile crane grumbled next to Doug, idling until it was needed. Today, Keystate was going to be rid of the rusted red tank. What the explosion initiated, a cutting torch would finish. Doug glanced at his watch and, realizing it would take some time to cut the tank into pieces, decided not to wait. There was – as always – a lot to do.

He entered the plant through the shipping dock. It was a sunny day and warm for late October. All six of the overhead doors were open wide. Early afternoon sunlight streamed in the open doors and lit the scarred, concrete floor. Later, when winter hit full bore, it would be dark as a tomb. Better lighting was one of the many things on Doug's *'to-do'* list.

Walking through the shipping area, Doug headed down the aisle that ran the length of the finished goods warehouse. It was a huge space of more than one hundred thousand square feet with a center aisle that ran for almost a thousand feet. A few months earlier, the warehouse sat mostly empty and cavernous under its thirty foot ceilings. Now, just ahead of winter, it was filled. Pallets containing cases of antifreeze, motor oils, windshield wash, brake fluid, automatic transmission fluid and sundry other automotive chemicals were double and triple stacked. All these noxious fluids were safely packaged in plastic bottles of various sizes and shapes. The only smell was the slightly sweet odor peculiar to cardboard boxes and freshly cut wood pallets.

Reaching the end of the aisle, Doug opened the door that separated the warehouse from the supplies storeroom. This space had the same height and width but it was only two hundred feet long. One side of the center aisle was filled to the ceiling with bundles of collapsed corrugated boxes. The other side was equally filled with boxes full of plastic bottles. There were round gallon jugs for windshield wash, squared-off gallon bottles for antifreeze, quart bottles for oil and various smaller bottles for miscellaneous automotive chemicals. Again, and since there were no open chemicals in the room, it had a surprisingly pleasant smell – different because the polyethylene bottles added a unique sweetness. Doug walked across the room and through another door into a different world.

The packaging area was a rush of constant motion and pungent smells. There were seven filling lines in a space of just under ninety thousand square feet. Each line had at least four hundred feet of motorized conveyors and each had rotary filling stations, cappers, labelers and drop packers. Despite the electric motors, spinning rollers, rotating fillers, pumps and miscellaneous equipment, the area was surprisingly quiet. The only abrasive noise was the constant drone of forklifts. The real nuisance was the smell. This was the only area in the factory where fluids were open to the air and the area had the acrid smell of chemical and petroleum products. Motor oil, transmission fluid and brake fluid were packaged year round and their combined smell laid down a base odor. This smell was adjusted seasonally. In the early spring, it was made more acrid by the bite of charcoal lighter fluid. From October through February, it was sweetened by the smell of washer fluid and antifreeze.

Keystate was a major producer of windshield washer fluid. Commonly known as *'wash'* - or more cryptically as *'blue water'* – the company produced about eight million gallons a year. Two lines filled and packaged wash into round gallon jugs. The other seasonal product was antifreeze and one line was dedicated to filling the squared-off gallon bottles. A fourth line filled quart bottles with various grades of motor oil, transmission fluid and brake fluids. The fifth - and final - bottling line handled myriad bottle sizes and fluids such as fuel treatments, dry gas and charcoal lighter fluid. In addition to the bottling lines, there were lines for filling pails and fifty-five gallon drums. At the moment, all seven of the production lines were in use. The constant motion of manpower and machinery was dizzying.

A small cluster of men were gathered at the end of the pail line. In the center of the group, Lud Rahl stood head and shoulders above the rest... literally. Lud - short for Ludwig - was six and a half feet tall with a head full of snow white hair and striking blue eyes. Nearing seventy, he had the carriage and energy of someone twenty years younger. Despite his size, or perhaps because of it, Lud was one of the kindest, most straightforward people that Doug knew. The two met eight years earlier when Lud, recently retired from a major chemical company, had been contracted as a management consultant at the plastics company where Doug worked. Lud quickly became Doug's mentor.

In addition to the nuts and bolts of manufacturing, Lud taught Doug how to make objective decisions. Most important, Lud's example showed Doug how to deal with people in a respectful, direct and unambiguous manner. Lud taught Doug to be a leader. In exchange, Doug gave Lud the respect and admiration he reserved for select people. Not surprisingly, Lud was the first person Doug called after he'd been given leadership of Keystate. It was also no surprise that Doug asked Lud to help with the turn around.

Doug walked over to the group and chatted with the men for a few minutes before pulling Lud aside.

"Did you decide whether you're heading home today or tomorrow?"

Lud still lived near Cleveland. He only spent two or three days a week at Keystate.

"Tomorrow." Lud replied. "I want to get one more thing done on the cost spreadsheet before I go. Besides, I don't want you to screw up anything before the weekend."

"Good for Lois," Doug shot back, referring to Lud's wife. "You know she pays me on the side to keep you away. Of course, I have to use that money to feed you. I'm assuming you're going to want dinner... again?" He feigned a despondent face. "The things I have to do to keep you married and Lois happy. I'll look for you around quitting time. Any idea where you'll be napping?"

With that, Doug headed for his office. It was almost two-thirty on Thursday afternoon and he had half a dozen phone calls to make. Before he had gone ten steps, however, he turned back to the group, "Hey, have any of you guys seen Stoli? I saw his truck this morning but haven't seen him anywhere."

"You just walked past him," Lud answered with a laugh.

"No I didn't"

"Yes, you did. Maybe if you get your head out of your ass once in a while you'll pick up on these things."

Doug was certain he hadn't seen Stoli. It wasn't as if Stoli was someone you'd miss. He was a burly, hirsute presence and his robust personality matched his appearance. Certainly, Stoli never missed the opportunity to come up to Doug and bust his balls. No, if Doug and Stoli were in the same building, Doug would know.

"Whatever." He responded to the group. "If you see him, tell him I'm looking for him. They're cutting up that tank and I think he'd like to see that."

The only response from the group was a collective, slight and knowing nod of their heads. Especially from Andy, the maintenance foreman. He'd been the one that, two months earlier, told Doug the story behind the destroyed tank. The tank had been specially designed to hold two-cycle oil; a particularly viscous liquid. About the only way to get it to flow was to heat it. The double walls of the tank created two chambers. The inner chamber held the thick oil and the outer allowed steam to circulate and heat the oil inside. Over time, a small leak developed on the inside wall. The repair was not something Keystate's maintenance crew could handle so the company hired a contractor who happened to be Stoli's brother and nephew.

Stoli's nephew, Jack, was a particularly skinny kid. That, and the fact that he was immune to claustrophobia, served him well in the many tight places he and his father contracted to work. They were talented steel workers and constantly demanded by the industrial companies that filled the valleys surrounding Pittsburgh. The tank at Keystone was a small job and one they would have passed over except as a favor to Stoli. Perhaps because they considered it a minor job, they got careless.

Stoli's nephew had wedged himself between the inner and outer walls of the tank in order to get at the bad spot. The inner tank had been emptied of everything but fumes. When young Jack used his welders' hammer to knock off rust from around the bad spot, he struck a spark that went through the small hole and ignited the fumes. The explosion did not erupt through the outer tank shell but did rupture the inner lining, crushing Jack between the walls and piercing his body in several places. They never determined whether he suffocated or bled out before the rescue crew cut through the outer wall to extract him.

Stoli blamed himself for his nephew's death and, although he dealt with it stoically, was never quite the same. He didn't talk about it and didn't complain; he just stopped going up on the platform. Doug remembered the brief conversation he and Stoli had on the day Doug took over and understood why Stoli said: "I never go up there."

"That was the day Stoli stopped shaving," Andy recalled. "He let his hair grow longer, too. Other than that, you wouldn't know his nephew got killed. He don't talk about it but I know it eats at him. Every time he sees that tank, it reminds him."

"Why didn't anybody take it down?" Doug asked. He was horrified when Andy told him the story. "It just sits there taking up space. And if it is such a morale killer, it shouldn't be there."

"You'd think so, wouldn't you," Andy responded. "But that was just before we went bust. There wasn't any money for stuff like that. Then your guys came in and bought us. Just kind of got lost in the shuffle. There's a lot of stuff like that around here. Stuff that just is left over and of no real use to us."

That was the day Doug started cleaning house. He started with people. He started by hiring or promoting people that weren't afraid of change. He and Lud interviewed several candidates for the plant manager's job. They lucked out and hired Dave Borner away from the company that supplied Keystate plastic bottles. Dave had the ability to let other people shine. He actively pushed people to think and take responsibility. Jim and Andy's new pail filling apparatus was the latest manifestation of Dave's leadership.

Large and small project ideas were popping up all across the plant floor. The less costly ones were easily funded and carried out. The larger ones took more planning and time. The really big ones, like adding a second filling station to the oil line, would need serious money and approval from the owners. That one would have to wait until the company proved itself profitable. They wouldn't know that until the spring and that would depend on the winter. Keystate was so dependent on antifreeze and windshield wash that the entire year's profit depended on a cold, nasty and long winter.

Doug could do nothing but be prepared for the season. After this week, he didn't know what else he could do to get ready. The tanks were topped off, the shifts fully staffed, bottles queued up at contracted prices and commitments garnered from key distributors and customers. The riggers were finishing the last of the capital improvements for the summer. A new double-walled tank for the two-cycle oil had just been installed and piped. The very last thing to do was to remove the old one.

He glanced at his watch again. It had been a little more than an hour since he left the tank farm and started towards his office. He knew that the riggers were probably well into cutting up the old tank. He still had all those calls to make but didn't want to miss seeing the tank come down. He stopped before he reached the door that led out of the plant and into the offices. Giving a little sigh, he turned around and started retracing his steps back to the tanks. He met Lud coming the other way.

"I thought you had some calls to make?"

"I do. And you have a spreadsheet to finish but we're both going out to the tank farm to watch them get rid of that damn tank."

"We won't be alone," Lud said. "The word's out that it's starting to come down and all the maintenance guys and blenders are headed that way.

A lot of the operators that remember will probably be there, too."

When Lud and Doug stepped out of the shipping bay door, there were fifteen to twenty people gathered around. The old tank had been cut into four pieces; two of them were already on the flatbed truck. The third swung gently in midair as the crane moved it into position over the truck. Doug looked at the faces in the crowd but didn't see Stoli.

"I guess he didn't want to see it coming down," He said somewhat to Lud but mostly to himself.

"Sure he did," Lud answered. "He's right over there." Lud nodded in the direction of the river.

Standing alone, Stoli leaned against one of the large pipes that carried methanol and glycol from barges to the large tanks. He was holding his valve wrench. A little more than an inch thick, the wrench's narrow end provided a two-fisted grip. It flared out over its three foot length to a large ratchet wrench designed to fit the many valves in the tank farm. Since only blenders were authorized to turn valves, they were the only ones with wrenches and they were seldom seen without them. Stoli's was red. If it wasn't for the red wrench, yellow Steeler's cap and pot gut Doug wouldn't have recognized him. The scraggly beard and long hair were gone!

"That's Stoli?!" Doug got out. "Holy shit! I can't believe it."

"Believe it," Lud's replied. "I told you that you'd walked past him a couple of times earlier today. Of course, I don't think he really wanted you to see him. He's been kind of keeping to himself all day."

"Well," Doug said. "I guess I'll wander over and see how he's doing. He's a big part of the reason this damn tank is coming down."

Lud grabbed Doug's arm as he turned to go. "Be nice." He said with his voice but his eyes said: '*Don't fuck with the man.*' "Think before you say anything. Better to not say anything at all. If he's got something to say to you, he will."

Doug put his hand over Lud's. "Thanks. I'll be careful," He said and walked over to Stoli. When he got there, he leaned up against the pipe next to Stoli and together they watched as the hoist lifted the remaining piece.

"So," Doug started. "The Amish finally excommunicate you?"

"Ha!" Stoli couldn't contain a short laugh. Then, without turning to look at Doug, "You're an asshole, you know that?"

"Sure, who doesn't. But I'm a good one. It comes from years of practice." They sat for a few seconds as the crew fastened the lifting straps to the last shard of the tank. As the crane revved its engine to begin the lift, Doug had to ask: "Seriously, what's with the shave and haircut? It's going to take me some time to get used to you like this. And I'm not entirely sure I like what I have to look at."

"You really are a good one... asshole I mean. I guess you're just going to have to get used to seeing me this way. I won't be having a beard for a while. You'll get used to it." Then, as the last piece started down, Stoli's face turned sorrowful and his voice quivered "You can get used to almost anything."

Doug let his hand rest on Stoli's shoulder. "I'm sorry about what happened to your nephew. From what I've been told, it was a freak accident. Nobody's fault."

"That's not true," Stoli said. "We should have vented and flushed that tank better. Jackie didn't have to die that way. There was fault."

"It was an accident. A lot of people got careless. It wasn't your fault."

Stoli turned to look at Doug, his eyes were shining from suppressed tears. "Is that what you think or is that what you've been told?"

"Both. But from what I've learned, I believe what I've been told."

"Thanks for that." Stoli looked back as the last piece clanged in place on the scrap truck. "And thanks for getting rid of that fucking tank. I suppose somebody also told you I stopped shaving the day of the accident?"

"Yeah. Andy."

"I don't know why I did that. Grieving I guess. I felt like shaving it off a few times but, after a while, it just didn't seem right to cut it off."

"So what made you shave today?"

"My son."

Doug was surprised. "Your son? Did he ask you to shave because we're scrapping the tank today?

Stoli burst out laughing. "No! He doesn't know what goes on here. You *really* are an asshole. John - that's my son - asked me to clean up because I'm meeting his fiancée's parents tonight. Her dad is some rich guy up in Erie. The kids met in school and now my boy's got a job working for her dad. Sounds like a fucking train wreck to me but what do I know. At least after they get married I'll have a rich kid for a son."

Doug didn't know what to say. He was embarrassed and it showed. He wondered if he'd ever learn to just keep his mouth shut. He figured now was a good time to start. He watched as the scrap haulers secured the load. It didn't seem like much now that it was just so much scrap metal. *'I guess I sort of overestimated what getting rid of that tank would mean.'* He thought to himself. Then, looking at all the people that gathered to see it go, he knew that was wrong. *'No, everybody's happy to see it go.'*

It was now a little past three and he still had calls to make. He'd ignored his cell phone for the past half hour while it buzzed in his pocket; there were undoubtedly several new calls and emails that would need his response. He got up to go. Stoli got up with him and casually put his red wrench on his shoulder.

"You know," Stoli said. "I would have shaved today even if John hadn't asked. Today would have been the right day to do it." As he watched the scrap truck turn the corner and go out of sight he added, "I'm serious about you being an asshole. But you're our asshole. You guys seem to have your shit together and might make something of this place. Depends on the winter. If you do get this thing going, I'll be coming at you for more money and better benefits."

"Thanks, Stoli. We'll talk about that next spring. Have fun with the in-laws."

Stoli followed the group back into the plant and Doug headed to his office. This time he walked around the outside to avoid getting sidetracked. On the way, he listened to three new voice mails. Back in his office, Doug sat down in his one new piece of furniture. He'd ordered a new chair on his second day on the job. The rest of the furniture were cast off pieces he'd found laying about the place. There was an old, black leather couch, a walnut credenza, two matching, albeit it threadbare, side chairs and a small oak conference table that Doug used as a desk. Nothing matched but it was functional.

Doug hit the refresh key on his laptop and powered up his email. There were fourteen new messages. He scanned through them quickly - deleting six and forwarding three to the people that should have been copied in the first place. He shook his head at that. He still was having problems with some people that didn't want to take responsibility or make decisions on their own. If that didn't change in another couple of months, he'd have to make some new hires.

The remaining five emails didn't require his immediate attention so he set them aside for later and turned to the list of phone calls he needed to make. The first on the list was a return call to Mark Duff, the VP of marketing at Sotex Chemical. Sotex was Doug's supplier of ethylene glycol - the base ingredient for making antifreeze. Keystate's annual buy from Sotex was just shy of nine million dollars.

Doug and Mark talked frequently and always returned each other's calls promptly.

"Hey, Mark! What's happening in Houston today?" Doug led off.

"Afternoon, young man," Mark drawled. "Nothing much. Still trying to clean up after the hurricanes. It's been a bitch!"

Mark was referring to Hurricanes Rita and Katrina. The two storms had pummeled the Gulf Coast and played particular havoc with refineries and shipping channels. It had been a couple of months and barge traffic was still snarled around Baton Rouge. Keystate had been lucky. Doug had ordered his first two barges to be delivered in September and October. The second load was to hit Keystate's dock in a couple of days. Doug figured that Mark's call today was to confirm delivery.

"I'm sorry to hear that. I suppose all this has put a crimp in your game?" Like Doug, Mark was an avid golfer. They had already played a couple of rounds. The first was in Houston the previous July. They'd hit it off on the first tee. The second round was played at Firestone when they'd negotiated commercial terms and scheduled shipments.

"Yeah, but there's a sliver of light in the distance. Enough that I'd like to bounce something off you. Would you be interested in storing our product in your tanks? It would be our juice and you could draw off it as you needed."

"Are you talking about consigned inventory?" Doug asked. If so, that would be a godsend. Doug had considered asking for consignments but not for another year. It was unexpected that Mark would offer.

"Actually…, no," Mark replied. "Something better. We want to get inventory away from the Gulf after what just happened with the hurricanes. We figure if we can rent tank space from you, we could place material out of harm's way and closer to our customers. You wouldn't be the only one to draw from the stock – that's why we'd pay you for storage and handling. We'd bill you for what you use and credit you for the use of your tanks. You'd be getting your ethylene glycol below market price."

"Let me think about that for a minute… OK!" Doug laughed. "Seriously, I'd better think about this for a couple of days. Why don't you put your proposal on paper and give me a chance to review it with the owners. Sounds like a no-brainer but I need to put it through the mill."

"Good enough. I'll have it to you by the middle of next week. When do you think we can get together to nail it down?"

"I'm going to be in Las Vegas week after next. I could swing by Houston on the way there or back."

"Are you going to the AAPEX show?" Mark asked. "If so, I'm going to be there too."

Doug was surprised by this. AAPEX - the Automotive Aftermarket Products Exposition - was a huge show for anybody involved in automotive maintenance and customization. Keystate was a regular exhibitor. So were hundreds of other companies that supplied everything from fuzzy dice to high performance engine components. It was held every November at the Sands Expo Center in Las Vegas.

"Why are you going to that show?"

"You aren't the only person making antifreeze, you know!" Mark laughed. "Just my favorite. I suppose you're just about done golfing for the year? We should schedule a round when we're in Vegas"

"Yeah. It's beautiful here right now but a cold front's coming. There's a possibility of snow tonight or tomorrow."

"I hope so," Mark offered. "An early and long winter would be just what we need."

"There's a perverse thought," Doug agreed. "But you're right. I'll call you tomorrow to set up a meeting in Vegas. Talk to you later. Hit 'em straight."

Doug hung up the phone and immediately reconnected to make several other calls. By the time he was done, it was a little after five. He could hear Lud in the outer office talking basketball with Pete Sawyer - the new sales manager. Both had played college ball and were comparing notes on their favorite pro and college teams. Doug poked his head out of his door.

"Guys, I'm going to be another half hour or so. Do you want to just meet at the restaurant?"

"Sure," Lud replied. "We'll see you there." Turning to Pete, "Looks like we have time for you to buy me a beer... or two!"

The two headed for the door and Doug ducked back into his office. He was tempted to follow after them; a cold beer would taste good. Unfortunately, the few emails he pushed aside while he made his phone calls needed answering. It took him about fifteen minutes to respond to the half dozen emails that needed attention. He answered three with a *'Yes'*, one with a *'No'* and two with *'Call me on this.'*

He shut down his laptop, stuck it in his backpack, slung it over his shoulder and took a last pass through the plant. It was quieter now - only the wash and antifreeze lines were running. One forklift could be heard in the distant warehouse. Doug stopped periodically to chat with an employee. Doug always made time for anyone that want to talk. Most of the guys were quick-witted and smart. The quick wit made for fun and challenging repartee. The smart part gave rise to a number of process improvements. Doug had already padded several pay envelopes with gift cards for good ideas. Tonight there were no such revelations and, after a couple minutes of casual chat, Doug headed for the exit.

The walk to his car was dark and blustery. The promised cold front was cutting into the area with low clouds, a twenty degree temperature drop, building winds and a few, fat raindrops. Doug hit the remote door unlock halfway across the gravel parking lot so he wouldn't have to fumble with the keypad. As he shut the door, the rain came down in earnest.

The car was a late model Lexus and was Doug's one extravagance after he got the job. He'd bought it used but it was the nicest car he'd ever owned. The color was a pale metallic blue and not one he would have chosen but, other than that, he really liked the car. As he turned the key, the head lights automatically popped on to cut an arc across the parking lot as he headed to the exit.

He entered traffic on Grand Avenue and exited on the entrance ramp to the I-79 bridge. Once cross the bridge on the north bank of the Ohio River, he headed east on Ohio River Boulevard towards downtown. He bypassed Heinz Field, PNC Park and the many bridges that could have dropped him in the city. He drove through several small towns that lined the east bank of the Allegheny River. Sometimes it was the north bank depending on the bend of the river. Eventually, Doug wound his way to the small burg of Aspinwall.

His predecessor, Vince Pirelli, had leased a two-bedroom apartment in Aspinwall. It was a newer apartment and overlooked the Allegheny river. Doug took over tenancy when he took over the company. Although new and nicely furnished, the apartment had required heavy-duty cleaning and fresh paint. Pirelli was a chain smoker and the remnant stench still emanated from the black leather sofa and twin recliners. Doug considered buying new furniture but was too frugal. Besides, he was in the apartment only to shower, sleep and eat breakfast and an occasional late dinner. Tonight's dinner would be eaten out with Lud.

Doug pulled into the parking lot of the restaurant a little past six thirty. Fortunately, Thursday was not a busy night and Doug found a parking spot near the door. The cold front had passed and, although the rain had eased, the temperature had dropped another ten degrees. It now hovered in the mid-thirties. Doug jogged the few feet to the door to avoid getting wet and cold. Since it was a small restaurant and Lud a large man, Doug had no problem spotting his friend. He was alone so Pete apparently wouldn't be eating with them.

"Pete had to answer the call tonight?" Doug asked.

"Guess so," Lud answered. "He had his usual two Heinekens and headed home to Barb and dinner. Lucky him! He gets to go home to his wife and I'm stuck with you."

"You poor baby," Doug feigned sympathy. "Let me get you martini and you can tell me all your troubles."

The waitress came by for a drink order. While she was there, they both ordered bowls of wedding soup. It seemed that every restaurant in a fifty mile radius of Pittsburgh served some variation of Italian wedding soup. The version at this eatery was particularly good. It wasn't too salty and they splashed a little wine in the broth. It took only a couple of minutes for the drinks and soup to arrive. As they touched glassed in their familiar toast, Lud asked,

"So tell me about your conversation with Stoli."

"Not too much to tell. He thinks I'm an asshole."

"He called you that?"

"Four times. Five if you count the time he said I was the company's asshole."

"Well," Lud said mocking thoughtfulness. "That confirms what I thought."

"What? That I'm an asshole?"

"Oh, hell no! I've known that for years. It confirms that Stoli is a bright and perceptive guy!"

"Now who's the asshole?" Doug countered before telling Lud the details of his earlier conversation with Stoli. Over dinner, they recapped all the significant events of the past week and the open items left to do. They had a comfortable camaraderie. Not quite that between father and son and more than just between peers, it was a unique relationship that allowed them to broach almost any topic freely and without fear of reproach. After almost two hours, they rose to leave - sated and slightly drunk. Outside the temperature had dropped enough that the rain had changed to pellets of snow. The wet ground was warm so there wouldn't be an accumulation. As they got into their respective cars, Lud commented on how much the day had changed from the sunny, warm afternoon.

"Good Keystate weather," Doug noted. "Never thought I would see the day when I looked forward to shitty weather! Oh well, see you in the morning."

Lud got in his car and headed to his hotel. Doug got into his Lexus and drove the few blocks to his apartment. There was no garage but he did have a reserved spot in front of his building. He entered the small foyer that served the four apartments in his unit and, out of habit, checked the mailbox. He never got anything except the occasional flier. Tonight, it was empty.

The hall smelled of noodles and cabbage. It was either that or sauerkraut. Maureen and George

Rubinski were a retired couple that lived in the apartment across the hall. They were nice enough but nosey. And flatulent. Doug felt sure his comings and goings were pretty well documented. He felt a guilty pulse of relief as he turned the key to enter his apartment and heard the soundtrack for *Wheel of Fortune*. As long as Pat Sajack held sway, George and Maureen would be glued to the TV. Doug wouldn't have to feign interest in a ten minute chat with George tonight.

He flipped on the light and dropped his backpack on the leather couch that still smelled of stale cigarettes. His laptop would stay there for the night. He was too tired to do any more work that night. He turned on the TV for company. The Golf Channel was Doug's choice for ambient noise.

Stripping down to his underwear, Doug dropped his dirty clothes in his laundry bag before stepping into the bathroom to turn on the shower. Once the water was up to temperature, he shucked his boxers and stepped in. Finished, he walked out to the living room in his bathrobe and switched the channel to the nightly news. Doug learned that the war in Iraq ground on, there would be a rain-snow mix tomorrow and the key match-ups for the upcoming Monday night game against the Ravens favored the Steelers. The locals would appreciate the bit about the Steelers and Doug liked the weather forecast. He turned off the TV, went to bed and was asleep in minutes.

Chapter Seven

Carmen Risotti sat at his usual table in Campo di Bocce. A swarthy, thick-necked man entered the restaurant. Large and obviously muscular under his dark suit, he walked directly to Carmen. The back of his right hand, which he extended to pass Carmen an envelope, was covered by a tattoo comprised of an eagle's head suspended under a parachute. He handed Carmen the envelope without a word, turned and left. Inside was a terse note:

> *Carmen,*
>
> *Unable to make it. Sent a driver. Please come.*
>
> *Y.P.*

Carmen paid for his unfinished drink and went outside expecting to find a limousine. He was surprised to see the thick-necked man standing beside the open side door of a large, black van. Carmen to stepped into the lushly appointed interior and sat in a swiveling captain's chair. His escort got in, slid the door shut and sat in a matching seat. As the van pulled into traffic, Carmen couldn't see who was driving; a solid partition separated the cab from the rest of the van. In fact, Carmen couldn't see much of anything. There were no side or rear windows. The only outside light came from a slightly open vent in the roof. Apparently, Carmen wasn't to know where they were taking him. He smiled to himself at the many turns and stops the van made on the half hour trip. They could have saved a lot of trouble if they'd know he had a terrible sense of direction.

When the van finally stopped, another very large man in a suit opened the sliding door from the outside. He exchanged a couple of words with Carmen's escort in what sounded like Russian and gestured Carmen to follow. They were inside a dimly lit and damp basement garage. A couple of high end cars, small trucks and vans were scattered about.

Carmen was led to a cylindrical booth that stood to the right of an elevator. He was instructed to put all his electric devices into a bag and step into the tube. The full body scanner was a tight fit for his portly body. Once x-rayed, Carmen stepped into the wood paneled interior of the elevator. He noticed that the polished brass panel had only two unmarked buttons. When his escort reached to pushed the top button, Carmen noticed he also had the eagle and parachute tattoo. This one had three Cyrillic letters under the eagle's head. The doors closed and the elevator smoothly accelerated; the downward pressure on Carmen's knees and lower back told him it was a high speed lift. It took more than fifteen seconds to reach the top so he guessed the building was at least ten stories high.

The door opened onto an elegant hallway of wood paneling and gilt sconces. The carpet pile was so thick that it made walking awkward. It certainly made it quiet. Although the hall was more than fifty feet long, there were only five doors; two on either side and one at the end. Carmen was ushered into the last room on the right. It was a conference room with a long walnut table, six chairs, a side table and a wet bar. The hall decor carried into the room and it was lit by several wall sconces and a large, ornate chandelier.

In addition to the door he entered, there were two other doors - one on either side of the room. Carmen assumed they led to offices. The wall opposite the entry door should have had windows. It didn't. Yuri Pandropov was obviously a man that didn't want to be seen. Apparently, he was also a man that didn't keep people waiting; he burst in the room before Carmen could find a seat.

"Carmen, my friend!" He pumped Carmen's hand enthusiastically. "How have you been. You look prosperous." He poked Carmen's ample belly.

"I'm fine, Yuri. I've been better as you know." Carmen figured there was no point gilding the lily. Michael undoubtedly briefed Yuri on his situation. "I'd probably feel better if I could get a little sunshine once in a while," He continued. "It's been so hard lately finding any windows in this city." Carmen swept his arm across the room in an obvious reference to the windowless van and room. "It also doesn't help my constitution to have my meals interrupted." He referenced the fact that the meeting was to be at Campo di Bocce.

"I apologize for that," Yuri replied. "I'm afraid that the nature of my business is such that I'm not allowed public meetings. Obviously, I am also careful to keep my whereabouts under wraps."

"Seems like a lot of trouble for a distributor of farm equipment," Carmen baited.

"So, we get right down to business, do we?" Yuri countered. "I like that. Does your business protocol allow for a drink?"

"If you will. I'm not one to let a man drink alone."

Yuri stepped to the small wet bar built into the paneled wall. He looked at Carmen as he reached for the scotch. "Are you still a single malt guy? When Carmen nodded, he poured a healthy two fingers of Glen Fiddich.

"Neat?"

Again Carmen nodded, impressed that Yuri either didn't forget or that his information was extremely detailed. Yuri mixed himself a vodka martini. Bringing the drinks over, he sat down in one of the side chairs next to Carmen and lit a cigarette. If it was an attempt to create a casual atmosphere, the informality was shattered by his next comment.

"Carmen, you know we're not talking about tractors. I believe you are in a position to help me with my other business and I can make you very rich. But you must know that it is an all-in proposition. If I tell you more, it means you are committed for the rest of your life. It can be a rich life but not without risk. If you're healthy, it can be as long a life. If you chose to join me and later betray me, you will lose your health very quickly. Should I continue?"

Carmen placed his drink on the table and sat back in his chair. He sat in thought for a moment staring as his finger idly circled the rim of his glass. He felt remarkably calm given that he'd just been threatened. Other than the van ride, body scan and mystery location, the meeting had stayed on script much as Carmen had anticipated. Looking up from his glass, his black eyes locked directly with Yuri's.

"Yuri," He began. "We both know that I put all my chips on the table the day I met with Michael. Once I discovered that you are more than a tractor distributor I became a threat to you. The fact that I'm here indicates that I might be a bigger asset than liability. I don't know any details of your other businesses other than they are illegal and Michael has made at least one clumsy attempt to launder the proceeds. I can do better. More important, you think so, too, or I wouldn't be here. Yes, I want you to continue."

This time it was Yuri's turn for a few seconds of thoughtful silence. The two didn't break their eye lock. Finally, Yuri broke a thin smile. "I have had people tell me that they don't like negotiating with me because my eyes reveal nothing. Now I know what they mean." Then, as if speaking to the air he said: "Michael, you can come in now."

Michael Cole walked through the remaining unopened door. Carmen wasn't surprised to see him. The two exchanged greetings and Michael sat down across from Carmen. Yuri moved to the head of the table. He left his drink untouched. Carmen wished he hadn't done that; he really wanted the scotch that sat in front of him. He'd just tasted his wine before leaving of Campo di Bocce. The only other drink he'd had that day was his morning Bloody Mary. Unfortunately, and following Yuri's lead, he pushed his drink away to focus on the business at hand.

Carmen asked Michael if the door he'd come in led to his New York office. Yuri cut in brusquely.

"Carmen, the less you know about this building - who and what is involved - the better for both of us. In fact, you will never be invited here again. After this meeting, you are not to attempt to contact me. Michael will be your sole contact. You can speculate all you want about what we do here but you are never to ask and you will never be told." He looked pointedly at Michael before continuing. "Your role is to take the money that Michael provides and turn it into legal profit. Now suppose you tell me how you propose to do that?"

Carmen gave Yuri a sly smile and asked: "Do you care if it's an *ethical* profit?"

"Look around!" Yuri laughed. "Do you see anybody ethical in here! All I care is that you generate clean cash. As long as it's done according to the law, I don't care if ignorant people get screwed. Now get on with it."

"I'm glad you brought up ignorant people," Carmen began. "The fastest and easiest way to generate cash is by taking advantage of ignorant people. Even better if they are ignorant and greedy. Remember all the 'dot.com' schemes in the nineties? Millions of people willingly forked over billions of dollars to invest in nothing more than an idea. No equipment. No inventory. Nothing physical. Much of the time, investors knew nothing about the companies or the technology behind them. How many people really know how the internet functions? All they saw was the ass end of the lemming in front and the promise of big returns. For a while it worked, too. A lot of people made a ton of money… on paper. In the end it all collapsed and the millions lost their billions. But where did all that money go?"

"To the people that got in early and cashed out before the bust," Michael answered.

"Correct!" Carmen affirmed. "But how did they know when to get out?" Facing silence from the others, Carmen answered his own question. "Because they had the inside information that only comes from insiders. The people that made money were the people that formed all those 'dot.com' companies and took them public. It was a scam. Maybe not in every case - there were probably some sincere people that really tried to create legitimate businesses. But I'll bet most of the late comers were flat out scams."

"This is all very interesting," Yuri cut in. "But how does this pertain to my situation. You're not suggesting that we create a fictitious internet company? I have to believe that SEC investigators are keen to spot those."

"You're right," Carmen answered. "I don't propose we go down that path. I do propose, however, that we borrow the concept. The difference is that we do it with brick and mortar companies. There are thousands of privately held manufacturing companies in this country. Most have sales of less than a couple of million dollars. There are a lot with sales up to fifty million. With rare exception, the owners make no more than four or five percent net profit. I propose we buy three or four similar companies, put them together under a corporate banner and package it for sale as a publicly traded company."

"Sounds like a lot of work," Yuri grunted.

"Yeah," Carmen replied. "But it's my work. You just have to provide the money."

"Before we get to that, tell me how financing the acquisition of small companies and creating a holding company is going to clean up large amounts of my cash. I see how you want me to spend it but I don't see how I'm going to get it back. And I sure as hell won't settle for a four percent return."

"You're missing the point, Yuri. We don't care if the company is successful. We just want other people to think it will be. We'd be creating a façade that gives the illusion value. Think of it as a Potemkin Village. Once we get people thinking there's a bandwagon, they'll jump over each other to get on. The first thing that happens is that you get your money back… laundered."

"How much money are we talking about?" Yuri interjected.

"I can't give you an exact amount," Carmen answered. "But to create a company that will get the interest of private and institutional investors will take at least ten million.

"And I get it all back?"

"Yes." Carmen made a mental note that Yuri didn't balk at the amount. "There's a risk that investors won't buy in but, if we sell it right, we shouldn't have any trouble raising seven to ten million. There's a lot of cash out there right now looking for a place to invest. A *real* company that people can come, see and touch would be attractive."

"Okay. But that's maybe only ten million dollars. It still seems like a lot of effort and some risk for just ten million."

Carmen put a mental asterisk next to his mental note. Apparently Yuri had a *lot* more money than Carmen realized! He continued to lay out the plan.

"Setting up the company and taking it public is only the first phase of the plan. The second phase is when you really clean up your cash. You'll also generate new cash - all nice and legal. This is where Michael's expertise comes into play." Carmen nodded in Michael's direction. Michael was caught a bit off guard. He knew the broad strokes of Carmen's plan but didn't expect to be drawn into the presentation.

"What expertise are you talking about? Michael asked.

"You need to set up legitimate trading companies that will invest Yuri's money."

"More of my money?" Yuri asked agitated.

"Yes," Carmen calmly answered. "Some you will invest as Yuri Pandropov, private investor. This will establish you as a shrewd investor. It's hard to track cash that successful investors hold as assets. The companies that Michael sets up will be institutional investors of your dirty money. And they will invest a lot… and lose it."

"What do you mean lose it?" Yuri asked, surprised. "I didn't risk all those years making money to lose it on some stock deal!"

"True," Carmen replied. "But all that money's no good to you, is it? Isn't that why we're talking?"

"Point taken," Yuri scowled. "Now suppose you tell me how losing money on a stock trade is going to clean up my cash."

"I'll tell you in a second. First, I have a question for you," Carmen paused. "Do you think you have absolute control over a couple dozen people?"

"Do you mean they will do precisely what I ask, when I ask?

"I mean that they would *'lose their health very quickly'* if they cross you," Carmen quoted Yuri's earlier threat.

"Yes."

"I thought so," Carmen smiled. "Those people will be individual investors. They will also use your dirty money to buy stock when the share price is high. The trading companies that Michael creates will do the same thing on a larger scale.

Yuri and Michael looked puzzled as Carmen continued.

"We're going to manipulate two stock price run ups. The first we've already discussed. In order to have a second, we have to drive the price of the stock back down. But before we do, you will have purchased a huge number of shares. When the share price collapses, the cash value of those shares will disappear but the actual number of shares won't. Just like that." Carmen snapped his fingers. "All your dirty money will vanish."

"And when the share price goes back up," Yuri cut in. "It will be with legitimate money."

"Exactly!" Carmen finished the thought. "All you have to do is sell the stock and take out clean cash."

"Carmen, you're a genius!" Yuri blurted. "I love it!"

Yuri got up from his chair and came over to stand by Carmen. "I have two questions. First, how are you going to control when the price goes up and down?"

"Well, I can't control exactly when or how much the share price will move. Remember there will be many other investors that we can't manipulate. However, I will release information to the market that will move the price generally up or down."

"You can do that?" Michael asked.

"Hey," Carmen replied with bitter irony. "I used to be an investment banker. It's what I do."

Turning back to Yuri, he continued. "The important thing is that you cash out when the share price is the same as when you bought it. You might be tempted to wait until it goes higher. Don't do that. In the first place, you will have to claim the extra money as a capital gain and I don't think you want to get the IRS interested. Secondly, the longer we stay in, the more likely we'll be caught. What's your second question?"

"What's your interest?" Yuri asked pointedly.

"Do you mean how do I get paid?"

Yuri nodded.

"I take five percent of the money you take back when you cash out your shares of stock."

Yuri's massive eyebrows shot up. "You're talking about millions of dollars, Carmen."

"For you or for me?" Carmen asked.

"Both."

This time Carmen's forehead twitched. He had no idea that Yuri had this kind of wealth. He decided now was the time to press the point and close the deal.

"That is a lot of money," He agreed. "But it's only five percent. That's a reasonable fee for providing a service. And it is a unique service. I don't think you'll find anyone else that can provide it."

Yuri thought about it for only a couple of seconds. "Okay. I agree. But Michael will keep the books and handle all the financial transactions. He will control all the money."

Carmen felt a jolt of excitement. '*He bought it!*' He exclaimed to himself. '*I'm going to be fucking rich!*' Then, as calmly as he could muster. "Thanks, Yuri. You won't be sorry."

"I take it you have an exit plan in mind?" Michael asked.

"At some point, I will step down as CEO and appoint some sucker to take the fall," Carmen answered. "Then, when the company fails, the management team, the economy, the weather - any plausible excuse will take the blame - and we'll be long gone."

Yuri stared intently at Carmen for a long moment before asking: "When can you get started?"

"Today," Carmen answered. "I already own a corporate structure that is set up for over-the-counter trading."

"Really?" Michael asked. "What is it called?"

"Houston Medical Products. It traded under HMT.PK on the pink sheets. It hasn't traded in years but it is still viable. I just have to fill the shell and activate it. I have to change the name to something more appropriate."

"Fill it with what?"Yuri asked. "Since you seem to have thought a great deal about this, I assume you already have some companies in mind to buy."

"Indeed I do. In a nice, insignificant and inconsequential industry. Packaging lubricants and chemicals for the automotive aftermarket."

Both Yuri and Michael looked bewildered and then broke out laughing. "What the hell is that?!" Yuri asked. "I never heard of such a thing!"

"Exactly," Carmen said.

Laughing, Yuri reached for his neglected martini. "To our success and your long health!" He toasted Carmen before draining his glass. Carmen followed suit wishing wistfully for a refill. The meeting, however, was over. Yuri sat his glass down before turning to Carmen.

"Remember, you are not to try to contact me. If I need you, I will send a message through Michael. If by chance we meet in public, it will be as casual business associates from your old days as a loan officer." Yuri Pandropov walked out of the room, closing the door behind him.

Michael walked Carmen back down the long hallway and put him in the elevator. He pushed the down button but held the door open.

"The driver's been instructed to take you anywhere you want to go. I'll call you tomorrow to set up a meeting for next week. We can map out what we're going to do and figure out how much money we'll need to get started."

"By next week you'll be a week behind," Carmen replied. "By tomorrow, I will have a deal in place for the first company and it'll cost Yuri a million bucks. Call me the day after tomorrow and I'll fill you in on the details."

With that, the doors slid shut on the elevator taking Carmen down to his future.

****** ****** ****** ******

Yuri sat behind his massive, carved desk. He was told that it had imperial origins. It did have the double-headed eagle crest of the Romanov dynasty engraved on the front and side panels. Of course, that could have been done by a skilled carver at any time. It didn't matter to Yuri. He liked the desk. It gave him a sense of stability and majesty. Besides, it went with the red carpeting and the paneled walls covered with masterpiece paintings. Those he knew were authentic. He'd been told he shouldn't smoke with them in the room but he did anyway. He did now as sat quietly contemplating a Rubens; the smoke from the cigarette between his yellowed fingers curled lazily toward the ceiling.

After several minutes, he pivoted his chair to look at the outside view provided by two-way mirrored windows. Though sunlit, the heavy décor made the space feel cloistered. All the furniture was large and leather. One of the two side chairs on the opposite side of the desk was occupied by Yuri's eldest son, Josef. He was clad in an expensive, light grey suit, stiff white shirt and red tie as he waited for his father to speak. Finally, Yuri turned to his son.

"What do you think of Risotti's idea? Can it work?"

"It's a Ponzi scheme," Josef answered with a shrug. "Ponzi schemes always work until they collapse. The trick is to get out before they fall apart. Risotti's plan is complex and that bothers me," Josef continued. "But perhaps complexity is a good thing in these matters. It would be difficult for the authorities to investigate such a scheme. Of course, that also makes it difficult to manage. Risotti will have to be a very smart guy."

"He is," Yuri vouched.

"But is he clever? If he's smart enough to construct a maze that the Fed's can't crack, then neither can we. The danger is that he might be that smart and also think himself clever enough to get into your pocket. You already know I don't trust Michael Cole. Can you trust Risotti?"

"It doesn't matter. If his system works, it's a tool we really need. If he stays a trusted ally, so much the better and we can have a long relationship. If not, we will have learned his methods and he becomes unnecessary."

"I thought he was a friend of yours?"

"And I thought you were smart enough to know there are no friends in this business. I want you to run this operation with Michael. Stay close to him and Carmen. Learn what they do and how they do it. If it works, I want you to be able to run it without them. I hope we won't have any problems with Cole and Risotti but if it becomes necessary to deal with them, you'll be a position to take care of it."

Chapter Eight

By mid-October, Carmen had renamed his shell company PetroChem Packaging Company and acquired two subsidiaries. The first was a small business called Sprayzon. Located in Newark, the company filled spray cans with carburetor cleaner, degreaser, and lubricants. Years earlier, the owner, Sean Tompkins, took the very first loan Carmen had underwritten.

It wasn't much of a loan and, as Carmen's portfolio grew over the years, had paled in comparison with the rest. However, because Sean was Carmen's first client, the two had stayed in contact over the years. Consequently, Carmen knew when Sean was ready to sell. Carmen also knew that Sean possessed a sizable streak of larceny. He wasn't above watering down his products or calibrating his scales a bit light.

While negotiating to buy Sprayzon, Carmen told Sean just enough of his plans for PetroChem that Sean accepted stock in PetroChem in lieu of an all cash deal. The final sales price was two hundred thousand cash and three million shares of PetroChem. Carmen got all the assets of Sprayzon and assumed the company's debt which amounted to just over two hundred thousand dollars. He retained Sean as the manager in order to keep the company running.

The second company Carmen bought - Union Automotive Products - was owned by two recognized cheats and liars. There wasn't a product that brothers Sol and Harvey Rosen made that wasn't watered down, adulterated, underweight or made with dubious raw material. In short, they were just the kind of people Carmen wanted as partners.

Carmen had to pay more for Union Automotive than he did for Sprayzon. In addition to being unscrupulous, Sol and Harvey were frugal and shrewd and had created a lot of equity in the business. The asking price was one and a half million dollars. When Carmen shared with them the scheme to manipulate PetroChem's share price, they gladly accepted shares in lieu of cash. The deal settled at four hundred thousand cash for each brother and the rest in shares of PetroChem. As was the case with Sprayzon, Carmen assumed the debt load.

All told, Carmen spent only one million of Yuri's dollars to buy two companies with combined sales of about twelve million. It was a good start but not yet big enough to take PetroChem public. Carmen needed to acquire a company that was better known. Harvey Rosen knew of a company that might fit the bill. He told the others about it at the inaugural meeting of the board of directors of PetroChem Packaging.

The nefarious gathering met at the Dark Horse Pub in north Philadelphia - a favorite haunt of Michael's. Carmen was elected chairman and chief executive, Michael as vice-chairman and legal counsel, Sean as chief operating officer and Sol and Harvey as vice presidents of marketing and acquisitions, respectively. It was a pretty façade but they all knew the sole purpose of the group was to orchestrate and execute fraud.

"The company is located in Pittsburgh," Harvey began. "It has been in business for more than forty years under different owners - all private. The past six or seven years it has been in and out of bankruptcy three times. Most recently, it was bought by a couple of private investors from Cleveland. Neither is directly involved in the business. I heard they picked it up for a song. I'd guess they got it for less than a million."

"What are the sales?" Carmen asked.

"Best guess, thirty million," Harvey answered. "They hired a professional management team to turn it around. The president cleaned house. That's how I heard about it." Harvey digressed. "The sales manager he fired came to me looking for a job. I didn't hire him.

"What do you know about the guy running the operations?" This time it was Michael.

"Almost nothing. I know he didn't come from the industry. Nobody I talked to knows anything about him."

"Yeah," interjected Sean. "But no one in our industry wants to talk with you!"

If he meant it as a jibe, Harvey didn't take it that way. He didn't retort but scowled as he continued. "They have a pretty good market presence east of Chicago and north of the Mason-Dixon. They have their own brand of motor oils, antifreeze and miscellaneous chemicals. They're not in the same league as the big, national brands but they hold their own. They also do a fair amount of contract packaging for bigger retail stores."

"The northeast region puts them square in the sights of the New York investment community," Carmen mused. "I should be able to spin a pretty good story around these guys." Then to Harvey, "Sounds good. What's the name of this company and how can I get in touch with them?"

"Probably the best way would be to arrange a meeting at the AAPEX show in Las Vegas. I know they'll be there. They always are. The company is called Keystate Oil."

Chapter Nine

Doug Reardon stood looking down. His room on the tenth floor of the Venezia Tower faced north. The view up Las Vegas Boulevard overlooked the construction site for the Palazzo tower. Once completed, this latest addition to the Venetian complex would block his current view of the Wynn and the bizarre, saucer shaped canopy of the Fashion Show Mall. It would also hide the mauve foothills of the Sheep Mountain Range. During the day, it was quite a vista. At night, however, the northern horizon was lost in the glare of the Strip. Fireworks, marking the end of the midnight pirate show at the adjacent Treasure Island, added to the blaze of lights.

His suite was unlit save for the thin strip under the bathroom door but it was far from dark. The Vegas glow illuminated Doug as he leaned, nude and nonchalant, against the large window. He figured that any light coming at the window would be reflected making him invisible. Even if that didn't work, there were no nearby buildings that permitted a view to his room. If there were, it was Vegas for chrissake! Nudity was de rigueur.

Not that any of that mattered. Doug was naked simply because he flat out didn't care. For the first time in a long time, he was comfortable in his own skin. He was the president of a decent sized company and enjoyed the role. He definitely enjoyed the special attention he was getting at the trade show. Keystate customers and suppliers attending the AAPEX show sought him out. He'd already played two rounds of golf with suppliers and had another scheduled with a key customer. In the morning, he and Mark Duff were going to play a round and ink their deal.

Over drinks earlier that evening, they reviewed the final changes to the agreement before being joined for dinner by Mark's wife and the surprising addition of the most remarkable woman Doug had ever met. Mark had also managed to get tickets for the Cirque du Soleil production of Le Rêve at the Wynn and the four were enthralled by the aqua-gymnastics. After the show, Mark and Doug each bought a round at the Tryst nightclub before they parted for the night.

When Doug went to call for a cab and escort his date back to her hotel, she suggested that they make the short walk back to the Venetian. Once there, she hinted that she'd like to see the view from his suite. They started kissing in the hallway outside his door. Inside, they groped and grappled like teenagers and were naked by the time they hit the bed. Fifteen minutes later they lay tangled together glistening and breathless. For a few moments they lay panting while she ran her fingers through his hair and he lay motionless, one hand resting on her pubic mound. When she eventually got up to go to the bathroom, Doug walked down to the lower level and stood leaning against the window - nude and nonchalant. If anyone could see him, they'd be looking at a supremely happy man.

The toilet flushed and he heard the shower go on. The bathroom door opened and she padded down to where he stood. From behind, her arms went around his waist. He could feel her breasts rubbing against the small of his back. The fingers of one small hand traced rings around his left nipple before dropping down across his stomach to encircle his penis. It hadn't gone completely flaccid and immediately sprang back to life. Doug turned and folded her in his arms. The top of her head nestled just under his chin as, facing each other, her breasts pressed warm against his belly, one nipple snug in his navel. He dropped an arm to cup his hand under the curve of her butt. His now fully erect penis pointed up between them.

"I thought you were going to take a shower," He murmured, his cheek resting atop her head.

"I am," She replied. "I came to ask if you'd wash my back."

"I think you came out here looking for trouble."

"Did I come to the right place?" She looked up at him playfully.

"Oh, yeah!" He looked down into Julie's face.

It was beautiful. More beautiful than he remembered. She had cut her dark hair short which startled Doug each time he looked at her. She had always worn it shoulder length. Now it was just slightly longer than Doug's and he kept his very short. The new look almost cost him the opportunity to be with her.

Earlier that day, Doug was walking the aisles of the show with Mark Duff. They were discussing their pending deal and not really mindful of what was going on around them. Julie came up from behind and followed them for a number of minutes. They were in deep discussion and she didn't want to butt in. Even so, she was disappointed when Doug occasionally looked in her direction and didn't seem to recognize her. Finally, she walked up to him.

"Hello, Doug."

He was startled. He couldn't believe she was there. And what happened to her hair?

"Julie! It's great to see you! You look wonderful. What are you doing here? What happened to your hair?" It came out as a run-on sentence.

"I'm here because of my new job. Same company but now I'm the technical liaison for new product development. I cut my hair right after...," She stole a glance at Mark. "...Well, you know when. I just felt like a change."

Doug remembered Mark then and turned to introduce him. "Julie, this is Mark Duff. Mark, this is one of the world's great people, Julie...," Doug stopped short. He didn't know how to finish her name.

"Reardon," Julie finished for him. "As in the former Mrs. Doug." She didn't say it with any degree of sarcasm or maliciousness. She figured she might as well put it out there. It didn't bother her and if anyone else was uncomfortable or judgmental, that was their business. It didn't seem to faze Mark at all.

"Good to meet ya!" He said in his thickest Texan drawl as he shook her hand. "A friend of Doug's is a friend of mine. Although I'm startin' to question his judgment if you're his ex. Mebbe you and I should be friends and I'll dump him?"

Julie and Doug laughed - she freely and he with some embarrassment. She reached into the pocket of her blazer and pulled out a business card for Doug. "My cell number's on it. Give me a call when you two wrap up. We'll make some plans to get together." She put out her hand for Mark. "Nice to meet you. You should stick with Doug. 'Better the devil you know' as they say." Doug watched her walk away until she disappeared in the crowd.

"Now there's a story you're going to have to tell me about someday," Mark said.

"Not much to tell. There was a time when I wasn't good enough for her. That's not a slam on her. It's just that she's a dynamo and, at the time, I couldn't keep up. I lied to her a couple of times. Nothing big. Just stupid stuff to make me look more important than I was. Broke her trust, though. When it was time to split, we did."

"Well, she sure seem interested in getting reacquainted. I think we'd better finish our talk so you can give her that call."

A half hour later, he made the call which led to a meeting for coffee, then drinks, dinner and a show. Ultimately, it led to a midnight embrace on the tenth floor of the Venezia Tower overlooking the Strip. Everything about it was a wonder to Doug. The room was extravagant. The view surreal. Julie was gorgeous and, as he held her close, she felt and smelled wonderful. A combination of perfume, perspiration and pheromones. His swollen penis gave an inadvertent throb against her belly. She back away with a bright laugh. With one hand, she gave him a little push while the other again took hold of his penis.

"Come on," She said turning and heading to the bathroom. "We both need a shower before I let you rub this thing on me again."

They passed a couple of mirrors as she led him into the bathroom. Doug would have thought the reflections comical except he'd pretty much stopped thinking. Julie led Doug like a bull with a nose ring wearing only a silly grin and a faraway look. In her late thirties, she was petite and incredibly fit. It was obvious that she regularly worked out. Doug didn't. He wasn't in bad shape but the late dinners and sedentary lifestyle were starting to show across his belly and lower back.

The bathroom was thick with steam as they stepped into the oversized shower stall. She handed him a bar of soap and turned her back to him. He lathered her toned shoulders and worked down to her slender waist. Dropping to one knee, he washed one foot and then the other as she balanced herself against the wall. Her calves and thighs were smooth as he worked his way back up. He stopped short of her crotch assuming she would want to do the sensitive areas herself. Standing erect, he reached around her belly to raise a lather in her pubic hair. He didn't have much luck. He was surprise to discover that Julie kept *all* her hair short. He felt a momentary pang of jealousy. He had asked her several times during their marriage to shave. She would have none of it. Now, she was trimmed high and tight and there was no hair at all around her lips. He wondered what - or who - had prompted that.

Jealousy quickly gave way to lust as his hands slid up her stomach to soap her breasts. They felt heavy and alive as his hands slipped under and around them. Finally, he washed her underarms and arms. She took the soap from him and washed her vagina and butt. After she rinsed carefully and completely, she turned to wash him. She went straight to his erect penis. The light touch of her lathered hand almost drove him over the edge. Seeing that he was about to climax, Julie handed him the soap and, stepping out of the shower, turned the water to cold. Doug dropped the soap and danced away from the piercing spray. His erection disappeared much faster than it popped up. He tried unsuccessfully to stay out of the stream as he reached around the icy water to turn the heat back on. He rubbed himself vigorously as the warmth returned to the water and his body. Julie's laugh bubbled from the other side of the door while she toweled off.

"What the hell was that for?!" Doug asked half pissed and half laughing.

"You needed to cool off and save it for the bed. Besides, I don't do showers. Way too many hard surfaces. Mind if I borrow your toothbrush?"

Doug was surprised and flattered that she would want to use such a personal object. "Go ahead," He answered, "The way my teeth are chattering, it will be a while before I can use it anyway."

She brushed her teeth and was in the other room before he stepped out of the shower. She had thrown one of the complimentary terrycloth robes into the bathroom for him. It felt good to slip it on. Still chilled from the cold shower, the heavy robe was warm. He walked into the bedroom still rubbing a towel across his hair.

Julie was in bed propped up on a stack of pillows. She, too, was wearing a robe but had it arranged for maximum effect. Loosely tied around her waist, it was open to show her navel and breasts. She was laying partially on her side with one leg over the other. As Doug approached the foot of the bed, she rolled on her back and coyly spread her legs a few inches. Doug dropped his robe and crawled up the bed, kissing her body as he went. He spent several luxurious moments nuzzling and kissing her inner and outer lips before moving up to her stomach, breasts and neck.

Raised up on his elbows, he cradled her head in his hands while she gently dragged her fingernails up and down his spine. Doug felt a subtle movement as she arched her hips. Reacting to her acceptance, Doug shifted to probe with the tip of his penis until he slid effortlessly inside. Julies wrapped her legs around his lower back and pulled his body onto hers. They held each other in this full embrace for a few seconds before Doug started long and slow thrusts. He pulled back until all but the tip was out then pushed in full length. When she matched his movements, they gradually increased the tempo, breathing short gasps in unison. He pushed himself up on his hands and looked down as she threw her head back. Her mouth opened to a low groan. Almost unexpectedly, her body jerked violently as she wrapped her legs more tightly around him. Her arms went around his neck and pulled him into a passionate kiss. Her spasms extended deep inside her body and Doug felt the grab and release of her orgasm. The joy of feeling her full release triggered his orgasm and they rocked and clutched each other for several second of sheer ecstasy. The waves of their simultaneous climax subsiding, they stay balled up in their embrace as their breathing slowed and hearts quieted.

Eventually, Julie softly pushed him away and he reluctantly rolled off. She turned on her side facing away and Doug pulled himself close. With his arm over her waist and hand under her left breast, he could feel her heart slow and her breathing deepen. A short while later, breath and hearts beating as one, they were asleep.

***** ***** ***** *****

Doug woke to Julie getting out of bed. She did not climb back into bed when she returned from the bathroom. Doug watched as, silhouetted against the window, she put on her panties and bra.

"What are you doing?" He sat up. "What time is it?"

"It's five-thirty. I've got to go."

"Why? Come back to bed and I'll take you back after breakfast." It was only a slightly gallant offer. Her profile in the shadowy light had him thinking about another tryst.

"Not now," She read his thought. "I really have to go. I have an eight o'clock breakfast meeting and I can't go with wrinkled clothes and no makeup."

"Hang on and I'll go with you." He started to get up.

"No. You stay here. I can get a cab from the lobby. I'll be all right." She sat on the edge of the bed to put on her shoes. Doug crawled across the bed to sit next to her.

"What time do you want me to call you?" He asked. "I have to play golf this morning and then we can have lunch."

"I don't know." There was a hint of dismissivness in her voice. "Call me when you're done with golf and I'll see if I'm available. I've got a lot planned for today."

Doug felt a little put off by her tone and the light kiss she gave him as she stood to go. He was still sitting on the edge of the bed as she said goodbye and the door closed behind her.

Since there was no going back to sleep at this point, he got up and showered. It wasn't nearly as fun this time but at least it was hot. He combed his hair and, after using the drier to defog the mirror, shaved.

Walking back to the bedroom, he picked a robe up from the bed. It was the one Julie wore the night before and smelled of her. He slipped it on before opening the hallway door to fetch the morning's papers. He placed the Wall Street Journal on the small table in the foyer and glanced at the front page of the USA Today. The riots in Paris and Saddam Hussein's trial were the headline. He learned from the sidebar that the Steelers were odds-on favorites to take the AFC Central Division and the weather for the northeast called for colder and wetter than normal. These last two items were of marginal interest. He put the paper with the other on the table so he would remember to take them to be read over breakfast.

Down on the lower level, he looked out the window. The sun was beginning to rise on what promised to be a glorious day. There was scant traffic on the Boulevard below. Early morning was about the only time Las Vegas drowsed. He thought of calling Julie to make sure she got back but decided to leave her alone. He dressed and headed down for breakfast.

The Venetian boasted several good restaurants but Bouchon was Doug's favorite. It served French cuisine in a recreated Parisian bistro complete with tin-topped bar and marble tables. Doug had eaten breakfast there every morning since he'd arrived. He sat in his regular spot facing the terrace. It would have been nice to eat al fresco but the morning had a chill. He gave his order to the waitress and sat back to drink his coffee and read the newspapers.

He barely made it through the headlines on the front page of the Journal when he was distracted by the loud conversation of two men walking in the door. There were actually three in the group but only two of them were talking. Doug groaned when he recognized them. The tall one with the hawkish nose, stooped shoulders and grey complexion was Sol Rosen. His brother, Harvey was the polar opposite - short, round and red. The only physical features that identified them as brothers were watery blue eyes and bad comb overs.

Keystate's sales manager, Pete Sawyer, had pointed them out to Doug the first day of the show. As they walked past the Union Automotive booth, Pete told him several stories of the brother's dubious business practices. If only a small percentage were true, Doug decided it would be wise to give the pair a wide berth. Unfortunately, the brothers visited the Keystate booth later that day and trapped Doug in an agonizing five minute conversation. He made several attempts to extricate himself before his cell phone mercifully rang in his pocket.

He excused himself and walked away to take the call. He wasn't ashamed that he feigned conversation for a few minutes after the caller hung up and until the brothers walked away. It wasn't just that their reputation made him uncomfortable. They were asking some damn probing and confidential questions about Keystate. He deflected those easy enough but the way they asked gave Doug the uneasy feeling they knew something he didn't.

Doug buried his nose in the newspaper in the hope that they wouldn't notice him or, if they did, would respect his privacy. He should have known better. The brothers walked directly to his table with their companion in tow.

"Good morning, Doug!" Harvey leaned in with his chubby right hand. Doug made a point of slowly folding his paper before reaching up to shake his hand. He was very glad he was seated at a small table. There was no way the three could join him. He fervently hoped they would not ask him to join them and started mentally searching for an out should they ask.

"Good morning, Mr. Rosen," He answered and looking at his brother, nodded. "Good morning."

"Have you eaten yet?" Harvey continued. "If not, why don't you join us?"

Damn.

"Thanks for the offer but I'm just here for a quick bite. I have to meet some folks shortly. Besides," He figured he'd just lay it on the line. "I avoid private meetings with direct competitors at trade shows. The organizers frown on it for good reason. Best not to open ourselves to any of that."

"I appreciate your position," Sol stepped in. "But at least allow us to introduce someone to you." Sol stepped aside as Harvey reached back and, guiding the third member of the group to the front said, "Doug, this is Carmen Risotti. He's the CEO of a company called PetroChem Packaging and the new owner of Union Automotive."

"Hi," Carmen said quietly and unobtrusively. "I'm sorry we've interrupted your breakfast. We won't bother you just now." As always, he had on his khaki pants, polo shirt and blue blazer. He was smiling his best, banker smile. He looked almost elfin with his round face, pudgy nose and bushy hair and eyebrows. Doug was a bit surprised by Carmen's polite demeanor. It was quite a contrast to the Rosen brothers' abrasiveness. He felt his guard relax a trifle as he stood to shake hands. But just a trifle; there was something disconcerting about the way he'd said 'just now.'

"Good morning, Mr. Risotti," Doug put out his hand. As he did, he looked into the blackest, most unreadable eyes he'd ever seen. He almost recoiled his hand but managed to complete the greeting. "What did you mean when you said you wouldn't bother me 'just now?' I meant it when I said I don't have private discussions with competitors."

"Well," Carmen began. "That's the thing. I don't think we should be competitors. I'd like to buy Keystate. I was hoping to chat with you about that."

This time Doug did jerk his hand back and it took a conscious effort not to plop back down in his chair. This was totally unexpected.

"Sorry about that," He said referring to his reaction. "That was a bit of a surprise. Especially before coffee." He tried to camouflage his shock with some weak humor.

"Not a problem. I probably shouldn't have sprung it on you like that," Carmen lied. He'd wanted to provoke a reaction from Doug and the one he got told Carmen what he needed to know. Doug might not be a willing participant.

Doug regained his footing. "In any case, I really have nothing to say about this. I'm just an employee. You need to talk to the owners and they're not here."

"I understand," Carmen answered. "I was hoping you'd arrange a meeting to introduce me. I understand they are in Cleveland. I'd gladly meet them there."

"Do you have a card?" Doug asked. "I'd be happy to give them a call later this morning to let them know of your interest." It was his turn to lie. "I'll let you know what they say."

"Thank you. That's all I ask. We'll let you get back to your breakfast. It was a pleasure meeting you," Carmen put out his hand.

"Same here." Doug lied for a second time in a matter of seconds. He summarily shook hands with Sol and Harvey before the three turned and left the restaurant. As he sat down, his waiter brought out his food. He picked at his eggs and had a couple of small bites of the croissant before he put his fork down and pushed his plate away.

"Fuck!" He sighed under his breath as he ran his fingers through his hair.

****** ****** ****** ******

Every major trade show has three or four areas where they sell lousy food and bottom shelf drinks at exorbitant prices. Doug found an empty high top table at the one off the main lobby. He nursed a Jack Daniels on the rocks. The lemon twist was the only nod to the eight bucks he paid. It was shortly past two o'clock and he was in a foul mood. Earlier that day, as he was headed to his golf outing, he'd reluctantly called Jim Harding to tell him of Carmen's offer. He was dismayed by how pleased Jim had been to hear of Carmen's interest in buying Keystate. Jim said he would call Ken to give the *good news* to his partner. Doug was to keep his mouth shut and wait for Jim's return call. He didn't have to wait long. He was in the tee box on the third hole when the call came. It was a short conversation. Ken and Jim wanted Doug to set up a meeting in Cleveland as soon as possible. Not surprisingly, Doug's game went in the toilet after that. It was the first time he'd lost money on a golf course in years.

On the way back to town, he called Julie. She was at lunch when he called and couldn't talk. When he eventually did get her on the phone, she said she was jammed but would meet him at two in the lobby bar. Doug glanced at his watch and took another sip of his drink. Finally, he saw her walking across the lobby toward him. She moved quickly - almost breaking onto a trot. Her apparent haste to be with him lifted his mood.

She wore a beige business suit with a skirt that came to just above the knee. She had on dark brown pumps and a pink blouse. In was an outfit that belie the beautiful body Doug knew was underneath. Doug left his drink and closed the remaining steps to her. He put out his arms to hug her only for her to take his hands in hers and offer up a cheek for a kiss. It was an awkward moment as he went to hold her and she avoided his embrace. She even dropped his hand and, as they walked to the table, glanced around the bar area as if she was looking for someone.

"What's going on?" He asked confused.

"What do you mean?" She answered a question with a question.

"I mean you're acting like we've just met. When we talked earlier, I felt like it was inconvenient for you to meet me - not the most pleasant location, I might add. And the way you bolted this morning. I almost checked to see if you'd left me a couple hundred dollars on the nightstand."

"I told you I had to get ready for my meetings this morning. And please keep your voice down about last night." She took another quick glance around the area.

"Oh, for crying out loud! Who are you looking for? You have a boyfriend here or something?" Doug was joking but the way she quickly looked away and blushed told him he'd hit pretty close to the mark. He felt sick."Oh, my God! You have a boyfriend? Here?"

She looked up at him with a mixture of embarrassment, fear and regret. "Yes. And no," She answered. "Yes, I am sort of seeing someone but, no, he's not here. He works where I do, though, and other people from the office are here."

Doug was stunned. That explained her actions since early this morning but left him at a loss to explain what happened yesterday and certainly last night.

"I don't get it. If you're seeing someone else, why did we have last night?"

Julie looked away again. "I don't know. Maybe it's because I wanted to see if there was still something there. I mean, the way you were acting yesterday talking with people at the show. The way people were acting toward you. The way I overheard you and Mark negotiating. I don't know. It all made you seem so... so..., I don't know - different somehow. More confident and responsible. I can't explain it. I know I shouldn't have come on to you like that. It was a mistake. It's just that you were so attractive and sexy."

"And today, I'm not?"

"No, I mean yes!" She was tongue tied again. "I mean yes, you're still attractive. No, I'm not going to do anything about it… not again."

"You said you're 'sort of seeing someone.' What does that mean? Is it serious?"

"Not really. We just started dating. I'll probably break it off anyway. I don't want to date anyone where I work. I just got this promotion and don't want to screw it up. That's why I don't want anyone to know what happened last night. I don't want to be known as the slut that went to Las Vegas to get laid."

"You'll never be known as that," He defended her honor. "Worst case, you're a woman that reconnected with her ex. If this other guy is not going anywhere, where does that leave us?" Doug was hopeful.

"Not right now," She dodged and dashed his hopes. "I want to focus on my job. And long distance relationships don't work. Besides, you must be incredibly busy doing what you do. I imagine running a company is pretty consuming."

Julie's reference to Keystate reminded him of the morning's events. He wondered how much longer he'd be a president. That made him wonder if that would make him less attractive to her. Probably. Doug was tempted to tell Julie about Jim, Ken, Carmen Risotti and the Rosen brothers. Then he realized he couldn't. He could have five minutes earlier. She would have been a good sounding board for him to unload his concern and frustration. Now she couldn't be a confidant. It wasn't allowed for him to trust her. At that moment, the illusion of what the previous night was, or might become, dissipated.

"Yes it is," He answered. "And I need to get back to it." He leaned over and gave her a soft kiss on the cheek. "It was great seeing you, Julie. Take care of yourself. I'll call you sometime when I'm in the area. Who knows, maybe by then you'll be running the show and I'll get to seduce you."

"Doug," She called after him as he walked away. "I'm sorry."

He shrugged as he looked back over his shoulder. "What the hell. It's Vegas, right?"

Doug retreated back to the Keystate booth. It was the last afternoon of the show and foot traffic was sparse. Around four o'clock, Doug told the guys to pack it up and he headed back to his room. The keycard slid easily into the door. The night before he had struggled to find the slot while he and Julie wrestled against the door.

Doug was disappointed by the cleanliness of the room. There was no evidence that Julie had ever been there. The shower had been scrubbed, trash can emptied and new shampoos, lotions and soaps filled the silver tray on the bathroom counter. There were fresh, plastic-wrapped glasses by the sink. Even the top sheet of toilet paper was pleated into a decorative twist. All the magazines were stacked and pillows fluffed in the seating area. The big window that overlooked the Strip had been washed. The bed was crisply made and, in the wardrobe, two terrycloth robes hung neatly side-by side. The ties crossed in front as if they'd never been worn.

Doug closed the wardrobe and walked to the window. It was twilight and he could still see the distant mountains. Down below, streetlights, headlights and marquees were becoming crisp in the approaching dusk. Doug reached to turn on a table lamp and then decided against it. His mood darkened as he stood in the dimming light.

Why were Jim and Ken so eager to pull their support from Keystate just when it was poised for success? He knew that they stood to make a lot of money by selling the company but didn't they realize it would ruin everything? And to sell to the Rosen brothers. What would that mean for all the employees and their families? Doug felt a great responsibility to them. It had taken time, hard work and persistence to get them to start believing in the company and each other. He thought they believed in him. Was all that about to disappear?

And Julie! Why did she take him to such emotional heights only to drop him so callously? It was unlikely that it was just about the sex. She said she found him attractive because of his role as Keystate's president. Was it possible that she really was just screwing his title? He hoped not. That would be demeaning to both of them. Julie had always been a climber. Her whole life was a mission to improve her station. The fact that Doug wasn't on that track had been the root cause of their marriage falling apart. The possibility that she now found him attractive only because of his current job was maddening.

He felt deceived. That thought forced him, for the first time, to understand how badly Julie must have felt the times he had deceived her. He finally felt true remorse for lying to her in order to build himself up. It was ironic. Now that he truly had some status, he felt diminished that she was attracted only by his title.

The epiphany explained why he was so distraught by the day's events. The trust he had placed in Julie, Jim and Ken had been violated. In Julie's case, he grudgingly accepted the kismet that had been levied against him. He wasn't happy about it and was angry if she had slept with him because of his current status. If that was true, her perception of his worth would evaporate should Keystate sell and he lost his job.

Although it wasn't certain that Keystate would be sold, it was clear that Jim and Ken were interested. Doug had always known that this was a possibility. Now he knew it to be a probability. The time, energy and emotion he poured into rebuilding the business and people would all be for naught. That Ken and Jim would be well within their rights to do so, and there was nothing ethically or morally reprehensible about it, didn't make it any easier to stomach. Doug - and all the other employees at Keystate - were just along for the ride.

Doug reached into his pocket and pulled out Carmen Risotti's business card. He turned it over in his fingers for a few second before looking up and out the window at the gathering gloom. Sighing, he took out his phone and punched in the number.

"Hello, Mr. Risotti. This is Doug Reardon. I'm calling to let you know that the owners of Keystate would like to meet you."

Chapter Ten

It was only the first week of December and already a foot of snow lay across the eighteenth green of the Oakdale Country Club. The staff and some volunteers were putting the finishing touches on the Christmas decorations. The club always went all out for the holidays and the ballroom was a blaze of green, red and gold. It was late afternoon and already getting dark. Heavy grey clouds dropped oversized snowflakes. Some might have found the scene festive. Doug just thought it was dreary. The others, Jim, Ken, Carmen and Michael Cole were still in the upstairs boardroom. Doug had been asked to leave while they discussed some final details of the deal. He hadn't wanted to stick around anyway. He felt like he'd been sold down the river, albeit on a gold raft with silver oars.

Carmen proposed to buy Keystate for three and a half million dollars. It was a deal Jim and Ken couldn't turn down. They'd paid only a half million dollars two years earlier and they wouldn't turn their backs on that kind of return. Doug assumed the four were discussing what role he would play in the transition of ownership. They had agreed to try to close the deal the last day of March. That would provide a clean break on a fiscally significant date. Doug had recommended to Jim that they pick that date for another reason. March was the end of Keystate's busiest period. Virtually all the company's profit was generated between October and March. Since the purchase agreement stipulated that Jim and Ken would keep any profit until the close of the deal, they stood to pick up an additional few hundred thousand dollars.

He heard them laughing as they came down the stairs. Jim waved him over as the four entered the ballroom on their way to the bar. Pat, the club's septuagenarian barkeep, had already started to set up drinks for Jim, Ken and Doug. Pat was a fixture behind the bar. He was the most senior employee by at least ten years and seemed always to be working. He had receding gray-red hair and bushy sideburns that framed a rugged face. His nose had been broken several times. Always genial and polite, Pat nonetheless gave the impression he wouldn't take crap from anyone. He always wore his black vest open and the sleeves of his white shirt rolled up just below his elbows revealed a 'birdie-on-the-ball' tattoo on his right forearm. He did acquiescence to the employee dress code in that his hand-tied, bow tie was always neatly done under his chin and his shoes gleamed. Doug assumed the shoes were a carryover from Pat's time in the Corps. After he took care of the members, Pat accepted drink orders from Carmen and Michael. It irritated Doug that Carmen also ordered scotch. Doug's was on the rocks with a splash of water. Carmen's was a neat three fingers.

Ken, Jim and Carmen engaged in casual conversation. They talked little of the deal preferring instead the more arcane topics of banking and finance. Doug and Michael said little. They were not principals in the deal nor were either attuned to the world of finance. While not architects of the deal, they were the ones that would have to execute it. Michael was already mentally girding himself for the legal manipulations to protect his side. Doug had already mentally checked out. He was a pissed off and unwilling participant. After forty-five minutes - and, Doug noted, two more drinks for Carmen - Michael and Carmen said their goodbyes. Jim ordered another round and asked Pat to bring the drinks to the small lounge off the bar.

The lounge was an octagonal gazebo that had been insulated for year round use. Of the eight walls, one had a fireplace, two had built-in bookshelves and four held floor to ceiling windows. Three leather chairs were arranged facing the fire. Jim, Ken and Doug entered through the door on the remaining wall and sat down. Jim offered Doug the center seat leaving him flanked by the other two. Doug knew Jim well enough to know this was neither a courtesy nor mistake. A minute later, Pat delivered the drinks and upon leaving, closed the door. From his seat, Jim looked out of the window as the snow continued to fall. It was heavier now.

"This must be good Keystate weather," He said to Doug.

Doug looked away from the fire and towards the window. "The best," He answered. "It's been like this since late October. You know we made about seventy-five thousand dollars in October. We're closing the books on November this week but it looks like we'll net a little over three hundred and fifty thousand."

That got a grunt from Ken and raised eyebrows from Jim. "Really?" The former asked. And then to Jim: "Maybe we should rethink selling?"

Doug felt a glimmer of hope at that and decided to press the point.

"I wish you would," He started. "Keystate is ready to be a cash machine for you guys. Everything is lined up - customers, suppliers, equipment, people - everything. You don't have to sell. You've got a nice business here and it will just get bigger and better. Why not just stand pat?"

"Apparently, you're forgetting about all the months we lost money. If I remember the math, we're still upside down by a quarter million."

"Not as of the middle of this month," Doug replied. "With what we've already invoiced and what is on the books for December, we're up by one hundred and thirty thousand. If the weather stays shitty for February and March, we'll have made over a half million bucks."

"If," Jim said. "That's a big if. I'm not a big fan of relying on the weather to make money. Might as well be a farmer. No thanks, I'll take my three and a half million from Mr. Risotti and keep the money Keystate makes between now and the close."

Doug knew he was arguing uphill but he had to try. Unfortunately, he knew the numbers were against him. Lacking logic, he had only sentiment.

"Do you have any idea what kind of people you're selling to? These guys are crooks!"

"Carmen seems like a decent fellow," Ken chimed in. "What do you know about him?"

"Nothing, really," Doug admitted. "But I do know the other people on his board. They are widely known as frauds and cheats. No legitimate people in the industry deal with them."

"Have they ever been charged with anything?" Jim asked.

"Not to my knowledge," Doug had to admit again. "The industry is pretty lax on setting and enforcing standards. But everyone knows they water down their product."

"I guess that's a bad thing," Jim agreed. "However, I'm not doing business with them. I'm selling to Risotti. I've got no dog in any fight the others are in."

"What about the people at Keystate?" Doug pulled out his last argument. "There are hundreds of people that stand to get screwed by these guys. These people are your employees!"

Jim and Ken said nothing for a minute before Ken responded. "Listen, Doug," He started. "I appreciate that you care for those people. I really do. I've got my own employees - and their families - that I worry about so I resent your implication that I don't care about the people at Keystate. In the first place, you don't know that things will be bad for them when Risotti takes over, do you?"

Doug had to admit that was true and shook his head in agreement.

"Secondly," Jim joined in. "And I shouldn't tell you this but I will. I need the money. I just got a large, new customer that required me to buy a building and a bunch of new equipment for my fabricating business. That took a large chunk of my cash and I still need to buy material and supplies for the job. Risotti's offer to buy Keystate is a godsend.

The cash I get will support my business and *my* employees. These are the people I care about. I am empathetic for the folks at Keystate if it turns to shit but I have to take care of *my* business and *my* people."

Doug knew that was the end of the discussion. There being no point in pushing the issue farther, he sat back in his chair and sipped his drink while he waited for Jim and Ken to get to the real reason they sat by the fire. He didn't have to wait long.

"You know, Doug," Jim started again. "I consider you one of my people, too. Ken and I intend to care of you after this deal settles. You've already done a hell of a job getting Keystate to this point and we're going to pay you one hundred thousand dollars at the close. In addition, we're going to give you ten percent of each month's profit starting from November through the close. Looks like you already made thirty thousand for November."

He paused to let this sink in before continuing. "We asked you to leave the meeting earlier because Risotti wanted to discuss what it will take to keep you at Keystate. It's important to him that you stay there for at least a year. Important enough that he wants to offer you a one-year contract for two hundred thousand plus the usual perks. He's also giving you an option on half a million shares of his company at four cents a share. He says he's going to make the initial public offering at ten. That's at least another thirty thousand dollars."

Doug was surprised. He had expected to get handsomely compensated for his role during the transfer. He was, after all, the face of Keystate to the industry, customers and suppliers. The latter would be particularly nervous with the change of ownership because of the involvement of the Rosen brothers. A big part of Doug's job would be to keep them on board. Jim and Ken also needed him there to watch their backs. Doug was not a trained auditor but he would be the first to see or sense anything amiss. Yes, Doug had anticipated a big payday because of the sale of Keystate. But the numbers Ken just cited far exceed his expectations.

Momentarily, Doug felt a surge of excitement and accomplishment. Then he remembered the money was payment for facilitating the sale of Keystate to Risotti. The lucre instantly lost its luster. Thirty pieces of silver or several hundred thousand is merely a matter of scale. The principle being the same, he felt dirty for his part in what was about to happen to the people of Keystate.

Julie was right; he had become more responsible and he felt no greater sense of responsibility than he did for his co-workers and their dependents. Stoli, too, was right. Doug *was* their asshole. He was about to prove it in spades. *'What the hell.'* He thought. *'It's going to happen anyway. I might as well be the one to deliver the coupe de gras.'*

        "Doug?" Jim reached over to touch his arm and pull him out of his reverie. "Are you in there?"

        "Yeah… yes," Doug answered. "That's a lot of money."

        "Yes it is," Ken said. "You earned it."

Doug was fully back in the moment. He wanted to be angry at Ken and Jim for selling Keystate but knew that they were doing nothing wrong. The men on either side were not thieves. They were sincere and honest businessmen executing a legitimate deal. They were not - nor should not - be concerned with the future actions of the buyer.

Doug wanted to be angry at himself for the ease at which he rationalized the money. But he was beyond being angry. He was just resigned. He would do his best to facilitate the deal. He would look out for Jim's and Ken's interests during the transition and maximize the company's profits for the remaining months of their ownership. Once Risotti took over, he would do his best to protect the business and employees from any shenanigans the Rosens might try. All he could do at this point was his best. That and take the money.

"Well," He said lifting his glass. "I guess that's that. Here's to you guys. Thanks for giving me the opportunity. I've had a great time."

"Jesus!" Jim said. "You make it sound like someone died! We're about to make some serious money here. Cheer up! Besides, the hard work is about to begin. These negotiations and paper chases are a huge pain in the ass. You've got to keep your head in the game."

"Don't worry, Jim. I've got you covered." Doug stood up and set his drained glass on the fireplace mantle. "Unless there's something else, I think I'll be heading back. It's going to take a while in this weather."

"Maybe you should stay here tonight?" Ken suggested. The club had a few guest rooms upstairs for occasions like this or when members overindulged. "Do you need really to head back tonight?"

"Unfortunately, yes. I had a lot to do before this deal and things just got busier. Do you guys have any suggestions or preferences about when and to whom I break the news? I assume we're going to have to provide financials pretty soon so I'll have to involve accounting."

"Why don't you give me a call in the morning," Jim said. "We can discuss the timing then. I suppose you're going to talk this over with Lud?"

"You know me too well," Doug replied. "You know I will… even if you ask me not to." He broke a weak smile. "What are you going to do, fire me? Don't worry, he's been around the track more than a few times. He knows how to be discreet. More than likely, he'll make sure I am! See you later."

Doug crossed the small room to the door. Before he could open it, Jim called to him. "Doug?"

"Yeah?"

"Thanks."

******* ******* ******* *******

Carmen Risotti had a great nose for cioppino. After leaving Oakdale, he asked Michael to drive the short distance to Cleveland's Little Italy neighborhood. It was still snowing as they drove down the hill past Lakeview Cemetery into the heart of the enclave. Red, green and white lights glowed on lamp posts and stretched across the street. Carmen made a joke to Michael about how Italians got double duty out of the decorations for Christmas and Columbus Day. When Michael gave him a puzzled look, Carmen tried to explain.

"Italians make a big deal out of Columbus Day because he was Italian. It's kind of our version of St. Patrick's Day."

"What's that got to do with the lights?" Michael asked.

"Red, green and white are the colors of the Italian flag. I was joking that they left the lights up after Columbus Day for Christmas."

"Oh," Michael replied. He either didn't get the joke or didn't think it funny. Carmen shook his head. Michael was one of the most humorless people he knew.

"We're here," He said. "Find someplace to park."

Snow plows had left piles of snow on the sides of the street so there was no parking. Michael pulled the rented Cadillac up to a valet stand and, after paying the attendant, stepped over the snow bank to follow after Carmen. Although both sides of the street were lined with restaurants, art galleries and shops, proprietors made no effort to shovel snow off the sidewalk. Michael slipped along a narrow, slushy footpath to where his portly companion had stopped. Carmen was reading a menu that was posted in the window of tiny ristorante. As Michael approached, Carmen poked a chubby finger at an entrée.

"Cioppino! I told you they'd have it here. C'mon, let's get out of the cold."

They stepped inside a tiny foyer that lead to a very small restaurant. There were only a half dozen tables and no apparent bar. Carmen was about to leave when a waiter came out of the kitchen carrying a bottle of wine. They waited while he opened the bottle and poured for the elderly couple that were the only other diners. Since it was Tuesday and the weather vile, it was likely to be a slow night.

The waiter left the bottle on their table before coming over to Carmen and Michael. He turned to scan the room as if to find an empty table. Carmen pointed to the table farthest from the old couple.

"We'll take that one."

He took off his coat, handed it to the rebuffed waiter and walked to the table. Michael apologetically handed over his coat and followed. A few minutes later, a smiling waitress came over to deliver menus and take drink orders. Carmen ordered his usual scotch - he had to settle for Glen Levitt - and Michael asked for water. He'd had enough to drink at Oakdale and he still had to drive across town to the airport.

They were flying out early the following morning and had booked rooms at the airport hotel. Michael was headed to Philadelphia to work on the Keystate deal and Carmen was going to an investor conference near Los Angeles to drum up interest in PetroChem. Michael needed to stay clear-headed. As he often did, he wondered how Carmen could function given his alcohol consumption. On cue, the waitress came back with their drinks and asked if they were ready to order. Carmen ordered the cioppino and a glass of cabernet. Michael asked for linguini with clam sauce. After she left, Michael asked,

"How'd you know they had that stuff here?"

"What stuff?"

"Whatever it was you ordered. You seemed to be sure they served it here. How did you know?"

"That *'stuff'*, as you call it, is cioppino. It's the Italian version of bouillabaisse. You'd be surprised at what I know about Cleveland. Or a lot of cities, for that matter. I have contacts in just about every major city. You meet a lot of people doing what I do for a living. That's how I met you, remember?"

"Yeah, I guess so. So you remembered that this restaurant serves that particular dish?"

"No. But I did talk to a friend last week to tell him I was coming to Cleveland. He's one of the people I'm using to get the word out on PetroChem. He reminded me of this place. I do know a lot of trivia about Cleveland, though. Did you know that Rockefeller got his start and lived a few miles from where we're sitting? In fact, he's buried in that cemetery we passed on the way here."

Michael neither knew nor cared but was polite enough to carry the conversation. "No, I don't know much about that. I've never been a big history buff."

"I am," Carmen replied. "Especially about Rockefeller. I've read a couple of his biographies.

The first one when I was a teenager. He was the archetype of the 'rags-to-riches' story. You can learn a lot by studying his life. In fact, we used one of his favorite ploys when we bought Sprayzon and Union Automotive."

"Really?" Michael was interested now. "How's that?"

"Well," Carmen explained. "Whenever old John D. wanted to buy out a competitor - which he did often - he always offered them shares of Standard Oil in lieu of cash. The ones that took the deal got rich."

"And the ones that didn't?"

"Got crushed."

Michael thought about this for a minute. "So was Rockefeller a stock manipulator?"

"I don't know. Probably not at first. Later on, when he was richer than God… maybe. That kind of wealth can certainly be used to influence events. A big part of it comes down to the people you're dealing with. I knew Sean and the Rosens would want to take shares of PetroChem because they are willing to be manipulative."

"What about the owners of Keystate?"

"I offered them the same deal and they turned me down flat. Said it had to be an all cash deal or no deal at all. Frankly, I think Reardon pissed in my soup. He knows about the Rosens' reputation and probably scared his bosses off."

"I don't like him," Michael groused. "The last thing we need is a choirboy running loose inside our organization. He's going to be trouble for us and I don't know why you offered to pay him so much."

"I'm paying him a lot to keep him around during the transition." Carmen answered. "We need him as window dressing in order to run up the share price. In a few months, we'll drive down the company's profit and blame him for the poor operating performance. At that point I'll fire him for cause and void his contract. Relax, we're not going to pay him half of what was promised."

"So you're planning on crushing him because he won't play ball?"

"That's right."

"Just like Rockefeller?"

"Not exactly like Rockefeller. We differ on a couple of key issues"

"Oh? What's that."

Carmen paused the conversation as the waitress approached with his wine. He picked up the remainder of his scotch and asked her to wait a moment before he continued.

"First, he had the nasty habit of giving away large chunks of his money to charity." He smiled at Michael over his drink, polished it off and handed the empty glass to the waitress. "And second, he didn't drink!"

Chapter Eleven

The following morning dawned crisp and bright. The front had passed during the night leaving a cloudless sky over Pittsburgh. Doug picked up Lud outside the hotel and drove the short distance to Denny's. Breakfast had become part of their routine and Marcie, their regular waitress, met them at the door when they entered.

"Usual?" was all she asked, putting the coffee back on the warmer plate.

"Yes, please." They answered in unison and, after hanging their coats on the tree, headed to their table. Marcie had already set them up with piping hot coffee. The two had known each other long enough for Lud to see that something was bothering his younger friend. He was also wise enough wait for Doug to open up. It didn't take long.

"Keystate is being sold." It came out flat and blunt. Doug was surprised by Lud's lack of reaction. "You're not surprised?" He asked.

"No. Not really. Disappointed but not surprised. Ken and Jim are absentee owners and Keystate is just an investment for them. It's always been a matter of time before they sold. I am surprised that it's selling so soon and before we've shown any sustained profit. Who's the buyer?"

Doug told him the story over breakfast. He started with the initial meeting in Las Vegas and ended at the events of the previous evening. Lud listened attentively, interrupting only to share Doug's concern that the Rosen brothers were part of the mix. When Doug finished, Lud asked whether it was a done deal and if so, when would it close? Doug answered that Jim, Ken and Carmen had agreed on price and, barring anything unexpected, the deal would close at the end of March.

"That's a pretty aggressive timeline," Lud said. "Did they say when people are going to start showing up for due diligence?"

"A lawyer named Michael Cole will be in next week to give me a list of documents I have to provide. I'll need John and Rose for some information so I have to let them know what's going on." Doug referred to the company's controller and IT manager. He continued. "Other than that, I want to keep it quiet until after Christmas. No point in getting people nervous going into the holidays."

"Did they offer you a contract to stay?" Lud's asked.

Doug hesitated before answering. He felt guilty about the money he would be paid to oversee Keystate's demise. He was also disappointed that Lud didn't ask how he felt or what he was going to do about the situation. Doug instantly knew those were pointless considerations. It didn't matter what he felt and there sure as hell wasn't anything he could do about it. Lud had asked the only significant question regarding Doug's role.

"I haven't been offered a contract yet. Risotti did talk it over with Jim and Ken last night and they ran me through his proposal. It's very generous."

"Good," Lud answered. "Now listen to me carefully. There's nothing you could do - or should do - to change the situation. Keystate has always been a turnaround proposition. You did a good job helping to get it back on solid footing. You should be proud of that. However, and despite the sense of ownership you feel, you are not - and never were - an owner. Don't take any of this personally. Take the money both sides are going to give you to manage the transition. Do the best you can do to keep the company running smoothly. Unless I miss my guess, you'll be gone within a year of the new owners taking over. That's just the way these things go."

"I know, Lud, I know. I'm just mad that all our hard work is probably going down the crapper when those guys take over. And that's only the half of it. What really pisses me off is what's going to happen to the employees. I'm telling you, the Rosens are cheats and liars. Unless Risotti gets rid of them, the place is going to crater."

"If it does... it does," Lud consoled. "There's nothing you can do about it. That may not be fair but no one ever said life is fair. You have to look out for yourself. Make sure you document everything. If the new owners are as bad as you make out, cover your ass by keeping a record of everything. Other than that, just keep doing the right things the right way. That's the only way to keep your nose clean and do the best you can for the employees."

Lud rose from the table, put his coat on and went over to the register to pay. Doug left the tip before he put on his coat and headed to the exit. He waited for Lud to join him before opening the door to go out. The sun was blinding as it bounced off the snow. Although it was cold, black patches of asphalt showed here and there as the sun warmed the parking lot. Lud rested his hand on Doug's shoulder as they headed they headed to the car.

"There's one more thing I forgot to tell you."

"What's that?" Doug asked.

"If this whole thing really does turn to shit, you have to make sure I get paid before you get canned!" Lud answered with a smile.

Doug gave a low chuckle at Lud's graveyard humor.

"I'm not so sure I should do that." He answered. "Aren't you the one that's always telling me that no good deed goes unpunished."

Chapter Twelve

It was a beautiful day for flying. A massive high pressure system dominated the center of the country making for a clear, smooth ride. Carmen looked out the window of his first class seat at the few cumulus clouds drifting below. The plane was headed east so the sun, which always glared at this altitude, didn't stream blindingly through the port. It was easy to make out the Appalachian foothills as the plane started its initial descent across Ohio to touchdown in Pittsburgh. The countryside had the fresh, green look of early June.

Carmen was on the red eye out of Los Angeles. He'd spent the early part of the week at a conference successfully pitching PetroChem to eager investors. It was surprisingly easy. There seemed to be a limitless supply of gullible people with cash. In most cases, Carmen just had to run through his computer presentation to attract new investors. Occasionally, he'd grab the attention of an institutional investor. When that happened, he had to arrange a tour of the Keystate facility. Today was one of those occasions. The pension administrator for the Indianapolis municipal workers was driving in to meet Carmen at the plant. It was exactly the type of fund Carmen wanted to reel in - large enough to give credibility to his scheme but not so large as to be intrusive.

Carmen reached up and pushed the call button. He'd finished his fourth Bloody Mary and wanted another before the galley closed for the final approach. He intercepted the flight attendant halfway down the aisle by raising his empty class.

She smiled, nodded and turned back to the front of the plane. A moment later she delivered his fresh drink. Carmen took a long pull before setting the glass on the tray table to pick up the draft of the latest PetroChem prospectus. He'd read it through on the flight and made a couple of notes in the margins. It was a good piece and painted a pretty picture of the company. Too bad it was mostly lies. He put the draft in his briefcase and sat back to rest his eyes for the remainder of the flight. His mind, however, raced on. Mostly, he was very pleased. Except for a few minor hitches, everything was unfolding to plan.

After he publicly announce the acquisition of Keystate, the price of PetroChem shares took off. It had been trading between six and seven cents a share. Three months later, it was selling around fifteen cents. So far, the company had issue just over six million dollars worth of shares. Carmen used four and a half million to repay Yuri for the money he'd advanced putting the company together. Of course, he took his five percent out of the sale of that stock. Yuri didn't object because the money he got back was clean. Yuri plowed a million dollars back into the company with the stipulation that the money not be used without his explicit permission. This stipulation created a problem for Carmen.

It was taking a lot of money to create the PetroChem story. He needed to raise another million dollars in order to fund the company's on-going operations. He wasn't interested in running it as a long term business but he did need to keep the golden goose alive.

Once he got that million dollar cushion in place, it would be time for Michael to start buying shares at the high point before releasing negative news to drive the price down. Once the price of those shares bottomed out, he would fabricate news to once again run the share price up. Carmen hadn't yet concocted the bad news he would report to drive down the share price. That was one of the open items that kept him awake at night. The other was Doug Reardon.

For the moment, Doug was contributing significantly, albeit unwittingly, to the success of Carmen's stratagem. Earlier in April, Doug and Lud had laid plans and set a timeline to consolidate everything in Pittsburgh. In early May, they were dismantling equipment at all three locations. Before the end of the month, new electrical and pneumatic runs were in place and the plumbers had started installing hundreds of feet of new pipe from the tank farm. It was now the end of the second week of June and concrete contractors were busy erecting new shipping docks and pouring foundations for additional tanks. The plant buzzed with energy and enthusiasm. Keystate had all the earmarks of a going venture. Potential investors got caught up in the excitement when Carmen led them through the plant. It was easy for him to peddle his snake oil.

Unfortunately, the rapid pace of change also presented him with a couple of headaches. The first was the cost of all this activity. Doug had already run up over two hundred thousand dollars of expense. It wasn't that the cost was unusual or unwarranted. Carmen expected the need for window dressing and had approved the budget that

Doug presented. He hadn't anticipated the speed or scope of change. There were a lot of bills coming due and Carmen was loath to give up the cash. All the money that Doug was spending - and he still had a few hundred thousand to go - had been earmarked for Yuri. Carmen hadn't yet told Michael about the growing need for more of Yuri's cash. He wasn't worried that Yuri would be particularly annoyed. Yuri had plenty of money. Carmen was concerned that the profligate spending would be just another reason for Michael to be pissed at Doug. There were plenty of those already.

Carmen finished his drink and handed the glass to the flight attendant. She was making her final pass down the aisle, collecting trash and reminding her wards to stow tray tables and bring their seats upright. Carmen looked out of his window as the plane flew over the western edges of Pittsburgh. He recognized Neville Island and thought he could make out Keystate's tank farm before the plane banked into a slow left turn as it descended towards the airport. The sun, momentarily bursting through the window, blinded Carmen as the plane arced north before settling into its final, westbound approach. This would be the first time Carmen had traveled to the plant alone. Michael, Sol, Harvey or Sean had accompanied him on earlier visits. One time, the entire cohort was there. Carmen grimaced at the memory.

Carmen had invited a significant, potential investor to tour the plant. The investor wanted to meet the entire board of PetroChem so Michael, Sean and the Rosens were there. Before the investor arrived, Carmen asked Doug and Lud to update the others on the progress of the consolidation. That turned out to be a mistake. It seemed Sean, Michael, Sol and Harvey each had strong and divergent opinions about how and when the plan should be executed.

At first, Doug and Lud were bewildered because Carmen had already approved their plan. When Doug said as much, the other four turned on Carmen to ask how he could approve a plan without discussing it with the board. Carmen made short work of that argument. With black eyes blazing, he reminded Sean and the Rosens that they'd been bought out and that Michael was just legal counsel. He then turned the floor back to let Doug and Lud continue.

Sean and the Rosens sat and sulked in silence. Michael, however, who considered himself both an equal partner in Yuri's plan and personally invested in Keystate, couldn't keep still. He peppered Doug and Lud with increasingly trivial and meaningless questions. For the most part, Doug bit his tongue and answered as best he could. Lud was not so diplomatic and he eventually let Michael have it.

"So, Michael," He began. "Where did you say you got your engineering degree?"

"I'm a lawyer," Michael responded indignantly but not missing the point.

"Oh," Lud paused for effect. "So you must have gone on to get an MBA. Where did you get that?"

"I didn't."

"Really?" Lud feigned surprise. "Doug did. He went to Case. Perhaps you've heard of it. He got his degree while he was working at a manufacturing business. In fact, he's spent about twenty years in manufacturing. Me? I've only got about fifty in it. Before that, I got a B.S. in Electrical Engineering."

Michael had turned beet red by this point. The others were smirking at his discomfort. He tried to fight back.

"I may not have the background or experience you have…"

"That's right." Lud loomed over him to cut him off. "You don't know shit! You don't even know enough to keep your mouth shut when it's obvious you have nothing to contribute. Now why don't you sit there like a good little lawyer until someone has a legal question. God willing, that won't happen."

Lud towered over Michael for a few seconds glaring while the castrated attorney nervously doodled on a legal pad. Looking up and around to the others at the table, Lud asked: "Does anyone else have anything meaningful to add to this conversation?" When no one responded, he concluded. "Well, then, if you'll excuse me, I have things to do."

Michael found his courage the instant Lud left the room. "I want that old fucker fired! I want him gone today!"

"That won't happen," Doug answered quietly. His voice was calm and even but with an unmistaken edge. "He has a contract with me and I have a contract with Carmen. Unless Carmen fires me, we both stay. I don't think Carmen is going to fire me. In the first place, he doesn't have cause. In the second place, without me, you don't have this." He waved his arm in the direction of the Keystate plant. "If anyone here is expendable, Michael, it's you."

The two men glowered at each other in pure hatred. The others sat in an awkward silence as painful seconds passed. Finally Carmen spoke.

"Michael, we agreed that Doug would be responsible for all manufacturing. This is his show to run. We have to give him the authority and responsibility to do what he thinks is right. That goes for all of us. Each of us has a different job to do." Looking at his watch, Carmen thought of the visiting investor. "My next responsibility will be here in fifteen minutes. I suggest we get our shit together and project a united front." He adjourned the meeting but asked Michael to stay after the others left.

"Let's not forget the bigger picture," He began after the others were gone. "Why are you getting so worked up about this place? It's not as if we have a long-term future here."

"I know and I'm sorry," Michael apologized. "That fucking Reardon and his mutant friend just get under my skin. They treat me like I don't know what's going on."

"That's because you don't. At least not where manufacturing is concerned. But don't forget that *you* know something far more important. Let them have their day. It won't last. Besides, we've got a much bigger problem I need you to work on."

"What's that?" Michael asked.

"You know we took over the debt when we bought Sprayzon and Union Automotive, right?

"Yeah, it was about eight hundred thousand," Michael answered.

"Eight hundred and fifty, to be exact. If you recall, the previous owners kept the debt when we bought Keystate and we had to negotiate a new line of credit."

Again, Michael knew the situation and wondered where this was heading. He answered: "I know, the bank gave us availability for one and a half million to get us started. They said they would raise it to two million this fall and as high as three once we prove our credit worthiness. What are you getting at?"

"We're already one point two million into the line of credit."

Michael was flabbergast. "What!" He exclaimed. "How did that happen?"

"I used the line to pay off the eight hundred and fifty thousand debt from Sprayzon and Union. The other four hundred has gone to cover the daily expenses and expansion here at Keystate."

"What about the money you've been raising from selling stock. You say it's been going great. Surely there should be a lot of cash from that?"

"That was Yuri's money. We used that money to pay him back the four and a half million he put up to buy the companies. We're in a tight spot with cash. It's getting worse because Reardon has spent another two hundred thousand dollars that due next month. Basically, we're out of cash."

"I suppose you want me to ask Yuri for more money?" Michael asked grim faced. "How much?"

"We need the million." Carmen referred to the million dollars Yuri had conditionally invested "Tell him that it's almost time to invest ten times that amount. The stock price is going through the roof and we should execute the second phase of the plan in a couple of months."

"Okay," Michael answered. "He's not going to like spending more to keep PetroChem afloat but he will be glad it to hear it's time to accelerate the laundering process."

******* ******* ******* *******

That had been three weeks earlier. Carmen was relieved that there hadn't been any more outbursts among his management team. After the episode, he forbade Michael and the Rosens from visiting until the transition was complete. Sean still made regular trips because Doug and Lud admittedly didn't know anything about packaging aerosol cans.

Although Michael had talked to Yuri, the money was just dribbling in. Yuri had decided not to release more than two hundred thousand at a time. He made it clear that he was not going to indefinitely fund the company. As a result, Carmen was constantly dealing with cash flow problems. He even dipped into his personal funds once or twice.

The plane's landing gear squealed against concrete and Carmen lurched forward as the pilot applied the brakes and reverse thrust. Settling down into a more relaxed taxi, the plane bumped across the runway to park at the gate. The bell chimed and the other passengers crowded the aisle to retrieve their belongings from the overhead bins while Carmen turned on his phone to call Doug who was parked at the cell phone lot.

It only took a few minutes for Carmen to make the short walk from the gate area to the sidewalk outside baggage claim. Doug pulled up to the curb just as Carmen came out the exit. As he opened the door of the blue Lexus he thought, *'God, I hope he doesn't ask me for money again.'*

"Morning," Doug said as he pulled back into traffic. He followed with the customary, "How was your flight?"

"It was good. No bumps and no storms. I caught a little bit of sleep on the way," Carmen answered.

"How was the investor conference?" Doug asked. "Did you sign up any new investors?"

"I think it went well. People seemed interested and I collected a bunch of business cards. I think we'll pick up a few. Are you ready for today's guest?"

"As ready as we can be given that the shop's all torn up. We're not putting much juice in any bottles the way things are. We have made a lot of progress reconfiguring the plant, though. It's a lot different since you were here three weeks ago. We haven't any distractions since then." Doug made an obvious reference to the fact that Michael and the Rosens had been banned.

"Glad I could help," Carmen replied sarcastically. "Michael's not a bad guy, you know. He's just under a lot of pressure."

"Michael's an asshole," Doug said matter of factly. They were on the freeway now and he took his eyes of the road for the moment it took to meet Carmen's glance. "We're all under pressure. That doesn't give him license to be a jerk. Just keep him away and we'll be fine."

"I'll bear that in mind. Anything else I can do for you?" Carmen maintained his sarcastic tone.

"You mean besides getting rid of the Rosens?"

Carmen groaned. He realized too late that he'd given Doug the opening to take that shot. "Yes, I mean besides that. We've already been down that road."

"Well," Doug replied. "If I'm stuck with the Rosens, the next best thing you can do for me is to pay for all these expenses we've been running up. Some of the contractors are really starting to complain about not getting paid. If we don't pay them soon, they'll walk off the job. I also have suppliers that put us on ship hold for parts we need to keep moving ahead. Pretty soon we're going to be at a standstill."

"I'm working on it," Carmen snapped back irritated.

They rode in silence for the remainder of the short ride to Keystate. Carmen turned the charm on as soon as he stepped into the plant. He made the rounds, chatting up the employees and commenting on the rapid pace of change. He was genuinely impressed and had one of those fleeting moments when he got caught up in the enthusiasm of legitimate enterprise. The moment passed as soon as he walked outside to the tank farm and ran into Stoli. Carmen had no idea who Stoli was and made the mistake of trying to bullshit a bullshitter. He bent over Stoli's shoulder to watch as Stoli tightened the nuts on a flanged union.

"What are you doing?" Carmen asked cordially.

"Wasting fucking time waiting for the valve I need to finish the antifreeze piping." Stoli was not one to be overly impressed by owners. He'd seen too many come and go over the years. To his credit, Carmen maintained his composure.

"Why are you waiting for a valve? Why don't you just go and get one?"

"Because you haven't paid the supplier and he cut us off. If you've got five hundred bucks in your pocket, I'll gladly get in my truck and go get one."

If Stoli was surprised, he didn't show it when Carmen called his bluff, reached into his pocket and pulled out a roll of cash. He counted out five, one hundred dollar bills and handed them to Stoli. Stoli looked at the crisp cash and then back at Carmen. He handed the money to Doug who had been standing nearby watching in amusement.

"That's a start," Stoli said to Carmen. "It'd be nice if you kept it coming. People are getting nervous."

"Tell them not to be," Carmen replied curtly. His black eyes flashing, he looked at Doug. "If you've got a minute, we need to talk before our guest arrives.

They made the short walk to Doug's office in silence. Carmen was fuming and shut the door behind him as he followed Doug into the office.

"What the fuck was that about?" Carmen hissed. "Who the hell was that and why is he asking me about money?"

"That's Stoli. He's the lead blender and the union steward. More important, he's one of the best employees you have."

"The union steward! Why in God's name does a union employee know anything about the company's finances."

"It's a small community, Carmen. Most of the contractors we have working in the plant are friends or relatives of the employees. We're a couple of weeks behind paying some of them. People talk. Why do you think I keep bugging you about cash to pay them. And you just heard that some of the equipment vendors shut us off. You've got to cough up some money if you want to keep this project on track. Either that or we slow the pace. If we do that, we definitely won't be ready for the winter."

Carmen didn't say anything for a few seconds and then closed his eyes to lean back into the well-worn couch. He clasped his fingers to rest his hands on his stomach and crossed his short legs. He held that pose for a few minutes while Doug sat and watched silently from behind his desk. When Carmen finally sat up, he was calm and his black eyes had once again become unreadable.

"I can't have people like that Stoli guy shooting his mouth off. Especially when I've got investors in the place. We have the money. Without boring you with the details, I just had to retire some long term debt and legal fees associated with all the acquisitions." Carmen paused for a few seconds before continuing. "If you don't mind, I need to use your office for the next half hour or so. Why don't you go and make sure we're ready for the plant tour."

Doug was glad to be excused. Carmen was right, he wasn't interested and didn't care to hear about the company's financial issues. He walked back to the tank farm. Stoli was where he'd left him and Lud was also there.

"Did I get you in hot water with your boss?" Stoli asked as Doug approached. He had a sly smile but was truly concerned that he'd caused trouble for Doug.

"You sure did," Doug replied. "But only a little. I guess he's getting tired of hearing the same song. Maybe you did some good. It sounds like he's going to free up some cash."

"Hell of a way to run a business," Lud grumbled. "So far I'm not too impressed by these guys."

Doug shrugged. "It's not our show to run anymore. All we can do is try to keep the wheels from falling off. At least for as long as we're here." Turning to Stoli, "Speaking of not being here, maybe you should be gone when Risotti gets done in my office. I don't think he wants you around when he's trying to woo potential investors."

"Why not? Look at how pretty I am!" Stoli joked. "Oh well, I know when I'm not wanted. I have to leave any way. The wedding's tomorrow and I promised Helen I'd be home early."

"I forgot about the wedding," Doug said. He had forgotten that Stoli's son was getting married the following and he was taking an extended weekend."I guess you shouldn't worry about impressing Risotti. It's much more important for you to suck up to the new in-laws," Doug joked.

"Maybe the old man," Stoli admitted. "He's an impressive guy. I guess he used to be in the Red Army and was a colonel when it was their turn to play in the Afghani-sand box. He must still be pretty well connected. My kid told me he got an exclusive deal selling Russian tractors over here. Must be a good business judging by the fancy cars and the size of his house. They've got a huge place on the lake. His wife's a piece of work, though. She's nice enough when she's sober but most of the time she lives in a bottle. At least she didn't drive my wife crazy planning the wedding. It's a really good thing that they're Russian Orthodox. I don't really care but my wife would have shot the boy rather than let him marry outside the church."

"I didn't know they were Russian," Lud commented. "I thought you said the bride's name was Linda or Cindy or something like that?"

"Her name's Lindsey," Stoli answered. "At least that's what they call her. She has a Russian name but I don't remember what it is. She's got two brothers, Joe and Sam. All the kids have two names - one Russian and one for here. Not surprising, I guess. Most of us have changed our names to fit in.

My last name is really Stalichovik. I don't think they changed their last name. It's Pandropov. The mother's name is Elena and his is Yuri. That's about as Russian as it gets."

Chapter Thirteen

Stoli stood with his arm around his wife's shoulder waving goodbye. Behind them, Yuri Pandropov stood stoically on his expansive front porch as the limousine carried the newlyweds away down the circular drive. He raised his hand in a gesture that was more of a salute than a wave just before the white Lincoln Town Car pulled into traffic and disappeared behind the hedge. Dropping his hand, Yuri slipped his index finger behind his sunglasses to wipe a small tear. Stepping off the porch, he walked up behind his new in-laws and put a hand on each of their shoulders. Stoli dropped his arm and his wife, Helen, turned to allow a space for Yuri to stand between them. They stood there for a second, the tall former colonel flanked by his shorter in-laws.

Helen wiped her eyes with the wad of wet tissues she held in her left hand. When it became evident they wouldn't suffice for both her tears and runny nose, she turned away to pull fresh kleenex from her purse and gently blew her nose.

Stoli didn't move. He had danced and drank too much and too late and was paying the price. The midmorning sun glared off any shiny surface and was killing his eyes. Every joint and muscle in his fifty year old body ached and his head pounded. He just wanted to go back to the cool darkness of the guestroom. Unfortunately, he had to drive back to Pittsburgh. It didn't help that they'd made the drive in Helen's Buick; his sunglasses hung from the rearview mirror of his truck back at home.

"Are you sure you won't stay for lunch?" Yuri asked them for the third time. "God knows we have enough food! Maybe you'd like a little hair of the dog? A Bloody Mary, perhaps?" He asked Stoli with a smile. Stoli blanched. The last thing he wanted was more alcohol. He wondered how Yuri could handle it. They'd matched each other drink for drink the previous night at the reception.

It had been a hell of a party. The backyard of Yuri's house had been turned into a sea of lights all the way to the lakeshore. There was an enormous white tent in the middle of the lawn that easily held the three hundred attendees. A bandstand had been erected by the pool. Wisely, Helen had suggested that they cover the pool with the dance floor. There were several bars set up across the property. Stoli and Yuri spent the latter part of the evening at the one by the boathouse overlooking the lake. It had been a clear, moonless night with a starry sky. Stoli and Yuri had killed the better part of a bottle of vodka.

"No, thanks," Stoli answered. "We'd better get going. Fortunately, it's a short drive. I just wish I didn't forget my sunglasses."

"Here, you can use these," Yuri took off his glasses and handed them to Stoli. "I've got more in the house."

They walked over to Helen's car and Yuri reached down to open the passenger door. Helen extended her hand and Yuri took it in both of his.

"Thank you for such a wonderful time," She said. "It was a beautiful wedding and your home was the perfect place for the reception."

"Thank *you* for all the planning you did to put it together. I'm sorry Elena couldn't have helped more. She just hasn't been well, lately. She sends her apologies for not being here this morning to see everyone off," He added weakly.

Helen and Stoli allowed Yuri his lie. They knew that Elena probably wouldn't get out of bed for the rest of the day. They also knew her illness lay in the bottom of a bottle. Yuri closed the door for Helen and walked to the driver's side.

"Ivan Stalichovik," Yuri used the Russian translation of Stoli's given name. "It was good being with you this weekend. You have raised a fine son. He makes my daughter happy. With luck, we'll soon have some grandkids, eh?"

"That would be good," Stoli answered. "But you know kids these days. We may have to wait for that."

"I hope not too long. I don't know about you, but after last night, I feel really old this morning!"

That finally got a bit of a laugh from Stoli. "Really?" he asked, surprised. "You don't act like it."

"Believe me - it is a great act. As soon as you leave, I'm going to go lie down."

"Goodbye, Yuri." Stoli got in the car and fastened the seatbelt. He opened the window before closing the door. "Thanks for the sunglasses. I'll mail them back."

"Don't worry about it," Yuri answered. "You can return them next time we meet."

Yuri waved as they pulled away and immediately lit a cigarette. He knew that Helen abhorred smoking and, out of courtesy, refrained from smoking when she was around. When the Stalichs made the turn onto the road, he walked through the house to the backyard and stepped out onto the flagstone pool deck. A crew was already busy disassembling the platform that covered the pool. There were more men folding and stacking the chairs and tables under the tent. The tent, itself, wouldn't come down until the following day. Other than that, Yuri expected most evidence of the reception to be gone by late afternoon.

He went over to the cabana where the pool supplies were kept and retrieved another pair of sunglasses from the cabinet. He also grabbed a bottle of water from the wet bar. Donning the glasses, he walked across the lawn to the boathouse. Yuri turned an Adirondack chair to face the water and sat down. The midmorning sun felt good on his face and a slight onshore breeze coming off the lake kept it from getting too hot. Though June, the lake temperature was still relatively cool. Yuri reclined in the chair and closed his eyes. It would have been a perfect moment of contentment were it not for the sun penetrating his sunglasses and forcing a squint. Even then, the insides of his eyelids glowed a reddish-orange.

The wedding had gone off beautifully and his daughter was obviously very much in love with John Stalich. Yuri was not one to be overly concerned with the happiness of others except where Lindsay was concern. One of the few, true pleasures of his life was her happiness. He had been concerned about her new husband before he got to know him and met Stoli and Helen.

They certainly didn't boast an aristocratic background but they did possess what Yuri wanted most for his daughter - legitimacy and respectability. It didn't bother him at all that Stoli was a factory worker. It was evident that he was intelligent. He must also have some leadership traits to have become the head of his union. Helen was a surgical nurse at the University of Pittsburgh Medical Center. Her specialty was assisting with organ transplants. She was both highly skilled and intelligent.

John seemed to have inherited their compassion and brains. Yuri could provide him the opportunity to make money. John had already shown good business acumen while selling farm equipment. Yuri could easily arrange for him to take over the business someday. For a brief moment, Yuri forgot that he was one of the country's largest heroin dealers. He was just a proud father. The moment didn't last long.

The shadow darkening his face eased the penetrating sun on his eyes. Even so, Yuri shielded his face with his hand to look up at the hulking silhouette of Alexandar Alexandrov. Yuri wasn't surprised that he hadn't heard Alexandar approach. He was remarkably stealthy for a man of his size. The skill was one he'd undoubtedly learned as a member of the Vozdushno-Desantnye Vojska - Russia's elite special forces unit.

Alexandar had literally parachuted into Yuri's life during their joint stint in Afghanistan. Under the cover of darkness, Alexandar's platoon had dropped behind the enemy's line and eradicated the fierce group of mujahedeen that besieged Yuri's outpost. When the sun came up, Yuri watched through his field glasses as a Russian flag came down out of the hills held aloft by a limping Alexandar. He'd broken his ankle during the drop but still manage to lead his unit's attack. Though commended for his actions, his injury forced him from his unit. Yuri's request for Alexander to be assigned to his command was approved and Alexander had been Yuri's driver and bodyguard ever since.

"I'm sorry to disturb you, Colonel, but Michael Cole is here to see you," Alexandar spoke in Russian.

Yuri groaned as he closed his eyes and fell back in his chair. It had to be about money again. This would be the third time in a little over three weeks that Michael had asked for more cash. It was unprecedented for him to show up without advance notice. It was also odd that he'd come on a Sunday and especially the day after the wedding.

"Where is he?" Yuri asked, also in Russian. Although Alexandar spoke a halting English, the two spoke almost exclusively in their mother tongue.

"He's in your office," Alexandar answered. "Dmitri is with him."

"Have him come out here. And ask Dmitri to bring some food. I'm starting to get hungry." Yuri sat up in his chair to light a cigarette.

Alexandar stepped away a few paces before using his cell phone to call Dmitri. Yuri looked toward the house and watched as Michael stepped outside and walked toward him. Yuri smiled when he saw that Michael wore a suit and tie. The man never relaxed.

"Good morning, Michael," Yuri said as the lawyer neared. "Have a seat."

The chair Yuri pointed to had remnant dew and dirt from the previous night's reverie. Someone must have stood on it at one point because it was smeared with soil and grass clippings. Michael pulled a handkerchief out of his pocket and wiped it off before sitting down. Yuri and Alexandar exchanged brief smiles.

"This is highly unusual for you to come unannounced," Yuri began. "Surely, Carmen doesn't need cash so badly that he'd send you out on a Sunday morning. You do recall that yesterday was Lindsey's wedding, don't you?"

"Yes, I do and I'm sorry to come like this. It's just for once, I have good news."

"That is a switch," Yuri answered. "So you don't need more cash?"

"Not for the moment, no. The good news is that Carmen got a large pension fund to invest three million dollars into the company. The share price is now up to thirty cents. He says it's time for you to start buying and you can spend up to ten million without raising suspicion. I'm here to ask you how high you want to go."

"Ten million."

"Really?" Michael was surprised. "Ten million dollars? Just like that?"

"Of course," Yuri replied. "Isn't that why we're doing this after all? If Carmen says now is the time, then now is the time. So far, he's done what he said he would do. How long do you think it will take to spend the entire amount?"

"A month. Maybe six weeks," Michael replied. "We control thirty-two different individuals and businesses that will be buying stock. We can't have them all buy at the same time. That would definitely be suspicious."

Yuri thought about that for a moment. "Have you discussed this with Josef?" He said, referring to his eldest son. "He's the one you need to coordinate the money transfer."

"Not yet. I expected to see him here this morning. That's why I came. Alexandar told me he went back to New York early this morning."

"He should be landing soon. Make sure you call him," He paused. "So, by the end of September, I will be the proud owner of about thirty-five million shares of PetroChem?"

"If all goes according to plan, yes," Michael nodded. "At that point, Carmen will drive down the stock price. He's planning on getting it below a dime. You will still have thirty-five million shares but they'll be worth less than three million dollars."

"Does Carmen know yet how he's going to drive the price down? More important, how he will he drive it back up?"

"The second part is easy. We start buying and that will drive the price up. He hasn't told me how he's going to drive it down. He just said he has to report some bad news that will make investors nervous. Right now, he's been filling them all with stories about how great the company is and what wonderful changes are happening."

"Changes that have been costing me money!" Yuri grunted. "What is going on that keeps Carmen asking for cash?"

"They're spending a lot of money consolidating companies and fixing up the plant in Pittsburgh. There's a guy running things - his name's Doug Reardon - that thinks it's his mission in life to make this thing work."

"He's not one of Carmen's guys?"

"No. He's clueless. He's just some manufacturing jerk spending your money like there's no tomorrow."

"But he doesn't know it's my money?" Yuri shot Michael a querulous look.

"No, of course not. But at some point, Carmen has to rein him in and put a stop to it."

"Why doesn't he do it now?"

"Because now the investors love the guy. When Carmen brings them to the plant to see the changes he's driving, they can't fork over their money fast enough."

"So, if he's the reason for the stock price going up, what would happen if he's not there?" Yuri asked pointedly.

"It could have a deleterious effect on the price."

"Something to consider, is it not?"

Chapter Fourteen

Doug Reardon stepped out of the cab and into the cool shadows of Park Avenue. The morning air was moist and the bright, breezeless sky promised a hot, humid afternoon. It was unusually warm for this late in September and the still air was heavy with the smells of the city. Doug craned his neck to take in the façade of the Waldorf Astoria. It wasn't as impressive as he thought it should be given its storied past. Just a few paces from the curb, the building rose straight for twenty stories of dirty granite and limestone. Only the canopy that jutted out over three sets of entrance doors gave pause to the otherwise vertical facade. It looked more like the marquee of a theater than the portal of a grand hotel.

Doug crossed the noisy sidewalk and entered the building through a revolving door. A short set of stairs took him to the Park Avenue Lobby. Immediately he understood why the hotel had its opulent reputation.

The anteroom for the main lobby was an art deco masterpiece in white. Towering fluted columns and pilasters supported the coffered ceiling that gleamed with gilding. The floor, completely covered with mosaic tile, featured a spectacular circular panel. Overhead, a monumental crystal chandelier glistened. Panels that complimented the floor adorned the entablature of the colonnaded hallway to the main lobby.

Through the hall, Doug entered the grandeur of the main lobby. His footsteps, which clicked across the mosaic tiles, hushed as he stepped onto plush, patterned carpets. Wood panels and dark furnishings gave the space a muted elegance. Eight massive, stone-faced columns carried the soft white ceiling which was heavily paneled and decorated with gilt patterns and motifs. The famous, ornately carved, octagonal clock anchored the room. A miniature Statue of Liberty crowned the timepiece.

Doug looked at the time. He'd taken the early morning flight into Newark and a train to Penn Station before hailing the cab that dropped him in front of the hotel. Carmen had called an emergency meeting of the board of PetroChem Packaging and summoned Doug to attend. The meeting was scheduled for eleven o'clock in a meeting room on the fourth floor. It was a quarter to ten and Doug figured he had time to grab something to eat.

He crossed the lobby and past the clock toward the Peacock Alley Restaurant. The smell of breakfast - bacon, eggs and coffee - got stronger as he drew closer and whet his appetite. There weren't many people eating breakfast. A few late arrivals - mostly lone business men - were scattered across the room nursing coffee and reading newspapers while the staff bussed tables and tidied up in preparation for the lunch crowd.

As soon as he crossed the threshold, Doug saw Carmen sitting at the bar off to his right. He, too, was alone and reading a paper but his beverage was scotch. Doug stopped at the door and waved off the hostess while pretending to look for someone in the room. He gave her a weak smile and shrug before beating a retreat. He had no desire to spend more time with Carmen than absolutely necessary.

All their encounters over the past six weeks had been testy to the point of adversarial. Doug walked back through the lobby stopping only to ask a passing bellhop for directions to the Brassiere.

He found the less frequented eatery and, after glancing around the room to make sure no PetroChem executives were there, followed the hostess to a secluded corner. Doug gladly accepted coffee from the waitress bearing a carafe and menus. He grimaced at the thirty dollar price tag before ordering a grapefruit juice and continental breakfast. He was appalled at the extravagance. It galled him that Carmen picked the Waldorf as the site for this morning's meeting.

Since the agenda dealt primarily with the effort to consolidate manufacturing at Keystate, the session should have been held at the plant. Thirty dollars in Pittsburgh would have provided coffee and pastries for the entire board! Doug suggested as much to Carmen but was weakly rebuffed and reminded that Michael and the Rosens had been banned from the site at Doug's request. Doug knew this was bullshit.

The opulent venue was typical of Carmen's modus operandi. Carmen made no secret of his lavish lifestyle. Doug was aware of the first class air travel and five-star hotels. He also knew that Carmen had a Manhattan apartment somewhere nearby and had overheard him tell Sean that he'd recently bought a Bentley sports coupe. Doug had no particular beef about Carmen's personal finances. He did have a problem with the lavish corporate expenses since little cash was available to fix up the plant. In fact, the process had just about come to a standstill. That was ostensibly the reason for the emergency meeting.

Doug pulled a small, spiral notebook from his breast pocket and reviewed the items he wanted to cover. There weren't many but they were important. First was the persistent lack of funding to upgrade the plant and purchase raw materials. Second was the shoddy condition of the equipment and inventory that was coming in from Union Packaging. Third was the general lack of cooperation he was getting to accomplish his assigned task. Since the cooperation should be coming from the people on PetroChem's board, he knew his was a failed mission.

Sighing, he pocketed his notes as the waitress returned with a fruit cup, English muffin and a scant selection of jams and jellies. He ate without relish while he scanned a copy of the *New York Times* he'd picked up at the train station. Finished, he paid in cash before heading back through the lobby to the elevator that whisked him to the fourth floor.

Carmen had reserved a room with a view of Park Avenue. Doug got off the lift and headed to the bathroom. He figured it would be a long session and he'd already had several cups of coffee. He looked at his reflection in the mirror as he washed his hands and combed his hair. He looked tired. Certainly a part of it was the early morning flight but mostly it was just the strain of dealing with Risotti and his cronies.

He'd considered quitting a couple of times but was deterred by his sense of obligation to the employees and his contract. Looking at himself, he also had to admit that he wanted to get vested in his shares of PetroChem. The past few weeks, the share price had held around thirty cents. Doug had only a week until he was able to exercise his option. He could hold out until then. After that... well, he figured he'd done his good deed.

It was a few minutes before eleven when he walked into the meeting room. There were six executive chairs around a table large enough to accommodate twice that many. All but one were occupied. Carmen sat at the head of the table and Michael occupied the opposite end. The Rosens sat together with their backs to the door. Sean sat across from Sol leaving the empty chair across from Harvey for Doug. He had to walked behind Carmen to get to the other side of the conference table. Perhaps not surprising, there was a wet bar set up at that end of the room. Tellingly, the seal had been broken on the bottle of scotch.

A continental breakfast assortment was set up behind Michael. Doug could have saved himself thirty bucks. Of course, that would have meant eating with the board. Considering that, the expensive breakfast seemed like a bargain.

The table in front of Michael held only a bottled water. Doug meanly mused that Michael wouldn't risk staining his expensive suit or purple tie. Coffee stained the tablecloth in front of Sol and the area between Harvey and Carmen looked like a food fight had broken out. It was strewn with plates, glasses, cups, crumbs and flatware. Carmen's was the sole setting with a rock glass and his customary scotch. Doug grabbed a bottled water from the wet bar and took his seat. The silence that fell on the room when he entered was broken by Carmen.

"Now that we're all here, let's get started. First the good news. As of this morning, shares of PetroChem were selling at thirty five cents a share. The company has issued more than fifty-five million shares so the market capitalization is a little more than nineteen million dollars. Obviously, the market loves what we're doing."

Smiles broke out around the table as the directors mentally calculated their gains. Recognizing this, Carmen continued. "As I recall, the average share price when issued to you was less than ten cents. I think you all can do the math."

"What was the average issue price for all fifty-five million shares?" Doug asked nonchalantly.

Carmen instantly saw where this was headed. Doug was obviously leading everyone to calculate the actual cash generated by the company. He looked darkly at Doug before answering. He'd intended for this discussion to be part of the agenda but wanted to hold it off until later. Now that Doug put it on the table, Carmen had to respond.

"Thirteen cents."

"So, the company has generated more than seven million dollars in cash from the issuance of stock." Doug quickly did the math.

"That's correct," Carmen answered expecting Doug to follow up with his usual request for cash to fund the plant improvements. He was surprised when Doug said nothing and merely wrote the figure on the tablet in front of him. Hoping to head him off Carmen continued.

"That seven million will come in handy as we continue our strategy to grow the company through acquisitions. Harvey, why don't you bring us up to date on your work to find new targets?"

Harvey Rosen launched into a fifteen minute report on three companies that, in one form or another, were related to packaging liquids or aerosols for the automotive market. He proudly distributed a bound prospectus on each company to the group. Doug quickly scanned his copies and noted that they were long on product and market information but very short on manufacturing, cost and pro forma financial statements. He piled his copies in a neat stack and didn't refer to them for the balance of Harvey's presentation.

The obvious slight was not lost on Harvey or Carmen. Doug didn't care. His focus was on dealing with the present situation at Keystate. Future acquisitions were just a distraction. He didn't understand why the board was looking to buy more businesses when the ones they had were disintegrating under their feet. The others didn't seem to share his concern and spent an additional half hour asking broad questions about whether the prospective companies would add or detract from PetroChem's share price.

Eventually, the discussion turned to operational issues and Doug became the center of attention. This was the moment he'd been dreading for weeks and he braced himself when Carmen turned to him.

"You made great progress in the early going but things seem to have slowed considerably in recent weeks. Can you give us an update on what's going on and your plans to consolidate operations in Pittsburgh?"

Carmen posed the question blithely but Doug instantly recognized the malicious intent. Since he had anticipated the moment, he had a rehearsed response. Reaching into the breast pocket of his sports coat, Doug pulled out the note pad he had reviewed over breakfast. He made the group wait a few pregnant seconds as he thumbed it open a couple of pages and scanned his notes. Every item he was about to present would antagonize one or more of the men at the table. By the time he was done, everyone of them would be angered. *'What the hell,'* He thought. *'Might as well go out in a blaze of glory.'* He put his notes on the table and began.

"We've gone as far as we can go considering the lack of money and cooperation we've received from this board."

Harvey Rosen and Sean immediately lurched forward in their chairs; Sol rose to his feet. They were talking at once in an unintelligible garble. Michael and Carmen were silent as they exchanged an amused glance across the table. Carmen used his rock glass as a gavel and rapped the table several times. The three aggrieved directors quieted one at a time; Sol was the last to stop sputtering and sat down. Doug sat passively in his chair for the entire tirade. When a measure of calm returned to the room, he look at Carmen.

"Would you like me to continue?" He asked.

"Do you think you can without pissing off people?"

"Not if you want me to tell the truth," Doug answered. "I could tell you what you want to hear but that wouldn't help us fix the problems. It may already be too late for us to salvage this year. I doubt we can be ready for the season."

"That's precisely the reason we're here," Michael spoke for the first time "We'd like you to tell us why you won't be ready."

Doug ignored the deliberate jibe. He and Michael hadn't been in the same room since their falling out in June. The mutual animosity still scorched. As calmly as he could, Doug began again.

"There are several reason why *we* are in trouble," He emphasized the word. "As you know from your visits and the reports you've been given, most of the site preparation work has been completed. All the electrical, pneumatic and hydraulic systems are in place. We started work on expanding the shipping and receiving areas but had to stop when the contractors - excavators and masons - walked away from the job."

"Why?" The question came from Sean.

"Because we stopped paying them. The same for the riggers we contracted to install the equipment and tanks. They'd heard that we weren't paying for work already done. The riggers want us to pay in advance before they come on site."

"Why didn't you pay them?" Sol asked.

"You'll have to ask Mr. Risotti. He has denied numerous requests for money to pay for the project."

Sol, Harvey and Sean looked at Carmen. Michael seemed to be intensely interested in the cufflink on his left sleeve. Doug's glance alternated between Sol, Harvey, Sean and Carmen. He tried to keep a straight face but couldn't completely contain the wisp of a smirk. Carmen stared darkly at Doug; his black eyes smoldered. However, he too had anticipated the direction the meeting would go and was prepared.

"Consolidating the operations of Sprayzon and Union Automotive with Keystate was always intended to be a self-funded activity," Carmen stated tersely. "Doug, you always knew this and yet you continue to ask the parent company for funds to cover your shortfall. By my math, we have already advanced you more than half million dollars to cover your expenses."

Doug was floored by the outright lie. He had always assumed that money to expand the plant would come from the issuance of company stock. Carmen had never told him - verbally or in writing - that he expected Keystate to pay all the expense of the project. Of course, that also meant there were no documents that said the parent company *would* pay. Doug immediately saw that he had been outmaneuvered. Faced with danger from a lie, all he could do was tell the truth.

"That's news to me," He said. "Even if that was your intention, it would be impossible to fund the plant expansion from operating profit. You know the business loses money between April and September. You also know there was no cash when you bought Keystate. The previous owners took it all."

"What about earnings from Sprayzon and Union Automotive?" Sol interjected. "I know we've always made money year round. I think Sprayzon is even less seasonal than we are." He look to Sean who nodded in agreement. "I know all of our profits have been going to the corporate kitty. Hasn't that helped fund the consolidation?" Sol addresses the question to Carmen.

"No," Carmen answered. "That money went to pay debts to your suppliers and bank. Same for Sprayzon. In fact, we had to take money from our new line of credit to pay your old debts."

This was more new information to Doug. He had not been privy to financial information since PetroChem took over. He never really knew how much cash the company had. Doug did know they were strapped because he regularly got calls from Keystate's suppliers looking for money. It was personally and professionally embarrassing for him to have these conversations.

He, and the previous owners, made sure that Keystate stayed current with creditors. It was just good business and it earned them better pricing, terms and service. Now, Doug had to refer any payment questions to Carmen. He could tell by the decidedly chilly receptions he got that the suppliers weren't happy. While that was bad enough during the off season, it would prove deadly when business picked up. That, combined with the stalled project, was a real threat to the company's survival. Doug had to press the point.

"How much money is left on the line?" He asked referring to the line of credit.

"That's a corporate finance matter," Michael replied for Carmen. "Your responsibility - which you seem to failing - is manufacturing and making a profit."

Doug was incensed and incredulous. *The little prick,* He thought. *He really doesn't know what he's talking about!* Before Doug could react, Sean stepped in.

"Maybe Doug doesn't have access to that type of financial information - which he should, by the way - but I do. So I'm asking, how much cash is on the line?

"We have three hundred thousand left," Carmen answered resignedly. "The original line of credit was one and a half million."

This was much worse than Doug imagined. The previous winter, Keystate regularly carried a float of three to four million. Three hundred thousand dollars of available cash going into the busy season was only a fraction of what they'd need. Worse, the tanks were mostly empty. He would have nothing going into the season and a shop that was half torn up. Keystate was doomed; his prediction had come true.

"We're fucked," He said thinking about the employees back at the plant. He really didn't give a shit what happened to the men around the table.

"Not necessarily." It was Sean. "We have cash from the sale of PetroChem shares. I suggest we make that money available to finish the plant, pay down the line of credit and get current with critical suppliers." He turned to Doug. "How much do you need to finish the job?"

"Three hundred thousand dollars to pay what we owe for work already done and another two hundred to get the rest finished. But there's no guarantee that we'll be ready in time. We need to get the equipment moved from Union Automotive and I'm not sure what condition it will be in when it arrives. The stuff we've got so far has been crap."

Doug was referring to the equipment and inventory that had been shipped to Keystate from the Union plant in Wilmington. The equipment should have gone straight to the scrap dealers. It was old, broken and rusty. There was one filling line still at the Union plant that Doug thought could be salvaged. The rest was unusable. Same for the packaging supplies that he'd received - bottles, caps, labels and boxes were likewise garbage. They were dirty, crushed, and out-of-date. He had received several truckloads of the useless material and stuck it in a corner of the warehouse for eventual disposal. Factual though it was, Doug's comment got the anticipated response from the Rosens.

We didn't send you any junk!" It was Harvey. "We didn't send you anything we haven't used ourselves."

"That's probably true," Doug answered. "But it's still crap. The packaging materials are not anything we should use if we want to keep customers happy. The equipment just isn't usable. There isn't anything that has any value. I'm amazed you guys were able to stay in business with that equipment." Doug meant it as a back-handed compliment but neither the Rosens or Michael took it that way.

"Your assessment of Union Automotive's value is not needed or wanted," Michael retorted. "It was worth what we paid for it!"

Doug was surprised by the remark. He hadn't intended to comment on PetroChem's purchase of Union. He was talking only of the operational value of the material and equipment. Now that Michael raised the issue, it did seem to Doug that Carmen had probably grossly overpaid for Union. He wondered why?

"Never mind that," Carmen cut in. "Right now we're dealing with the immediate problem. How much money do you really need?" He asked Doug.

"Half a million," Doug repeated the number he'd just given Sean. "That doesn't cover what we'll need for materials and supplies to make product."

"I know!" Carmen snapped. "I'll take care of that. You'll get the cash you need."

"It's not what *I* need, Carmen. It's what the company needs it you want it to succeed." Doug tried to smooth it over.

"Of course we want it to succeed! Why would you think we wouldn't?" It was the second time Michael jumped in with a seeming non sequitur. Doug's common sense finally succumbed to his meaner nature and he let loose.

"So far, it's been a blueprint for failure," He shot back. "You've asked me to execute an expensive project but won't give me any money to do it. This despite telling me the company's shares are selling like hotcakes. Today, I learn that I am to fund this project with profit I'm supposed to earn from a crippled plant, with no materials or supplies and no working capital. Finally, I discover that the cash I thought was available has been spent to pay the previous debts of Sprayzon and Union Automotive. You ask me why I question your commitment to success? Maybe it's because you manage working capital like a Ponzi scheme and hoard investment capital like it was your own!"

Because Doug directed his tirade at Michael, he didn't see Carmen's spastic reaction. Carmen shot up straight in his seat, tipping over an empty coffee cup.

"God damn it!' He exploded. "That's enough of this horseshit! Doug, you'll get the money you need to finish the project and make product. I don't want to hear anymore comments about anybody's lack of commitment to making this work. I've got too much tied up in this not to have it succeed. If you doubt that, or if you can't work with the members of this board, I will accept your resignation. Michael, that goes for you too. If you two can't work together, I want to know now!"

Doug and Michael glowered at each other. Carmen was on his feet; his clenched fists supported his upper body as he leaned over the table. Sol and Harvey exchanged nervous glances as they cowered back in their chairs like schoolboys hoping the teacher wouldn't look in their direction.

Sean maintained his composure as the awkward seconds ticked by. He was trying to come up with a way to defuse the moment when Michael's cell phone went off. He had set it to vibrate and placed it on the table when the meeting started. In the silence of the moment, the soft buzz was jarring.

Michael picked it up, glanced to see who was calling, and excused himself from the room. The call and Michael's departure eased the tension by eliminating the need for either side to back down. Carmen, however, was left unanswered. With Michael out of the room, he pressed Doug.

"Are you in or out?" He asked, his black, bottomless eyes boring in.

Doug didn't return his stare. Instead he got up and went to the window. He stood there with his hands in his pockets looking down on the flags that hung limp over the entrance to the hotel. He thought about the project yet undone and the employees and their families that relied on Keystate. Selfishly, he thought of his own ego and ambition. He also thought of the stock options that would vest the following week. Turning back to the room, he saw Carmen, the Rosens, Sean and Michael's empty chair. *'Was it worth it?'* He asked himself. *'How much good could come from working with this bunch? At best, they were incompetent. At worst… well, what could be worse?'* Cursed with the dual burdens of obligation and responsibility, Doug knew he really had no choice.

"I'm in."

Carmen sat down in his chair and drank the last of his scotch. The ice had melted and it was mostly water. He swiveled his chair to reach the bottle on the side table behind him. Turning back around, he poured a drink before asking Doug if there was anything more he wanted.

"No," Doug answered. "If there's nothing else you need from me, I'd like to head back." He looked at his watch. "I have a chance to catch an earlier flight if I get going now."

Carmen had had more than enough of Doug. He had developed a splitting headache from the squabbling.

"I think we're done with operational issues," He said. "Unless anyone else has something for you, I think you can go."

Doug glance around the table. Neither of the Rosens returned his look and Sean just shrugged his shoulders. Doug picked up his notepad and bottled water from the table before saying his good-byes and heading for the door. He closed the door behind him and was relieved that Michael was not in the hall. In a few minutes, he was crossing the lobby, past the clock and through the marbled foyer to the street.

It was half past noon and the sun, now directly overhead, scorched the sidewalk. Despite the heat, Park Avenue bustled with lunchtime foot and street traffic. Horns blared occasionally and diesel exhaust mingled with the smell of cigarettes and restaurants. The doorman hailed a waiting Checker and Doug gratefully slid into the air conditioned backseat.

It had been a hectic and harrowing morning. He retrieved his notepad from his jacket pocket to review his jottings. He'd managed to cover all the important points and the board had acceded to all his requests. But at what cost? A rue smile passed across has face as he realized that he now knew how Pyrrhus must have felt. No point in worrying about that. He was committed to seeing this through unless, of course, they fired him first. If that happened, at least he'd given it his best shot.

***** ***** ***** *****

Carmen and Michael faced each other across the long table. They were alone; the others had gone for lunch. Only one person could have summoned Michael from the board meeting with a phone call and Carmen wanted to know what he wanted.

"I take it that was Yuri?" He asked.

"No. It was Joe," Michael responded.

"Same thing. What did he want?"

"He wants to know when we're going to start driving the share price down. We just bought the last block of shares and Yuri wants to know when to expect the next phase to begin."

"Tell him it will start next week. By the week after, the share price will start to tumble."

"He will be happy to hear that. Do you mind telling me how you're going to make that happen?" Michael asked.

"I think you already know."

"Reardon?"

"Yeah," Carmen nodded. "He's just given us the excuse to terminate his employment contract. I don't think anyone can argue that he's not hostile to the board."

"Do you think he has an idea of what we're doing?" Michael was truly worried. "I mean, his comments about a Ponzi scheme and hoarding cash hit pretty close. It's as if he knows."

"I don't think he has a clue. He's not the type that thinks along those lines. But he's not stupid, either. It's time to get rid of him before he stumbles on what we're up to."

"What about Keystate. If he's right, we stand to lose a lot of money."

"We've already lost a lot of money," Carmen answered. "Getting rid of Reardon will only start driving share prices down. Next month, we'll report a significant loss for the quarter. That will be two quarters in a row that Keystate lost a lot of money. We'll blame that on Reardon, too. After we report those losses, the share price will drop like a rock.

"What about all the money you just committed to spend?" Michael asked. You know we can't use any of that money without Yuri's approval."

"I know," Carmen nodded. That had always been the deal back to his first meeting with Yuri. Michael controlled all the financial dealings of PetroChem. That meant that ultimate control rested with Yuri. All the company's proceeds from the issuance of stock had been deposited in several international banks. None of the banks were obligated to divulge depositor information to authorities in the United States. Only two people had the authority to access the various accounts: Michael and Yuri. Only Yuri could authorize withdrawals.

"I have no intention of spending another nickel on that plant until next spring," Carmen continued. "At that point, we'll announce a new management team and fresh capital to execute a turn around. Investors will be all over that story and the share price will go back up."

Michael smiled in appreciation of Carmen's scheming. There had been moments when he'd questioned whether Carmen could pull it off. It was beginning to look like he would. Carmen pushed back from the table and stood up. He contemplated pouring another drink but decided he that could wait until he and Michael joined the others for lunch. Unless he missed his guess, Sean already had ordered him a scotch.

"I have a favor to ask," Michael said as they waited for the elevator.

"What's that?"

"Let me terminate Reardon."

"You'd like that, wouldn't you?" Carmen said wryly.

"Of course. But it's more than that. There is a legal side because of his contract. I just want to make sure it's done cleanly."

"Go ahead," Carmen was grateful to get out from under the task. He didn't have much experience firing anyone and really didn't want to start learning now. "Just make sure it's done before next Thursday."

"I will but what's important about that day."

"Reardon's stock options vest on Friday."

Chapter Fifteen

From his vantage point, Alexandar Alexandrov had a clear view into Keystate's parking lot. It was an industrial neighborhood and the truck he'd stolen blended in with the other pickups in the gravel lot. He'd been there ever since he'd followed Doug Reardon back from the airport. The three hours since then had given him time to mentally run through his plan. He had also called Dmitri twice an hour to make sure the line functioned and Dmitri was awake. It was raining and the dark clouds hastened the evening sky. Alexandar was grateful; wet roads and poor visibility would be allies for the evening's work. He'd been told that it had to look like an accident. That point had been driven home by Michael Cole.

Alexandar was surprised that Michael was involved. This was the first killing Alexandar had planned with anyone other than Yuri or Josef. He recalled that Josef had been involved with the decision to kill Doug Reardon but had left the details to Michael. Thinking back, Alexandar couldn't remember whether Josef had specifically given the order to kill Reardon. But then, Alexandar hadn't been in on the entire conversation. He'd been summoned to Josef's office in New York City on Monday and had entered the room in time to hear Michael finish a sentence.

"… and Yuri thinks it would be a good idea to get rid of Reardon. After our board meeting last week, Carmen agrees that it's time to terminate him. I've been given the responsibility to carry it out but will need some help from you."

"If that's what my father and Carmen think, then I agree." Joe had looked over at Alexandar at that point and waved him in. "Alexandar, we have a job for you in Pittsburgh." He switched to Russian. "Michael asked for your special assistance. You're to do as he says." Turning back to Michael, he reverted to English. "I don't know why you need Alexandar's help getting rid of this guy. What kind of trouble do you expect from him?"

"With Alexandar's help... none. That's why I want him along"

"Alright," Joe finished. "Just make sure he's back at my father's house before Thursday. My parents are planning a party for Lindsay on Friday. She's pregnant, you know. Alexandar has to provide security that night."

Joe dismissed the pair and Michael led the way to his office down the hall. That's when he had stressed that killing Doug Reardon had to look like an accident. They'd discussed several possible scenarios and decided that a car accident would be best. Alexandar reminded Michael that the risk of failure was high. There were too many uncontrolled variables. Michael reminded him that this was the highest priority for Yuri and that failure was not an option.

Alexandar flew to Pittsburg later that same day. He'd spent the next day, Tuesday, reconnoitering the route between Doug's apartment and Keystate. He determined that the likeliest place to stage an accident was the interstate bridge that transected Neville Island. There were several sections where old guardrails had been removed in preparation for installing new ones. The bridge, which normally carried six lanes of traffic, had been reduced to four. For safety reasons, the outside lanes were closed and concrete barriers had been erected to separate traffic from the work area. However, road crews had left openings in a couple of sections to allow construction trucks access to the work zones. There, the only thing between the bridge deck and the Ohio River forty feet below were flimsy, orange pylons. Alexandar planned to herd Doug and his car off the bridge at one of these spots. This would require a second vehicle so he'd called Dmitri and told him to drive down from Erie.

That night, Alexandar slept in a rented car near Doug's apartment. The following morning dawned overcast and humid. It was still unusually warm for late September but a cold front was moving in from the west and expected to cross overhead by mid afternoon. Alexandar woke with a start at the noise of a passing car. He was parked on a side street that provided a view of the parking lot in front of Doug's apartment. A quick look assured him that Doug's car was still there.

Alexandar stretched as best he could behind the wheel. He wanted to get out, stretch his legs and take a piss but that was not possible now that it was getting light. He would have to wait until Doug was ensconced in his office. At that point, Alexandar would break surveillance in order to steal a truck. The rented car wasn't heavy enough for the job. Besides, it could be traced back to him. He would grab something to eat and relieve himself after he stole the truck.

Shortly after six, the courtesy lights on the Lexus blinked as Doug unlocked the doors with his key fob. A second later, he came into view carrying his backpack. He dropped it into the back seat and slid behind the wheel. Alexandar watched the car back out of its spot, leave the parking lot and turn into traffic. He waited for Doug to get a few hundred yards down the road before he pulled away from the curb to follow. Traffic got a little heavier when they turned onto Ohio River Boulevard and Alexandar let a few cars get between them. He didn't follow Doug when he turned into the parking lot of a hotel. Instead, he went a short distance past and turned into a gas station. In the rear view mirror, Alexandar watched as a large, white-haired man left the hotel and got in the car.

Doug pulled back onto the main road and past where Alexandar sat. As they went by, Alexandar could see they were laughing. Again, he let Doug go a short distance before following. They didn't go far before they stopped at a Denny's restaurant. Alexandar sat across the street in the parking lot of a beer distributor for an hour until the pair emerged. He was struck by the size of Reardon's companion. He knew that Doug was just over six feet tall. The other man was a good head taller. Not that it mattered. The hit was designed to take out the car and whoever was inside. It would be unfortunate if there was an extra occupant in the car. But only for that person.

Doug didn't make any other stops on the way to Keystate and drove through the gate a few minutes after eight. Alexandar watched from the lot across the street as the pair walked into the building. He waited another half hour before he drove away to get something to eat, relieve himself and steal a truck. He left Neville Island to do all three. The first two he accomplished at a McDonald's five miles down the road. He went another ten miles before he spotted a vehicle that suited his needs. It was a battered, gray Ford pickup that sat in a Home Depot parking lot. It was parked away from the building and Alexandar assumed it belonged to an employee. He parked his rental in the lot of a small strip mall a few hundred feet away and walked back to the truck. A minute later, he was back on the road in the hot-wired truck. He was very pleased to see the gas tank was half full. More than enough to suit his purpose. He took a different route back to Neville Island and was in position by ten o'clock. Thankfully, the Lexus hadn't moved. A short time later, however, it did.

Doug came out of the building at quarter past eleven, got in his car and drove through the gate. Cursing under his breath, Alexandar followed him up Grand Avenue before turning onto the bridge. On the other side of the river, Doug continued south on the interstate before turning west towards the airport. Alexandar definitely did not care for this turn of events. He hadn't intended to be out and about in a stolen vehicle and he hoped it had not yet been reported. He also cast a glance at the gas gauge. There was still almost a half tank of fuel but he didn't know where Reardon was headed. If he went too far, Alexandar might lose him.

He nervously followed the Lexus for several miles and was relieved when Doug took the exit for the airport. Alexandar followed him to the passenger pickup area but did not stop. As he drove past, Alexandar saw the man open the passenger door of the Lexus and bend to get in. Following the loop back to the highway, Alexandar drove slightly slower than the speed limit to allow Doug to catch up and pass him. Alexandar finally relaxed when he saw that Doug was retracing his path back to the plant. He settled in several cars behind and followed. As soon as he crossed over onto Neville Island, Alexandar pulled to the side of the road. He knew where his quarry was headed and there was no point in following too close. Ten minutes later he parked across the street from Keystate Oil. The truck he'd stolen blended in with the others in the gravel lot.

****** ****** ****** ******

Doug, Lud and Mark Duff stood on the loading dock and watched the pounding rain. Mark had flown in earlier that afternoon at Doug's invitation. Now that Carmen owned the company, Doug encouraged Mark to keep a close watch on the Sotex material. The men had been down by the river watching Stoli's crew unload a barge of ethylene glycol when the skies opened up. Doug and Mark managed to make it inside the warehouse without getting too wet. Lud, despite a surprising sprightliness for his age, wasn't fast enough and got drenched.

It was just after four o'clock and the warehouse was quiet save for the rain on the roof. Compared to the previous year, it was sadly empty. They passed through the warehouse and plant on the way to Doug's office. Mark commented on the dearth of finished goods and the unmanned plant. They were down to only one shift.

"Now that we have a full tank of glycol, we probably will restart the antifreeze line on second shift," Doug answered Mark's question. "We still have motor oil coming in and an occasional truckload of brake fluid or isopropyl. With luck, I'll get a barge of methanol in three weeks. Until then, we barely have enough material to keep the first shift going. Not that we need the raw material. You can see that we still have empty spots where the new equipment is supposed to go."

"You were going like a house afire when I was here in July. What happened?" Mark asked.

"The money dried up," Doug answered. "Risotti told me that I'd get the money needed to finish the plant and buy raw material. That was a week ago and I still don't have the cash."

"What are you going to do?"

"Wait, I guess. That and keep making what little we can."

They had covered the distance to Doug's office and Mark plopped down on the couch. Doug sat behind his desk and Lud stood uncomfortably in the doorway. They had dinner plans at an upscale restaurant that overlooked downtown from trendy Washington Hill. Mark and Doug's attire was still passable but it was obvious that Lud would have to change. Doug looked at his watch.

"Lud, the reservation isn't until six thirty. Why don't you take my car and get some dry clothes. Mark and I will take the company car to the restaurant. You should be able to make it back in time. I promise to have a martini waiting for you."

Lud make a one handed catch of the keys Doug tossed his way.

"Thanks. Is there enough gas to get me there and back? I know how you always run it down to fumes."

"I think so," Doug answered. "If not, you remember how to pump gas, don't you? I can see how you might forget since I'm always driving your dead ass around!" He rolled his eyes in mock consternation. "I buy you dinner, buy you drinks, lend you my car and you still complain."

"Hey," Lud smiled. "No good deed…"

"… goes unpunished," Doug finished the sentence. "So you've always told me. There's an umbrella behind that door. No point in you getting any wetter. See you later."

Lud grabbed the umbrella, waved goodbye and disappeared down the hall.

****** ****** ****** ******

Alexandar peered through the heavy rain as the light blue Lexus drove across the parking lot and swept through the gate. As it turned past him and onto Grand Avenue, he could see only the one head of the driver. Alexandar gave a passing thought that fate was being kind to the other men that had travelled with Reardon earlier that day. He put the truck into gear and pulled into traffic a few cars behind his target. Dmitri answered the call on the second ring.

"He's headed your way," Alexandar told him."Get ready."

The car immediately in front of Alexandar turned off the road leaving only two cars between Alexandar and Doug's car. The rain was heavier now and he had to turn the wipers on high speed. It was difficult to see very far down the road and Alexandar wasn't sure how far they'd come. He started to panic that they'd already passed Dmitri's position.

"I see him," Dmitri's voice came through the earpiece. "I'm pulling out now." A few seconds passed before Alexandar got the confirmation he needed. "I'm right in front of him and I see the entrance ramp to the bridge."

Alexandar watched as the turn signals flashed on three of the four cars ahead of him. The car directly in front went straight leaving only one car between him and his prey. Dmitri deliberately slowed so the vehicles bunched together going up the curve of the ramp and maintained the slow speed as he merged into traffic on the bridge. The car behind the Lexus accelerated into the passing lane and Alexandar sped up to follow. When he came abreast of his target, Alexandar slowed to match speed. He and Dmitri had their prey in a box and the three vehicles sped just under fifty miles per hour across the rain-slick bridge. Alexandar stole a quick glance in the rearview mirror; the nearest car was a quarter mile back. He gripped the wheel more tightly as they approached the section where there were no barriers.

"Not yet... not yet... NOW!!" He yelled into the phone.

Dmitri slammed on his brakes sending his car into a controlled skid. At the same moment Alexandar laid on his horn and steered the truck towards the Lexus. Lud hit the brakes and swerved to avoid the car in front. The blaring horn caused him to throw a look over his left shoulder only to see the looming gray fender of a truck bearing down on him. He reflexively threw the steering wheel the opposite direction and towards side of the road. He realized too late that there was no guardrail and he was going too fast to stop in time.

Lud tried to turn back but the truck slammed into him and kept pushing him toward the edge. The right front wheel dropped off the bridge deck and the crunch of the car's frame on concrete almost brought the Lexus to a sudden and complete halt. Were it not for the driving force of an assassin, the car might have stopped and cantilevered over the dark river.

Alexandar stomped the accelerator to the floor and, tires spinning on wet pavement, pushed the car over. Lud started screaming as the car slowly pivoted upside down and dropped towards the water. His large hands gripped the steering wheel and he screamed until the force of the impact collapsed the roof around his snow white head.

Alexandar turned the wheels of the stopped truck toward the edge of the bridge and, leaving it in gear, calmly opened the door and stepped out. The truck drove itself into the abyss. Alexandar didn't see it go. He had turned and was jogging the short distance to Dmitri's car.

None of the cars ahead of them saw what happened. The few cars that were behind stopped and the occupants ran over to cautiously looked off the bridge. The Lexus and stolen truck were already submerged. No one gave chase as the taillights of Dmitri's car faded into the rain-dimmed twilight.

It had taken less than two minutes from beginning to end. Alexandar wiped the rain from his face and dried his hands on the inseam of his trousers before pulling his cell phone from his jacket pocket. He punched in a phone number and waited through three rings for it to be answered.

"Hello."

"It's done," He said and hung up.

Chapter Sixteen

The phone went dead in Michael's hand. Alexandar hadn't said much but it was enough. He smiled grimly and placed the cell phone the on the table next to his plate. As usual, it was the only plate set at the table. Michael ate as he lived - alone in a large brownstone in downtown Philadelphia. The house had belonged to his parents and his grandparents before them. Michael was likely to be the last Cole to live in the elegant townhouse on the tree lined corner of Delany and Philips streets.

The only child of Ira and Miriam Cole, Michael had three female cousins but they had all married and moved away. He doubted any of them could afford to buy the place anyway. No, he was the only Cole that had made it. He had taken what his parents provided and multiplied it several times over. Not that his parents hadn't given him a good head start. The Cole family had operated a successful jewelry business in Philadelphia for over seventy-five years. Established in 1920, the business had passed from father to son until Michael broke the chain. He'd simultaneously broke his father's heart.

Michael lost count of the times his father told him the family history. It starting with great-grandfather Isaac Kolek escaping the pogrom during the Russian Revolution. He'd fled to America where an immigration official on Ellis Island arbitrarily changed his name to Cole. Isaac begged scraps on the streets of New York City for a few months before migrating to Philadelphia where he found work at a grocery store. Eventually, he earned enough money to set up a business selling trinkets and paste jewelry.

The business took off during the Roaring Twenties and Isaac made the jump from costume to fine jewelry. There were tough times during the Depression but, since the very wealthy always have money to spend, high end jewelers like the Coles managed to make it through relatively unscathed. The business prospered through the rest of the century until the advent of malls, discount and on-line retailers took away younger customers. Michael recognized this trend and decided he would rather make his way in life through the law.

He'd done well enough as a young corporate lawyer but really hit pay dirt when he was retained by Yuri Pandropov. He couldn't, and didn't, discuss his professional life with his parents but when his father found out he was working for a Russian, the old man went berserk. Already frail, Ira soon succumbed. Michael's mother passed away a short time later leaving Michael both bereaved and a pariah to his family. Ironically, his standing as an outcast served him well in his relationship with Yuri.

Since he had no close family to be interested in his work, he didn't have to worry about divulging the nature of his employment. Michael was a paid great deal of money to keep his mouth shut while he bridged the gap between Yuri's illegal and legal activities. He had earned Yuri's confidence and, for the most part, had been left to his own devices. That was, of course, before Carmen Risotti came on the scene.

It had been two years since Carmen had burst into his life and Michael often rued the day he bought into CARMA. The insignificant Hollywood tech firm provided Carmen the opening he needed to ingratiate himself with Yuri. To be sure, Michael remained the conduit but even that had been diluted. He now had to report through Joe and he knew that Yuri's eldest son had a palpable dislike for him. He didn't know what he'd done to merit Joe's distain. Ultimately, he passed it off as a general animosity for lawyers or, worst case, anti-Semitism.

Whatever the cause, Michael found himself thrice removed from Yuri because of Carmen and Joe. Michael knew that Yuri and Joe respected Carmen because of the plan to launder Yuri's money. True, it hadn't yet been fully realized but the plan had, thus far, gone according to schedule. As Carmen's star had risen, Michael's had waned.

 Feeling marginalized, Michael felt compelled to contribute in some meaningful way. What better way to re-establish his standing than by advancing the plan while eliminating a threat? That's why he took it upon himself to kill Doug Reardon. Carmen just wanted Reardon fired and Yuri had been ambiguous but Michael considered Doug a real threat. He didn't think the comments Doug had made at the board meeting about a Ponzi scheme had just been a coincidence.

Besides, if Doug met an accidental death, Carmen wouldn't have to make up a story to explain to investors why Reardon needed to be fired. Firing him would have been messy. If investors liked him, they would question the board's wisdom for firing him. If investors didn't like him, they would wonder why it took so long for the board to take action. Either way, the board would lose.

Michael concluded that it was much better that Doug died. And he made it happen without any help from Carmen and Joe. He'd shown them - and Yuri - that he was just as capable of decisive action as they were. He doubted Carmen would have had the balls to develop and execute a plan to kill someone. It didn't matter that Michael hadn't actually participated. After all, Alexandar was just the weapon that Michael aimed and fired.

No, he, alone, was responsible for killing Doug Reardon. He couldn't wait to tell Yuri and Joe how he had killed the two birds with one stone. And he had no remorse about it. Far from it. After the events of the previous months, he was glad the prick was dead.

He got up from the table and went into the kitchen to clean up. It only took a few minutes to wash and dry the dishes and put them away. It wasn't late but he decided to go to bed. He was going to drive to Pittsburgh the following morning and wanted to get an early start. On the way up the stairs, he contemplated calling Carmen but decided against it. If Carmen knew that Doug was dead, he'd want to fly to Pittsburgh.

Michael wanted to be the first and only PetroChem executive at the plant while the company digested the news. The desire was equal parts proprietorship, narcissism and morbid curiosity. Despite Carmen's admonishment - or perhaps because of it - he still felt ownership of Keystate and felt he deserved respect for the role. Michael decided Carmen could wait to hear the news until after he'd told Yuri and

Joe what he'd accomplished. It gave him a delicious satisfaction to know that, for once, he had privy information and could decide when and to whom it should be released. It was the second time that night he'd had the sensation of power.

Chapter Seventeen

When Lud didn't show up for dinner or answer repeated calls to his cell phone, Doug asked Mark to take a taxi to his hotel. Doug drove back to Keystate and, finding neither Lud nor the Lexus, drove to Lud's hotel. The trip took longer than usual because bridge traffic had been reduced to one lane at the site of an accident. Flashers of several police cars and some high intensity lights lit up the scene. It seemed strange to Doug that the search lights were aimed off the bridge and down to the river.

He looked back as made the right-hand to run parallel to the river. A flotilla of small boats circled the waters under the span. Flashing strobe lights on two indentified them as police boats. A barge with a crane was making its way down river. Doug's stomach turned with dread at the conclusion that some poor bastard had driven off the bridge.

A premonition caused him to speed to the hotel where the girl behind the desk said was sure she hadn't seen Lud that evening. She joked that he was hard to miss as she placed a quick call to his room. When the call went unanswered, Doug convinced her to let him into the room. The momentary relief of discovering that Lud had not collapsed in the room was replaced by the concern of not knowing where he was. Doug looked in the bathroom and closet for the wet clothes Lud had on. They weren't there. That's when Doug decided he had to call Lois.

"No," She answered. "I haven't heard from Lud tonight. He called me a couple of hours ago to tell me you were having dinner and said he'd call me when it was over."

Doug decided not to tell her that Lud had been missing for those two hours. He joked that he would kick Lud in the ass when he caught up with him and asked Lois to give him a call if she heard from Lud before then. Still at the hotel, he asked to borrow the phonebook to look up the number for the local police.

He was connected to a desk officer and reported Lud and the Lexus missing. He implied that the car was stolen. He wasn't sure how fast the police would respond to a missing person report but figured a stolen car would immediately find its way onto a data base. Once he'd provided his contact information, there was nothing more he could do so he drove the short distance to his apartment.

He tried several times over the ensuing two hours to call Lud. The battery of his cell phone was running low so he walked into the bedroom where he kept the wall charger. He was about to plug it in when the phone rang in his hand. He looked at the screen; it was Lois.

"Hi, Lois," He answered a cheerily as he could. "Has the big guy surfaced?"

"No." Doug picked up on the tenseness in her voice. "I was hoping he was with you. Doug, I'm getting worried. He never goes this long without calling me. Should I call the police?"

"I already did that," Doug confessed. "A couple of hours ago after we talked. I didn't want to worry you."

"Well, I'm worried now. Is there anything else we can do? Should I come there?"

"I don't think that's a good idea," Doug answered. "It's late and you shouldn't be driving the turnpike in this rain. There's nothing to do here but wait." He cringed to himself at the last comment and quickly added: "I'm sure he'll call one of us soon. He probably had a flat tire or something and will chew me out for loaning him my car." He tried to sound reassuring.

"Doug, it's been over four hours. I know something's happened."

"No, you don't. Try to get some rest. I'll call you as soon as I hear from him."

As soon as she hung up, Doug plugged his phone into the charger and walked back into the living room. It was time for the late news so he switched the channel to the local station. He was a few minutes late and just caught the last seconds of the lead story about the accident on the Neville Island bridge.

He quickly tuned into a competing station where a beat reporter stood under an umbrella and broadcast from Ohio River Boulevard. The camera panned to the river where a barge with a crane was hoisting a pickup truck from the water. Cables were fastened to the front and rear axles so the truck was suspended upside down. The driver side door swung open and water poured from the cab. Doug watched the scene play out as the reporter provided sketchy details.

"Authorities report that the truck you see being pulled from the river - an older, Ford F250 pickup - was one of two vehicles involved in a collision on the I-79 bridge. Eyewitnesses say the other vehicle was a late model sedan believed to be a Toyota. The vehicles were headed north on the interstate at around five-thirty this evening when the truck appeared to lose control and slam into the sedan causing both vehicles to plunge off the bridge into the river below. Reports are that police divers found a body still in the car. There has been no sign yet of the driver of the truck.

PennDOT crews have been replacing the guardrails on the bridge for the past several weeks. Although barricaded, it appears that the car and truck unfortunately found the one unprotected spot. There will undoubtedly be a full investigation into the incident. Reporting for KDKA, Channel two news, this is…"

Doug flipped through stations to see if any others were still reporting the story. They had all moved onto national news items. He felt that there should be something he should be doing. It was innervating that he could think of nothing so he paced up and down the narrow hall between the living room and bedroom. On the fifth lap, his cell phone rang. He ran into the bedroom and grabbed it from the nightstand. The display announced the Ohio Township Police.

"This is Doug Reardon," He answered out of professional habit .

"Mr. Reardon, this is Officer McMeans of the Ohio Township Police. I have information on the car you reported stolen."

"Where is it?! Where's the guy that was driving?" He blurted out.

"The car has been impounded. I'm afraid it's been involved in a fatal accident. Can you come the police station in Sewickley? We can have someone come pick you up if you need transportation or don't know where we are.

Doug was stunned.

"Did you say the driver was killed?"

"There was a fatality but we need you to come to the station in order to ask you some questions and give you the information on your car. Is it possible for you to come now? Again, we can send a car for you if you'd like."

"No. I'll get there as soon as I can. Can't you tell me about the driver?" Doug implored. "His wife knows he's missing and is worried sick."

"No, sir. Not over the phone. We'll answer your questions when you get here."

It was not quite midnight when Doug walked into the station. It had been a quiet ride to Sewickley. The small town sits on the north bank of the Ohio River just west of the bridge to Neville Island. That late at night there was no traffic and the rain had almost stopped. He introduced himself to the officer at the front desk and she punched a number on the phone. A minute later Officer Dan McMeans stepped into the lobby. Before Doug could ask any questions, the officer led him back to a small conference room and asked him to sit down. Doug refused a proffered cup of coffee and instead reached for a large clear bag that was on the table. Inside appeared to be a wallet and watch. McMeans picked the bag up before Doug could get to it.

"Does that belong to the to the man who was driving my car?" He asked. "Where is he?"

"Your car was involved in a two-car accident this evening on the interstate bridge leaving Neville Island. Both vehicles ended up in the river. The driver of your car was killed. We haven't found any sign of the driver of the truck." McMeans watched as Doug visibly cringed in his chair. "Did you know the man driving your car?"

"Yes. His name was Lud Rahl. He's a friend of mine. Lud is short for Ludwig"

"The blotter says you reported your car was stolen."

"I reported it missing. Which it was… along with Lud. He got wet from the rain earlier today and needed to go back to his hotel to change. I lent him my car."

"What time was that?"

"Between five and five-thirty."

"And that was the last time you saw him."

"Yeah." Doug felt tears well up but manage to hold them back. "I have to call his wife."

"I understand. Before you do that, we need to positively identify the body. Here are his personal effects." The office opened the bag and dumped the contents on the table. He picked up the wallet, extracted the driver's license and handed it to Doug. "Is this your friend?"

"Yes." Doug looked at the picture and handed it back.

"Do you think you can go with me to the hospital to identify the body?"

Doug nodded his head numbly. McMeans stood to go and held the door for Doug. He blanked out getting into the police cruiser, during the short drive to Sewickley Valley Hospital and riding the elevator that took him to the basement morgue. He felt a moment of panic as they swung opened the heavy doors and walked him to the table where the large body bag lie. He'd never been in a morgue or seen the body of an accident victim much less that of a friend. The attendant unzipped the body bag and Doug wobbled at seeing the battered image of Lud's broken body.

It struck him as odd that Lud's hair was still wet. It was soaked the last time he saw his friend alive. That had been from the rain. Now, his once white hair was matted and stained pink by blood, bits of brain and river water. McMeans grabbed Doug firmly under the left arm and swung him back toward the door. There were a couple of chairs in the corridor and the officer plopped Doug down in one and sat next to him.

"Was that him?"

Doug nodded.

"I'm sorry to do that to you, There wasn't much question about his identity but we'd needed a positive identification from somebody that knew him."

They sat there silently for a few moments under the glare of fluorescent lights. Eventually, McMeans asked,

"Are you ready to go?"

Doug nodded again and the two men got up and headed to the elevator. They didn't speak on the way back to the police station where McMeans guided Doug back to the small conference room. This time Doug accepted the strong coffee as he waited for McMeans to retrieve a couple of forms that needed Doug's signature. He was starting to regain his wits and was thinking of calling Lois when McMeans returned. One of the forms let him know his car was impounded and where it was located. The second confirmed that he had identified the deceased.

"What's going to happen to my car?"

We have to hold it until the investigation is over," McMeans answered. "After that, it's yours to do with as you please. There's nothing to do with it except the shredder, though."

"What kind of investigation?" Doug asked.

"There is always an investigation after a traffic fatality," McMeans answered. "In this case it will be extensive because the Highway Patrol and PennDOT will get involved. There are several loose ends we have to tie down involving the other vehicle and driver."

"What's that?"

"For starters, and I shouldn't tell you this, but the truck was reported stolen. Secondly, the driver of the truck is missing. We haven't found him or his body. We have an unsubstantiated report from an eyewitness who says she thinks she saw the driver of the truck walk away from the scene. The investigation will have to stay open until we determine what happened to the driver of the stolen truck."

Doug finished the last of his coffee. "Are you finished with me?"

"Yes, sir. Are you going to be okay to drive?"

Doug assured McMeans that he was and left. An hour later, he stood in his shower. Arms raised, he gripped the shower head as he leaned forward to rest his forehead on the tiled wall. He felt as though his head was stuffed with wadding and there was pressure at the base of his neck and behind his eyes. Not quite a headache, the sensation was uncomfortable and alien.

The hot water was relaxing as it pelted the back of his head and neck. For an instant, he felt as though he was having an out of body experience before being completely overwhelmed by loss and despair. Lud had been his best friend and had been a stalwart listening post and source of encouragement. He had helped Doug navigate previous job losses and the sense of betrayal when Jim and Ken sold Keystate to Risotti and his gang.

There wasn't much either of them could do once those miscreants took control but Lud tried to provide Doug some perspective as his position, status and prestige were stripped away. Through it all, Lud had been a bulwark of support and respect. Now that he was gone, waves of remorse and loss crashed through the breech that Lud's absence ripped in Doug's emotional bulkhead.

In an instant, Doug was sobbing violently as the water ran down the sides of his face to mingled with the tears, snot and drool that fell freely from his eyes, nose and mouth. Periodically, he gasped in hot, humid air that he exhaled in a low, guttural moan ending in a breathless, silent scream. His body wracked through this cycle for several minutes until, spent, he dropped to his knees. Leaning forward into a fetal position, he rocked back and forth with his arms wrapped across his chest and his face pressed against the shower floor.

Eventually, the small water heater ran out of hot water and cool water chilled him back to awareness. He reached up to turn the water off before rising to stand on wobbly legs. Grabbing a towel, he dried, stepped out of the shower and put on his bathrobe. Plodding into the living room, Doug collapsed in the recliner that smelled of stale cigarettes. The TV was still on and Doug stared at it blankly. He had to make the call; there was no one else to do it. He picked up his cell phone and dialed the number with leaden fingers. It was almost two in the morning but she answered on the first ring.

"Lois, its Doug."

Chapter Eighteen

The season changed seemingly overnight. There was a crispness to the morning air and, as Michael crossed over the Laurel Highlands, there was frost on the ground and color in the trees. The sun was an hour over the horizon behind him and bathed the way ahead with a diffused light that was easy on his eyes. He had been on the road for two hours and had three more to go before arriving in Pittsburgh. Figuring an hour for lunch, Michael should be at Keystate around one o'clock.

At some point, he'd have to call Carmen and break the news that Doug was dead. He decided that he would wait until he got to the plant. Any sooner and Carmen would want to know how he found out. Besides, he didn't want to give Carmen the opportunity to catch a flight that day. For the next three hours, Michael didn't have anything pressing to do.

He turned his phone off and squirmed into the leather seat of his dark green BMW. Freed from emails and phone calls, he wrapped his gloved hands around the wheel and accelerated down a grade into a sharp turn to speed past a tractor-trailer. The high performance car squatted as it gripped the road coming out of the turn and purred as the grade rose to climb yet another hill. Michael was enjoying the moment and started to sing along with Madonna as she warbled from the car's CD player.

Chapter Nineteen

Doug woke up at eight-thirty feeling like shit. He sat up to a headache and eyes that felt like they were full of sand. It took him a few seconds to remember that Lud was dead. When the realization hit, he fell back on his pillow. He didn't cry but did tear up enough to moisten his eyes. When he opened them again, they didn't feel quite as scratchy. Getting out of bed, he went straight to the refrigerator for orange juice. Eschewing a glass, he drank directly from the carton in gulps. Sated, he threw the empty container in the trash and walked to turn on the television. It took twenty minutes of watching the pseudo-news show for the talking heads to mention the accident that killed Lud. The authorities hadn't released the identities of the deceased. Doug knew more than they did.

He went into the bathroom and the reflection in the mirror told him why he felt like shit; he looked the same way. He splashed some water on his face before sticking his head under the faucet to wet his hair. It hadn't been that long since he'd showered and he didn't have the enthusiasm for it. After drying and combing his hair, he went to the closet and got dressed. In the bedroom, he picked up his phone to call the office. Doug exchanged pleasantries with the receptionist before telling her not to expect him until the afternoon. Then he asked to be transferred to Stoli.

"Late night out partying with the big boys?" Stoli's cheery voice came over the phone. He knew that Doug and Lud went out the previous night. "What's this I hear about you not coming in this morning? If you can't hunt with the big dogs, better stay on the porch." It was Stoli's way of ribbing Doug for not yet being at the plant.

"Stoli, I've got bad news. Lud's was killed last night in a car wreck on the interstate bridge."

"Sweet Jesus!" Stoli muttered. "God damn it! I saw the news this morning on TV. They were showing the car they pulled out of the river." Stoli had a flash of recognition. "Was that your car?"

"Yeah. He borrowed it last night to go back to his hotel to change clothes. He got soaked yesterday watching you unload that barge."

"Where are you?" Stoli asked. "Do you need a ride?"

"I'm still at my apartment. I picked up the company car yesterday," Doug answered. "Lud's wife and son are driving in this morning and I'm going to meet them at the police station. After that, I guess we have to go to the hospital to make arrangements to move him. I don't know."

"Is there anything you need me to do?" Stoli offered.

"Not really. I should be in late this afternoon. We can talk then unless it gets to be too late. In that case, we'll get together tomorrow."

"I'm not going to be at work tomorrow," Stoli answered. "Helen and I are going to Erie this afternoon. My daughter-in-law is pregnant and her parents have asked us up for a family get together. It starts tonight and goes through the weekend."

Doug was struck by the irony that he was dealing with death this morning while Stoli was planning to attend a party celebrating the beginning of a life.

"Congratulations on becoming a grandfather, Jack," Doug used Stoli's given name. "That's good news. Do they know if it's a boy or girl?

"It's a boy. Either that or a three-legged girl." Stoli couldn't resist the shop humor.

Doug was happy for Stoli and appreciated the attempted joke. It was the first time he felt anything other than dread, sadness or despair since the night before.

"Good for you. If I don't see you later today, enjoy the weekend and we'll talk on Monday."

"Okay. Doug, I'm really sorry about Lud. Everybody knows how close you were."

"Thanks, Stoli."

Doug had one more call to make before he headed back to the Sewickley police station. He didn't really want to talk to Carmen and thought about sending an email but decided Lud's death was worthy of a conversation.

"Good morning, Doug," Carmen answered. He must have seen Doug's name pop up on his phone's display. "I don't often hear from you this early in the morning. What's up?"

"I hope I didn't wake you," Doug began. "I never know whether you're on the East or West Coast."

"I'm home this morning in New York. What can I do for you?" Carmen was all business.

"I'm calling to let you know I won't be in the office for a few days. Lud Rahl was killed in a car accident last night and I have to help his widow move his body back to Cleveland. I'll probably miss a couple of days next week for the funeral. Sometime during all that, the police want to speak with me again."

Carmen's mind instantly kicked into high gear. He almost didn't answer Doug's call because he feared it might have been in response to being fired. Obviously, Michael hadn't done that yet and probably wouldn't now that Doug was going to be unavailable. *'Looks like Doug is going to vest his stock options, after all.'* Carmen thought. *'It doesn't really matter but it would have been tidier.'* However, what really riveted Carmen's attention was Doug's comment about the police.

"I'm sorry to hear about Lud," He began. "I didn't know him well but I know he was a good friend of yours. I understand why you need to take time away. Take as much as you need." Nonchalantly, he added: "You said the police want to talk to you. Why is that?"

"Lud was driving my car when he was killed. Apparently, a pickup truck ran him off the bridge leaving Neville Island. Both vehicles ended up in the river. The truck was stolen and they haven't found the body of the driver yet. I guess the police are investigating until they do. I don't know why they want to talk to me. Funny, the cop said he shouldn't have told me that the truck was stolen. Now that I think about it, that hasn't been reported in the news."

Chapter Twenty

It was one-thirty when Michael drove through Keystate's gate and crunched across the gravel lot. He stopped in front of the office building and deliberately chose the spot where Doug usually parked. There were no sounds coming from the plant and he'd noticed several employees in the smoker's shack as he drove past. None of them waved although most turned to watch him drive by.

He walked the short distance to the office and entered the small lobby. The receptionist was not in her chair so he walked, unannounced, down the hall that led to Doug's office. Hearing voices from the cubicles that held the sales department, he headed that direction. He walked past three empty offices until he came to the one occupied by Peter Sawyer. Pete, the receptionist, three sales clerks and Rose, the IT manager were crammed into the small space. The receptionist and Rose were weepy eyed and sniffled frequently into wads of tissues. Pete had been speaking but fell silent when Michael appeared.

"I heard," Michael said, although he really hadn't. "It's a terrible, terrible tragedy. How is everybody?"

"We're doing as good as can be expected," Rose sniffed. "He was such a nice man. I'm really going to miss him."

"Yes, he was. We're all going to miss him," Michael lied. "But it will be all right. These are tough times but we'll get through somehow."

They looked at him as though he had three heads. Most knew of the enmity between the two men. Besides, the news of Lud's death was less than two hours old. People hadn't had time to process the news much less begin grieving and Michael was already talking about recovery and moving on. He looked from face to face for some acknowledgment. They just stared at him blankly for long, uncomfortable seconds. Michael became nervous as the awkward silence stretched out. He could feel himself redden.

"I'll be in Doug's office," He stammered weakly.

He spun on his heel and hurried down the hall into Doug's empty office and shut the door. He was embarrassed and angry that they had rejected his overture of compassion. '*What did these people want from me?*' He fumed. '*Why did it always seem so easy for them to like Reardon? What did he have that I don't?*'

He set that aside for now. It was a pointless consideration anyway, now that Doug was dead. Michael decided it was time to call Carmen and hit the speed dial on his cell phone.

"Where are you?" Carmen didn't bother to say hello. "And why haven't you fired Reardon like we planned?"

Any other day and Michael would have been back on his heels. But not today. Today, he had the upper hand over Carmen Risotti.

"To answer your first question, I'm at Keystate in Doug's old office. In answer to your second question, it's kind of hard to fire a dead man."

"What are you talking about?" Carmen was incredulous. "Reardon's not dead."

"Yes, he is," Michael answered calmly. "You wouldn't have heard the local news but he was killed last night in a car accident on the bridge leaving the island. Somebody in a stolen truck ran into him and they both ended up in the river."

"Maybe I didn't hear the local news, but I did talk to Doug this morning. About a half hour ago he called me to tell me that Lud Rahl was killed in that accident. Reardon is very much alive."

Michael was instantly afraid. If Doug was still alive that meant Alexandar had failed. If Alexandar had failed, that meant Michael had failed. Yuri was not one to suffer failures. Especially if the failure was the result of a rogue plan such as the one Michael hatched. The confidence and power Michael felt earlier evaporated. He stammered: "That's not possible. I know he was killed! I had confirmation!"

Carmen was confused. He naturally assumed Michael meant the television newscasts. Then it struck him that Michael had referred to the 'stolen' truck. He recalled his earlier conversation when Doug told him the police hadn't released that information to the public. If that was true, how could Michael know the truck was stolen? Maybe Doug told someone at the plant and that person told Michael. But, if that were the case, there wouldn't be any confusion that it was Lud that was killed.

"What do you mean you had confirmation? Who told you that? And how did you know the truck was stolen? Doug told me the police didn't report that."

Michael felt trapped and defenseless. This wasn't going at all the way he'd planned. He wanted to tell Joe and Yuri that he'd killed Reardon because Carmen didn't have the guts to do it. He wasn't going to tell Carmen until he'd collected his just rewards. Now it looked as though he was going to have to tell Carmen.

"Alexandar Alexandrov called me last night when it was done. I knew he was planning on stealing a truck. He said he needed a heavy vehicle."

"What the fuck are you talking..." Then it hit Carmen just what Michael had done. "Oh, you ignorant bastard! Do you realize what you've done?! You just killed us!"

"What do you mean? I just did what had to be done. Reardon was...is a threat to us because he knows. Yuri and Joe will thank me for having the guts to do what needed done."

"Do you really think Yuri and Joe want the police sniffing around their operation? Doug is on his way to the police station right now. There will be an investigation because of the stolen truck and missing driver. An investigation that could lead back to Yuri."

"Oh, God," Michael groaned. "I didn't think of that. What am I going to do. What should I do?"

"Right now, get the fuck out of Keystate before Reardon shows up. How many other people saw you there?

"I don't know. Maybe a dozen."

"Okay. On your way out, make sure to tell someone that you're going to the bank to arrange to transfer some money. That will explain why you're there. Now get out of there. I'll call you after I have a chance to think."

Michael hung up the phone, grabbed his few things and went to let someone know he was leaving. The same people were still in the cubicle he'd left earlier. He told no one in particular and everyone in general that he was leaving to go to the bank. The only response was a blank look from Pete followed by: "Do you want Doug to call you if he shows up or calls in?"

"Only if he needs me," Michael replied, groaning inwardly at the confirmation that Doug lived. "I should be back later."

He turned and walked away from the small group angry that they always made him feel so awkward. But then, just about any group made him feel that way. He made his way back through the small lobby and was just about to step outside when the door swung open. Doug stood in the doorway.

"What are you doing here?" Doug demanded. "I thought Carmen told you to stay away."

Michael felt the anger and resentment swelling inside him. *'I hate you, you arrogant fucker!'* He thought. *'You should be dead right now instead of standing here questioning me.'* He took a step back so they both were standing in the lobby.

"I'm here to get you the money that was promised at the board meeting," Michael managed to sound civil. "I'm on my way to the bank right now. I just stopped by because I heard about Lud and I wanted to convey my condolences."

Doug doubted Michael's sincerity. Although Lud hadn't wasted thought or emotion on Michael, Doug knew the resentment Michael carried for Lud after the episode earlier in the year. It galled Doug that the little prick showed up the day after Lud's death with hollow sentiment. Still, he had to be gracious.

"Thanks for that," He said. "You said you were going to the bank for money. How much is going to be available and when?"

"I don't know," Michael hesitated. Carmen hadn't done that much thinking for him. "I have to coordinate that with Carman. I'll get back to you. Are you going to be here the rest of the day.

"Yes and all day tomorrow, too."

"Okay. I'll call you."

With that, Michael walked out of the building and got into his car. He was headed toward the gate when his cell rang. It was Carmen.

"Did you leave Keystate yet?"

"I'm leaving now. I ran into Reardon on my way out the door. I told him I was going to the bank to arrange to transfer funds for the project."

"All right," Carmen sighed. "Here's what you need to do." There was a weighty pause. "Finish what you started."

"What do you mean?"

"I mean that Reardon is a threat now that the police are involved. They will probably ask him if he can think of anybody that might want to kill him or Lud. The obvious answer is *you*."

"Why would the police ask him that."

"Because I would. It's a logical question. It doesn't take much imagination to think that Doug's car was deliberately pushed off the bridge. It was a stolen truck and the driver is missing. We both know there's no body to be found. The police are bound to start asking questions. The only way we can keep Reardon from answering them is if he's not around."

Michael was feeling panicked and it showed in his voice. "I agree. But how do we do it."

"There's no *we* in this conversation. You got yourself into this mess; you get yourself out. I suggest you call that henchman of Yuri's. You'll have to do what you can to convince him to keep his mouth shut. You are in more danger from Yuri than the police if this gets out. So am I. Tell Alexandar that he failed in his mission and you won't expose him if he stays quiet. Then hope he's smart enough not to say anything."

Carmen's decisiveness and instructions made Michael feel a bit better. He was still in danger but at least he had the beginnings of a plan. "Okay," He said. "Is there anything else I should do?"

"Yeah. Don't call me for a few days. I won't answer your calls if you do. You fucked up big time and I don't plan on going down with you if you can't fix this."

The phone went dead in Michael's hand. Carmen had said a lot but it wasn't nearly enough. Michael wanted reassurance that everything was going to work out. He wanted someone else to take the lead, develop the plan and tell him what to do. He felt exposed and alone. And powerless.

He pulled into traffic on Grand Avenue and then up the entrance ramp to the interstate bridge. The BMW accelerated through the curve of the ramp. He was already doing sixty by the time he merged into traffic and had to hit the brakes as he neared the construction zone. Traffic was down to one lane and Michael slowed to a crawl as he passed two sets of skid marks that led over the edge of the bridge. Yellow, crime scene tape was stretched across the gap and the evidence of a police investigation caused the knot of fear to return to Michael's stomach. He stayed on the interstate after he left the bridge and headed north to Erie.

Chapter Twenty-One

Stoli was alone in his truck. Helen had driven to Erie earlier in the day to help organize the party. He had showered and changed clothes at Keystate but still got a late start. It was now two-thirty and he was only slightly more than halfway to the house by the lake. He'd been following the same semi for fifteen miles. As usual, the freeway was under construction and long sections had been reduced to one lane.

When the line of traffic finally reached the end of the construction, the big rig signaled to pull over into the right lane. Stoli stayed in his lane in anticipation of it clearing out. The semi started to drift over and then unexpectedly swerved back to the left. Stoli slammed on his brakes and glanced into his rearview mirror in time to see a dark green BMW coupe fly up the right lane to pass him and the truck.

'Fucking asshole!' Stoli swore at the driver under his breath. The trucker blasted his air horn in agreement before once again steering into the slow lane. This time, he made it without incident. With the lane clear ahead, Stoli accelerated to seventy. The offending coupe was far down the road. *'He must be doing ninety,'* Stoli thought. *'I hope he doesn't kill anybody but himself.'*

It had been only a few hours since he had learned of Lud's tragic accident and death. Stoli was surprised by the magnitude of shock and sadness he'd felt when Doug broke the news. Despite his reservations and attempts to stay apart from management, Stoli realized that Lud had become a friend. So had Doug. Both treated Stoli honestly and with respect. They listened to what he had to say, implemented his ideas when they agreed and took time to argue when they didn't. Once or twice, he's won an argument and Lud or Doug backed down.

As he thought on it, Stoli realized that Lud treated everyone the same way. There wasn't anybody in the plant that he hadn't spent time trying to know. There were a few that weren't interested in talking and a couple of union stalwarts that wouldn't give Lud the time of day. But those that took the time to talk discovered Lud an interested and respectful man. It was easy to see how he'd influenced Doug. Now that he was gone, it was clear to Stoli how much of an impact Lud had on him, too.

By the time Stoli turned into the circular driveway of the Pandropov house, it was four-thirty. He pulled into the large, bricked area in front of the four car garage and parked his truck beside Helen's Buick. There were two other cars, a Mercedes and a Volvo, that Stoli assumed belonged to Lindsey's brothers. He felt a twinge of jealousy as he turned off his Dodge Ram. The truck was only a few years old but showed the scars of a working man's vehicle. As he stepped down from the cab, Stoli saw Yuri coming out of the house with his hand outstretched.

"Ivan Stalichovik! It is good to see you again. A great day, is it not?"

"Yes it is," Stoli answered. "Other than the rain yesterday, we've been having pretty nice weather for this time of the year."

"What? No, no!" Yuri responded. "I'm not talking about the weather. I'm talking about Lindsey and John. You and I are going to be grandfathers! I knew they wouldn't disappoint us!" He had his arm firmly around Stoli's shoulders and was leading him to the front door. "Come. We need to share a drink to our good fortune."

The two men walked into the house. They passed through the spacious foyer and down a short hall to the kitchen. The rest of the family was gathered around a glass topped table. Joe stood apart at the far side of the room. He was married but his wife, Sybil, was not with him. She was a real beauty but in a plastic sort of way; always immaculately coiffed and attired. Normally, her blonde hair was pulled up into a French twist and, unless she was going out, she almost always wore navy slacks, a light cashmere sweater that complimented her curves and a single strand of large pearls. She made sure Joe was appropriately and similarly attired in slacks and a sweater. He didn't wear pearls but had the male equivalent - a large, gold Rolex. They had no intention of children and she seldom left Manhattan. To her, the continent ended west of the Hudson.

Lindsay's other brother, Sam was still a bachelor. He was single mindedly pursuing his medical degree and wouldn't make time for women. He was relaxed in a pair of worn jeans and surgical scrubs. His hair was curly and on the long side. He was sitting with Lindsey on his lap and they were laughing at the type of inside joke that only close siblings share. John Stalich sat next to them with an amused, puzzled look on his face.

The two grandmothers-to-be were in the kitchen proper. Helen was showing Elena how to make baked pierogies. It was Helen's one, secret recipe and Stoli was surprised to see her give it up. Unlike the boiled and fried variety, baked pierogies are more like puff pastries. Light dough is stuffed with a mashed potato and cabbage filling and then baked. Out of the oven, they are put in a large bowel and drizzled with melted garlic butter.

Helen had already baked a couple of dozen and the kitchen smelled of baked bread and garlic. It was the Russian equivalent of ambrosia. Elena was uncustomarily animated and engaged. She had her shirtsleeves rolled up and was kneading dough. Stoli couldn't concentrate on what they were saying but it was obvious that the women were enjoying a conversation periodically punctuated by bubbling laughter.

Standing in the doorway, with Yuri's arm still across his shoulders, Stoli took in the vignette. It was a happy and infectious scene. As he looked at Lindsey and his son, he broke into a grin. It felt good to be standing among family celebrating the coming of a baby. The beginning of a new life brought to mind the ending of another. The grim thought of Lud's death erased Stoli's sense of happiness. Yuri noticed Stoli's change of countenance.

"What's wrong, Ivan?"

"It's nothing. And I'd prefer if you'd call me Jack or Stoli. Nothing personal but I can't get used to being called Ivan."

"Okay, Jack," Yuri acceded. "What do say we leave the kitchen to the women and kids and go outside for a drink and a cigar. Since Elena found out that Lindsey is pregnant, I have been forbidden to smoke inside the house. Not even in my office! I guess babies trump everything."

That brought a smile back to Stoli's face and he followed Yuri down another hallway to the office. Once there, Yuri went to the wet bar and poured two brandies. There was a small humidor on the bar and Yuri extracted two Cuban cigars. He trimmed the ends of both cigars before handing one to Stoli. Reaching into his pocket, he pulled out a butane lighter, lit it and held it out for Stoli.

"I thought you weren't allowed to smoke in the house?" Stoli asked.

"I'm not. We're just lighting up in here before we step outside. It's my little rebellion," He finished with a sly grin. "I can't let them think I don't rule my own house."

Leaning into the lighter, Stoli drew on his cigar until a three inch flame sprung from the lit end. Yuri did the same and great puffs of smoke started drifting to the ceiling.

"Come on, we have to get out of here before the smell makes it to the kitchen."

Yuri opened the door that led from his study to the pool deck. Stoli grabbed the brandies from the bar and followed him out. They scampered across the patio like a couple of kids that just stole a cookie jar. As they headed to the boathouse by the lake, the smile was back on Stoli's face. They covered about half the distance when they were approached by two very large men wearing coveralls.

Stoli was impressed by their size and bearing. Not quite as tall as Yuri, both men had extremely broad shoulders, muscular necks and walked ramrod straight. They both wore their hair cropped close and, although shaven, were heavily bearded. The most striking similarity Stoli noticed was the strange tattoo both had on the backs of their right hands. Though not identical, the tattoos were of an eagle's head suspended under an open parachute.

Yuri excused himself from Stoli for the few minutes it took him to walk the men several paces back toward the house. They stopped just out of earshot and talked for a few minutes before Yuri returned to accompany Stoli the rest of the way to the boathouse.

"Sorry about that," He explained. "Those are the grounds maintenance guys we use. I asked them to come over today to make sure everything is set for this weekend. They'll be here on and off the whole time. They're very good and discreet. You probably won't even notice them around."

"Those are some impressive looking yard guys. I wouldn't want to run into them under a dark trellis or anything," Stoli joked. "They look like they'd be good guys to have on your side in a fight."

"Yes, they do," Yuri shot Stoli a sideways glance.

They walked the rest of the way to the boathouse and sat in the Adirondack chairs. It was much cooler now than it had been the previous June during the wedding. Fortunately, Lake Erie now offered up her warmth. Heated by the summer sun, the lake's shallow waters warmed to almost eighty degrees. Even during the short days and cooler temperatures of fall, the shoreline was noticeably warmer than just a few hundred feet inland. The two men sat watching the sky over the lake. It would be another couple of hours until sunset but the light over the lake was already beginning to soften and turn the water shades of light blue, silver and lavender. There was no wind and the lake was dead calm. A light fog hung over the lake and the combination of haze and still water blurred the horizon.

Sipping on brandy and puffing a cigar put Stoli back into a contemplative mood. He once again though of the juxtaposition of the baby's coming and Lud's death. This time, when Yuri asked what was troubling him, he answered.

"A friend was killed in a car wreck last night. Somebody ran him off a bridge and they both ended up in the river. It was a stupid accident. I didn't want to bring it up back in the house. Everyone is having a good time."

"Was he a good friend?" Yuri asked.

"We were becoming good friends," Stoli nodded. "He was someone I worked with. A good man. It seems so senseless and such a waste."

"Death is a bitch," Yuri said without emotion. He had seen and caused too much of it to react to the death of a stranger. Still, Stoli was now family and protocol demanded a consolatory gesture. "You have my sympathies and I respect and appreciate that you didn't burden the others with your loss."

They sat there in a comfortable silence for several minutes. Yuri finished the last of his brandy. He was about to reach into his pocket for his phone to call Dmitri when he remembered the pretence. Not wanting his in-laws to learn he had armed bodyguards and servants, Yuri had to tend to his own needs for the weekend.

"I seem to have finished my drink," He announced. "I'm going back for a refill. Do you want me to bring you one?"

Stoli hadn't quite finished his brandy. Truth be told, he didn't like the taste and was having a hard time drinking it. He'd been sipping it just to be polite.

"No thanks. I think I'm going to sit here for a few minutes before I head back inside. I'm sure Helen and Elena are going to want us to come to supper soon. You go ahead and tell the others I'll be right there."

Yuri got up and left Stoli looking out over the lake. Stoli turned to watch his host step onto the pool deck before nonchalantly pouring the remainder of his brandy on the ground. The cigar had gone out so he dropped the butt into the empty snifter. As he stood to return to the house, sunlight reflecting off the copper weather vane atop the boathouse caught his attention. He been out by the building a couple of times now but hadn't really looked at it.

It was a handsome structure built to resemble a Cape Cod cottage. The roof had shake shingles and supported a vented cupola that sported the nautical weather vane. The building itself was also shake sided and was stained grey with white trim. Three of the four sides had large, mullioned windows. The arched opening on the north side held double doors that swung out over a concrete ramp that extended well into the lake. The doors were open and Stoli walked inside.

Perched on a cradle was a sleek boat that appeared to be about thirty feet long. The boat and cradle sat on steel rails that were embedded into the concrete ramp. The whole apparatus was mechanized so that the boat could be launched and retrieved with the push of a button. Stoli paced the length of the boat and confirmed his estimate. Not counting the twin, four hundred horsepower outboard engines, the boat was about thirty-two feet long. The name, *Horsing Around*, adorned the full length on both sides of the hull. Stoli didn't know much about boats but he could tell this one was expensive and well maintained.

His curiosity satisfied, he started toward the doors but stopped when he heard the voices of two men in a heated conversation. One of them had a heavy Russian accent but Stoli could tell it wasn't Yuri. The other was an American and Stoli felt sure he recognized the voice. They weren't close enough for Stoli to hear what they were saying but it was obvious from the rapid exchange that it wasn't pleasant. Stoli didn't want to be accused of eavesdropping and was about to step into the open when the American voice stopped him in his tracks.

"You killed the wrong man. Reardon is still alive. Someone else was driving his car. You failed in your mission for Yuri."

"I will fix this," The accented voice answered.

Stoli scurried back into the boathouse and crouched behind the boat just as the two men stopped in the open doorway. His heart pounding, Stoli cautiously peered from behind the boat's transom. He couldn't see the Russian but the American stood in full view, illuminated by the setting sun. Stoli drew an inaudible gasp when he saw who it was. He knew he had recognized that voice.

It belonged to Michael Cole.

Chapter Twenty-Two

Michael had made the drive to Erie in just under two hours. It would have been shorter were it not for construction traffic. He'd almost caused an accident by illegally passing a slow moving truck on the right but the nervy move got him clear and on his way. He tried calling Alexandar several times from his car before the laconic Russian answered.

"Where have you been and why haven't you answered?" Michael barked even though he knew exactly where Alexandar was. "I'm on my way to Erie. We need to talk."

"I am at the house and we are talking now," Alexander answered. "What do you want?"

"I just talked to Doug Reardon. He is very much alive."

"He is in the hospital?" Alexandar was incredulous thinking Doug had somehow survived.

"No, you idiot! He wasn't in the car. Somebody else went off the bridge and now you have to finish the job. I'm coming to you. We have to talk."

Quick thinking wasn't Alexandar's forte but he knew that Michael shouldn't come to Yuri's house. He also knew that he couldn't leave the property to meet Michael. Since this was definitely not a conversation to have over cell phones, he and Michael needed a secure and private place to meet that was close to the Pandropov estate.

"Are you there?" Michael's voice over the phone interrupted his thoughts.

"Yes. You can't come here. There are too many people here now. There's a restaurant called the Parthenon on Lake Road. Do you know it?"

"No, but I'll find it," Michael answered.

"Go there and wait. I will call you with a time and place to meet."

Michael was put off that he was taking orders from a foot soldier but knew he had no choice. He couldn't risk having Yuri or Joe find out what he was doing. Since Alexandar was in the best position to set the rendezvous, all he could do was find the restaurant and wait.

He found it on a lightly traveled road in a residential neighborhood. Driving around to the back of the building where his car was less likely to be seen, he sat for fifteen minutes before deciding that might appear suspicious. He went inside and sat at a small table next to the window.

The waitress, a lithe young woman with raven hair and dark eyes, brought him a menu. Michael wasn't hungry but took the menu and ordered a coffee. The Parthenon served eastern Mediterranean fare and there wasn't much on the menu that appealed to Michael. In fact, there wasn't much that he could identify other than hummus. When the waitress returned with his coffee, he ordered the appetizer portion.

As she headed back to the kitchen, Michael pulled his phone out of his inside coat pocket and fruitlessly checked for incoming calls or voice mails. There were none and he set the device on the table. He hated the wait but it at least gave him time to mentally work on the suicide note he was composing.

Michael had decided that an apparent suicide was the best way to kill Doug. Distraught over the death of his dear friend and the collapse of Keystate and his career, he would choose to end it all. Michael didn't know much about Doug's personal life but he did know he was single and never heard him talk of anything other than work. Not that he and Doug ever talked about much of anything. Still, if there was a romantic component of Doug's life. Michael would have known something. 'No,' Michael thought. '*Reardon is a lonely, depressed man with nothing to live for. No one would be surprised if he killed himself.*'

At least that's what he'd concluded on the drive from Pittsburgh. Once he'd made that decision, Michael sketched the outline of a plan to carry it out. It wasn't a great plan because he had to be directly involved. He wouldn't actually do the killing - that was still Alexandar's job - but Michael had to somehow gain access to Doug's computer in order to type and send a suicide note. The beauty of email was that no one would know it was Michael - and not Doug - that sent it.

His phone buzzed on the table a fraction of a second before the ringtone. Michael grabbed the device before the first sequence of electronic tones ended. He looked at his watch as he connected the call. It was almost five o'clock.

"Hello."

"Are you at the Parthenon?" Alexandar asked.

"Yes. Are you going to meet me here?"

"No. I can't leave the property. But everyone is inside eating. You can come here."

"That's too dangerous. Somebody might see me. We can't risk that."

"You must come here," Alexandar insisted. "They put in a temporary road when they built the boathouse. It is in the woods and can't be seen from the house. Park your car there and walk the rest of the way. I will meet you at the boathouse in fifteen minutes."

Alexandar hung up before Michael had a chance to object. Figuring there was no point in calling back to argue, Michael pulled out his money clip and left a twenty on the table. He waved to the waitress as she came out of the kitchen with the order of hummus and a puzzled look.

It was three miles from the Parthenon to Yuri's house and Michael covered the distance in less than five minutes. The construction driveway was just east of the main drive and, while it might have been gravel at one time, was now mostly mud. Afraid of getting bogged down, Michael cautiously drove in only a few dozen feet until he could no longer see the main road in his rearview mirror.

Getting out of his car, he made a futile attempt to avoid the puddles. He considered changing out of his driving slippers and into the shoes he's packed in the trunk. In anticipation of an overnight stay in Pittsburgh, a change of clothes was in the back along with a ridiculously expensive pair of Ferragamo loafers. He decided he'd rather sacrifice the driving shoes and headed down the muddy track in the direction of the boathouse. He'd gone about fifty yards when Alexandar suddenly loomed out of the underbrush. Michael was startled by the large man's abrupt appearance.

"Follow me," Alexander's command left no room for debate as he ducked back into the woods. He walked quickly and purposefully and Michael struggled to keep up. His driving shoes were useless in the terrain and completely trashed. The cuffs of his expensive trousers were muddied and he'd pulled several snags in the sleeves of his suit coat. They finally broke free of the woods and emerged a short distance from the boathouse. Michael was relieved to get back to open ground but his suit was ruined.

"Was that necessary?" He almost whined. "We could have just as easily talked back there."

"I need to be where I can see the house," Alexander answered curtly. "This is not a good time for you to be here."

"I wouldn't be here at all if you'd done your job in the first place. Now we're both in trouble if Yuri finds out you screwed up."

"I did my job."

They had walked to the north side of the boathouse and stood in front of the open doors.

"You killed the wrong man. Reardon is still alive. Someone else was driving his car. You failed in your mission for Yuri."

"I will fix this."

"Tonight," Michael said.

"That is not possible," Alexandar protested. "I have to stay here."

"We have to do this as soon as possible. Tonight. We can't allow Reardon to talk to the police. That could lead to me, then you and ultimately Yuri. Do you want that to happen?"

"No," Alexandar grudgingly agreed. "Do you have a plan?"

"I have the beginning of a plan," Michael answered and laid out what he'd devised. When he was finished, Alexandar agreed that a staged suicide was the best alternative although there were several aspects he didn't like. He didn't like not having time to plan better. Michael wanted to do it within the next few hours. He didn't like that he had to subdue his victim without harming him. There could be no evidence of a struggle and he certainly couldn't shoot or stab him. That left poison, drowning or concussive impact. Alexandar had never been to the Keystate but Michael told him there were several high storage tanks. That would have to do.

"You can get Reardon to the plant?" Alexandar asked.

"Yes. I have something he wants and he will come," Michael answered, thinking of the money Doug needed to complete the project. "I'll tell him I need his signature on some documents. He'll come."

"You will be there?"

"Only to lure Reardon in and to send the suicide note. After that, I will go to my hotel. I'm staying at the William Penn downtown. You can call me when it's over. Just make sure it's done right this time. Is there anything else we need to talk about?"

"No," Alexandar answered. "I will go and tell Dmitri that he has to cover for me for the next few hours. He won't like it but he has a hand in this, too. I just hope Yuri or Joe don't look for me before I get back."

"So do I," Michael agreed. "But that's a chance we have to take. Let's get going. The sooner we leave, the sooner you can get back. I'll meet you back at the Parthenon and you can follow me to Keystate from there."

Michael retraced his path through the woods to his car and Alexandar headed towards the house to find Dmitri.

****** ****** ****** ******

Stoli waited for a few minutes before creeping from behind the boat to cautiously step outside. He peered around the corner of the boathouse to watch Alexandar disappear around the side of the main house. He waited a couple of minutes more before jogging across the yard and into the house.

Helen looked up from the stove when Stoli walked into the kitchen. She knew in an instant that something was wrong. He beckoned her with a subtle jerk of his head and, together, they walked a few steps down the hallway.

"I have to leave," He began. "There's an emergency at the plant and they need me."

Helen was dubious. "How could the plant call you? She asked. "You don't have a phone."

"I gave Doug the phone number here just in case," He lied. "Please, Helen. There really is an emergency and I need to leave now. Just tell everyone that I'll be back. I'll call you as soon as I can."

Stoli walked though the foyer and let himself out the front door. He didn't want to take the time to say goodbye before he left and certainly not to his host. He didn't know how or why, but he knew that Yuri was somehow involved in Lud's death. The thought both sickened and angered him. More important, Doug was in danger and Lud's killer was on his way to finish the job.

Stoli's first instinct was to call the police but he couldn't do that from Yuri's house. As he turned out of the driveway onto the street, he tried to think of where he could find a phone. There were no phone booths in the residential area and he didn't want to start knocking on doors. He headed towards the more commercial area near the interstate thinking he would find a public phone. He didn't. '*God damned cell phones!*' Since the advent of mobile phones, pay phones had become scarce.

Stoli pulled off the road by the entrance ramp to the highway leading to Pittsburgh. He needed to quit running around like an idiot, stop and think. It had been about fifteen minutes since he'd left the boathouse. It was likely that Michael and the Russian hadn't rendezvoused yet and were still behind him. They wouldn't be for long.

Stoli remember the urgency with which Michael goaded the Russian to immediate action. Then it hit him that Michael's biggest concern was that Yuri might discover what they were doing. '*Yuri didn't know!'* Stoli thought. *'But if he didn't know, what was Michael doing at his house and who was the other Russian?'* Stoli was starting to ask himself more questions than he could answer. The biggest was whether he should still call the police. Without a doubt, Lud had been murdered by Michael and the Russian. But was Yuri involved? If not, Stoli could falsely accuse his in-law. There would be hell to pay for that.

"Fuck it," He decided out loud and went up the ramp to the freeway. *'I have to warn Doug. The rest can get sorted out later.'*

Chapter Twenty-Three

The first round had been on the house. When the owner of the corner bar discovered that the small group of Keystate employees had gathered an impromptu wake for Lud, he set them up for free. Doug bought the second round and Pete the third. By the fourth, Dave, the plant manager, only had to cough up enough to cover himself, Pete and Doug. Everyone else had gone home.

Doug had switched to beer after downing an initial vodka martini in Lud's honor. The bartender put a fresh longneck bottle in front of him next to the half-empty one he was nursing. Doug wasn't a big beer drinker and he was already feeling the effects of the martini and beer. Then, too, he was operating on less than three hours of sleep. The bar clock chimed and he looked up to mark the time. It was six o'clock; twenty-four hours since the accident.

The three men said little as they sat at the bar. It was just as well. Doug was so wrapped up in his thoughts that he would have heard little that came his way. It was a strange sensation. The events of the last day had gone by in a blur but he could remember every detail of every moment. The worst had been taking Lois back to the hospital to claim Lud's body.

They tried in vain to dissuade her from looking at the body until a funeral home had the chance to clean it up. Doug was better prepared this time when they unzipped the body bag and didn't waver. He was surprised by Lois' stoicism and strength. She merely put a trembling hand on Lud's chest, murmured something unintelligible, turned and walk out of the room. Doug said goodbye to Lois and her son in the hospital lobby and promised to return to Cleveland early the following week.

He drove back to the Sewickley police station where Officer McMeans waited to take him to the impound lot. There wasn't much left of the car. The crush of the impact had compressed the roof and shattered all the glass. None of doors opened and Doug had to reach through what had been the passenger door window to retrieve some water-soaked documents and personal items from the glove box and center console. They had to jimmy the trunk open in order to get his golf clubs. Once Doug had collected everything he wanted from the wreck, he signed the police report that would be submitted to his insurance company. Handing the form back to McMeans, he asked if there would be anything else.

"No, I don't think that will be necessary," McMeans answered. "We checked your story about where you were last night and who you were with. I got the names and addresses of the people that confirmed your story."

Doug was surprised. The cop was talking as if Doug was under investigation. "Are you investigating me?"

"Not you, specifically. We just need to gather all the facts. We still haven't accounted for the driver of the truck. There's a lot more work to do on this case. I think we're through with you, though. For what it's worth, I'm sorry about your friend. That's a tough way to go."

Doug thanked McMeans for the condolences and drove back to Keystate. His bad day got worse when he ran into Michael Cole. The encounter had been mercifully short and somewhat sweetened by Michael's announcement that he was headed to the bank to transfer the long awaited money. Doug spent the remainder of the afternoon walking through the shop and offices talking, consoling and commiserating with his fellow employees. He closed the plant and sent everybody home at four o'clock. That's when he and a few others went to the bar.

He managed to finish off his third beer and was reaching for the fourth when his cell went off in his pocket. He pulled it out and groaned when he saw it was Michael Cole.

"Hello, Michael. What do you want?"

"I need you to meet me at your office in an hour and a half. Say around seven-thirty," Michael answered.

Doug was tired, tipsy, hungry and depressed. The last thing he wanted to do was to meet with Michael Cole.

"Why."

"Because I need your signature on a couple of forms in order to transfer the money. Carmen wants you to be able to write checks against the line of credit."

Doug sighed. '*Well, at least that's some progress and a little good news to end a shitty day.*'

"Okay, Michael. I'll see you in my office at seven-thirty. Goodbye."

Doug put his phone back in his pocket and stood up. Turning to Pete and Dave, he asked: "Would either of you ladies care to join me for dinner? It seems I have an hour to kill."

***** ***** ***** *****

Stoli threw the flat tire in the bed of his truck, wiped his hands on a rag he kept in the crewcab and climbed back into the front seat. He shot a quick glance in the side mirror before stomping on the accelerator to shoot back into traffic. Whatever his tire had picked up in the construction zone cost him half an hour. It was a quarter to seven and starting to get dark. He had about another hour to Keystate assuming he went the speed limit. A twinge of panic in his stomach told him he had to do better than that.

Stoli goosed the Dodge up to seventy-four and set the cruise control. There was very little traffic at this hour and he didn't want to attract a cop. He couldn't afford to get pulled over. It would take too long to tell his story and convince the cops to go the plant. His only hope was to get to Keystate before Michael and the Russian. He constantly glanced down as the dashboard clock ticked off the minutes seemingly faster than he could click off the miles.

***** ***** ***** *****

Doug pulled his chair up to the oak table that served as his desk and, out of habit, lifted the lid of his laptop. He was about to turn it on but decided that would be a waste of time. He was very tired and didn't plan on being at the plant one second more than the time it took to sign Michael's damn documents. It had been a miserable, long day and he just wanted to go to bed. He certainly didn't want to spend any time with Michael. Not surprisingly, Michael was already late. The ubiquitous, round office clock showed seven thirty-five.

Doug was about to walk to the lobby for a look when he heard the front door open. The offices were dark except for the fluorescent glare that lit the lobby, hallway and Doug's office. The click of Michael's expensive shoes bounced a shallow echo as he came down the hall. The footfalls stopped just outside the door and Michael surreptitiously leaned his head in the doorway. He glanced around the room as if afraid of being ambushed before he entered. When Michael finally stepped into the office, he was followed by the most hulking, dangerous looking man Doug had ever seen. He was wasn't as tall as Lud had been - Lud had to duck to enter most rooms - but this man's breadth completely filled the doorway. He was intimidating as hell and Doug felt a reflexive pang of fear.

"Who are you?" He asked ignoring Michael.

"He's here for security," Michael answered.

"Security for what? You didn't bring cash did you? We have no safe here."

"No. No cash," Michael answered." Just some documents we need to execute."

Doug noticed that Michael was nervous. His gaze darted around the room and he hadn't yet looked Doug in the eye. He also looked disheveled. Michael was in the same suit Doug had seen him wearing earlier in the day but it was wrinkled and soiled. The dried mud on the cuffs of his slacks contrasted sharply with the high gloss of his shoes. Doug almost asked Michael about his appearance but didn't want to open the door for unwanted conversation. Instead, he opted to get to the point.

"Where are the documents?" He asked. "I'd like to get this done and get out of here."

"I scanned and emailed them to you," Michael answered as he sat down in one of the side chairs. Alexandar remained in the doorway. "Didn't you get them."

"I turned my computer off this afternoon and haven't checked since then. I didn't get anything on my phone, though." Doug reached over to turn on his laptop. He didn't see the look of relief flicker across Michael's face as the machine hummed to life. He did notice that Michael took his phone out of his pocket and typed a few strokes on the keypad.

It took a few seconds for Doug's computer to boot and another minute to open his email folder. When he did, several new emails popped up. Doug quickly scanned them for any from Michael. There was only one and it was addressed to Doug and Carmen. Doug looked at the time it was sent and then at the digital clock in the bottom corner of the screen.

Both said seven forty-two. There was no subject line to the email but there was an attachment. He opened the email and was surprised to see that the attachment was titled *'Reardon Termination of Agreement.'*

"What's this?" He looked up at Michael.

"You are being terminated," Michael replied flatly. He nodded his head in the direction of Alexandar. "This gentleman is here to see that you leave the premises immediately and quietly."

"Bullshit!" Doug sprang from his chair flush with anger. "You don't have the authority to fire me! I report to Carmen." He came around his desk and stood over Michael. The move put him just a few feet from where Alexandar stood.

"I am acting for Risotti in this matter," Michael looked up at Doug. "He doesn't have the stomach for this type of work." Michael was completely focused on Doug now and his eyes were wide. Not with fear but with a malevolent intensity. His face was dark and contorted with hatred. "Alexandar," He spoke through the gritted teeth of an evil smile. "Please take him out."

Alexandar took one step into the room and planted his left foot. His right arm swung a massive fist through a viscous uppercut that caught Doug just under his ribcage. Perfectly placed, the blow forced the air out of Doug's lungs and paralyzed his diaphragm; he collapsed to the floor unable to breathe. The pain was excruciating and tears welled up behind his clenched eyelids. Strange clicking noises came from his throat as he struggled to breathe. Alexandar grabbed Doug by the hair and pulled his head back. The new pain caused Doug to open his watery eyes in time to see Alexandar cock a fist. The fierce blow crashed into Doug's left temple and his world went black.

Alexandar bent to one knee over the limp body and wrapped his hands around Doug's throat.

"Not here!" Michael screamed.

He looked like a wild man. His face and neck were bright red except for the white around his mouth where his lips were drawn back around snarling teeth. The muscles of his neck stood taught with strain and excitement. "Take him outside! It's has to look like a suicide not like you choked him!"

Alexandar loosened his grip and Doug's head dropped with a thud to the floor. Grabbing Doug under the arms, Alexandar lifted him upright before hefting him over a broad shoulder in a fireman's carry. He started for the door but stopped at the threshold to look back at Michael.

"Are you coming?" He asked.

"No." Michael was headed behind Doug's desk. His eyes were glassy and wide behind his rimless glasses. He was still flush and his hands trembled noticeably. Alexandar's ruthless efficiency had had a debilitating effect. It was one thing to fantasize about seeing Doug brought low. It was quite another to actually see it happen. Michael had never witnesses violence on this order. He had no desire to see it through."I have work to do here," He ended weakly.

"What do you want me to do with him?" Alexandar asked.

"I don't know," Michael sat down in Doug's chair. He noticed it was still warm. "You're the professional. Throw him in the river or off the building. I don't care. Just make sure it looks like he killed himself and do it right this time."

"You will be here?"

"No. I need only a couple of minutes and then I'm leaving. Call me when you are headed back to Erie."

Alexander threw a disdainful look at Michael, shrugged his shoulders and walked out of the office. *'Typical, fucking officer.'* He thought. *'Full of orders and ideas but no stomach for the real work.'* He walked down the narrow hall to the front lobby and outside into the chill.

With Alexandar gone, Michael tried to focus on Doug's computer. The email that contained the termination letter was still open. Michael reached for the keypad but his hands were shaking so violently that he couldn't type. He sat back and shook his hands in the air as if shaking off water. He took several deep breaths as he alternatively clenched his fists and wrung his hands. Finally, he sat on them for a minute and that seemed to work. Even so, he had to hunt and peck as he replied to the email.

I am sorry that you think I have failed you. It is nothing compared to the failure I feel for what happened to Lud. Neither he or I would have been in this position if it weren't for you. I hope you can live with the consequences.

I can't.

Doug

Michael reviewed the email twice to make sure it said what he intended before sending it off. He waited a minute and checked the sent mail folder. Satisfied the message was transmitted, he shut off the laptop and used a tissue to wipe down the keypad. He didn't bother wiping down any other surface. There were several witnesses that knew he'd been in the office earlier that day. It would be no surprise for his fingerprints to be all over. He glanced at his watch; it was five minutes before eight. Leaving the lights on, he walked out of the building, stepped into his car and headed for the gate.

Michael was starting to regain his composure and the act of driving provided a sense of normalcy and calm. Even so, he fumbled his cell phone as he pulled it from his pocket and it fell to the floor. He reached over to pick it up as he drove past the smoker's shack. He didn't see the Dodge truck parked in the shadows.

***** ***** ***** *****

When Alexandar walked out of the office building, Keystate was dark except for a few floodlights scattered across the property. He stuck to the shadows as he made his way toward the river. It was a clear night and a sliver of a moon hung low over the southern sky. There was no wind and very little noise save for the far off hum of traffic and throb of adjacent factories. The path to the river took Alexandar past the tank farm that rose high above the plant. Smaller tanks were stacked on top of larger to a height of about sixty feet. He stopped and looked up at the maze of storage tanks, pipes and walkways.

'If I was going to kill myself,' He thought, *'I'd jump from there instead of drowning in a cold river.*

The cold air was starting to make his leg hurt. That, and the fact that he was getting older, gave rise to another thought.

'On the other hand, it would be easier to drop him into the river than to carry him up the ladder.'

Alexandar sighed since he knew what had to be done. He'd screwed it up the first time and had to make it right. He started climbing. It took a several minutes to reach the top of the ladder. He shrugged Doug on top of the tank and paused a minute to catch his breath before pulling himself atop the tank. It was tricky because he had to use one hand to keep Doug from rolling off.

Once he was sure of his footing, he slung Doug over his shoulder and, following yellow lines that marked a path across tanks and rickety catwalks, made his way to the mezzanine that supported the highest tanks. Alexandar looked over the edge of the platform to estimate the drop. He figured it was about fifteen meters. Enough to kill someone if they fell on their head. But only if they fell on their head. He had to go higher.

The ladder that led up to the next level was at the opposite end of the mezzanine. Alexandar thought it looked makeshift and decided he'd better check it out before climbing. He let Doug slide down onto the open grate of the platform. His neck, shoulders and lower back ached from the strain of the climb and he rolled his neck and shoulders a couple of times to loosen the knots as he walked down the row of tanks. Stopping just short of the last tank, Alexandar put his hands on his hips and leaned back to stretch his lower back and look up at the ladder. He looked past the top of the highest tank to the stars beyond. It struck him that it looked like the night sky in Afghanistan. It was his last pain free thought.

*****   *****   *****   *****

There were three cars in the parking lot when Stoli drove through the gate. He immediately turned off his headlights. One of the cars he recognized as the company car. The BMW looked familiar although he couldn't place where he'd seen it. The last car, a Mercury Grand Marquis, was one he hadn't seen before. He realized with dread that he was too late to warn Doug and hoped he was not too late to save him.

Pulling his truck behind the smoker's shack, Stoli opened the center console and grabbed his hunting knife. Like most of the guys in the plant, he regularly hunted and the knife had field dressed many deer. It was razor sharp and had saw teeth stamped into the spine for cutting small bones and tissue. Stoli wished he had one of his rifles in the gun rack but deer season was still several weeks away. He went to the back of the truck to retrieve the tire iron. When he saw the red handle of his valve wrench poking from under a piece of cardboard, he grabbed that instead.

Sticking to the shadows, he made his way along the fence that surrounded the parking lot. It more than trebled the distance to the office building but Stoli didn't want to risk being seen. He made it about halfway around the perimeter when the office door opened. Stoli froze against the chain link fence and watched as a huge man lumbered out of the door with Doug thrown over his shoulder. Although he was too far away to get a good look, Stoli recognized the coveralls the man was wearing and knew this was one of the Russians he'd seen talking to Yuri earlier that day. Obviously, this man was not just a gardener.

Stoli breathed a sigh of relief when the man turned away from where he stood and headed for the river. Stoli waited for him to turn the corner of the office before jogging straight across the parking lot. He cringed at the noise his steps made in the gravel and fervently hoped Michael didn't choose now to leave the building. He made it to the corner of the office and peered around. The Russian had stopped near the tank farm and, after looking up for a few seconds, walked to the base of the ladder and started to climb.

Stoli watched until he was sure the Russian was committed to the climb before he ran back across the front of the office building and disappeared around the opposite corner. He scurried down a narrow passage that ran between the office building and factory and led to the tank farm. When he emerged from the passage, he was on the opposite side of the tanks from where the Russian was making his ascent. The area was filled with the pipes that fed the various liquids into the plant. It was also where the second ladder rose to the mezzanine.

Stoli had to cross several pipes to get to the ladder and, although his eyes had adjusted somewhat to the darkness, he had to slow down to pick his way across the array of pipes. Reaching the base of the ladder, he bent over with his hand on his knees to catch his wind. He hadn't exerted this much in years and his heart pounded and lungs burned. He rested for only a second or two before reaching down to pick up the rope that lay coiled at his feet.

He had learned long ago that it was easier to climb to the safety of the platform and haul up tools with the rope. He left the rope at the base of the ladder expressly for this purpose. Stoli tied one end of the line around his valve wrench and the other end to his belt before he started to climb. He stopped at the first rung and stepped back to the ground to kick off his shoes to minimize noise. The rough rungs hurt like hell as they dug into the soles of his feet but Stoli made the forty foot climb in less than a minute.

He stepped into the empty space on the mezzanine that once held the tank that had killed his nephew. The tank on Stoli's right supported the rickety ladder that led to the top of the uppermost tanks. He untied the rope from his belt and made it fast to the railing. Pressing his back against the tank on his left, he slid around for a look across the mezzanine to where the other ladder came up. Stoli was relieved that the Russian hadn't yet completed his climb. From the sound of grunting, he was getting close.

Stoli went back to retrieve his valve wrench. He managed to hoist it without clanging it against any of the steel surfaces. Clutching it against his chest, he again slid around the tank to get a look at the other ladder. This time, the Russian's head popped up over the edge.

Stoli watched as the his upper torso came into view. Doug was awkwardly slung over one shoulder. When most of his chest cleared the top of the ladder, the Russian shrugged Doug off. The limp body landed on the domed tank with a thud and started to slide toward the edge. The Russian quickly grabbed him and, apparently winded, remained perched on the ladder with one hand on the ladder and the other holding Doug. It seem like an eternity to Stoli, but it was barely a minute before the Russian awkwardly pulled himself atop the tank. Planting his feet, he bent to hoist Doug before starting the hazardous trip across the tanks and catwalks to the mezzanine where Stoli hid in the shadows.

Stoli was intimidated by the sheer size, strength and gracefulness of the man. He carried Doug effortlessly and came across the dangerous path without hesitation. When he reached the mezzanine, the Russian let Doug slid onto the platform and stepped to look over the edge. He stood for a few seconds as if in thought before turning to look down the length of the mezzanine to the ladder that was welded to the side of the last tank. He stepped over Doug's prostrate body and walked toward the ladder rolling his neck and swinging his arms. Stoli held his breath when the large man stopped at the gap where Stoli waited in ambush. The Russian placed his hands against his lower back and leaned back into a stretch with his head thrown back. The stance left his throat exposed.

Too late, Alexandar saw the flash of red as the heavy wrench sliced a lethal arc out of the shadows and crashed into his throat. The blow shattered his larynx and blocked his airway. It was a mortal blow that would have leveled a lesser man. Alexandar, though already dead, was not yet down. He staggered forward for a few steps clutching his neck with both hands. Eyes bulging, his soundless mouth opened and closed in a futile attempt to breathe. He didn't see Stoli's second strike - an thunderous shot to his abdomen. The force of the impact propelled the air out of Alexandar's lungs and forced blood, sputum and tissue from his gaping mouth. The blow doubled him over and finally dropped him to his knees. Falling forward, Alexandar caught himself with his right arm while his left hand remained clutching his throat. His massive head hung down and exposed the back of his muscular neck. Stoli squared himself, raised the heavy wrench high over his head and swung it down to the base of Alexandar's skull. The right arm collapsed and, still on his knees, Alexandar fell forward onto the side of his face. His lifeless eyes stared into the tattooed eyes of the parachuting eagle.

Chapter Twenty-Four

Stoli stood next to Alexandar's grotesquely genuflecting body; the wrench tightly gripped in both hands. His heart raced and chest heaved as adrenaline coursed through his body. His eyes, though open wide, didn't register sight. It was several seconds before he regained awareness. When he did, he dropped the wrench with a clatter and backed away from the body. He jumped, startled, when he backed into the tank that had hidden him seconds before.

The jolt of physical contact snapped him fully back into the moment. Remembering Doug, he ran to his prostrate friend and rolled him onto his back. Bending to put an ear to his chest, Stoli heard a heartbeat and felt Doug's chest rise and fall as he breathed. Relieved, Stoli grabbed Doug under the arms and sat him upright against a tank before sitting beside his friend to rest and gather his wits.

Although he killed many things in his life, this was the first time he'd killed a man. He knew this man had killed Lud and was about to kill Doug. He knew he didn't have a choice. It needed to be done and he'd done it. Had he taken the time to think on it, he might have been surprised that it didn't bother him more.

Stoli heard a car door shut and an engine jump to life. He pushed himself up against the tank and watched the green BMW back away from the office and turn toward the gate.

Michael Cole.

Stoli recalled the conversation he'd overheard at the boathouse. Obviously, Michael knew Yuri. The concern he voiced about keeping Yuri in the dark about Lud and Doug proved that. That, at least, suggested that Yuri was not directly involved. But it didn't explain the connection between Michael and Yuri and the dead man. Stoli couldn't be sure that Yuri wasn't involved.

And why was Michael trying to kill Doug? It was common knowledge that Michael hated Lud and Doug but Stoli thought it unlikely that personal animosity would motivate Michael to murder. And even if that's what it was, how could Michael recruit Yuri's man for the work. There had to be more to it. Much more.

It occurred to Stoli that he'd just interrupted a plan. Whatever started the series of events that led up to this moment wasn't over. That meant he was now in danger from an unknown source for unknown reasons. He needed answers and could think of only one person that might provide them.

Yuri Pandropov.

Not knowing Yuri's involvement made going to him a very dangerous proposition. Stoli realized that he couldn't go without protection. Normally, that would come from the police but Stoli couldn't involve them without explaining the crumpled body on the mezzanine or why he decided to take the law into his own hands. It also meant exposing Yuri and his family to investigation. Stoli intuitively knew that was something Yuri would want to avoid. And that, ultimately, gave Stoli the leverage he needed.

Somewhat rested, Stoli climbed down from the mezzanine, put on his shoes and went gather the tools he would need. Within minutes, he was back up on the mezzanine panting and kneeling in front of Doug.

He cracked small capsules of smelling salts under Doug's nose. The strong smell of ammonia did the trick and Doug's eye's fluttered open as he weakly tried to push Stoli's hand away. It took several minutes and a few more of the aromatic spirits before Doug was minimally coherent.

The left side of Doug's face was red and puffy and the eye was swollen shut. He complained of a headache and ringing in his ear. Stoli's suspicion that Doug had a concussion was confirmed when his friend leaned over to vomit.

Stoli left Doug sitting against the tank and walked past the corpse to the ladder. He used the rope to haul up a small canvas bag of tools. He grabbed a box wrench and walked back across the mezzanine and onto the top of the first tank.

An access hatch had been cut into the top to allow periodic maintenance inside the tank. The lid was secured by rusted bolts and it took Stoli several minutes to work them loose and slide the hatch open. Fortunately, the tank held ethylene glycol and there was no noxious odor. That done, Stoli made his way back to the mezzanine. Doug had regained a some measure of awareness and looked up as Stoli approached.

"What happened?" He asked. "I remember being in my office with Michael Cole. Somebody hit me. How did I get here? Is that the guy that hit me?" He pointed at Alexandar's body.

"Yeah," Stoli answered. "Believe it or not, he carried you up here. I think he was going on throw you off."

"What happen to him?"

"I killed him. He killed Lud thinking it was you. He came here tonight to finish the job. The only thing I know about him is that he was working for Michael Cole."

Doug tried to process this information. He couldn't. Even without the concussion it would have been difficult to register. No one had ever tried to kill him. He couldn't even imagine that anyone would want to. Now he was sitting, bruised and battered, on a steel platform forty feet in the air with the corpse of his would be assassin less than twenty feet away.

"Did you say that guy killed Lud? And he was working for Michael?"

"Yeah."

"How do you know?"

Stoli bent down to help Doug stand. When he had Doug upright and leaning against the tank, he told him of the conversation he'd overheard at the boathouse and his efforts to get to Doug before Michael and Alexandar. He told him of the flat tire and how he watched Alexandar carry Doug up onto the mezzanine. He described how he'd climbed the other ladder, hid in the shadows and ultimately killed the Russian.

"Did you call the police?" Doug asked.

"No," Stoli answered. "And I'm not going to."

Doug used his good eye to cast a questioning glance at Stoli.

"Did you say you weren't going to call the cops?"

"Yes."

"Why?"

"Because I would have to explain why I killed him," Stoli pointed at Alexander's crumpled body still kneeling absurdly on the decking. "I'd have to explain why I came here to warn you instead of calling them. I can't do that without telling them that I overheard Cole and that guy plan to kill you. That would drag my in-laws into it. I don't know if Yuri is involved or not but, for my son's sake, I have to find out."

"How are you going to do that?"

"I'm going to ask him."

"Just like that?"

"Just like that," Stoli replied matter-of-factly. "But I'm going to need leverage and you have to help me get it."

Doug had recovered enough of his wits to be scared. He was still digesting the fact that Michael Cole wanted him dead. Now Stoli intimated that there could be others involved in a plot that was getting deeper by the minute. Doug very much wanted the police involved.

"Stoli," He began. "I think we'd better call the police. There are two people dead already. You really haven't done anything wrong. Maybe you should have called the cops earlier but you can explain that you had to warn me. It wasn't your fault you got a flat and were too late. Nobody can blame you for what you did after that."

"My family can," Stoli said evenly. "I know it might not make any sense to you, but my son and his wife are going to have a baby. Her father may be involved in this. Maybe not. But I have to know one way or the other before I call the cops. It might not be the smart thing to do." He paused and stared purposefully into Doug's eyes before turning to look at Alexandar's body. "But, when family and friends are involved, sometimes you have to do the right thing instead of the smart thing."

Doug followed Stoli's gaze to look at the body of the man who shortly before had tried to kill him. There was no misunderstanding Stoli's message. Doug was alive because Stoli did what he thought was right. The outcome might have been the same had the cops been involved. Maybe not. There was no point playing that game. Doug was alive and Alexandar dead; both because of Stoli. Now Stoli needed Doug's help. *'It might not be the smart thing to do,'* He repeated the thought. *'But it was the right thing.'*

"All right," Doug sighed. "What do you need me to do?"

Stoli reached out and gently gave Doug's left shoulder a squeeze.

"Thanks," He said with a grim smile. "I'm glad you understand. Come on. We need to hide the body. I opened the access hatch on the glycol tank. We can dump it in there."

Stoli walked to the corpse and stood over it for a couple of seconds. He put his left foot against Alexandar's right hip and pushed the body over. He crouched down to go through the pockets of the coveralls and found a wallet and a wad of cash in the right front pocket. Stoli handed both to Doug. The car keys and a pocket knife were in the left pocket. He kept those.

Stoli ran his hands inside the coverall on either side of the still warm torso. As expected, he felt the nylon strapping of a shoulder holster. He was tempted to remove the pistol but decided it was better left alone. No point leaving his fingerprints on an assassin's weapon. The rest of Stoli's cursory search revealed nothing. Standing up, he reached to take the driver's license Doug had pulled from the wallet.

"I can't focus my eye," Doug said. "Who is he?"

"Says his name is Alex Smith from Buffalo," Stoli grunted. "You'd think he could have come up with a better name that that."

"What do you mean?" Doug asked.

"Our friend Alex is…was… about as Russian as they come. I heard him talking in the mother tongue. I don't know where he's from but it sure as hell isn't Buffalo. Grab his arm and let's get him over to the tank."

Doug and Stoli struggled to pull the body across the mezzanine. Alexandar weighed close to three hundred pounds. They managed to pulled him onto the catwalk that led to the tank. Doug carefully stepped over the body to get back to the mezzanine. Stoli stepped squarely on the dead man's chest. He walked back to where he'd dropped his valve wrench and bent to pick it up.

"Do you think you can get down the ladder by yourself?" He asked Doug.

"I think so," Doug answered. "My head's pounding and I'm a little blurry but I'll be okay."

"Can you see good enough to use your computer."

"Yeah," Doug was puzzled. "Why?"

"You need to write down what happened here tonight. Make sure you mention Michael Cole and Alex Smith and that they met at Yuri Pandropov's house in Erie. Tell how you got beat up and that Alex is dead and we hid the body. Don't say where. When you're done, make three copies. Those are our insurance policies. Can you do all that."

Doug gave a thin smile of understanding. "Yes. I suppose you're going to give the copies to your lawyer to be opened if something happens to us."

"Something like that. I don't have a lawyer but they will go to a couple of people I trust."

They were startled by a cell phone ringing. Doug reflexively reached for his phone but didn't have it on him. Stoli never carried a phone so they looked at each other in bewilderment until they realized the sound was coming from Alexandar. Stoli ran to get the phone but it stopped ringing before he got there. He retrieved it from an inside breast pocket of the overalls and brought it back to Doug. Doug flipped open the small phone and pushed a couple of buttons until he found the call log. Still unable to focus, he handed the phone to Stoli.

"It says the call came from Dmitri," Stoli reported. "That must be the other guy I saw talking with Yuri." He thought for a minute before asking Doug how to return the call. Doug took the phone, pushed the green send button and handed it back.

"Alexandar?" The voice on the other end answered before rattling off a rapid string of Russian.

"Alexandar is dead," Stoli interrupted. "This is Jack Stalich. I killed him. Tell Yuri he has ten minutes to call me back on this phone before I go to the police. Do you understand?"

There was a momentary silence from the other end.

"I understand. Yuri is to call you before ten minutes or you will tell police that you killed Alexandar," Dmitri succinctly repeated the instructions.

"That's right," Stoli answered and hung up. He looked up at Doug. "How do I make a call with this thing?"

Doug looked at it to make sure it was in the outgoing call mode before answering. "Just punch in the number and hit the green button."

Stoli did as instructed and seconds later was talking. The conversation was short and to the point.

"Steve, its Jack. I need you to come to Keystate right now. I'm in a jam and need your help." There was a pause as Stoli listened. "No, that's alright. Just as long as you're here within an hour. I need you to keep an eye on somebody." Another pause. "My boss… Yeah, that's the guy… Okay… Okay. Good. Thanks, Steve." Stoli finished and handed the phone back to Doug to hang up.

"Next time, just push the red button," Doug said and handed the phone back. "What was that about?"

That was my brother, Steve. He's coming here to pick you up and take you someplace safe for the night."

Doug was surprised. "He doesn't know me. Why would he do that?"

"Because I asked him to. Besides, I told him how you got rid of the tank that killed his boy. He figures he owes you. Let's go. We've got a lot to do before he gets here. What time is it?"

Doug held out his wrist so Stoli could see his watch. It was almost nine-thirty. Stoli stood at the top of the ladder and watched until Doug was safely on the ground before picking up the rope and valve wrench and walking over to where Alexandar lay.

The body was on its back and the eyes were still open. Stoli placed the heavy wrench on Alexandar's chest and tied the line to it. He measured off about twenty feet of the rope and, pulling his knife from where he'd shoved it in the back of his pants, cut the line. He carefully put the knife next to the wrench before tying the rope tightly around Alexandar's ankles. Stoli tied one end of the remaining piece of rope around the dead man's left wrist and the other end through a bolt hole in the cover plate.

Stoli stood up, sheathed his knife and stuck it back in his belt. He picked up the valve wrench and, crossing to the open hatch, dropped the heavy tool in the tank. It sank until it coming to a stop at the end of the line. Stoli was about to bend over to drag the body to the open hole when the cell phone went off in his pocket. The call connected as soon as he flipped the phone open.

"Hello, Yuri?" He answered.

"Mr. Stalich, this is Joe Pandropov. My father can't come to the phone. Can you tell me what this is about?"

"Are *you* involved in this? Stoli asked.

"Alexandar is an associate of mine, yes," Joe answered.

"He *was* an associate of yours. Now he's dead because he tried to kill a friend of mine. If you want to keep this a private, family matter, meet me in the lobby of the William Penn Hotel at midnight."

"That's not much time," Joe protested.

"Especially if you waste it talking," Stoli answered. "Midnight."

He hung up and put the phone back in his pocket. Bending over, he grabbed the body by the wrists and strained to pull it the few feet off the catwalk and onto the top of the tank. When Alexandar's shoulders lined up with the open hatch, Stoli positioned the tattooed hand over the opening and, unsheathing his knife, started cutting.

The knife was razor sharp but a wrist is crowded with bones, ligaments and tendons. Periodically, Stoli had to flip the knife over and use the saw to hack through sinew. Even so, it took only a couple of minutes to complete the gruesome task. Stoli reached the severed hand into the tank to rinse it in the chemical bath. Satisfied it had bled out, he walked across the mezzanine and put it in the canvas bag.

He walked back to the body and, after shoving the stump into a pocket of the overalls, positioned the body so its feet hung over the access hatch. Stoli sat Alexandar upright and, wrapping his arms around the dead man's chest, jostled the body into the hole. There was a tense moment when Alexandar's broad shoulders jammed in the opening. Stoli sat down and, with a foot on either side of the massive head, kicked him through the hole. The rope that was tied to Alexandar's wrist slipped through Stoli's fingers as the weight of the wrench pulled the body down. When the line went slack in his hand, Stoli tied it to an eyebolt on underside of the lid, slid the hatch back in place and bolted it down.

Stoli was exhausted. The adrenalin that had given him the strength and stamina to kill Alexandar and hide the body was gone. His muscles ached with fatigue and a few of his knuckles were bleeding. He'd banged them working the wrench on the stubborn bolts of the access hatch. He wanted to sit and rest but knew he couldn't afford the time. The meeting with Joe was a little over two hours away. Precious little time to get everything in place and Doug squirreled away someplace safe. Stoli got up from where he'd been sitting atop the access hatch and looked around. He grimaced when he saw the evidence of the night's events.

Even in the darkness, the scuffmarks from where they'd dragged Alexandar's body were obvious. So too, was the fact that he'd unbolted the access hatch. The only positive was that little blood had been spilled. Neither Doug or Alexandar had bled from their respective blows. Alexandar had coughed up a bloody mist from the shot to his sternum but that had been minimal and much had fallen through the open grate of the mezzanine. Stoli had been careful to butcher the tattooed hand over the open hatch so that blood and sinew from that gruesome bit of business dripped into the tank. There was little else Stoli could do to hide what had transpired. He trudged over to the ladder and dropped the canvas bag to the ground. He swung onto the ladder, took one last look across the mezzanine, and started down.

Chapter Twenty-Five

Doug finished typing the letter and hit the save button before sending the file to be printed. The document contained the little he could remember and everything Stoli had told him. There wasn't much but it had taken him almost a half hour because of his swollen eye and screaming headache. He also had scrapes and bruises on random parts of his body. He didn't remember how he got any of those. He did remember when he got the tender spot just under his ribs where Alexandar had sucker punched him.

Doug was still trying to come to grips with the fact that Michael tried to kill him. Their mutual animosity was well known but, at least for Doug, could never reach the point of attempted murder. This was no spontaneous crime. It was obviously pre-meditated because, having failed once - and killing Lud in the process - they tried a second time. That required planning and forethought.

'Michael has several flaws,' Doug thought, *'But being stupid isn't one of them. He wouldn't plan to kill me just because he doesn't like me. There has to be more to it.'*

Doug swung his chair around to grab the copies from his printer. He scanned them quickly before folding and putting them in envelopes. That done, Doug returned to his computer and opened the email Michael sent earlier that evening with the termination letter attached. He noticed that it had also been sent to Carmen.

'Was Carmen in on it?' He wondered.

Although Doug didn't like what Carmen was doing to Keystate, the two had no personal animosity for each other. If Carmen were involved in Lud's death and the attempts on Doug, that put a more significant, sinister spin on it.

'But why?'

Doug read the email and attached letter looking for an explanation. He got increasingly angry as he read the termination letter which accused him of insubordination, malfeasance and misappropriation of funds. It was obviously Michael's handiwork and further proof of the premeditative attempt to kill Doug. The lies and defamatory statements could only stand up if Doug were not alive to make a rebuttal.

He printed a copy of the letter and closed the attachment. He was about to close the email when he noticed someone had replied to the email. He knew he hadn't responded to it but he had a pretty good idea who had. He opened the sent mail folder and there it was. The top email on the list, it was addressed to Carmen and Michael.

I am sorry that you think I have failed you. It is nothing compared to the failure I feel for what happened to Lud. Neither he or I would have been in this position if it weren't for you. I hope you can live with the consequences.

I can't.

Doug

It was evident that Michael - and perhaps Carmen - were planning on killing Doug under the guise of a suicide. That still didn't explain why. Doug sat back in his chair and tried vainly to think. He was too tired and pained for the effort. He'd taken four pain-killers from the office medicine cabinet before he'd sat down at his computer. The pills were starting to take effect on his pounding head and, as he sat there, his one open eye closed and he started to drift off.

The door to the office building opened and he jumped with a start. There was a second of reflexive fear and dread until he recognized the sound of Stoli's shuffling gait.

"Did you finish the letter?" Stoli asked as he came around the corner into Doug's office. He was carrying a small canvas bag

"Yeah," Doug replied, handing the envelopes to Stoli.

Stoli took the envelopes. "These all say the same thing?"

"Yes."

Stoli took the notes out of the envelopes. One copy he folded over and stuck in his pants pocket. He added handwritten notes to the bottom of the other two.

"What are you doing?" Doug asked.

"I'm letting people know where they can find the body if anything happens to us."

"What do we do now?"

"You need to make yourself scarce for a few days until I get this sorted out with Yuri. We don't know if he's involved in this or why. All we know is that Michael wants you dead."

"And maybe Carmen Risotti," Doug added. He showed Stoli the emails with the termination letter and suicide note.

"Is there any way those emails could have also been sent to Yuri?" Stoli asked.

"Maybe the first one. Michael could have blind copied somebody. But not the reply with the suicide note. We would see if he sent it to anybody else."

"Well, my in-laws know you're alive. I told them as much when I told them I killed that guy," Stoli mused. "But Michael thinks you're dead. And so will Risotti as soon as he reads that email."

"But not if he doesn't see it." Doug sat up, animated by an idea. He quickly checked to see if Carmen or Michael had opened the email with the suicide note. They hadn't. He quickly set about recalling the transmission.

"What are you doing?" Stoli asked.

"I'm canceling the email Cole sent with the suicide note and replacing it with a new one." Stoli looked over Doug's shoulder as he typed.

Mssrs. Cole and Risotti:

I emphatically deny the content and substance of the attached letter terminating my Employment Agreement. I intend to vigorously defend myself against the slander and defamatory comments and will seek both the enforcement of the terms of the Agreement and punitive compensation.

Doug Reardon.

Doug smiled as he pushed the send button. Stoli was confused.

"Why did you do that?" He asked.

"Now everybody knows I'm still alive," Doug answered. "This will smoke out the rats. Michael - and anyone else that thinks I'm dead - will shit their pants and go quiet. If Carmen's not involved, I'll hear from him or his lawyer. He'll have to respond. One thing for sure, there will be a reaction."

"Yeah," Stoli replied grimly. "Can you make copies of those emails? We should stick them with the letter. They prove that Michael - and maybe Carmen - are involved. They don't mention Yuri or Joe so we don't know if, or how, they are involved."

"No, they don't. But you've already started that ball rolling. If we're lucky, we'll have some answers in the morning... if were still alive."

"I'm pretty sure you'll be alive," Stoli answered. As if on cue, the outside door opened and a large voice boomed and echoed down the hall.

"Hello? Anybody in here?"

"We're back here, Steve," Stoli called out.

The lithe man that walked into Doug's office belied the size of the voice that preceded him. Steve Stalich was a diminutive man of five feet four inches and weighed no more than one hundred and forty pounds. He had the same scruffy beard and long hair that Stoli sported in winter. Steve wore tight blue jeans that were jammed into the unlaced tops of scarred work boots, a plaid, flannel shirt and, because of the chill, the bright orange vest ubiquitous to deer hunters. The outfit would not have been complete without a ball cap. Steve's was black and yellow and bore the requisite Steeler's logo.

"So, what kind of trouble are you in this time?" Steve began jovially before he turned into the room an saw Doug's face. "Jesus! What the hell happened to you?"

"Steve, meet Doug Reardon," Stoli introduced the men. "Doug, this is my brother, Steve."

"Are you sure?" Doug asked sarcastically as he looked from Steve over to his much larger brother "It doesn't look like you two came from the same litter."

"Don't let his size fool you," Stoli answered. "He's ten times meaner than I am and could easily kick your ass."

"Looks like somebody beat me to it," Steve piled on. "Or at least got a good start. I take it this is why I'm here? Don't bother getting up," He said as Doug started to get up from his chair. Doug sat back down and extended his hand. Steve took it in a firm handshake and Doug couldn't help noticing the size and strength of the grip. These were hands that had seen more than their share of hard work. They were calloused, gnarled and so large that they were out of proportion to the rest of the man. Doug had no doubt that Steve could, indeed, easily kick his butt.

"Steve," Stoli said. "It's better if you don't know what happened. All I can tell you is that somebody tried to kill Doug tonight. The same guy killed a friend of ours last night."

"The car on the bridge?" Steve interrupted.

"Yeah. We know who did that. He's not in the picture anymore. Don't ask," Stoli cutoff Steve's question before it was asked. "There's another guy that's behind it but we don't know why. We think there may be more people involved but we don't know for sure."

"How are you going to find out?" Steve asked.

"I can't tell you how but I will know by tomorrow morning. Until then, I need you to take Doug someplace safe. I don't want to know where. I also need you to take these two envelopes," Stoli handed them to his brother. "Put one in a safe place and give the other one to somebody you trust. Don't tell me who. If Doug or I end up dead, give your envelope to the Sewickley police. Have the person you give the other envelope do the same thing if something happens to you."

Steve looked stonily at his brother and Doug. "It's as bad as that?"

"Afraid so," Stoli answered.

"I take it the police are out of the question."

"Yeah. At least until I get some more information. Even then, I may not be able to go to the cops," Stoli said thinking of the body floating in the tank. "I did something they wouldn't appreciate."

"I know," Steve finished his brother's thought. "Don't ask."

That brought a thin smile to Stoli's face. "That's right," He said. Then, looking at the clock on the wall, he shrugged his shoulders. "I guess that's about it. I have to get going. Is there anything else?"

"Yeah," It was Doug. "How are we going to contact you?"

"You won't. If everything is going to be all right at my end, I'll contact you. Do you have your cell phone?" Doug moved some papers on his desk and found the phone that had lain hidden during the events of the evening. He nodded to Stoli.

"Good. Even if things are good at my end, you will still be in danger until we find out about Risotti." He grimaced and turned to his brother. "You didn't hear that."

He returned his attention to Doug. "You're going to have to lay low until we know if he's involved. Steve can hide you for a couple of days but then you'll have to go someplace else. I don't want to know where. Just keep your phone handy. Anything else?"

The three looked at each other and shook their heads. There was nothing more to discuss. Doug shut down his computer and put it in his back pack with the few things he wanted to take with him. There wasn't much. He took a last look around his office and followed the Stalich brothers down the hall to the foyer. Steve and Stoli left the building while Doug turned off the lights and set the alarm before stepping outside and locking the door. The brothers had walked to the parking lot and were standing by Alexandar's car.

"I forgot about his car," Stoli said to Doug. "We can't leave it here." He thought for a second.

"I guess I'll take it. It probably needs to end up in Erie, anyway. Oh shit!" He looked at Steve. "You didn't hear that, either." He sighed before beginning again. "Doug, you drive my truck to my house."

"Okay," Doug answered. "I want to swing by the apartment first to get some stuff. Doesn't sound like I know when I'll be able to go back there after tonight. Your truck will come in handy. Do you mind if I leave some things with you. There won't be much - just some clothes and personal things."

"That's a good idea," Stoli replied. "You can put your stuff in the garage. Steve will show you where." He reached in his pants pocket for Alexandar's car keys and started to reach for the door handle but stopped midair. Walking to his truck, he opened the passenger door and, reaching behind the seat, pulled out a pair of cotton work gloves. He put them on before opening the door to Alexandar's car to slide behind the wheel. The canvas bag went onto the passenger seat. Steve had already climbed into his truck and started the engine. Doug waited beside Alexandar's car for Stoli to lower the window.

"Thanks for coming back for me tonight," He said through the open window. "Looks like I'm on the hook to you for a very long time. Your brother, too."

"You would have done it for me," Stoli replied. "We both would have done it for Lud if we'd known. Steve wouldn't have come if he didn't think you deserved it."

"You mean because of the tank? That was just a small thing."

"Maybe to you. Sometimes the small things mean a lot."

"I guess. I just hope he doesn't get in trouble because of this. I would think his wife, at least, would be pissed."

"Steve's divorced," Stoli answered. "They broke up right after Jackie got killed. Don't worry about him. He only answers to himself these days. Good-bye, Doug. Keep your head down until you hear from me."

"Good-bye, Jack. See you soon." Doug moved away from the car as Stoli backed up and drove away. Doug climbed into the cab of Stoli's truck and, as he drove across the empty parking lot, looked back at the dark plant and shadowy tank farm. He wondered if he would ever be back.

Chapter Twenty-Six

It was a quarter past eleven when Stoli crossed the Fort Duquesne Bridge onto the peninsula that is downtown Pittsburgh. The spit of land between the confluence of the Allegheny and the Monongahela forms a near perfect isosceles triangle. Streets and avenues that run perpendicular to the two rivers converge on Liberty Avenue in a series of angled intersections. Coming off the bridge, Stoli drove parallel to the Allegheny River for a few blocks before heading inland on Seventh Street. The streets were deserted which suited Stoli just fine. He seldom drove into the city and was relieved that he wouldn't have to contend with traffic on his way to the William Penn Hotel. A few cars plied Liberty Avenue when he pulled up to the red light before crossing the thoroughfare that served as the backbone of the city.

The streets on the other side of Liberty are defined by their relation to the Monongahela and Stoli made a forty-five degree turn onto Sixth Street and drove past the Presbyterian Church, Trinity Cathedral and Mellon Square Park to the William Penn. The park sits atop the roof of the underground garage for the hotel. Stoli maneuvered the Grand Marquis into the entrance and, after taking the ticket from the kiosk, drove through the gate into the confines of the garage.

He circled down several levels of the mostly empty garage until he spotted the green BMW. Stoli pulled into a spot well away from the sports car, grabbed the canvas bag and got out of the car. After locking the doors, he took off the cotton gloves and dropped them and the keys in the bag. As he passed the BMW, he casually put the back of his hand on the hood. It was still warm. Confidant it was Michael's car, he left the garage and walked up the slight incline that led to the hotel entrance.

Stoli had never crossed the threshold of the William Penn. It was Pittsburgh's premiere hotel and not a place he would normally go. He gave himself a quick once over before pushing through the brass revolving door. Although scuffed up from the earlier events at the plant, he figured he was presentable enough to not draw attention. He climbed the few steps that led from the foyer to the elegant main lobby.

Towering ceilings carried three massive, crystal chandeliers over the glossy patterns of the marble floor. This late at night, the chandeliers had been dimmed and the lobby was softly lit by floor and table lamps. A large banquette pouffe anchored the center of the lobby and was surrounded by groupings of side chairs and end tables. Large, square columns carried rounded arches around the perimeter of the lobby and created a side aisle and balcony that looked over and into the main space.

Stoli stood at the top of the stairs to take in the room and scan it for signs of Yuri or Joe. They weren't there but Stoli was neither worried nor surprised. He really didn't expect them to make the drive from Erie before midnight. The deadline he'd set was just intended to convey a sense of urgency.

Stoli found a small grouping of chairs off the main lobby. He chose a chair that provided an unobstructed view of the entrance and, placing the bag between his feet, sat down. There were few other people in the lobby. Three businessmen in suits occupied a cluster of chairs on the opposite side of the lobby and an elderly woman sat by herself reading a book and sipping wine. Periodically, one or two people would come up the stairs and click across the marble floor to the bank of elevators.

Fifteen minutes passed and Stoli, not wishing to look out of place, strolled over to the reception desk and took a complimentary newspaper from the stack. He returned to his chair and pretended to read while keeping an eye on the entrance. After another ten minutes had passed, Stoli started to succumb to the relaxing ambiance of the lobby. He folded the paper in his lap and closed his eyes.

*******   *******   *******   *******

There were three vehicles in the small motorcade that pulled up to the entrance of the William Penn Hotel. All of them black. A large sedan had the lead position and a panel van brought up the rear. Both carried two passengers. The gleaming SUV in between was driven by Dmitri. Joe Pandropov sat next to him in the front passenger seat and Yuri sat alone in the back. He'd been chain smoking since they'd left the house.

The caravan made the trip from Erie in astounding time - less than an hour and a half from the time they'd assembled the men and vehicles. The three passengers in the SUV had ridden in silence for the last half hour of the trip. The first hour had been spent under grueling questioning from Yuri.

"Jack Stalich told you he killed Alexandar?" Yuri started by asking Dmitri the question in Russian.

"Da."

"Did he say why?"

"Nyet," Dmitri answered. "He only said for you to call back in ten minutes or he'd call the police."

"Why did you tell this to Josef and not to me?"

"Because I assumed it had something to do with the failed mission to kill Doug Reardon."

"What!" Yuri exploded. "Who the hell is Doug Reardon and why were you trying to kill him?"

"Doug Reardon is the guy that's running the Keystate operation for Carmen," Joe answered. "Last week, Michael came to me and said you and Carmen agreed it was time to terminate him. It was part of the plan to start driving down the share price."

"I never authorized that! And Carmen sure as hell never talked to me about killing the guy!" Yuri and Joe had switched to English. "You say Michael is behind this?"

"Sounds like it, "Joe answered. "I certainly didn't approve it. He came to me and asked if he could use Alexandar as backup. I just assumed he was going to fire the guy and needed someone to walk him out. You know what a dickless coward Michael is."

"Dmitri," Yuri switched back to Russian. "Did you and Michael Cole plan to kill Doug Reardon?"

"No. That was between Alexandar and Michael. Alexandar called me later to help carry out the plan. I did what he told me to do."

"And you never talked to Michael? Yuri asked. Dmitri shook his head.

"You said it was a failed mission?" Yuri pressed. "What happened?"

"The plan was to cause an accident and force his car off a bridge into the river. It worked to perfection," Dmitri said with some pride. "But I guess the wrong person was in the car."

Yuri groaned. He quickly made the connection between what Dmitri just reported and Stoli's account of his Lud's death. Somehow, Stoli had made the same connection. That explained his abrupt departure from Yuri's house earlier that evening.

"So tonight Alexandar was to finish the job?" Yuri continued.

"Da. He told me to cover for him so he could go with Michael to kill Reardon."

"When did he talk to Michael?

"Tonight. At the house."

"Michael Cole was at my house? Tonight!?" Yuri was incredulous. "What the fuck kind of security are you running?" He screamed at Joe.

"Michael Cole is your man," Joe answered coldly. "You know I never trusted him. I don't know what he's up to but it obviously has something to do with the PetroChem deal. That means Carmen Risotti might be involved. I warned you about him, too."

Yuri was furious but he knew Josef was right. Michael Cole *was* his man. Yuri had brought him in to quietly steer his drug money into legitimate business. Now it looked like Michael was running a rouge operation that threatened to open Yuri to investigation. Worse, he'd somehow managed to pull Jack Stalich into the mix. *'My daughter's father-in-law, for Christ's sake!'* He thought. The whole purpose behind Yuri's legitimization effort was to free Lindsay and Sam from a future of drug dealing.

'How the hell am I going to do that now that Stalich thinks I'm connected with the death of one friend and the attempted murder of another? And what about Carmen? Was he working with Michael to kill Reardon?'

Yuri rode in silence for the next several minutes. He stared out the window into the blackness of the night as he calmed his mind to sort through the unanswered questions. He decide that he had to set the issue of Carmen aside and focus on Stalich. The immediate concern was to learn what he knew of Yuri's connection to Alexandar, Michael and Keystate. Yuri didn't think it likely that Stalich knew anything about his heroin empire.

'Still,' Yuri thought, *'He certainly knows I'm connected to a plot to kill people. Hell, up until a few minutes ago, he knew more about it than I did!'*

That was about to change.

"Josef, I am sorry to have lost my temper," He began. "You are correct that Michael is my responsibility. If, as it appears, he has put us in jeopardy, I will deal with it. However, I have some questions to ask him. I need to know if Carmen is in on this. But first, we need to find out what Jack Stalich knows."

******* ******* ******* *******

Stoli woke to gentle shaking. He opened his eyes and, bolting upright with a start, swatted the prodding hand away from his shoulder. Looking up, Stoli immediately recognized the intruder as the second gardener. The overalls were gone and replaced by dress slacks, a thin sweater that barely concealed bulging muscles and a light jacket that didn't hide the shoulder holster.

"Mr. Stalich?" Dmitri asked, although he knew full well it was.

"Yeah," Stoli answered as he looked at the lobby clock. It was twenty past midnight. He'd been asleep for less than ten minutes. "You're the other one from Yuri's house last night, aren't you?"

Dmitri nodded.

"Were you the one on the phone?" Stoli continued.

Another nod. Stoli looked at the tattoo on the back of Dmitri's right hand. "I guess you two were friends?" Stoli asked with some regret and more fear.

"We knew each other for more than twenty years. We were together in Afghanistan. He was my friend."

"Yeah. Well, he killed my friend and tried to kill another. I didn't want to kill him but I had no choice."

Dmitri stared intently into Stoli's eyes. There was no hint of regret or animosity in his face. "That is the way it is with soldiers. Kill or die." He shrugged his shoulders." It was Alexandar's time to die. Please, come with me." Dmitri turned toward the hotel entrance. "Mr. Pandropov is waiting outside."

"Yuri or Joe?" Stoli asked.

"Both."

Stoli grabbed the canvas bag from between his feet as he stood to follow. Walking a few paces behind Dmitri, he was struck by the physical similarities between this man and the one he'd killed. Like Alexandar, Dmitri had broad shoulders that supported a massive bull neck and a heavily browed, bullet shaped head. Equally hirsute, Dmitri's day-old beard was thick, black and only slightly shorter that his close cropped hair. Stoli wondered if Dmitri and Alexandar hadn't been brothers.

The lobby was empty except for the night clerk behind the reception desk. He gave a quick look and practiced smile as the two men crossed the lobby to the short flight of stairs that led to the foyer.

It was much colder outside and Stoli's breath was visible in the night air. So, too, was Dmitri's and that of the men standing next to the sedan and van. Stoli followed Dmitri to the black SUV and, after having the rear door opened for him, climbed inside. Yuri was still in the back seat and Joe in front

"Good morning, Ivan Stalichovik," Yuri had the solicitous tone of an undertaker. The end of his cigarette glowed red as he inhaled.

"I told you I would prefer to be called Jack," Stoli replied curtly. "And would you mind not smoking?"

"Yes, I would. And I would prefer that you had not killed Alexandar Alexandrov. Although I admit I find it difficult to believe you could. He was the best of the best," Despite his objection, Yuri cracked his window and tossed the unfinished cigarette.

Stoli said nothing and pushed the canvas bag across the seat. Yuri lifted the bag onto his lap and cautiously looked inside. Unable to see in the dim light, he reached inside and reflexively recoiled when he felt the cold hand. Grim faced, he pulled it from the bag and held it up to the garish light streaming down from the street lights. Turing the hand palm down, Yuri straightened the curled fingers to expose the tattoos of the skydiving eagle and Cyrillic letters. Stoli detected a slight slumping of Yuri's shoulders and a hint of sadness as he gently replaced the hand in the bag.

"You've made your point, Jack," Yuri said softly. "A bit dramatic, don't you think?"

"His wallet, keys and cash are also in the bag," Stoli replied. "I wanted to be sure there was no doubt about what I did and may yet do."

"Apparently, there are many things we do not know about each other. I can assure you that there are many things about me you do not want to know." Yuri's voice was thick with emotion and there was no mistaking the obvious threat.

"I am not a curious person," Stoli said. "I'm not here by choice."

"Then why are we here?" Yuri asked. "You killed Alexandar and summoned me here but you haven't told me why."

Stoli leaned back in the car seat, stretched out his right leg and reached into his pants pocket. Joe, who had been sitting quietly in the front seat, quickly reached back to grab Stoli's arm.

"Relax," Stoli said. "I'm just getting some pieces of paper. I left Alexandar's gun where I found it."

Pulling the documents from his pocket, Stoli unfolded and handed them to Yuri. Yuri took the small bundle with his right hand while his left hand went inside his overcoat to retrieve reading glasses. He adjusted them on his nose and, holding the note in the light, tilted his head to read.

My name is Doug Reardon and today is Thursday, September 22, 2005. Yesterday, Lud Rahl was killed when the car he was driving was forced off the Interstate bridge by a man known as Alex Smith. Officer Dan McMeans of the Sewickley police is investigating the accident. Alex Smith was working for Michael Cole. These men killed Lud Rahl because they mistook him for me.

Tonight, Alex Smith tried to kill me because
Michel Cole told him to. I met Michael Cole in my
office at Keystate Oil Company on Neville Island.
Alex Smith was with him. I was knocked
unconscious by Smith and was going to be
thrown off a tank to make it look
like a suicide. I was saved by Jack Stalich,
a co-worker at Keystate Oil Company, who
killed Smith to protect me. Jack overheard Cole and
Alex Smith plan to kill me at the home of Yuri
Pandropov near Erie.

I don't know why they are trying to kill me.
If they succeed - if there is anything at all
suspicious about my death - give this letter to the
Sewickley police.

Yuri handed the letter to Joe before quickly reading
through the accompanying termination letter,
Doug's rebuttal and the faked suicide note. He
handed these documents to Joe before putting his
glasses away. "I don't suppose those are the only
copies?" He asked rhetorically.

"There are two others," Stoli confirmed.
That one's yours to keep. The others say where I
hid the body."

"That's quite an insurance policy," Yuri
looked over. "Or is it a threat?"

"I don't think I'm in a position to threaten
you. I just want my family and friends to be safe."

"Why didn't you just go to the police?" Yuri
asked. "That would have been the safe thing to do."

"Because I wanted to find out if you're involved," Stoli answered. "If it was just you and me, I would be at the cops instead of here. But your girl has my boy's baby in her belly. What happens to you involves them." He pointed to the canvas bag. "You're obviously involved somehow. I know Cole was giving the orders but I don't know if he was dancing for you or maybe Risotti. I don't give a shit about either of them but I'm hoping you can convince me that you had nothing to do with it."

"And if I can't?"

"To be honest, I haven't thought that far. I really don't want to go to the cops. I killed a guy tonight and don't want to go through all the bullshit that's involved with that. Nothing personal, but he killed a friend of mine and was going to kill another one. In my book, he deserved to die."

Stoli paused a moment as the memory of the wrench crashing into the back of Alexandar's skull flashed through his mind. "I guess it doesn't matter if you're involved," He continued. "Like I said, I just want my family to be safe."

The two men studied each others' faces in the dim light. Both were conflicted and it showed. Stoli wanted to believe that Yuri was not involved but knew the odds were against it. It was obvious that Alexandar worked for him. It didn't seem likely that Alexandar would have been sent off on an assassination mission without Yuri's knowledge. But that didn't explain how Michael Cole figured in the equation. Or Carmen Risotti. Stoli had played his hand; there was nothing he could do but hope that Yuri wasn't involved. If he was, Stoli prayed that the threat of Doug's letter would be protection enough.

Yuri had a different dilemma. He knew that he was innocent - at least of Lud's murder and the attempt on Doug. His problem lay in defending himself against that without unduly exposing his other criminal activities. His thoughts, too were on his daughter and unborn grandchild. His greatest ambition was to provide Lindsay and Sam affluent, crime-free futures. That aspiration was what brought him and Michael Cole together in the first place. It was infuriating that the little prick had put all that in extreme jeopardy. Yuri would deal with that later. At the moment, Yuri had to defuse Stoli's suspicions.

"Ivan... I mean, Jack," He began. "It appears we have a common problem in Michael Cole. He does work for me but I had no idea what he was up to regarding Keystate. Neither did Joe," He said with a nod to his son in the front seat. "We didn't figure it out until tonight after you called and we started asking questions."

That was the first time that Keystate had been mentioned in any conversation between the two men and Stoli was quick to take notice. '*So there is a connection between Yuri, Michael and Keystate.*' He thought. '*That means there must be a connection between Yuri and Carmen Risotti.*'

"I never said anything about Keystate." Stoli said. "In fact, I don't think you and I have ever talked about me working there. What do you have to do with it?"

"You work at Keystate?" Yuri was floored.

"Yeah. I run the blending area. I'm also the union steward."

Yuri was incensed and he shot a dark glance at Joe. This was another serious breach of security and lack of information. Had he known his daughter was marrying the son of a Keystate employee, he never would have approved Carmen's acquisition of the company.

'*What an incredible fuck up!*' He thought. '*It seems that both Michael Cole and Fate are working against me.*' Yuri set aside that line of thought for the moment. He would deal with it later when he and Joe were alone. At the moment, he had to deal with Stoli's question. It was a dangerous one.

If Yuri answered truthfully, he could open the door to the full extent of his illegal activities. He'd already accepted that Stoli was smart enough to suspect that he was dirty. Yuri entertained the thought of letting Stoli glimpse the truth. Stoli could be a valuable asset. He'd already demonstrated intelligence, decisiveness and the ability to take even the most extreme action.

Yuri discarded the notion as quickly as it came. In the first place, Yuri wasn't at all sure what Stoli would do with the knowledge. Besides, even if Stoli could be trusted to become part of the organization, Yuri's broader plan was to diminish - not extend - familial ties to the drug trade. Yuri and Joe were to be the last. With that in mind, Yuri opted to lie.

"I know that Keystate is a subsidiary of a PetroChem Packaging," He started. "I know this because I have invested several million dollars in the company. In all honesty, if I knew you worked there, I wouldn't have." Yuri shot another glace at Joe. "Michael Cole is my business agent in such transactions."

"Isn't he on the board of directors?" Stoli asked.

"Yes," Yuri replied. "He and Carmen Risotti put the deal together and I was one of the initial investors. Once the company went public, I became just another stockholder."

"So Risotti works for you, too?"

"In a manner of speaking."

"Is that legal?"

"According to who?" Yuri answered with a slight smile. "Strictly speaking - probably not. But that's how things get done."

The conversation was taking Stoli into waters well over his head. He was not at all interested in financial manipulation or intrigue. He knew that all this had, in some way, led to the events of the past two days but had no idea how or why. Ultimately, he decided that it didn't matter as long as he could be assured that he, his family and Doug would no longer be swept up in it. If Michael was, indeed, a rogue actor, he had to be stopped. That was Yuri's responsibility.

"You said Michael was acting on his own - that you didn't know anything about him trying to kill Doug. Do you know why he would want to do that?"

"No," Yuri told a half truth. He knew of the plan to remove Doug in order to drive down

PetroChem's stock price. He just didn't know that Michael was planning to kill him. "That's the first thing I'm going to ask when I find him."

"You've found him," Stoli said softly.

"Where?" It was Joe. "He's here? In Pittsburgh?"

"In the hotel." Stoli jerked his thumb toward the building. "I heard him tell Alexandar that he was staying here tonight. When I got here, I parked in the hotel garage. Cole's car is there. I checked, the engine was still warm."

Yuri and Joe switched to Russian for a lengthy conversation. Yuri did most of the talking. When it was over, Joe got out and walked to the sedan. Stoli watched through the front window of the SUV as Joe conveyed Yuri's instruction to his men. One crossed the driveway and entered the hotel. Another went down the ramp in the direction of the garage entrance. A third went with Joe and climbed into the back of the windowless van. The last, Dmitri, came and stood next the window where Stoli sat.

"What's that all about?" Stoli asked.

"Joe is going to call Michael and invite him to come and have a chat with me," Yuri answered.

"Do you think he'll come? I heard him tell Alexandar that he didn't want you to find out what he was up to."

"I think you know all you need to know," Yuri responded flatly. "Now I need to know something from you." Yuri turned the full force of his black eyes on Stoli. "I will take care of Michael

Cole. He won't be a threat to you anymore. What happened shouldn't have happened. It was stupid and unnecessary. I don't do stupid or unnecessary things. Do you?"

"I try not to," Stoli answered. "I suppose you're talking about me going to the police."

"Yes. That and the copies of the letter. I need those."

"I won't go to the police. You can trust me on that. But I'm going to keep the letters. I don't know if I can trust you."

"And Alexandar's body?"

"I'll keep that, too. Without a body, everything else is just a story, isn't it?"

Yuri had to smile despite the seriousness of the moment. "You're a shrewd man, Ivan Stalichovik. You've got me by the balls. At least you're decent enough not to twist them." Yuri looked out the window before continuing. "What about this friend of yours, Doug Reardon. Can I trust him to keep his mouth shut?"

"Yes."

"What assurance do I have of that?

"Because I asked him to and he said he would."

"And that is enough?" Yuri asked skeptically.

"Yes. He's a man of his word. Besides, he figures he owes me. I saved his life last night."

"I understand a debt of honor," Yuri's gaze fell to the canvas bag still in his lap and his thoughts drifted to a distant morning and a flag waving soldier limping out of Afghan mountains. "I think we are done here. Dmitri will take you back to Erie." He smiled wanly. "There is some vodka in the car. You'll want to have a few drinks before you get there."

"I'll have no problem with that but why?"

"When you called earlier, we had to come up with an excuse to tell the women why we were leaving. Joe and I told them that, since you weren't there to drink with us, we were going to come here to drink with you. They were pissed. Especially Helen," Yuri gave a mirthless chuckle. "You'll have a few bad days with her but it's better than telling her you killed somebody," That thought sobered him. "You'd better go."

"One last thing," Stoli hesitated as he reached for the door latch. "What about Carmen Risotti. How do you know he's not behind this whole thing?

"I don't," Yuri admitted. "That's one of the things I hope to find out from Michael."

"You saw the email Doug sent to Cole and Risotti saying he wouldn't quit and was going to sue?"

Yuri nodded.

"Doug did that to see if Risotti involved."

"What do you mean?" Yuri asked.

"If Risotti just intended to fire Doug he will have to respond to Doug's threat to sue him. If he was part of the plan to kill Doug, he won't."

"I see," Yuri mused. "Sounds like this friend of yours is pretty shrewd."

"He's all right," Stoli agreed.

"Anyway, I'll get what I can out of Michael," Yuri said. "If he says Carmen's involved, I'll deal with it. If not, I'm sure I'll hear from Carmen soon enough. Either way, it's not your problem anymore."

Stoli opened the door and stepped out. He turned and leaned into the open door. "Helen and I will be leaving in the morning," He said referring to the weekend plans that had now become untenable. "You're right that she will be pissed about our 'boy's night out.' I'll use that as an excuse to leave."

"I understand," Yuri answered. "I will contact you when this is settled. You have nothing to fear from me."

Stoli nodded and, stepping back, closed the door to the SUV. Dmitri obsequiously waved his arm toward the sedan and, leading the way, opened the rear door. Stoli stepped in and, as promised, found a bottle of expensive vodka lying on the backseat. He cracked the seal and had already pulled down a couple of hard swallows before Dmitri had started the car and headed for Erie. By the time they crossed the Fort Pitt bridge, Stoli was drifting off to sleep.

Chapter Twenty-Seven

In his dreams, Michael Cole was always a second too late. Whether running through airports, train stations or after taxis or people, the recurring theme was that, just before he got there, a door slammed shut in his face. This night, it was an airport.

He ran, gasping, through the gate area to make his flight but he couldn't run fast enough. His legs had the numb weight of lead and barely budged. Looking down, he was horrified to see Doug Reardon hugging his right thigh and Carmen Risotti on the left. *"Can't you see you're making me miss my flight?"* He screamed in the dream. But it was too late. By the time he made it down the jet way, the door to the plane slammed shut. Yuri Pandropov, dressed as a flight attendant, peered out at him through the small port as the jet backed away.

Michael was left standing alone. He looked back up the ramp to see Doug and Carmen doubled over in laughter. Standing at the edge of the jet way, Michael looked down at the tarmac. Except it wasn't the tarmac any longer. Now it was a bottomless pit. A bell started ringing and the jet way jerked under his feet. He lost his balance and pitched forward into the abyss while the bell rang on and on and on.

Terror jerked Michael awake with pounding head and heart to the harsh ringing of the phone. He sat upright on the edge of the bed and grabbed for the handset.

"Hullo," He mumbled as he spanned his free hand across his forehead and rubbed his throbbing temples.

"Michael, it's Joe."

A fresh surge of fear, cognizant this time, sent a wave of blood coursing into his already overloaded brain. The ensuing migraine was instantaneous and blinding. He pulled the phone away from his ear and, wide-eyed, looked around the room in an effort to get his bearings. It took a couple of seconds for him to survey in the room and remember where he was. He looked at the phone in his hand and recognized it as the hotel phone. Another wave of panic hit him when he realized that Joe knew where he was.

"Hello? Michael? Hello?" The small, static voice of Joe Pandropov came out of the earpiece. "Are you there? Michael?"

Michael put the phone to his ear. "Hello, Joe. Sorry about that," He spoke tentatively. "I was asleep. Where are you? What time is it?" He grabbed his glasses from the nightstand and put them on to look at the clock.

"It's twelve-thirty. I'm down in the lobby. Alexandar told me you'd be here," Joe lied.

"Alexandar told you?"

"Yeah."

"Did he tell you about tonight?" His voice was plaintive, almost pleading.

"Why do you think we're here?"

"*We're* here?" Michael asked. "Who else is here?"

"My father. He's out front in the van. He would have come in but you know he doesn't like to be seen."

"Why is he here?" Michael's voice cracked with fear.

"To congratulate you."

"Really?" Michael's response was flooded with relief.

"Really. You sound surprised. Why wouldn't he congratulate you."

"I was afraid he wouldn't understand."

"To be honest, he was angry at first," Joe said. "He wasn't happy that you didn't consult him. Frankly, I was more pissed than he was because I thought you were going to terminate the guy... not *terminate* him," Joe stressed the word. "After we thought about it, we realized what you did was the right thing to do Anyway, come on down."

"Okay. I'll be right there. I have to change clothes," Michael looked down and realized he was still dressed. "I fell asleep in my clothes."

"Don't worry about that," Joe replied. "We won't take long. Just come as you are. See you in a minute." Joe hung up.

Michael went over to the wardrobe and took his jacket from the hanger. He slipped it on and knotted his lavender tie before stepping into the bathroom to quickly brush his teeth and drag a comb through his thin hair. He gave himself a swift appraisal in the mirror and decided that would have to do. His headache had dissipated but his heart still raced. Now, however, it was with excitement.

'Yuri was pleased!' He thought. *'I knew he'd agree that getting rid of Reardon was the only thing to do. Carmen didn't see it but I did!'*

Michael was inordinately pleased with himself as he strode to the door and, once in the hall, strutted to the elevator. The doors slid open to the ground floor and Michael walked across the lobby to the entrance where Joe stood. They shook hands before walking outside to the waiting van. It was the only vehicle there; the SUV had been driven away and out of sight. As Joe and Michael neared, the driver stepped out of the van and slid open the side door. Joe gestured Michael inside and followed him in. There were four plush, leather captain's chairs in the back of the van. Yuri sat in the one directly opposite the door and, gripping Michael's hand in fraternal shake, steered him to sit in one closer to the back. Joe sat in the one closest to the door.

"So, Michael," Yuri began. "What's this I hear about you showing some initiative and dealing with this little problem of ours?"

"With all due respect, Yuri," Michael preened. "It wasn't a *'little'* problem. I think Reardon was onto our scheme. Since it was time for him to be removed anyway, I thought it would be smart to eliminate him completely."

"And Carmen agreed?" Yuri asked.

"Carmen didn't know about it. I don't know if he's got the stomach for this sort of thing?"

"And you do?" Yuri asked. "You were there to watch him die?"

"Well, no," Michael stammered. "That was Alexandar's job. But I did the planning. I was the brains."

"Both times?" Joe asked.

"What do you mean?"

"I mean did you do the planning the first time when the wrong man was driven off a bridge?"

"No," Michael began to feel the familiar rise of fear. "That was Alexandar's fault. He had the right car but didn't make sure who was driving. That was a mistake."

"I see," said Yuri. "So you take credit when things go according to plan but not when there's a screw up."

"It's not like that," Michael defended himself. "It's just that I wasn't there on the bridge. I can't be responsible for that."

"I guess that's true," Yuri conceded. "But an innocent man is still dead and the police are investigating. You say Carmen wasn't involved in any of the planning for this?"

"No," Michael confirmed. "Like I said, he doesn't have the balls for it."

Michael didn't like the way the conversation was turning. Apparently, Alexandar had told the whole story. At least Alexandar hadn't known that Carmen was involved after the first screw up. Michael could still take full credit for eliminating Reardon.

"What about Joe and me? Do you think we lack the balls?" Yuri asked pointedly.

"I didn't say that!"

"Then why didn't you consult us?" Yuri's eyes were starting to storm over. "Did you think something like this wouldn't interest us?"

"I did consult Joe," Michael replied weakly. "I went to him to get Alexandar's help."

"You made me believe that you needed Alexandar to help fire the guy. Not to kill him," Joe said.

"I can't help it if you didn't understand," Michael cowered.

"Bullshit!" Joe exploded. "You also made it sound like you'd talked to Carmen and my father and they approved it."

"They did! They both wanted Reardon gone," He turned to Yuri. "Tell him. That day by the lake. You said it would be good if Reardon was gone."

"But not dead," Yuri said coldly. "That was your idea. And it was a bad one. I warned you once before about not consulting with me on everything you do. Do you remember?"

Michael recalled the day Yuri had reprimanded him for not disclosing that first encounter with Carmen over the CARMA dealings. That was the beginning of the path leading to this moment. Michael shrank back into the leather seat and weakly nodded his head.

Yuri said nothing in reply. Instead, he bent over to lift the canvas bag from the floor. He sat it on his lap, reached in and pulled out all that he had left of Alexandar Alexandrov. He held the severed hand in his own as if shaking the hand of an old friend and extended it inches from Michael's face. Michael trembled at the macabre sight.

"This right hand served me loyally for over twenty years," Yuri's voice was thick with emotion and dark with menace. "Never once did it give me cause for mistrust or concern. I have known you for a fraction of that time and you have disobeyed me and put me in danger. Because of you, Alexandar is dead, Reardon is alive and I am threatened with exposure and investigation. You were supposed to help me legitimize my business and secure my family's future. Instead, you have opened me to investigation and thwarted my plans. You have failed me in every way possible. I think it is time to *terminate* our relationship. Josef will see to the details."

Yuri put the hand back into the bag and nodded to Joe. His son rapped twice on the door of the van and it slid open. Yuri rose from his seat and stooped to crossed to the door and step out. From outside, he cast a last look at Michael Cole whimpering in the back of the van.

"Please, Yuri," Michael moaned. "Don't do this.

Yuri put a cigarette between his lips. The glow of the lighter illuminated a face that held no compassion; the black eyes seemingly swallowed the light from the flame. He wordlessly turned away and the door slid shut. Inside, Joe stared stonily as Michael wept; his tears dropped freely onto a lap already wet with warm urine.

*******   *******   *******   *******

Michael Cole stood in the silted sand of Lake Erie and looked up into the inky blackness over his head. His expensive suit, already blemished from the events of day, was now completely ruined. The silky mud rose to just below his knees and stained both the trousers and his outrageously expensive Ferragamo loafers. The shoes had been destroyed. The rough chain that wove its way around Michael's calves and feet had scuffed the polish and marred the leather. His silk tie had, at least, retained some flair as it floated gently with the current. So, too, did his unbuttoned jacket as it billowed up and away from his torso. Normally, Michael would have been distraught over such wanton destruction of his wardrobe. At the moment, however, he just seemed resigned.

His arms, palms turned slightly up, stretched out and up in a sign of surrender. At last, he was placid and his face calm. Except for his eyes. They were crossed and slightly rolled back in their sockets as they stared with incredulity at the small round hole in the middle of his forehead.

Sixty feet above, Joe Pandropov turned the key and the twin, four hundred horsepower outboard motors purred to life. Dmitri finished coiling the hose he had used to wash Michael's blood off the deck and came to sit next to Joe. Both were bundled in sweaters and heavy jackets against the chill and damp. The cold, predawn air formed a dense fog over the warm waters of Lake Erie. Not that it would matter in the pea-soup, but they would keep the running lights off for the ride home. Joe flipped on the radar as he pointed the bow of

Horsing Around toward shore and waited for it to complete a circuit to be sure the course was clear. Confident it was, he pushed the throttles forward and the boat accelerated smoothly to plane across the placid lake for home.

Below the surface, an ancient and enormous channel catfish picked up the scent of blood and swam up current to the source. In the blackness, his whiskers caressed the contours of Michael's face.

Chapter Twenty-Eight

Carmen Risotti cupped his scotch in both hands as he leaned across the stainless steel railing of the balcony and watched the people watching the sun set into the Pacific Ocean. Some of them were on the pool deck directly below his room and many more stood on the crescent of beach that gave the town its name. Laguna Beach, a small town south of Los Angeles, is a happy convergence of artists, musicians and the multi-millionaires that make art possible.

The mix of affluence, bohemia and idyllic climate also attracts a sizable influx of tourists. Carmen recognized that many of the people watching the sun disappear over the horizon fell into this later group. They wore clothes - usually khaki or white shorts and polo shirts - that they thought the locals would wear. The footwear almost always gave them away. The men usually wore boat shoes and the women crisp, new sandals. No local would be seen thusly clad. T-shirts, cargo shorts and sandals were de rigueur for the young and artsy. The rich sported designer fashions that complimented their exotic Italian, British or German automobiles.

Carmen was a hybrid; he wore his trademark khaki slacks, polo shirt and deck shoes but drove a rented Bentley Continental. He was staying at an inn on the northern edge of the beach where he'd been a regular guest since the days he and his then wife habituated the area. The hotel and staff appreciated Carmen's frequent business and heavy tipping. There was always a fresh bottle of Glenn Fiddich in the room and ice in the bucket when he arrived.

He'd flown in the previous Friday afternoon to attend an investor conference at the luxurious Montage resort a few miles south of town. The resort was a regular stop on the conference circuit and Carmen had attended several sessions as both an investor and presenter. Earlier in the day, he had made another pitch on behalf of PetroChem Packaging. It was the third such presentation he had made in the past year. If things went according to plan, it would be the last for quite a while. However, things were most definitely not going to plan.

It had been four days since Michael's debacle and Carmen hadn't a clue what was going on. He regretted telling Michael to not call. It had been a knee-jerk reaction and one of the rare times Carmen felt panicked. Now, he wished he'd been more involved in planning Doug's murder. At least he would know what was going on. The only communication he'd received was the email Michael sent with Doug's termination letter and Doug's response telling Carmen and Michael where to shove it.

Carmen had been on the plane to Los Angeles when those emails arrived and hadn't read them until the following day. When he did, Carmen noted that a couple of hours had passed between the time Michael sent his email and Doug's response. Doug's was sent late in the evening; long after he should have been dead. Worried, Carmen made several unsuccessful calls to Michael's cell phone. When that failed, he tried email. Thus far, he'd received no response. Carmen even went so far as to contact the Rosens and Sean Tompkins. They had not heard from Michael since the board meeting the previous week.

More troubling, Carmen had no idea whether Doug was dead or alive. He'd searched through the on-line media sites in Pittsburgh for any story about Doug's demise. Nothing. Most telling, the share price for PetroChem held steady. Carmen obsessively monitored the company's share price and it was holding at around thirty-five cents. This, more than anything else, worried Carmen. Sooner or later - and probably sooner -Yuri would want to know why the share price was not dropping as planned. That was a line of questioning Carmen definitely didn't want to follow.

All things considered, Carmen had to assume the worst - Michael had somehow screwed up - again - and Doug Reardon was still in the picture. *'Fucking little princess!'* Carmen cursed Michael under his breath. All of Carmen's scheming, effort and expense over the past couple of years was in peril of blowing up.

He thought back to his initial meeting with Yuri and the inherent danger of approaching such a man. Then there was the real work of setting up PetroChem and negotiating the acquisitions of Sprayzon, Union and Keystate. Following that were the endless months of promoting the company in order to drive sales of the stock and boost the share price. More than once, he had almost run out of cash. When Yuri balked at advancing the necessary funds, Carmen had to dip into his own money. He was now nearly broke and living week to week on his salary and expense stipend. As if all this had been hard enough, he'd had the additional grief of dealing with the people surrounding him.

Sean Tompkins had been a benign ally and the Rosens not much more than a nuisance. But the virulent animosity between Michael Cole and Doug Reardon was something Carmen hadn't anticipated and was unable to diffuse. The best he could do was keep them separated.

Carmen kicked himself for granting Michael's request to fire Doug. He never thought that Michael hated Doug so much that he would attempt murder. To make matters worse, Michael had been foolish enough to recruit Yuri's man for the deed and, most damning of all, they had failed so flagrantly in the attempt that they drew in the police. And because of that, Carmen was now in real danger. He had no doubt that Yuri would ruthlessly cover his tracks should that be necessary. Anything that could connect Yuri to PetroChem would simply disappear.

Contemplating that, Carmen shuddered, pushed himself upright off the railing and drained his glass. He walked off the balcony and into his room to refill the glass with ice and scotch. The glass was halfway to his lips when a sharp knock rattled the door. Carmen lowered his arm to look at his watch. It was six-thirty and the bellman was right on time.

Carmen was taking the redeye from John Wayne airport to LaGuardia. Earlier in the day, he'd asked the concierge to arrange a bellman for his luggage and a taxi to take him to the airport. Carmen opened the door and pointed to his bag laying on the bed. Picking it up, the bellman held the door while Carmen took a last look around the room.

Spying the nearly empty bottle on the desk, Carmen glanced at his glass, gulped half of it down and poured the remnants of the bottle into the glass. He dropped the empty bottle into the garbage can where it clanged noisily against the one he'd thrown away that morning.

Chapter Twenty-Nine

"How many shares did we sell today?"

Yuri Pandropov stood at the window of his study and peered through the black night towards the lake beyond. It was ten o'clock and he had been on the phone with Josef off and on all day. He was tired and the fatigue was evident in his voice.

"Just under a million," Josef answered. "At an average price of thirty-three cents a share, we got back about three hundred and twenty-five thousand dollars. Last Friday, we got back just over four hundred thousand."

"Hmm," Yuri quickly did the math. "Not quite three quarters of a million in two days. Not bad. If we can hold this pace, we'll get my money back in a couple of weeks."

"I wouldn't count on that," Joe countered. "We have to be careful or the other investors will get nervous. If they smell a run, the price will drop."

That brought an ironic smile to Yuri's face. A few days earlier and that would have been the intended result. Now he was just trying to get his money out without too much of a loss. The only silver lining was that, whatever amount he got back, it was clean. It has been laundered through the transactions.

"How long do you think it will take to get it all out?" He asked Josef.

"A month. Maybe more."

"We don't have that much time," Yuri responded. "Now that Michael is out of the picture and Carmen is missing, people are going to start wondering what's going on. We need to make it appear as though the company is operating as usual if we have any hope of getting my money back." Yuri anxiously ran his fingers through his hair. The movement was reflected in the dark window and startled him. *'I'm getting to be an old woman.'* He thought. He sat down at his desk and turned his chair away from the window before continuing.

"Did you send some people to Philadelphia to sanitize Michael's house?" He asked his eldest son.

"Yeah. It was pretty clean when they got there. They didn't find much information that linked Michael to you or to PetroChem. Lucky for us, he conducted most of his business from here." Josef was calling from New York. He had driven back to the city earlier in the day after the aborted weekend party. Stoli and Helen had left early Saturday morning and were obviously not speaking to each other or their hosts. Not surprisingly, the festive atmosphere deflated with their departure.

Lindsay spent most of Saturday and Sunday mad at John and crying in her room. Elena hit the booze and hadn't come out of her room since Friday night. Sam went back to Cleveland on Sunday and Josef left for New York Monday.

With his family scattered, distraught or drunk, Yuri retreated to his office where he set about cleaning up the mess Michael had thrown at his feet. The most important task was to recover the ten million dollars he had invested in PetroChem. Josef had been selling shares since the market opened on Friday morning. It was a tedious process. It had taken many weeks for Josef and Michael to purchase the shares through the network of individual and corporate investors they had created. Now Josef had to reverse the process. He had to be very careful to sell fairly small blocks of shares. If he tried to sell too many shares at any one time, he ran the risk of spooking the market. What they needed was the perception that PetroChem was stable and operating normally. That was difficult, if not impossible without Carmen Risotti or Doug Reardon.

"Have you heard anything from Carmen?" Josef asked his father.

"No," Yuri answered.

"Are you going to call him?

"Not yet. I want to see if this ploy of Jack Stalich and Doug Reardon works. If they don't hear from him in the next couple of days, it's likely he was involved in the plan to kill Reardon."

"And if that turns out to be true…?" Josef asked.

"Don't ask questions when you already know the answer," Yuri flatly reproved his son. "Let's hope he's still on our side. We need him to keep the lid on this mess until we cash out. Anyway," Yuri continued. "If he is part of that idiotic plan to eliminate Reardon, I have another idea of how we can flush him out without me getting directly involved."

"How?"

"I'll let you know if it works."

Chapter Thirty

Helen Stalich dried the last plate from dinner and reached into the cupboard to put it away. She happened to glance out the window over the kitchen sink and saw the black SUV pull up to the curb. It sat and idled for a few moments before the driver got out to open the rear door. Yuri Pandropov stepped down and crushed his cigarette under his heel before walking briskly through the chilly evening to cross South Evaline street and onto the porch. He was carrying a very large bouquet of flowers.

Helen quickly took off her apron and smoothed her hair with her hands. She called to Stoli on her way to the front door and stopped for a moment to check herself in the hallway mirror. Her anger from the events of the weekend, which had just begun to subside, was reignited by this unannounced visit.

She was at the door of the row house and pulled it open before Yuri had a chance to ring the bell. Helen had thought of many things she wanted to say to Yuri for cavorting with her husband in Pittsburgh when they should have been in Erie. In her mind's eye, she reduced him to a limp pile of remorsefulness with her well placed and pointed verbal assault. All those thoughts vanished when she opened the door onto a mass of roses, lilies and chrysanthemums.

"Helen," Yuri's muted voice came from behind the floral display. "I'm here to apologize for taking your husband away from you the other night.

I should have know better. I should have left my old customs back in Russia."

Helen reached out and took the bouquet with both hands and lowered it so she could see Yuri. She almost laughed; he looked so contrite.

"You should be sorry," She began. "Last weekend was for our children and their child to come. It was not for you and Jack to act like children." She had to get in at least one shot before stepping back to allow him to enter. "Come in. You're letting in the cold. I'll get Jack for you."

Yuri wondered if she really saw through his ploy that easily. He figured he'd better play it out. "No. Really, I am here to apologize to you," He said. "I suppose I hope my apology also helps Jack get out of the trouble I caused. He wanted to come right back home but Josef and I coerced him into have a drink… or two… or three."

This time, Helen did laugh. "Come in, Yuri, and take off your coat. I don't believe you for a second but I appreciate the flowers. I'll go put them in water." She walked out of the room and passed Stoli in the hall on the way to the kitchen. "Your drinking buddy is here," She said snidely but with enough of a smile in her voice that Stoli knew the storm had passed.

"Thanks for the flowers," Stoli said to Yuri when he walked into the small living room. Helen and Stoli lived in a row house on Pittsburgh's near north side. It was actually two row houses put together. Stoli had purchased and remodeled the two spaces into one comfortable home.

"I didn't bring the flowers for you," Yuri objected. "They are for Helen."

"Trust me," Stoli replied. "If they make her happy, I get the benefit. You know what they say about mommas and happiness."

Yuri chuckled. "Yes. That expression is universal."

Helen came back into the room carrying a small tray with coffee cups, cream and sugar. "I put on a pot of coffee. It shouldn't be long." Turning to Yuri: "So how is Lindsey? She seemed pretty upset the other day."

They talked for fifteen minutes about Lindsey and John and another half hour on sundry small talk. In between, Helen got up to bring the coffee and some store bought cookies from the pantry. When she was out of the room, Yuri shot Stoli a furtive glance that let him know this was not purely a social visit. Yuri finished his coffee and, looking at his watch, refused a refill.

"Thank you, no, Helen," He stood. "I don't want to take any more of your evening. I just came to apologize and make peace. Did it work?

"Yes," Helen laughed. "Just don't do it again!"

"I promise," Yuri smiled down on her. "Now good night."

"I'll walk you to your car," Stoli offered and went to the hall closet for a jacket. Putting it on, he held the door before following Yuri out. As soon as he closed the door, Yuri was all business.

"I dealt with Michael Cole. He won't bother you - or anyone else - again," Yuri reached out and put his hand on Stoli's shoulder. "You and Doug Reardon have nothing to fear from me, either. Just as I have nothing to fear from you."

They had walked down off the porch and were nearing Yuri's vehicle."Aren't you forgetting the letters?" Stoli asked, referring to the letters he'd given his brother.

"Not for an instant," Yuri replied. "But you aren't going to need them. In fact, you might want to get them back."

"Why would I want to do that?" Stoli asked.

Yuri took his hand from Stoli's shoulder and put it in the warmth of his coat pocket before answering.

"You know I'm a retired Russian military officer, don't you?"

Stoli nodded his head.

"Here's a bit of history for you," Yuri continued. "Back during the cold war, the United States and the Soviet Union both had enough nuclear weapons to completely eradicate each other. The fear of that happening kept the peace for several decades. Do you know what they called this insanity?

Stoli shook his head.

"Mutual Assured Destruction. MAD, for short," Yuri chuckled. "I never knew if the acronym was an accident or on purpose.

Stoli wasn't smiling. "I know what weapon I have pointing at you. What gun do you have to my head?"

"Several, actually." Yuri answered, "You have killed a man and didn't report it. That's at least obstruction of justice. Maybe manslaughter. Secondly, you didn't want to report it for the same reason you are in no danger from me. Neither one of us want to shit on our kids' futures. Finally, and most important," Yuri brought his face close to Stoli's, his black eyes oozing malevolence. "I obviously know where you live. If you fuck me, no one you know will be safe."

If Yuri expected Stoli to cower from the threat, he was disappointed. Stoli stood his ground and returned Yuri's withering stare. Slowly, a wry smile formed at the corners of his mouth. This took Yuri by surprise.

"You find this amusing?"

"The threat? No." Stoli replied. I was just thinking of a joke."

"A joke!" Yuri was abashed. "What joke?"

"A guy goes to see his dentist. As he sits down in the chair he reaches over and grabs the dentist by the balls and says, 'We're not going to hurt each other, are we?'"

This time it was Yuri's turn to smile. "I like your analogy better. So? Are we going to hurt each other?"

"No," Stoli replied. "But I still think I'll keep my letters as a deterrent."

"Now you sound like a politician. Very well, détente it is. Since we have established diplomatic relations, there is something else we need to discuss.

"What?"

"Michael told me that Carmen Risotti had nothing to do with killing your friend or the attempt on Reardon."

"I guess that's good," Stoli grunted.

"It would be if I can confirm that it's true. I keep thinking of Reardon's refusal to be fired and how he said Carmen would have to respond to that. Do you know if Carmen contacted Doug yet?"

"No. I haven't talked to Doug since that night. I don't know where he is and I don't want to know. I can't be forced to tell you something I don't know."

"Please see if you can find Reardon and ask him to get in touch with Carmen. I never had any direct contact with him. Michael was my connection to PetroChem. If Carmen was involved in the plan to kill Reardon, I can't have anything that could tie me to him. It's ironic, but it seems your friend is the only person that can contact Carmen without raising suspicion."

"You want me to find Doug and ask him to find Carmen for you?" Stoli asked.

"Yes. If Carmen helped Michael plan the killing, I need to deal with it and move on."

Stoli cringed inwardly at the cold and calculating manner with which Yuri dealt with murder. He made it seem like a simple business decision. Just another obstacle to overcome or a competitor to outmaneuver.

"If he wasn't involved," Yuri continued. "I need to get him and Reardon back to work as soon as possible. I told you that I have a large amount of money invested in PetroChem. Right now, the only thing standing between the company and collapse is Doug Reardon and Carmen Risotti. It might survive without Risotti but wouldn't without Reardon. I need to get this resolved now."

"What if Risotti was involved in trying to kill Doug?" Stoli couldn't leave the question unasked.

"Do you really want me to answer that?" Yuri lit a cigarette and stepped into the SUV.

Chapter Thirty-One

Doug turned the collar of his overcoat up against the driving rain as he stood between Lud's two sons and watched the undertaker swing open the door of the hearse. Pelting rain spattered the mahogany casket as the first two pallbearers pulled it across the rollers to be passed down the line. When all six bore their share of the load, they began the slow walk through the wet grass to the gravesite. Because of the unseasonably raw weather, a green canopy had been erected to cover the bier and two rows of folding chairs.

There were several dozen people lining the path to the grave. Most of them held aloft umbrellas and tried, as best they could, to shelter the passing casket and attendants. All the same, the pallbearers were soaked through by the time they set the casket on the bier. Lois's two sons took their seats on either side of their mother. Their wives sat next to them and they all held hands as they huddled together. Doug took a seat at the end of the second row of chairs. He sat alone.

The graveside service was mercifully short compared to the funeral liturgy at St. Patrick's. The sanctuary, one of the largest Catholic churches on Cleveland's near west side, had been filled to capacity. Several hundred people had gathered out of respect for Lud. The ripples of his life obviously extended far and wide. Lois had asked Doug to share the pew with the family and he did so reluctantly and remorsefully.

Through the service, the eulogies and condolences, Doug couldn't elude the thought that, were it not for him, none of this would be happening. Though a victim himself, Doug felt he had contributed directly to Lud's death. Each kind word of support for the family or remark on Lud's exemplary life hit Doug as an accusatory stab. It was a relief when the service ended and he retreated to his car for the drive to the cemetery.

Alone for the short trip, Doug's thoughts returned, as they so often did over the past week, to the events that led up to Lud's death and the attempt on his own life. Those thoughts always led back to Michael Cole and Carmen Risotti and left him with a burning desire for revenge. Once or twice, he'd tried to convince himself that he just wanted justice for his friend. Then he'd recall the gross injustices that Risotti and his crew visited upon everything and everyone they touched. In those moments, and when he was completely honest with himself, he knew his thirst was for vengeance

There was no question in Doug's mind that the two had conspired to kill him. Michael's guilt was obvious by his actions. Carmen's complicity had been proved by his inaction. Having received no response to his refusal to be fired, Doug was convinced that Carmen was a co-conspirator. What was troubling was that he didn't know why. He'd run through the sequence of events and jumbled facts through his troubled mind endlessly since the night he'd driven out of Keystate's parking lot.

That night, after they left the plant, Steve had followed him to the apartment and waited while Doug gathered a few personal belongings. They drove to Stoli's house where Doug stuffed his possessions into plastic garbage bags and stuck them in a cupboard in the garage. He'd left the keys to Stoli's truck in the visor before climbing into the cab of Steve's Chevy Silverado for the short drive to his house. Steve showed Doug to the room that once belonged to his dead son. There were several dusty trophies and medals from high school wrestling and a few faded photographs of a pretty blonde girl.

"That was Jackie's girl friend," Steve said when he caught Doug eyeing the photos. "I haven't seen her since the funeral. She was a sweet thing. I wonder what happened to her?" He shook his head. "Anyway, there's towels in the bathroom if you want to take a shower. Looks like you could use one. I'll get you some ice for that eye." Steve went in the direction of the kitchen to get the ice. When he came back to the bedroom, Doug was already asleep across the bed.

They'd gotten up before dawn the following morning and literally headed for the hills. The Stalich brothers owned a hunting cabin on a heavily wooded patch of Chestnut Ridge just east of Latrobe. It was really more of a shack than a cabin. There was no electricity or indoor plumbing. It did have a clean well and a hand pump in what passed for the kitchen. The cabin was obviously a man's world and Doug saw no evidence that a woman had ever stepped foot on the property.

The smell of stale air wafted out when Steve opened the padlock and swung open the creaking door. They opened three small windows and the cross draft quickly aired the place out. Although the late afternoon sun shone brightly, it was cold so Steve lit a fire in the small wood burning stove. The few pieces of wood stacked next to the stove were bone dry and in minutes the fire was crackling and throwing off heat.

On the way to the cabin, they had stopped at the grocery store in Latrobe to picked up enough staples to tide them over the weekend. Steve had to be back at work on Monday morning and Doug was planning on being in Cleveland for Lud's burial. He had no idea what arrangements had been made. Since Lud was Catholic, Doug assumed the funeral would be held Tuesday or Wednesday. He wanted to call Lois to see how she was holding up and get the particulars for the funeral but his cell phone's signal was weak and service was spotty.

Doug borrowed Steve's truck and ran down the mountain to get better cell service and access the internet. He found a McDonald's in the nearby town of Lawson Heights and, after ordering a coffee, sat down to log on. While his laptop was making the connection, Doug called Lois. She was holding up well, all things considered, and told him that the funeral was being planned for the following Wednesday in order for out-of-town family and friends to gather. Doug told Lois that he would be in the area on Monday and would stay for as long as she needed him. She thanked him and asked if he would serve as a pallbearer. Doug said he would be honored and thanked her for asking. They chatted for a couple of minutes more before saying their goodbyes.

By the time Doug had finished talking with Lois, his computer was connected to the internet and he opened his email. He scanned through the incoming emails quickly and didn't see any from Carmen Risotti. There was little else that got Doug's interest. The intra-company traffic was very light. It was early afternoon on Friday and things were ramping down for the weekend. The way things stood at Keystate, there wasn't much going on anyway. There also wasn't anything of note from suppliers or customers. The only email that caught Doug's attention and merited a response was from a man Doug had never met. It was from a stock broker that had been contracted by PetroChem to administer the employee stock option program.

The email informed Doug that he was now vested in the program and could exercise his option to buy up to five hundred thousand shares at a price of four cents per share. The administrator informed Doug that, for a nominal fee, the brokerage firm would advance the money to buy the shares for resale. Shares of PetroChem were currently selling for approximately thirty-five cents a share. It would cost Doug twenty thousand dollars to buy shares that he could turn around and sell for one hundred and seventy-five thousand. Doug would net over one hundred and fifty thousand pre-tax dollars and all he had to do was send a brief email authorizing the transaction.

It took him less than a minute to type the message and hit the send button. He hoped it would be as easy to bury the knowledge of what others had paid providing him the windfall. Doug closed his email and went online to book a rental car. That done, he turned off his computer and headed back up the mountain.

He and Steve spent the ensuing, uneventful weekend at the cabin in the woods. Any other time, it would have been a peaceful and pleasant retreat. As it stood, Doug was tormented by the events of the previous week and frustrated by the fact that, try as he might, he couldn't figure out why Michael, and, most likely, Carmen, wanted him dead.

For the life of him, Doug couldn't fathom the connection between Michael Cole, Alexandar and some man named Yuri. The fact that the man happened to be related to Stoli by marriage was mind boggling. Doug spent the weekend days stiffly walking the trails near the cabin and sleepless nights tossing on a musty cot trying to makes some sense of it all. He couldn't. There just were too many unknowns.

Early Monday morning, Steve drove Doug off the mountain and dropped him at the airport car rental. Doug thanked Steve profusely for the help and shelter. Doug shook Steve's gnarled hand through the open window of his truck, stooped to pick up the small duffle that contained a few clothes and toiletries and walked the short distance to the rental kiosk.

Three hours later, he pulled into the parking lot of a nondescript hotel on the southwest side of Cleveland that catered to traveling businessman. He checked in and rode the malodorous elevator to his home for the next few days at the far end of the third floor hallway. Once inside the room, he bolted the door and called Lois to let her know he was in town.

He spent the next three days shuttling between the hotel, Lois' house, the funeral home and the church.

Although he was in his home town, he made no effort to contact his own family. Doug had every reason to believe he was still in danger and didn't intend to put his family in harm's way. Doug checked his email several times a day and found nothing from Carmen. Same with the voicemail on his cell and office phone. He'd made several calls to various employees at Keystate and subtly asked whether Carmen or Michael had been seen in the plant. No one could remember seeing Carmen for weeks and Michael was last seen the previous Thursday.

A couple of people asked Doug if Stoli was with him. Apparently, the lead blender had not shown up for work. Doug knew why Stoli was missing work but didn't know where he was. He sorely wished he did. He hadn't heard from Stoli since they'd parted company at Keystate. Doug vacillated between anger at Stoli for not calling and fear that he couldn't.

Those two emotions - anger and fear - had been his constant companions. Now, as he sat by Lud's gravesite, he was angry. He was enraged by Lud's needless death and his own unwitting culpability. He was incensed that he was reduced to skulking about his home town constantly looking over his shoulder. The uncertainty was the most infuriating. Doug was a man that excelled at solving problems and coaxing clarity out of chaos. It was maddening that this time he couldn't.

Lost in thought, he sat and stared at the rain drenched and flower laden casket as the gathering of mourners thinned out around him. He didn't notice he was alone until two gravediggers came sauntering in from the rain. They waited quietly until Doug stood and walked the few steps to the bier.

"Goodbye, old friend." He said simply and turned away. He walked around the rows of chairs and had to duck under the edge of the canopy. It was still raining so he pulled up his collar and stooped his shoulders to partially cover his head. He didn't see the third worker and had to awkwardly sidestep to avoid walking into him. The man reached out and grabbed his arm.

******* ******* ******* *******

"Doug." Stoli stood in the rain with water dripping from the bill of his yellow Steeler's cap and onto the front of the black and yellow parka. "I figured you'd be here. Come on, we need to talk."

Stoli led the way down a row of headstones and through a clump of trees to where he'd parked his truck. He climbed in and started the truck while Doug walked around to the passenger side. Stoli handed him a damp towel as he climbed into the cab and pulled the door shut. Now that Doug knew Stoli was safe, he was glad to be angry.

"Where have you been? I thought you were going to call?"

"Sorry. I didn't want to use a phone," Stoli answered. "I knew you'd be here so I waited a couple of days. Besides, I wasn't done talking with Yuri."

"You talked to Yuri more than once?"

"Yeah. You know about the first time. He claimed he didn't know anything about what Cole was doing."

"So he knows Cole?"

"Cole was running Yuri's investments. Yuri says he has money invested in PetroChem. A lot of money. He said millions."

"What about Carmen? Does he think Carmen is in on this?"

"He's not sure," Stoli answered. "He said that Cole told him Risotti wasn't involved. I don't think Yuri believed him. In fact, that's why I'm here. Have you heard anything from Risotti?"

"No, and I'm convinced he's involved." Doug thought for a minute. "If Michael and Carmen were plotting to kill me and we don't know why, I guess I'm still in danger."

"Not from Cole," Stoli said knowingly

"What do you mean?"

"Yuri said he took care of him. He said that Michael won't bother us - or anyone - else again. I took that to mean he's dead."

Doug felt simultaneously glad, stunned, vindicated and appalled. "Yuri could do that?" He stammered. "He told you that he had Michael killed?"

"He didn't say that and I didn't ask. It's enough that we don't have to worry about him anymore."

"I guess," Doug said. "But that still leaves Carmen and we still don't know why they wanted to kill me."

"Neither does Yuri. And that's why we talked the second time. He's asking for your help."

"Me? What does Yuri want me to do?" Doug asked skeptically.

"He wants you to contact Risotti and set up a meeting with him."

"Does he want to kill him?" Doug surprised himself by asking the question. He was even more surprised that he wasn't repulsed by the thought.

"No. Yuri just wants to find out if Risotti was part of the plan to kill you. He actually hopes not. He said he needs you and Risotti to keep the company going and protect his money."

"I don't give a damn about his money," Doug was churlish. "If Yuri is so concerned, why doesn't he call Carmen himself?

"Yuri doesn't have any direct contact with Carmen. He ran everything through Cole. I don't know - and I don't want to know - the particulars, but, Yuri is into illegal shit up to his eyeballs. He won't risk coming out in the open. I've thought about it and Yuri is right. You're the only one that can contact Risotti without him getting suspicious. If he is involved, and you play your cards right, you might find out why this is happening."

Doug thought about that. If Carmen was innocent - which Doug highly doubted - there might be some salvation for the company. If Carmen was plotting to have him killed, Doug wanted to know why.

"All right. I'll do it. What if I find out Carmen was trying to kill me? What will Yuri do then?"

"Do I really need to answer that?" Stoli echoed Yuri's earlier answer to the same question.

Chapter Thirty-Two

Gary Kreisler sat in his delivery van at the corner of East 31st Street and Lexington. His windshield wipers were off for the moment. They'd been on and off - mostly on - all day as rain continued to pelt the city. New York, and the rest of the New England coastline, had been pummeled by a nor'easter for two days. The weather system was starting to slide east but bands of rain continued to harass the region. As a result, Gary was running late.

He'd been a currier for the past five years. He'd been a cabbie until the day he'd decided he'd had his fill of people. Nowadays, he drove silent parcels and envelopes in the back of his navy blue van. He still had to deal with the occasional customer shrieking that a package had to get across town *NOW!* Usually, he'd been able to accommodate even the most strident demands. Today, however, he was going to be late.

The lousy weather snarled traffic and was causing delays all across Manhattan. It was just after eight and he had two more deliveries to make. One around the corner on 31st Street and the last up on 61st Street. With any luck, he be able to make the deliveries and get home in time to watch the Giants play the Cowboys on Monday Night Football. The light changed and he made the turn onto 31st.

****** ****** ****** ******

Carmen Risotti sat at his usual table anxiously swirling the ice in what was left of his second scotch. Pepe, taking this as a summons for a third, approached with a questioning look. Carmen gave him a slight nod and Pepe diverted to the bar.

It was an unusually slow night at Campo di Bocce - even for a Monday. Carmen glanced at his watch. It was five after eight. Only three minutes later than the last time he looked. Doug was more than a half hour late. Any other time and Carmen would not have waited. He also would have been incensed at being kept waiting by a subordinate. This was not, however, a normal meeting. This was to be dinner with a dead man - or at least a man that should be dead.

Carmen had been in the city since arriving from California the previous Wednesday. He'd spent most of that time holed up in his apartment searching the internet for any sign of Doug's demise. There had been nothing. He considered calling Sean and the Rosens again to question whether they had heard from Michael or Doug but decided against it for fear of rousing suspicion. He hadn't discussed his intention to fire Doug with the other three PetroChem directors. He certainly didn't want them to suspect that killing Doug was part of the plan to drive down the company's share price.

The price continued to stay in the mid-thirty cent range amid heavy trading. To an casual observer, everything about PetroChem appeared to be normal. Carmen knew that the situation was not at all as it appeared. What was maddening was that he had no idea what the situation was.

Until his phone rang on Saturday morning.

"Hello, Carmen," It was Doug. "Surprised to hear from me?"

"Yes… um… no," Carmen stammered before regaining his footing. "You told me you were going to spend the week attending to Lud's funeral. I figured you'd call me when that was over. How'd it go?"

"It was a funeral," Doug replied. "Why didn't you respond to my email?"

"What email?" Carmen tried to act ignorant.

"Let's not play games, Carmen," Doug was terse. "The situation has changed over the past few days and I'm tired of being jerked around. You and Michael tried to fire me. That's not going to happen."

Carmen's flash of anger was tempered by Doug's defiant tone. "Where do you get off talking to me like that!?" He asked. "I can fire anyone I want anytime I want. You've given me plenty of cause."

"I suppose you have a legal opinion on that?" Doug baited. "Did you get that from Michael? As I understand it, he's not in a position to offer advice these days."

Carmen felt the first icy pricks of fear in his gut. Doug obviously knew more than Carmen about what had transpired the previous week. "I haven't talked with Michael since I left for California last week," He said.

"Then you might not know that he's been terminated."

"What!" Carmen exclaimed. "What are you talking about. I'm the only person that could fire him and I sure as hell didn't!"

"I didn't say Michael was fired," Doug replied. "I said he was terminated. It appears you have a major shareholder that has the ability to eliminate members of your board. I understand that he is very concerned with some aspects of your recent management style. He's also concerned about the long term health of the company"

Carmen blanched and almost dropped his cell phone. His breathing became laborious and his knees weak as fear consumed him. He suddenly felt very unhealthy as he remembered Yuri's words of admonition against betrayal. He looked at the phone in his hand as Doug's voice emitted from the device, tinny and faint. "Carmen? Are you there?"

"Yeah. I'm here," Carmen responded as he put the phone to his ear and dropped into the Barcelona chair. "What do you want?"

"A meeting."

"What?" Carmen was surprised.

"It seems that, although the shareholder didn't care for Michael's tactics, he likes you. I can't say I agree with him. Still, he believes it is in his best interest if you and I continue to work together. I will be in New York on Monday. We need to meet."

"Of course." A wave of reprieve swept through Carmen. "I have just the place. It's called Campo di Bocce. Say six-thirty?"

"No," Doug replied. "I'll see you there at seven-thirty." Doug disconnected the call without saying goodbye.

Carmen spent the ensuing weekend trying to glean how Yuri and Doug had connected. Obviously, Michael's plot to kill Doug had gone awry. Undoubtedly, Carmen's plan to launder Yuri's drug money had also unraveled. That made him question why he wasn't already dead. Whatever the reason, it was apparent that Doug Reardon would be the messenger. Consumed by worry and doubt, Carmen drank more and slept less than usual.

By Monday evening, Carmen was a wreck and was already slightly drunk as he sat at his table in Campo di Bocce. The fatigue from sleepless nights showed on his face. He looked at his watch again. It was eight fifteen and he was halfway through the third scotch. Pepe was hovering nearby and Carmen was about to signal for the chit when he saw Doug enter the restaurant.

The maître de took Doug's wet trench coat and pointed him to Carmen's table. Doug ran his fingers through his wet hair as made his way across the restaurant. Neither man attempted the gesture of a handshake as he sat down.

"Did you get lost?" Carmen grumbled and pointedly looked at his watch.

"I took a cab from the airport," Doug replied. "The traffic was bad because of the weather. Sorry you had to wait."

Doug wasn't at all sorry. In fact he'd been in Manhattan all day and he'd spent the past hour in a coffee shop around the corner on 2nd Avenue.

Doug had intended to arrive significantly late and for Carmen to spend time alone in the restaurant. More to the point, he wanted Carmen to be alone with his booze.

Doug was on a crusade to discover the truth and he'd recruited scotch as his ally. As he sat and looked across the table, he could see that the normally impenetrable black eyes were fuzzy and lacked focus. Pepe sidled up to the table and Doug, taking the opportunity to call in reinforcements, ordered a scotch on the rocks. Pepe looked to Carmen and, with a slight nod, another round was added to Doug's arsenal.

Doug glanced around the room as he reached for the menu. Coming full circle, his eyes came to rest on the photographs on the wall. They were the same pictures Michael had seen a couple of years earlier and they elicited a similar response from Doug.

"I take it you're a regular?" He pointed to the photograph over Carmen's right shoulder.

"Yeah. I've been coming here for years. It's convenient and the food's good," Carmen craned around to look at the picture. It had been taken years before and his ex-wife was in the picture. It was New Year's Eve and, other that the party hats, they wore formal attire. They were in a crowd and everybody was laughing. It had been some time since Carmen had taken the time to really look at the picture. As he did now, he was struck by how happy he looked. And young. And about seventy-five pounds lighter. The man in the photograph bore little resemblance to the reflection he'd seen in the mirror lately.

The difference wasn't lost on Doug, either. The Carmen sitting across from him now was disheveled in his wrinkled blue blazer and khaki pants. It looked like he hadn't shaved for a couple of days or slept for a good deal longer. The polo shirt he wore under his jacket looked to be two sizes too small with a frayed collar and stains where food had dropped on Carmen's ample belly.

"What's good?" Doug's casual reference to the menu broke Carmen's reverie.

"Huh? ... Oh," Carmen drifted back. "Anything with veal in it. I always go for the saltimbocca. The calamari is good for an appetizer."

Doug closed his menu and put it on the table just as Pepe returned with the drinks. Carmen finished the one he was drinking before swapping the empty glass for the fresh one in Pepe's hand. He immediately took a pull on the drink before setting it on the table. Pepe placed Doug's drink on the table where it remained untouched while Doug ordered. Ignoring Carmen's recommendation, he ordered a salad, eggplant parmesan and a glass of Chianti. Carmen also ordered a glass of wine to accompany the calamari and veal.

Their meals ordered, the two men sat in a stilted silence for several minutes. Carmen nervously toyed with his silverware and sipped his drink while Doug sat quietly. Carmen was unaccustomed to this type of situation. Heretofore, he had been the one in charge. The one with all the information. The one with the upper hand. Now, his ignorance and confusion - exacerbated by exhaustion and alcohol - left him somewhat befuddled and tense. Finally, he broke the silence.

"I gotta tell you, Doug," Carmen's speech was slightly slurred. "I'm surprised a Boy Scout like you is involved with a guy like Yuri Pandropov."

"I've never met the man," Doug ignored Carmen's derogatory tone.

"Now who's playing games?" Carmen snorted. "If Yuri wants you and me to play nice, we'd better learn to get along. You can start by not trying to bullshit me. Yuri is the only person that could - and would - get rid of Michael. Don't try to tell me that you don't know him or that he's not behind this."

"I didn't say that," Doug answered coolly. "I said I never met him."

Carmen wasn't yet so drunk that he missed Doug's verbal sparring. He smiled briefly and raised his glass in recognition before speaking.

"I'm not surprised. I haven't seen him myself in a couple years. Michael was always the intermediary." Carmen thought for a second. "Now that he's dead, who are you getting your orders from? Joe?"

"I don't know Joe and I didn't say Michael was dead," Doug continued to flirt around the edges of the truth. "I was told that he was terminated and won't be bothering me anymore."

"If it's not Joe or Michael - and you can be assured Michael's dead - who's the go-between?."

"That I won't tell you," Doug answered. He smiled grimly. "You wouldn't believe me if I did."

"I guess it doesn't matter who the messenger boy is," Carmen grunted. "He's just doing what he's told, anyway. Same as you and me." He paused to take another drink. "So, just what is it that Yuri wants us to do?"

"He wants us to work together to save the company and protect his investment."

Carmen let out a derisive guffaw. "You really think he wants to save the company?"

"Of course. How else can he protect the money he invested."

"You really are a fucking choir boy!" Carmen shook his head and chortled maliciously. "Yuri doesn't give a shit about PetroChem or your precious Keystate. The only reason he invested in the first place is because I set it up for him to launder money. The company's a loser. That's why I picked it. Now, he probably wants to keep it propped up until he gets his money out. PetroChem is finished." Carmen abruptly stopped laughing. "So are you and I. As soon as Yuri gets what he wants, we're dead men.

"You created PetroChem to lose money?" Doug was confused. "Why would Yuri deliberately want to lose money? As I understand it, he's invested millions."

"Where do you think he got those millions... and many millions more? What do you think Yuri Pandropov is?" Carmen answered bitterly. His eyes stared into a faraway place as he thought of all that money drifting out of his reach.

"I heard he's a distributor of farm equip..."

"Jesus Christ, Reardon!" Carmen hissed as he interrupted and leaned over the table. "What legitimate businessman keeps Russian assassins on the payroll?"

Pepe returned to the table just then with the wine and appetizers. Carmen and Doug sat back in their chairs and said nothing for the awkward minute it took Pepe to place the food and drinks on the table. The silent moment gave Doug the opportunity to analyze Carmen's comments.

He's starting to slip. Doug thought. '*He forgot that I wouldn't know about Alexandar except for the fact that he tried to kill me.*'

He looked across the table. Carmen continued to nurse his drink.

'*That's right, you worthless piece of shit! Drink up. Let's see if we can get some more truth out of that lying mouth of yours*'.

"I don't understand," Doug baited aloud.

Carmen sat his drink on the table and slouched over his plate. He looked pensive and tired and beat down. He took another sip of his scotch and, replacing the glass on the table, looked sideways at Doug from under his massive eyebrows.

"You might as well know why you'll soon be dead," He slurred. "Yuri Pandropov is one of the biggest drug dealers in the country. Heroin. I set up PetroChem as a scam to launder his drug money. He bought a bunch of stock when the price topped out. We were going to drive the price down so all that stock would be worthless. Then," Carmen waved his hand in a limp flourish. "We would drive the price back up and, voila, he would have a bunch of stock he could sell for nice, clean cash. Dirty money in and clean money out. It was beautiful and it was working."

Carmen picked up his drink and finished it with a gulp. Pepe, watching from a distance, started toward the table. Carmen saw him coming and, with a bobbling nod of his head, sent the waiter to the bar for another. Doug had barely touched his drink and the wine not at all. He picked up his fork and started working on the salad. Carmen eschewed flatware in favor of his fingers as he made short work of the calamari.

"You know," Carmen continued. "I really have to thank you for helping me."

"Me?" Doug was piqued. "I had no part I this."

"Not on purpose, to be sure," Carmen answered. "But you played a big role in driving up the share price. I just had to tell investors what a big, shining star you are. After you showed them what was going on at your fucking plant, they bid up the share price. It was almost too easy."

Doug felt sullied. All his well intentioned efforts to create and run a successful business had been part of a criminal plan to launder drug money. He'd been played for a fool and he felt the part. All along, he'd thought Risotti and his cohorts were incompetent or, at worst, shiftless businessmen. He was dismayed and disgusted to learn how naïve he was.

"What about your board?" He asked. "Were they in on it?"

"Michael was, of course," Carmen answered. "The others were all in favor of driving up the share price but they didn't know anything about the rest of the plan or Yuri. Lucky them," He finished with a shrug.

Doug picked up his drink and took a large swallow. He didn't like what he was hearing but, at least the pieces were starting to come together. He cringed as he thought of the times he guided potential investors through the plant to show them improvements and introduce the employees. Although he hated the association with Michael and the Rosens, he'd taken pride in what the people of Keystate had accomplished in such a short time and with limited support. He now understood why Carmen was so niggardly about spending money for the project. It was never intended to succeed.

Doug had always anticipated the company would fail because of the incompetence of the board. It was disgusting to learn that Keystate's demise had been planned. It was sickening to discover that he'd abetted the scheme. At least insofar as driving the stock price up.

Then it hit him.

In a flash he understood why they killed Lud and tried to kill him.

If his leadership of the company had played a big part in the price run up, his death would surely have the opposite effect. Concerned investors would have sold their shares and the price would inevitably drop. Doug realized that he was the ultimate patsy. Carmen had used him to drive the price up and he was willing to kill him to drive the price down.

Sitting across the table from him now, Doug was filled with such hatred and loathing that, for the first time in his life, he knew he could kill. He might have taken the salad fork he gripped in his right hand and thrust it into the fleshy jowls of Carmen's neck had not Pepe arrived with the food. Doug relaxed his grip and the fork dropped to the table.

Again, an uncomfortable silence descended while the appetizer dishes were removed and replaced by the entrees. Carmen dove into his food and in a matter of seconds, the sauce from the saltimbocca blended with the leftover grease from the calamari on his stubbly beard. He was seemingly oblivious to Doug who sat, his food untouched, staring with malevolent disgust at the porcine display.

"So it was all about the money?" He growled through gritted teeth. "All the hard work and effort was just so you could launder Yuri's drug money? You never cared about the business or the people. Especially the people! You're willing to fuck up the lives of hundreds of people and their families to clean up drug money?"

"It's always about the money," Carmen took his napkin and sloppily wiped his chin before taking a sip of his latest scotch. "Don't be so self righteous. You've made a good chunk of money from the deal yourself. I saw how much you made exercising your options. What are you going to do? Give the money to all the wives and kiddies of the employees? Give me a break." He was derisively sarcastic.

"At least I didn't kill anybody." There was no masking the hatred in Doug's voice. "Couldn't you have just fired me?"

Carmen's face drained of expression. He made a feeble attempt to look Doug in the eye but was unable to hold Doug's withering stare. The once impenetrable black eyes were now just empty, black holes.

"I see you've figured it out," Carmen blankly stared at his plate. "Nobody was supposed to die. I only gave Michael instruction to fire you. Nobody was supposed to die." He repeated. "Michael went off on his own. He must have really hated your guts. I knew we were fucked the minute he told me what happened to Lud."

"He told you about Lud?" Doug saw the final piece click into place. "When?"

"The day after it happened. Right after you called to tell me about it." Carmen continued to stare at his half-eaten food. "He told me about recruiting Yuri's guy to kill you and that they killed Lud by mistake." He looked up at Doug. "I swear I didn't know about it. Michael was just suppose to fire you."

"But you knew about it before they came back a second time," Doug said accusingly. "That night, they came back to try again. Why didn't you call them off?

"And let Yuri know what Michael had done?" Carmen asked indignantly. "I might as well have put a gun in my own mouth."

"I wish you had," Doug pushed his chair back and stood over the table.

"Where are you going?" Carmen looked up.

"You and I are finished," Doug answered.

"What about Yuri? You said he wants us to work together. It's not a good idea to cross him."

"That's your problem. He already knows everything and he's not happy. I just came here to hear it from you. I'm not worried about Yuri, As far as I'm concerned, he can go fuck himself."

"You don't know what you're saying. We have to stick together. You can't go against a guy like Yuri Pandropov. You won't last a day."

"I already have," Doug answered. "Given all that's happened, why do you think he hasn't he killed me before now?"

"I don't know," Carmen was too besotted to try to figure it out. "You have a fucking guardian angel or something?"

"Yeah," Doug smiled mirthlessly. "Something like that. Good-bye, Carmen"

Doug turned on his heel and headed for the door. He waited with his back to Carmen while the maître de brought his coat. He put it on and slowly turned back for a last glance across the restaurant where Carmen sat under the festive photograph. Doug touched two fingers to his forehead in a mock salute before opening the door and stepping into the darkness.

Chapter Thirty-Three

Carmen sat at his favorite table in his favorite restaurant with his favorite meal half-eaten before him. He stared across the room to the closed door that just shut him off from his favorite city. Carmen suddenly felt very alone and vulnerable. He knew he was in mortal danger.

Before Doug called the previous Saturday, he'd held to the slim hope that Michael had somehow managed to pull off the murder. Then, when he'd learned that Doug was alive and Michael dead, Carmen figured that he, too, was a dead man. Yuri's edict that Doug and Carmen work together to save PetroChem rekindled the hope that he might yet make it out alive. That hope left with Doug when he walked out the door.

As soon as Yuri learned of the imminent collapse of PetroChem, he would eliminate anything linking him to the company. The fact that he'd also lost millions would add the impetus of retribution. Carmen and Doug wouldn't last a day.

Strangely, Carmen's fear wasn't paralyzing. In an odd twist, the inordinate amount of alcohol he'd consumed neutralized his nascent fear. He wasn't thinking clearly, but he could at least think. Rising from the table, he wove his way toward the door. The maître de met him half way.

"Do you want me to put tonight's dinner on your tab, Mr. Risotti?"

"Yeah, Sal. That would be great. And call me a cab, will you? Doesn't look like a good night for me to walk home." While Carmen shuffled to the men's room, the maître de picked up the phone to call a taxi. By the time Carmen returned from the restroom, the cab was idling at the curb.

"Good night, Sal, old man," He addressed the maître de. "Hope to see you again real soon.

"You, too, Mr. Risotti. Maybe tomorrow?"

"I sure hope so, Sal. I sure hope so."

Carmen stepped out under the small canopy that covered the entrance to Campo di Bocce. Since the canopy didn't extend all the way to the street, he'd have to walk the final few feet in the rain. As he turned up the collar of his jacket, he glanced up and down 61st Street.

Fear surged through him when he saw the dark van parked two storefronts to the left. He stepped back into the shadowed doorway and cautiously peered through the rain. A similar van had picked him up once before. Carmen had no desire to repeat the experience. This time the result would likely be drastically different. He open the door to the restaurant enough to slide his rotund body inside.

*******   *******   *******   *******

Gary Kreisler trotted out the of card shop two doors down from Campo di Bocce and hopped into the sliding door in the side of his van. He'd made his final delivery of the day and headed home to catch the second half of the game.

*******   *******   *******   *******

"Did you forget something, Mr. Risotti?" Sal asked when Carmen slid back into the restaurant. Carmen ignored the question and stumbled through the restaurant, into kitchen and out the back door. The restaurant had a small patio and bar in the rear courtyard that serviced the five outdoor bocce courts. Most evenings, there was a lively crowd playing or watching. The night's inclement weather had washed them out and Carmen was alone as he sloshed across the gravel courts. A small gate at the back of the property led to a narrow alley. Carmen stumbled through the gate and headed down the alley toward Lexington Avenue.

The rain had slowed to a steady drizzle as he turned south on Lexington towards Bloomingdale's department store. A few other pedestrians braved the weather and Carmen joined the small cadre waiting for the light to change at the intersection of 61st Street. When it did, Carmen huddled with the group to cross the street. Halfway across, he look back towards Campo di Bocce to see if the van was still there. It was.

Carmen had to cross Lexington Avenue in order to hail a southbound cab. He didn't know where he would go but knew he couldn't go home. If Yuri had people outside the restaurant, there would surely be another van staking out his apartment.

He walked the block to East 60th Street and caught the light to cross Lexington. It started to rain harder as he stood by the curb to hail a cab. He was looking north up Lexington when he saw the dark van pull out of East 61st Street and make the turn onto Lexington. It would drive right past where Carmen stood. Panicked, he looked for a place to hide. Directly behind him was the entrance to the 59th Street Metro Transit. He half trotted across the sidewalk and clumsily made his way down the steps.

Carmen almost never rode the subway. He'd given it up years before for taxis and limos. He did, however, possess a Metro Card which he swiped through the card reader before pushing through the turnstile and onto the platform. He had to wait only a few minutes before boarding the N Train that whisked him across the East River to Queens.

The train was mostly empty. There was a waitress, still in uniform, on her way home after spending the day serving overpriced sandwiches to chic Manhattanites. Two young men in hooded sweatshirts juked and jived to music only they could hear through ear buds. It was obvious by their mismatched movements that they were listening to different tunes.

The only other passenger was an obvious drunk with watery eyes, tattered clothes and mismatched shoes. Carmen sat across from him. The waitress made a passing note that, at least, Carmen's loafers matched.

Carmen disembarked at Queensboro Plaza and made his way down the stairs of the elevated platform. It was still raining and he was soaked through and shivering. Needing shelter and a place to rest and think, he saw the illuminated sign of the Queen's Burrow Gentlemen's Club less than a block away. The neon sign advertised liquors, wines and women.

Carmen barely rated a glance from the regulars when he entered the darkened bar. He looked like he belonged. His hair was plastered to his head and his clothes were a mess. His face was puffy and flushed from alcohol and the dash out of Manhattan. The scruffy beard and tired, blood shot eyes completed the picture. He was just another sad drunk come to ogle the bouncing, saggy tits of strippers well past their prime.

He sat at the bar and ordered a scotch. He pulled his phone from his pocket and used it to search for a nearby hotel. There was a discount hotel just around the corner and Carmen called to book a room for the night. That done, he turned back to his drink. It was a bottom shelf blend and he had to water it down to get it past his palate. As a result, he had five in rapid succession.

Carmen was as drunk as he'd ever been without passing out; a fact that was not lost on the barkeep or the man that sat three stools down. Sporting a pony tail and myriad tattoos, he started paying rapt attention when Carmen produced a large roll of bills from his pocket and stripped off two fifties for the drinks.

After the sixth drink, the bartender shut Carmen off. It was only a few minutes past ten and the bar would be open for another few hours but the experienced barman knew brewing trouble when he saw it. Besides, Carmen hadn't paid any attention to the girls; it didn't seem likely that they'd see any of Carmen's cash stuffed in their garters no matter how hard they bumped or ground. Carmen finished his last drink and stumbled for the door. A minute later, the tattooed man followed.

The mugging took place in an alley off 42nd. It was mercifully short but not painless. The tattooed man came up from behind and shoved Carmen into the alley and against a brick wall. The impact of his head bouncing off the wall would probably have been enough to render Carmen complaisant but his assailant added two quick blows to his diaphragm and one to the left side of his face. Carmen crumpled in a heap.

The thug rifled his pockets with ease and made off with Carmen's roll of cash, credit cards, watch, phone and identification. For good measure, and just out of meanness, Carmen received a parting kick in the ribs before the miscreant left him lying in the trash.

He lay unmoving for the agonizing seconds it took to regain his breath and then for several minutes more waiting for the pain to subside. When it did, Carmen pushed himself into a sitting position against the brick wall. It was a good thing that he was as drunk as he was. The booze numbed some of the pain.

He struggled to his feet and groped along the wall to the main street where he grabbed a telephone pole for support. He ran his free hand across his pockets in a cursory inventory and was disheartened to feel them empty and flat. The only thing his attacker left him was the Metro Card. Carmen pulled it out of his pocket and stared at it blankly. He knew it had some value but couldn't remember why.

Already numbed by scotch, his mind was further addled when the back of his head slammed against the wall in the alley. Severely bruised, his brain was starting to hemorrhage. The blood-thinning effect of alcohol accelerated the process.

Keeping his hand on the pole, Carmen slowly swung around to get his bearings. As he spun to face west, he looked up into the familiar red glow of the Silvercup Studio sign. A solid reference point, it was also a beacon of hope and he started the painful and slow trek toward the lighted sign.

It took twenty minutes for him to cover the three blocks. He was doubled over from a stabbing pain in his upper abdomen. The parting kick from his assailant had cracked a rib making it excruciating to breathe. His left cheek was swelling and a small smear of drying blood spread from the left corner of his mouth and congealed in the stubble of his beard. His head throbbed and his vision was blurred. The pupil of his right eyed had dilated and the glare from periodic street lights was blindingly painful.

When he finally reached the studio, he was heartened to see a party underway. The small parking lot was full and limousines stretched down both sides of the street. Carmen had attended many similar events during his halcyon days as one of New York's elite. As he approached the entrance now, his addled brain transported him back to that time.

All the guests were already inside and the press and hangers-on had disseminated leaving a clear path for Carmen to hobble up to the gate. Two very large and imposing security men flanked a petite intern holding a clipboard. Carmen knew from experience that the clipboard contained the list of invitees.

"Goo ebening," Was the best he could muster. "I'm Carmen Rishoti."

The intern, having seen more than her share of inebriated guests, dutifully checked her list. "I'm sorry, Mr. Risotti, but your name isn't on the list of invitees this evening."

"I know." Carmen responded. "But I have frenz in the bizniz. They'll wanna see me."

"I'm sure you do," The girl wanted to be kind. "But I can't let you in tonight."

"Shure ya can. Jus' lemme by an it'll be okay."

"Take a hike, buddy." One of the security guards stepped between Carmen and the intern. "If you're not on the list, you're not getting in."

"But I gotta get in. I needa talk ta somebuddy."

The security guard was not of a mind to be kind. He routinely dealt with drunks and people trying to crash events. Carmen was both. He waved to his associate and they advanced on Carmen in unison. Carmen was too heavy for them to lift so they each grabbed an arm and dragged him backwards away from the gate and down 22nd Street toward the bridge that carried car and train traffic between Manhattan and Queens.

As seemingly always the case, the bridge was undergoing repair and the ground underneath was covered with construction debris. A plastic clad, chain link fence had been erected around the site in a futile effort to secure the area and hide the eyesore. The two deputized thugs dragged Carmen through an open gate and roughly dropped him in the shadows amid the rubble.

"If you're smart, you won't come back," One of them said to the prostrate Carmen. As they walked away, he said to his companion, "Fucking drunks! Queens is crawling with 'em. The world would be better off without the worthless pieces of shit."

Carmen heard the man's words but was beyond comprehending what he said. His brain was a stew of hemorrhaged blood and scotch. He could no longer feel pain except the searing heat inside his skull. The rest of his body was numb from the combined effects of alcohol, unrequited synapses and the beginning stages of hypothermia. As he lay dying, he turned his head and, through a gap in the fence, glimpsed a sliver of the Silvercup Studio sign. The last thing he saw before lapsing into unconsciousness was the aura of a glowing red 'DIO' shining down on him.

******* ******* ******* *******

The cop took the glove off his hand before reaching down to feel for a pulse. He knew as soon as he felt the cold skin that the man was dead. In truth, he knew it the second he'd seen the corpulent body. The head was slightly tilted to one side and the eyes half open. One of the pupils was fully dilated although that was hard to discern because both pupils were coal black. The officer gave the body a quick pat down looking for identification. There was nothing. Standing erect, the cop called out to his partner seated in the warmth of the cruiser.

"It's a 10-100. Call in the meat wagon," He shouted to be heard above the noise of the traffic leaving Queens. "Looks like we got another John Doe drunk that didn't make it."

Chapter Thirty-Four

Yuri Pandropov stood by the open window and listened to his grandson's squeals of delight. The baby was eighteen months old and loved to splash in the pool. He particularly loved to be tossed in the air as his father was doing now to the chagrin of disapproving grandmothers. Both Helen and Elena voiced objections and, when Lindsey sided with the matrons, John had to acquiesce. The toddler started to pout until his dad pushed him through the water while making motorboat noises with his lips. That reignited shrieks of laughter.

It was the Friday before Labor Day and Lindsey, John and little Ivan - John Jr. to the Stalich side of his family - were spending the weekend at the house by the lake. John's parents would also be guests as would Lindsey's brothers. Helen was already there. Stoli, as usual, was working and would drive up later that evening. Sam, in his second year of residency, wouldn't arrive until Sunday evening.

Joe had just arrived and, after a cursory exchange of pleasantries with the family by the pool, went directly to Yuri's study. He found his father standing by the window watching the family relax and play. Smiling, Yuri turned from the window and walked slowly to his desk.

Joe sat on the couch adjacent to the desk and took note of his father's pallid complexion and shallow breathing. Especially the breathing. It was only a few steps from the window to the desk but the short distance took Yuri's breath and exacerbated the persistent cough. The light hack, which Yuri had had for several months, recurred every few minutes. He would cough two or three times as if clearing a tickle in his throat. At first, he'd thought that's all it was. Then he'd attributed it to allergies. Now, he considered it a nuisance.

He never considered easing up on his smoking and he lit up as he sat behind his desk. The moratorium against smoking in his study had been lifted once Ivan had been born. Unless, of course, the baby found his way to Yuri's sanctum. That rarely happened. Joe was the only member of the immediate family that regularly entered Yuri's world.

"Why don't you go see a doctor about that cough?" Joe asked. "It's not getting any better."

"It's not getting any worse, either," His father groused. "I'm not going to a doctor. They just look for something wrong with you. It's probably just allergies. I always get them in late summer."

Joe decided not to pursue the subject or to point out the illogic of Yuri's objection to doctors. There was no point in trying to sway a strong-willed character like his father.

"Then at least close the windows," Joe replied. " If you have allergies, there's no point in letting all the pollen and dust into the house. Besides, it's hotter than hell outside and the air conditioning is on. It's costing a you a fortune."

"I like it this way. I like to hear the baby laugh." He coughed lightly as he exhaled a stream of smoke. "Anyway, it's my money. I'll dump it out the window if I choose. But, since you seem to be so interested in my money, what's the latest status on your project."

Joe's *'project'* was the ongoing work to convert Yuri's drug money into legitimate assets. Joe no longer had any part in the heroin side of the business. After the PetroChem debacle, Yuri assigned him complete responsibility for laundering the cash garnered from producing and distributing the white powder.

Initially, Joe chaffed at what he perceived to be a demotion. He considered himself as a leader and man of action - not a pencil pusher or accountant. Eventually, Yuri convinced Joe that real power emanates from those with great wealth not large egos. Yuri put it to Joe that the power to be derived from converting the useless cash to useful assets far exceeded the authority of ordering around a few thugs and drug dealers.

The turning point came when Yuri disclosed the full extent of the family's illegal cash. The Pandropov cartel had accumulated over five hundred million dollars from the heroin trade. Less than twenty-five million dollars of that was considered clean. The rest were illiquid entries on statements from banks scattered around the world. Once Joe recognized that the family's enormous wealth was essentially useless until laundered, he zealously applied himself to the task of converting it into legitimate enterprise.

It started with the frantic effort to recoup the ten million dollar investment in PetroChem. Joe had managed to recover almost six million of the investment before the company went bankrupt. It took a herculean effort, but he'd been able to do that in less than the four months it took for the bank to call the note and take control of the company.

With Joe focused on financial matters, Yuri had reassumed complete control of the heroin trade. His organization was very solid and he had capable - and loyal - lieutenants to run the supply, production and distribution of the product. As titular head of the organization, Yuri was only marginally involved in daily operations. That left more time for him to oversee Joe's work. At least more of the little time Yuri knew he had left.

He knew that the persistent cough and fatigue were not caused by allergies. The effects from a life of heavy smoking had caught up with him. He'd know it for some time and it was, ultimately, the reason he decided to get out of the illegal drug business. His illness wouldn't allow him much more time to benefit from his life of crime but he damn sure would make it possible for the family to do so. That meant putting as much distance as possible between his criminal past and the legitimacy he craved for his posterity. Driven by this ambition, he relentlessly drove Joe to legitimize the proceeds from his life of crime while he worked on shutting down his drug operations.

The effort turned out to be much more difficult and than he anticipated. The pending vacuum of Yuri's abdication led to a bloody war between two of his lieutenants vying to take his place. It was inevitable that Yuri had to pick a side. Several former associates had to die before the matter was settled. Eventually, however, most of his authority and responsibility for the drug business had passed hands and the situation settled enough for Yuri to focus more on Joe and his work.

"How much have you cleaned up so far?" He pressed his son as they sat in his study.

"One hundred and fifty-three million," Joe answered.

"What did it cost us?"

"Twenty-two million," Joe answered.

"So, a little more than fourteen percent. Not bad."

Yuri referred to the amount of money they'd lost running drug money through various investment vehicles. Although the PetroChem scheme hadn't ended as planned, the money they did get out was laundered. The four million they'd lost became known as the laundering fee. Undeniably usurious at forty percent, the transaction proved epiphanic. It set the pattern that Joe had followed to run millions of dollars through the process.

Each subsequent sale of stock was recorded as a legitimate trade. If any particular trade was a loss - and Joe made sure many were - Yuri was able to take the deduction on his taxes. Having used the free market system to make his fortune supplying the demand for heroin, Yuri was now using capitalism to convert his ill-gotten gains into legitimate assets.

'*Not bad for a former soldier of a communist regime.*' He chuckled as he considered the irony.

"I thought you'd also like to know that I sold the last of the PetroChem shares this week," Joe added.

"Really?" Yuri was intrigued. "What did you get for them?"

"A penny a share," Joe laughed sardonically. "And I was lucky to get that. I can't believe there are people out there that think the company will rise from the ashes."

Though bankrupt, PetroChem was still an actively traded penny stock. The price ranged from as low as fractions of a penny to as high as three cents a share. After the bankruptcy, Yuri was stuck with a few million shares. At one time, those shares would have been worth over a million dollars. When Joe finally sold them, they were worth thirty thousand.

"So we're finally finished with PetroChem?" Yuri asked. "What was the final accounting?"

"Adding in the money from the last transaction, we recovered just over six and a quarter million," Joe answered. "The deal cost us three and three quarter million dollars."

"Not really," Yuri reached into the top drawer of his desk and pulled out a single piece of paper that he floated across the desk to Joe. "We actually made a nice profit."

"What's this?" Joe picked up the paper and turned it to read. It contained the names of six banks with respective account numbers. Next to each account were dollar amounts ranging from five hundred thousand to two million dollars.

"Those are the bank accounts that hold the proceeds from the initial issuance of PetroChem stock," Yuri answered. "There's a little more than seven million dollars in total. I had Michael open those accounts. Only he and I knew about it and only I have withdrawal authority. I'll arrange for you to have access. You can add these funds to the rest you have to clean up."

"So, you didn't lose money, after all?"Joe chuckled appreciatively. "You actually netted a three million profit on the investment in PetroChem. But aren't you worried about the SEC finding out?"

"Who's going to tell them? The only other person that knew about it is dead. You took care of that. It's been over a year since the company went bankrupt and the feds started nosing around. We'd already know it if they were going to come after us."

"You may be right," Joe said. "After we eliminated Michael and then Carmen disappeared, I heard that PetroChem was crawling with investigators from banks and the SEC. For a while there, I thought we were screwed. I figured Reardon would buckle and the feds would have found their way to us. I guess we were lucky."

"Possibly," Yuri replied although he knew that wasn't the case. He remembered the night outside the hotel in Pittsburgh when Stoli told him that Doug Reardon had promised to keep his mouth shut. Obligation can be a powerful motivator for some. Apparently, Reardon was one. Yuri sat quietly for a minute and pondered a frequent thought.

"I wonder if he killed him?" He mused.

"Who?"

"Risotti. I sometimes wonder if Reardon killed him."

"I would have if I was in his shoes," Joe responded. "If somebody tried to kill me the way Risotti and Cole tried to kill Reardon, I wouldn't think twice about taking them out."

"Yes, but Reardon's not you," Yuri answered. "We'll probably never know and I guess it doesn't matter. Risotti's disappeared and nobody knows what happened to him." Yuri reached for a cigarette and lit it before continuing. "Anyway, back to the matter at hand. Is there anything you can do to speed up the process? You've still got over three hundred million to convert."

"Not really," Joe answered. "I've got sixty-five million in active investments going now. I can't do much more than that. It looks suspicious if I execute too many trades at one time. We could do more if I had more people making trades but you put a stop to that."

"I had to. We can't rely on people outside the family. I made that mistake once. It won't happen again. Everything we do from here on out stays in the family. We can't trust anyone else."

"Even extended family?" Joe asked nodding toward the open window and the people around the pool. "I know you want to keep all this away from Sam and Lindsey but there are others that know more than they should."

"Ivan Stalichovik," Yuri nodded his head.

"And Doug Reardon. And Carmen Risotti, if he's still alive," Joe added. "All of them know too much. We need to tie up those loose ends."

"No," Yuri was adamant. "We don't touch Stalich or Reardon. Don't forget about the letter they wrote the night they killed Alexandar. And they still have his body hidden somewhere. If we make a move on either of them, all of that goes to the police. Besides, neither of them has done anything to make me think they're a threat. Just the opposite. If it wasn't for Reardon sticking it out at PetroChem, we would have lost a lot more. And John Stalich wants to protect his family as much as I want to protect mine. He's not likely to jeopardize that."

"I understand," Joe replied. "But I don't like it. Stalich may be family but only by marriage. We have no idea what happened to Reardon. He's disappeared just like Risotti."

"That's not surprising. We probably wouldn't see Stalich, either, if he wasn't married into the family. After what happened, I can't say I blame him," Yuri said with some regret. Stoli rarely came to the house by the lake and only when Helen insisted. He was due to arrive later that day. Since Stoli was driving up by himself, Yuri anticipated that he would leave the following day.

Yuri looked at his watch. It was nearly five o'clock. He got up from his chair and returned to the window overlooking the pool. John and the baby were out of the pool and Lindsey had the toddler wrapped in a plush beach towel. Elena was at the poolside bar fixing another drink. Helen was saying something indistinguishable to John as she looked at her watch. Yuri assumed they were talking about the pending arrival of their father and husband. Despite all that had happened between them, Yuri, too, found himself looking forward to Stoli's arrival.

Chapter Thirty-Five

The sweating workman straightened from his task. With a gloved hand, he turned the knob to shut off the supply of acetylene and his cutting torch extinguished with a pop. Taking this as the signal to quit, four others stood from their backbreaking work and four more pops marked the end of the work day. The lead man placed his brass torch on the cart that held the red and green tanks of acetylene and oxygen. Taking off his gloves, he sat them atop the torch before taking off a battered hardhat that once had been green. Now it was mostly a scuffed black except for the Steeler's decals on the front and back. They were new and still bright yellow.

Reaching up with calloused fingers, he pulled down the heavily shaded glasses that protected his eyes from the glare of molten metal. The glasses hung loose around a grimy neck darkened by years of exposure to sun, sweat and soot. His face matched the neck except where the glasses left circles of pale skin around his eyes. It was the face of a hard working man. It was the face of an honest man. It was the face of Steve Stalich.

Steve and his crew were cutting up the penultimate tank of what had been the tank farm at Keystate Oil Company. They would take down the last tank the following week. The very last structure to fall would be the mezzanine and that, at last, would mark the end of Keystate Oil. Without the tank farm, the property was just another empty industrial site in need of repurposing. The buildings, such as they were, would remain as would the barge facility on the Allegheny river. The bank appraisers felt these structures still had value. The tanks and piping, however, which once made the property uniquely Keystate Oil, had been scrapped.

The demolition had started the previous June. For most of the summer, Steve supervised a crew of fifty men and equipment as they tore into the three largest tanks. Several steelworkers had been suspended by harnesses and cut into the steel plating as they demolished the tanks from the top down. As sections were cut free, large cranes lowed them to the ground to be cut into smaller pieces and loaded onto trucks. It was highly dangerous work and carefully orchestrated. From a distance, it had the appearance of a colony of ants dissecting a much larger carcass. Gone, the absent tanks left a looming gap. Passers-by and workers at adjacent factories frequently commented how strange it was to look across Keystate's property and see clear through to the river.

Once the big tanks were dismantled, the crew started on the smaller tanks stacked next to the factory building. These tanks and corollary equipment proved to be a more difficult demolition. Steve and his crew spent many days planning the demolition before the suspense of actually cutting and removing sections of pipe, structural steel and tanks. By the middle of August, the bulk of work was done and Steve dismissed most of the crew. Now, the Friday before Labor Day, all that remained were Steve and four of his most trusted workmates…

"Hey, Steve!" The voice boomed out from behind a bushy, salt and pepper beard. "The trucks just got here for the last of the juice. Is it clear for them to drop their trailers by the last tank?"

... and Stoli.

The bank had contracted Stoli to supervise emptying the tanks of the noxious chemicals and oils so they could be cut up. It was probably the most dangerous and critical part of the operation. All the volatile liquids had to be carefully drained and loaded into to waiting barges, train or trucks. That was the easy part.

Empty, the fume-filled tanks were exponentially more dangerous. A small spark could easily ignite the vapors inside. It was such an explosion that had claimed the life of Stoli's nephew years earlier. The size of the tanks to be emptied during the demolition of the plant magnified the danger. An explosion in any one of the remaining tanks would likely flatten whatever was left of the plant. Anyone within a few hundred yards would surely be killed. Stoli was seldom more than a few feet away from what would be the epicenter.

After the chemicals and oils had been removed, Stoli refilled the tanks with water. The contaminated water was pumped out, loaded on a barge and shipped down river to a facility in Louisiana that specialized in cleaning up such pollutants. Emptied the second time, Stoli donned a hazmat suit and descended into the tanks for final inspection before releasing them to his brother to be cut into scrap. It was tedious, laborious and dangerous work. It suited Stoli.

Since it was better to vacate the area while Stoli did this work, he mostly worked evenings and weekends. That also allowed him to keep his day job. Stoli was working for a small oil company that had been a supplier to Keystate. Stoli's new employer bought much of Keystate's surplus oil at a steep discount. It benefitted everyone to have Stoli coordinate the transfer of the material. None more so than Stoli.

The bank had agreed to pay him based on double and triple his normal hourly rate since he was working off hours. He was making a killing. This weekend was to be the last of that bonanza. The two trucks that had just arrived would drop their tanker trailers before heading home for the holiday weekend. That would give Stoli Sunday and Monday to transfer the ethylene glycol from the last tank to the tankers.

There was, however, one other thing he had to remove first.

"Yeah, Stoli," Steve called back to his brother. "We're done for the day. Tell the drivers to drop their tankers next to the mezzanine. If you get them loaded over the weekend, we can start on the last tank and mezzanine first thing Tuesday morning."

While Stoli went to pass these instructions to the waiting truckers, Steve and his crew gathered up their equipment and dragged it inside the empty plant. The maintenance room was still intact and the gated tool crib provided a secure spot for Steve's crew to store their gear.

Steve snapped the padlock closed and followed the others to the locker room where they could wash off the top few layers of dirt and grime. It would have been nice to take a shower but the stalls were no longer fit for use. Months of abandonment and vandalism had left them broken and full of trash and animal detritus.

Stoli told the drivers where to drop their trailers, and entered the plant through the shipping dock. It was a sunny day, hot day and all six of the overhead doors were open wide. The late afternoon sunlight streamed in the open doors and lit the scarred, concrete floor. One by one, Stoli closed and locked the doors. Walking through the shipping area, he headed down the center aisle that ran the length of the finished goods warehouse.

The cavernous room dwarfed Stoli as he walked across the completely empty floor under the towering ceiling. Only the lingering, slightly sweet odor peculiar to cardboard and a scattering of broken pallets and crushed boxes gave evidence that the space was once stacked high with rows of antifreeze, oils, windshield wash, brake fluid, automatic transmission fluid and sundry other automotive chemicals.

Reaching the end of the aisle, Stoli opened the door that separated the warehouse from the supplies storeroom. This space was completely empty and had been swept clean. Only the oddly pleasant smell of polyethylene bottles remained. Stoli walked across the room and through another door into what had been the packaging plant.

Where screaming lift trucks, whirring motors, spinning rollers, conveyors, fillers, pumps and the miscellaneous equipment of seven filling lines once created a world of constant motion, there was only silence. All that remained to be seen in the yellow glow of two or three overhead lights were puddles of rainwater, stray pieces of electrical conduit and errant pipes hanging from the rafters. The most telling feature of what the room had been was invisible

The acrid aroma of chemicals and oil that had soaked into the floors, ceiling, walls, crevices and cracks permeated the empty plant. Stoli always thought that he hated that smell. Now, as he walked across to meet his brother and crew emerging from the locker room, he knew that, noxious though it had been, he would miss it.

"Are you all set?" Stoli asked.

"Yeah," Steve answered. "How long are you going to be?"

"Not long. It'll take about twenty minutes for them to drop their rigs and get out. It's a holiday and they're in a hurry to go home."

"What about you?" Steve asked. "Are you still going to your in-laws?"

"As soon as I'm done here," Stoli answered. "I won't stay for the weekend, though. I'll be back to empty that tank so it'll be ready for you on Tuesday."

"Are you going to need any help?" I could stay if you want." Steve offered.

"No, but thanks. You'd better get home to that new wife of yours. If you don't, somebody else will," Stoli joked.

Steve had remarried the previous year to a woman in her late twenties. She wasn't much of a looker but she was funny and had the freshness of youth.

She certainly made Steve happy and most nights he was anxious to get home to her.

They'd walked across the empty factory as they talked and were now outside. Steve and his four man crew waved goodbye to Stoli as they headed to their trucks. In a rush to start the weekend, there wasn't any of the usual banter of men leaving work. Five truck doors slammed shut in rapid sequence followed by the sound of revving engines. They formed a short line as they swung toward the gate and crunched across the lot. The last in line, who was also the youngest, threw up a cloud of dust and spray of gravel as he punched his accelerator leaving the gate.

Stoli shook his head and walked back to where the two truck drivers were dropping their tankers. One had already lowered his landing gear and was disconnecting the hydraulic lines and electric harness. By the time he was finished and was taking off his gloves, the other driver had his gear down.

"I'll have you guys loaded out by Monday night," Stoli approached the first driver. "You should be able to pick up first thing Tuesday."

"It'll probably be around nine o'clock, if that okay with you," The driver said. He and his partner were friends of Stoli's and had moved several loads from Keystate over the summer. "We have to come across town and the traffic's liable to be bad."

"That's all right," Stoli answered. "Just don't be later than that. Steve'll want to start cutting into that tank as soon as possible. You don't want to piss him off."

"Don't I know that," The driver chuckled. He'd seen Steve's temper flare on more than one occasion. "Don't worry. We won't be late." The driver climbed into his rig as he spoke. Closing the door, he called down, "See, ya, Stoli. Have a nice weekend and don't do anything I wouldn't do!"

'Not likely.' Stoli thought as the truck's diesels growled through the lower gears and accelerated across the gravel lot. *'I doubt you'll ever do what I'm going to do.'*

He reached into his pocket and pulled out his cell phone. Stoli still hated the damn thing but he'd grudging come to accept the value of having one. He wouldn't be doing what he was about to do if, two years earlier, he'd been able to call and warn Doug. He drew a heavy sigh, hit a speed dial number and put the flip phone to his ear.

"Come on in. Everyone's gone."

Chapter Thirty-Six

    "I'll be right there," Doug Reardon said and hung up. He sat in a rented car in the same parking lot Alexandar Alexandrov had used the night Lud was killed. Because of the sightline it provided, Doug was parked in almost the exact same spot. The view was different, though. Doug was saddened to see the hole where the large tanks had been and, while he couldn't see behind the plant, the fact that he no longer saw the stacks of smaller tanks poking up above the roof told him they were also gone.

He thought he'd gotten past the disappointment of what had happened to Keystate and the hatred he had for those responsible for its demise. The hour he'd spent looking over the dismembered corpse of the company reignited both the frustration and loathing. He was glad Michael Cole was dead and hoped worse for the missing Carmen Risotti. Howsoever bad their fate, it was no recompense for the loss of Keystate and the concomitant misery of the hundreds of people that had relied on the company.

As he drove through the gate and across the weedy, graveled lot, Doug imagined he saw the shadows of former co-workers standing in the ramshackle smoke shack and the open doorways of the plant and office. He parked the car in what had been his old spot in front of the office building, got out and went looking for Stoli

He found him standing at the base of the ladder that led up to the mezzanine. Doug was shocked to see that only the mezzanine and the tank containing Alexandar's body were left standing. The large, curved sections that Steve and his crew were cutting into scrap lay on the ground; evidence of what had happened to the rest. The only other sign that this had once been a thriving, active industry were the large, circular slabs of concrete that had supported the massive weight of full tanks.

"Pretty sad, isn't it?" Stoli asked rhetorically. "Looks a lot different than the last time you were here."

"Yeah, it does," Doug shook his head. "I knew it was over when I left but I never imagined it would end up like this. I hoped the bank would find a buyer for the business. I guess the place was just too old and tired for another go around."

"I guess so," Stoli lifted his ball cap by the brim and held it between his thumb and forefinger while he scratched the back of his head. "If it's any consolation, you and your group gave it a good run. Better than the other's I worked for. Too bad they sold it to Risotti. We sure as hell wouldn't be doing what we're doing." He put his cap back on and tugged the bill to adjust it lower over his forehead.

"Thanks for saying so," Doug was sincere. "I just wish it hadn't turned out like this. I wish there was more I could have done."

"Wishing about the past doesn't come to shit," Stoli was pragmatic. "You did what you could. More than most would have."

Stoli referred to Doug's return to the plant after his final meeting with Carmen. Doug told Stoli that Carmen denied involvement in the original attempt on his life but admitted knowing about the second. When Stoli asked if Carmen had conspired with Michael, Doug had to concede that he didn't think so. Stoli told Doug that he would report to Yuri and that was the last the two friends spoke on the matter.

They knew that there was no saving the company and set about, as best they could, to cushion the employees, customers and suppliers from the inevitable collapse. Doug made the rounds of the company's key suppliers and customers. The first call was to Mark Duff at Sotex Chemical. While his fiduciary responsibility to PetroChem and its shareholders barred Doug from being as forthright as he would have liked, he made it clear to Mark that Sotex needed to keep a close eye on their inventory in Keystate's tanks. Doug made similar calls to other major suppliers and customers to give them time to prepare.

Meanwhile, Stoli worked to find jobs for Keystate's remaining employees. There wasn't much he could do other than to counsel and encourage them to start looking for different work. It didn't take long, however, for the grapevine to work its inevitable magic and people started leaving for more secure jobs.

Doug was surprised that no one had interfered while he quietly orchestrated the shutdown of Keystate's operations. He half expected to hear from Carmen after the meeting in New York and spent the first few days anticipating a call. A week went by with no word. Then two. At the beginning of the third week, Sean Tomkins called to ask Doug his he'd heard from Carmen or Michael. Doug truthfully answered that he didn't know what happened to Michael and that he'd last seen Carmen at Campo di Bocce to discuss his contract. Finally, at the end of that week, Sean came to Keystate to tell Doug that he was taking over as the interim chairman of PetroChem. Doug and Stoli tacitly agreed that Yuri had done his work and Carmen would be heard from no more.

Two weeks later, the bank called to inquire why PetroChem was not paying on its line of credit and to inform Doug that the company was violating several conditions of the loan covenant. Doug told then that he didn't have responsibility for PetroChem's finances and referred them to Sean.

Three weeks later, agents from the Securities and Exchange Commission arrived to grill Doug on what he knew about Carmen, Michael and more than seven million dollars in missing cash. Apparently, the proceeds from the initial sales of PetroChem stock had disappeared. Again, Doug referred the SEC investigators to Sean Tomkins.

For several weeks he'd received regular calls from the investigators and Sean inquiring whether he had heard from Carmen or Michael. Eventually, the SEC lodged criminal charges against both Michael and Carmen for theft, fraud and conspiracy to commit fraud. Warrants went out for their arrests but were never executed. Everyone assumed that they'd left the country with the stolen money.

Four months to the day after Doug and Carmen had their final meeting in New York, the bank foreclosed. By then Doug had discreetly talked to all Keystate's key customers to encourage them to find new sources. He had similar conversations with the suppliers. The few people still willing to sell to Keystate were now demanding payment in advance. Most important to Doug, all but a few employees had moved on to other jobs. One of the last was Stoli to a job Doug had arranged for him

Years earlier, Doug had developed a friendship with the guy that would become Stoli's new boss. Not surprisingly, it had happened while playing golf. On the last round they would play, and knowing the end was near, Doug asked the fellow to give Stoli a job. Doug assured him it would be the best hiring decision he would ever make. The following week, Stoli started his new job. Doug left Keystate and Pittsburgh two days later when his contract was terminated.

There hadn't been much to pack and nothing to keep him. He travelled south until he reached the golfing Mecca that is the South Carolina seaboard. He rented a condo on one of the numerous golf courses and, within a month, got a job as an assistant pro at a posh country club. Six months later, he was the pro and before a year had passed, he was the course operations manager.

The hours and days he spent on the golf course were a balm for his battered psyche and ego. It was pure, honest work without a hint of corruption or larceny. If anything, he became even more of a purist of the game. A lie was either played or a stroke taken. Doug relished the black or white simplicity. For over a year, he lived this cloistered life and did his best to not dwell on the past. He never tried to contact any of his former associates but when Stoli called and said he needed Doug's help, he'd booked a flight for the following day. He hadn't bothered to ask why. Now, standing at the base of the ladder leading up to the mezzanine and the adjacent tank, his supposition was confirmed.

"He's still in there?" Doug asked, nodding his head at the tank.

"Yeah," Stoli answered. "I figured it was the best place to leave the body. When I found out they were going to tear the tanks down, I almost shit my pants. Lucky for us, they hired me to drain them. I could have asked Steve to help but I figured there's no point in getting him involved if I don't have to. I appreciate that you came."

"You'd do it for me," Doug said simply.

"Well," Stoli grunted as he bent to pick up the rope and tie it to his belt. The other end was already tied to a canvas bag containing some tools. "Let's get this over with."

He motioned for Doug to start the climb first and waited until he was halfway up the ladder before following. When they both stood on the mezzanine, Stoli hauled up the bag of tools. They stood for a minute to looked around. The view was extraordinarily different from the last time they shared the platform. Mostly, it was the sense of exposure.

The mezzanine was empty. All that remained of the row of tanks it supported were charred stubs of angle iron that had attached the tanks to the decking. Stoli and Doug had an unobstructed view in all directions. To the east, downtown Pittsburgh, which previously could only be seen from atop the highest tank, was clearly visible. The view in the opposite direction, where the three largest tanks once stood, looked even more destitute from the vantage of height. Even the gravel parking lot, never much to look at, seemed more forlorn. It was a panorama of desolation and abandonment.

Stoli crossed the mezzanine and rickety catwalk to the top of the remaining tank. Time and exposure to the weather had eliminated any trace of the events of almost two years prior. The nuts that secured the access door had rusted and there was no outward indication that the tank held anything other than ethylene glycol. The two friends knew better and Doug noticed a purposeful pause as Stoli kneeled momentarily atop the tank before starting to work on the nuts. In a few minutes, Stoli had them loosened and removed.

"Give me a hand with this," He said over his shoulder.

Doug carefully crossed the catwalk and, together, they grabbed the handles of the heavy lid and lifted it aside. Stoli was relieved to see that the rope was still attached to the underside of the hatch. He grabbed the line and gave it a slow and steady tug. It had heft; Alexandar was still attached. Stoli reached into the canvas bag and pulled out two pairs of leather gloves. Doug was staring at the rope stretching down into the tank. He could follow it about four feet into the liquid before it disappeared. Stoli slapped Doug in the chest with the work gloves to break his stare. Doug took the gloves put them on.

"Ready?" Stoli asked.

Doug nodded and, together, they bent to grab the rope. It was remarkably easy. Over time,

Alexandar's body had absorbed ethylene glycol and, other than his skeleton and the heavy wrench attached to his leg, he had attained the same buoyancy as the surrounding liquid. Within seconds, the left arm became visible followed by the top of his head and shoulders. When Alexandar's hand broke the surface, Stoli reached down and grabbed the wrist.

"Take this," He said to Doug when the arm rose above the access hole. Stoli dropped to his knees and reached into the hole to grab the collar of Alexandar's coveralls. "Okay. Now pull."

Together, Stoli and Doug leaned back and slowly pulled the preserved body out of the tank. It was a tight fit and the weight increased as the body lost buoyancy. The domed top of the tank got wet and footing became tenuous. It took several minutes before Alexandar Alexandrov lay free of the tank. Doug squatted on his haunches to catch his breath while Stoli took hold of the rope that was tied to Alexandar's leg and pulled the red wrench up and out of the tank. It was none the worse for the time spent submerged.

Doug studied the body. It was remarkable well preserved. The skin was rubbery and had darken considerably. The lips, which seemed to have shrunk, were drawn back to expose yellowed teeth. Although still black, Alexandar's eyes were no longer rounded. They stared, flattened, from behind half closed lids. Surprisingly, his hair and beard were intact. If anything, Alexandar appeared even more hirsute. Doug had read somewhere that hair and finger nails continue to grow after death. He looked at Alexandar's hand to see if this were true. It was missing.

"What happened to his hand?"

"Yuri's got it."

"What?!" Doug was surprised. "Why?"

"I needed to prove that his man was dead and I wasn't fucking around."

"Jesus, Stoli," Doug was taken aback by his friend's methods. "That's pretty gruesome."

"As gruesome as what happened to Lud?" Stoli was unapologetic.

"No," Doug answered as he recalled Lud's battered body laying in the morgue, pieces of brain and bone matted pink in what had been snow-white hair.

"As vicious as trying to throw you off there?" Stoli sat next to Doug and nodded toward the edge of the tank.

"No," Doug reflexively reached up and rubbed his temple where Alexandar's fist had knocked him senseless.

"He was a vicious, gruesome man that got what he deserved," Stoli continued. "So was Michael Cole. So is Carmen Risotti and so is Yuri Pandropov. It makes me sick to think that my son married into that cesspool. Now I'm in it up to my neck and so are you. We didn't ask for any of this. We were just doing our best to get by and maybe make something better. Those assholes brought this on us and we have to live with it for the rest of our lives. Did I have to cut off his hand? Probably not. Was I vicious? Maybe. Do I care? No fucking way!"

Doug said nothing. There was nothing to say. Stoli was right. Carmen, Michael, Alexandar and Yuri had brought them to this moment and had cast a pall over what remained of their lives. Everything that Doug had tried to accomplish had been destroyed by the avarice and ambition of three corrupt people. Far worse, the damage extended to hundreds, if not thousands of people. Everyone that was associated with Keystate had been victimized.

The recovery for the customers and suppliers had been relatively brief and mild. That for the employees and their families took longer. There was no relief for Stoli. He was literally married to the situation. All because he'd done what he thought was best for his family... and friend.

"No good deed goes unpunished," Doug said softly.

"What?" Stoli had only half heard.

"Just something Lud always used to say," Doug answered. "No good deed..."

"...goes unpunished," Stoli finished. "He was right."

"More often than not," Doug replied. "I sure miss him. Although, I don't know what words of wisdom he would have for this." Doug pointed at Alexandar. "What are you planning to do with the body."

"I'm giving it to Yuri."

"Is that smart?" Doug was surprised. "I thought this was part of our insurance."

"I don't think we need it anymore. Helen thinks Yuri is dying," Stoli answered. "Cancer."

"What about his son, Joe? Won't he take over the business?"

"I don't know. Maybe. I'm not sure it matters," Stoli continued. "The body always was just extra protection. We still have the letters you wrote that night. Even without the body, Yuri and Joe won't want the police investigating. I think we'll be all right. Besides, what am I going to do with a body?"

"What *are* we going to do with it?" Doug spoke to the practical matter at hand. They still needed to get it down to the ground. He looked at the prostrate and wet body of Alexandar Alexandrov resting on the domed top of the tank. Small streams of ethylene glycol ran from his soaked clothing and trickled down the curved top of the tank and over the edge. Doug had a thought that he buried as abusive and disrespectful until he glanced sideways at Stoli. He knew instantly that they shared the same idea.

"Why not?" Stoli asked with a shrug. "He won't feel it."

Simultaneously, they each stretched out a leg to push the body. Alexandar slowly started to slide down the curved top of the tank. The wetted surface was slippery and the body gained speed as it neared the edge. The head and torso reached the precipice first and, as it slid off, Alexandar's body did a half turn to plummet face first. The body landed on its head with a sickening thud and resounding crack. Had he not been already dead, the fall would have killed him.

Doug and Stoli replaced the cover over the access hole and Stoli hand tightened a few of the nuts. They walked across the empty mezzanine and stopped at the end of the platform for a last look around. This time, Doug knew he would not return to Neville Island. There was a slight breeze coming from the west and the air, which at ground level stung from the acrid smell of chemicals and industrial grime, was fresher and smelled of the river.

"What are you going to do now?" Stoli asked.

"Go home, I guess."

"To Cleveland?"

"No. I have nothing there except family. I swing by now and again but don't spend much time. I don't want to put my parents at risk until I'm sure this thing with Pandropov is over." Doug paused and grimaced. "That may be never."

"So where are you going?" Stoli asked

"South," Doug answered. "I'm the golf pro at a country club in South Carolina."

"That's it?" Stoli couldn't hide his surprise. "Is that enough?"

"It is for now," Doug replied. "Sorry to disappoint you."

"I'm just surprised," Stoli responded. "I figured you'd find another outfit that needs your help."

"You mean like I helped Keystate?" Doug asked bitterly. "Take a look around." He pointed to where the tank farm once stood. "I can't imagine there are many people looking for this kind of help."

"None of this was your fault," Stoli consoled. "You and Lud turned this place around. You got fucked just like the rest of us. You were doing the right things. Just keep doing that." Stoli turned to walk over to the ladder. Doug didn't move.

"You coming?"

"I want to take another look around," Doug answered. "I'll be down in a minute."

Stoli dropped the rope, canvas bag and red wrench to the ground before starting down. He stepped onto the top rung and paused to look at his friend. Doug was looking away into the distant skyline of the city. Stoli gave a sad shake of his head and disappeared down the ladder.

'The right thing.' Doug thought to himself: *'What is that?'*

He'd spent his life trusting that happiness and success came from doing the right things the right way. Ironically, Lud and Stoli shared the belief. Now, Lud was dead and Stoli and Doug had become two strands in a web of deceit. Never had good deeds resulted in such malevolence. Doug lamented exposing Lud to Keystate and would never forgive himself for putting Lud in his car on that dreadful night.

That night also turned Stoli, a man that wanted little more than the security and safety of his family and friends, into a killer. Now, in order to protect those dear to him, Stoli was forced to abet the very people that posed the threat. Albeit spun to protect the innocent, the web offered no hope of release. Stoli was literally wed to it.

It was rare for him to hold his grandson without thinking of Lud and Alexandar. Their ghosts swaddled the child with a ethereal blanket. Constantly surrounded by his extended family, Stoli would find no escape.

Doug, though not so intimately entangled, was similarly haunted. His ghosts, however, resulted from forced separations. He rarely spoke to his family for fear of putting them in harm's way. For the same reason, he did not allow himself the possibility of anything beyond casual relationships with women. That, he told himself, was the reason he hadn't tried to contact Julie. In truth, he knew it was because he didn't want to set himself up for more rejection. It had been a long, painful descent from that dreamy night overlooking the lights of Las Vegas to this night's view across the dregs of dismantled dreams.

'The right thing,' He repeated the thought.

Then, softly and to himself:

"How will I know what that is?"

Doug Reardon stood looking out. From this height, he could see straight into downtown Pittsburgh. His line of sight passed over Heinz Field and the adjacent PNC Park. Farther east, the setting sun bounced off the fortress-like edifice of PPG Place. The building glowed orange-red in the fading sun. Beyond, One Mellon Place, the city's second tallest building gleamed. Just north stood the U.S. Steel building. The surrounding sidewalk, rusted a darker stain of red from additional years of cascading rain, reminded passersby that this was Pittsburgh – a town built on sacrifice, sweat and blood.